"SON OF THE ICE," RUVANNA ASKED, "HOW DID YOU FIND US HERE?"

Korkoris, the Icewrought, looked at her carefully before answering. He knew her place among these people was important. He had seen how the wolves kept to her, obedient as hounds. He decided to tell the truth. "The music," he answered softly.

"Calling to you? Drawing you to these mountains?"

Korkoris nodded. "Like a beacon."

"Earthsongs," said Brannog. "Carac heard them as far away as Goldenisle. Now we have all heard them. Even you, Korkoris, from under the ice."

"The Sublime One," said Ruvanna. "He calls his people to him. But why?"

Brannog looked up. The clouds were coming, dark and laden . . . .

"AN INTRICATE, EXCITING TALE . . . SMOOTHLY AND SUPERBLY WRITTEN"
Robert Adams

ADRIAN COLE

BOOK THREE OF THE OMARAN SAGA

THE KING OF LIGHT AND SHADOWS

AVON BOOKS ◆ NEW YORK

AVON BOOKS
A division of
The Hearst Corporation
105 Madison Avenue
New York, New York 10016

First Avon Books Printing: November 1990

AVON TRADEMARK REG. U.S. PAT. OFF. AND IN OTHER COUNTRIES, MARCA
REGISTRADA, HECHO EN U.S.A.

Printed in the U.S.A.

RA   10 9 8 7 6 5 4 3 2 1

 **Contents**

Now we are scattered like dust in the storm, we who once ruled Omara and whose cities were its pride. Now we are creatures of the earth, the deeps of stone, and it is both womb and grave to us, and all between.

But there will be a better time, a reaching for the light, when overmen will put away their cruelty to us and share the light with us.

And we will sit again with pride in the halls of our ancestors.

CREED OF THE EARTHWISE

I shall cry out in my anguish and my anger, and every true child of the earth shall hear me. I shall speak for them all, and Omara will be my strength. Nowhere in all Omara will my songs not be heard. It will be a time of preparing and of gathering, and then, as a storm of storms, we shall rise up and fill the earth under the sky. We shall drive out the invader, the usurper of our glory. Omara shall be cleansed and we, her blood, shall be redeemed.

THE SUBLIME ONE

Do we kill those we foster, those who come to us for protection any more than we kill our sick, our wounded?

Do we lack compassion? I hear you saying no.

Then how should Omara judge those who fled to her from the great darkness? Let Omara first judge herself.

If she is to survive, she must do this. And the time is now.

Ulthor, the Faithbreaker,
Warlord of the Earthwrought

PART ONE

BRANNOG'S HOST

1
Carac

CARAC COULD SMELL the coming of the thunderstorm and knew with Earthwrought intuition that it would focus over the island of Medallion. From his vantage point high above what had once been the Hasp, the narrow opening to the island's Inner Sea that had been closed up by a colossal landslide, Carac studied the patterns of the clouds mirrored in an already darkening ocean. Like the Stonedelvers, he had a natural fear of the sea and he had never been completely at home on the island, in spite of its size. But now the restlessness of the water reflected the strange mood of the Empire, where the talk was of impending war and of terror in the far west. As the first rumble of thunder spread across the horizon, Carac could smell the rain hanging heavily overhead. In an hour there would be a deluge and it would be bad.

Below him in the shadows he could just see the vague forms of huge Stonedelvers, endlessly removing the rocks and rubble of the landslide, their sworn task to clear the Hasp and again open the Inner Sea to the sea lanes of Empire. Like the Earthwrought here on Medallion, they were loyal to the newly enthroned Emperor, Ottemar Remoon. Carac listened to the growling thunder progressing over the water and the many lines of his broad face spread. He had come to trust the overmen, where once, like all his people, he had hated them and seen only the cruel power of the invader, the tyrant. But the world of Omara had come into a new age, just as the Earthwise councillors had promised. Ianelgon, who had been Carac's Earthwise before his death at Rockfast, had himself

3

promised a new life for the Earthwrought, above ground.
Carac had fought alongside Stonedelvers and Men against the
enemies of Ottemar Remoon and had been well rewarded.
Even so, Medallion could never be his true home, and his
thoughts often took him back to the east and his birthlands.

He wound his way down the rocky slopes of Malador to the
first of the openings that the Stonedelvers had made and almost at once met two of Aumlac's burly warriors. The Stonedelvers recognized the squat figure and greeted him heartily.
Carac was a little larger than most of his kind, about half
the height of a Man, though as wide at the shoulder. He had
dark, weatherbeaten skin, and broad hands that the Stonedelvers knew had a grip almost equal to their own. His face
looked grim, whatever his mood, with its wide features, but
his heart was warm and his loyalty unquestionable.

"Carac! What brings you down from the Heights? You
spend so much time on watch up there, I swear you're turning
into one of us. Why, look, Elgan, hasn't he grown six inches
at least?" said the first of the huge figures.

In the early days, Carac would have shown his teeth and
retorted rudely to these two, regardless of their great height,
but he managed a grin. "Storm coming," he grunted.

They were used to his bluntness; Carac had always been
taciturn at best. But they read his concern in an instant.
"Heavy?"

Carac understood the dangers of heavy rainfall to the
countless tunnels below them. He nodded. "Aye. And the
eagles are circling. Already they are moved by what comes."

Elgan, larger of the two Stonedelvers, looked up at the
towering Heights of Malador. "Storms do not usually concern them."

"Something else then. I must go below."

Elgan, who had been frowning thoughtfully, suddenly
chuckled. "Yes, you'd better see that we've done our work
properly. But I think you'll find our fellows have prepared
enough drainage channels to bear any rainwater out to the
open sea."

Carac waved and disappeared, leaving the two large figures
to blend with the scattered rocks above him. The Earthwrought felt an inner glow as he went down into the tunnel

system, instantly wrapped by the earth, the smell of it and the knowledge that it lived and breathed for him as any animal might. He was attuned at once to its many life forms, large and small, sensing their abundance. It was true that he had come to love the upper air and the sky, a response he attributed to his people's remote past when they had lived on the surface, but he was a true Earthwrought and here he was most at peace. As he descended, his body began to glow in the fashion peculiar to his kind; they needed no artificial lights.

The upper tunnels were large, but as Elgan had said, there were well constructed minor tunnels running from them in a complex underground web. Teams of Stonedelvers and Earthwrought had spent many months removing the mountainous debris from this place, but had had to exercise extreme care in ensuring that the Inner Sea did not flood in too soon and cause a fresh collapse. It was true of any rain also and once, a month ago, two smaller tunnels had folded up, although no one had been killed. Earthwrought pride had been stung, of course, and Carac's anger was volcanic, but he had seen to it that the work had been repaired quickly.

Now, as he went below, Carac encountered a number of his fellows, speaking to them in his gruff way, telling them to be vigilant this night. There were Stonedelvers, too, and they were glad of his warnings. After a while he found himself alone in one of the newer side tunnels and he wondered why he should have come here. The construction was good, the earth solid and silent. He was far from the surface and the storm had become a remote whisper at the back of his mind. He turned, seeing a lone Stonedelver pass along a corridor that crossed this tunnel. Something about the manner of the stooped figure puzzled him. Carac would have hailed him, but voices were always kept muted down here, especially where there were new workings.

At the crossing, Carac saw the Stonedelver going below. He did not recognize the giant figure, which was strange, for he knew most of Aumlac's people. Perhaps there were newcomers, although only those who had survived the flight from Rockfast were known to be alive. As the Stonedelver went deeper down into the earth, Carac realized that he was moving in an odd mechanical manner, almost as if drunk or dazed. Perhaps he was injured? Carac was again about to call him, when the Stonedelver turned. Instantly Carac froze, blending into the earth wall beside him. To a Man, he would have been invisible, but to a Stonedelver he might not be.

Carac saw the face of the being ahead, a face almost devoid of expression, as though cut from stone and with no understanding of the life within that stone. Yet the Stonedelver was furtive, bearing a secret of some kind that suggested to Carac that he performed a private task and not necessarily one that his fellows would have approved of. But he had not seen Carac and so turned to continue his descent.

Carac followed, getting as close as he dared to the Stonedelver. At length he came out into a small chamber that had been clumsily scooped out of the earth with no regard for the feel of the surrounding rock. It was like an animal's lair, hastily constructed through flight. It was quite improper: no such working had been commissioned here. From its portal, Carac watched the Stonedelver laboriously probing at the loose soil of the walls. It took him a few moments to find what he sought and Carac guessed he must have hidden it here earlier. Although caked with soil, it could be seen as a length of metal, a rod about the length of a Man's short sword. The Stonedelver cleaned it of earth easily and pushed it through his belt. His face remained expressionless as he turned.

Carac had drawn back, puzzled as to why such a dull thing should be the object of secrecy. He hid himself expertly as the Stonedelver trudged past him; as the big figure began the ascent, Carac sensed the coming of a second, inner storm. This was evil work, he was certain. Instinctively he went down into the chamber and studied the disturbed earth. Clearly there had been much work done here, not of removing and of shaping, but of reckless hunting as if an animal had been trying to dig out its prey. Carac knew that he must follow the Stonedelver, but first he had to make a study of this place. Something about it spoke to him. He closed his eyes in deep concentration and saw beyond the shell of its walls.

Shock thrust him back. He had seen an intrusion. At once

he clawed away part of the wall and in a moment had touched something, withdrawing in horror. His fingers had prodded an outstretched hand, but even as they did so, he knew that the arm of the hand was attached to nothing else. And worse, it was not an arm of flesh and blood, although in some ways it seemed to be. Carac's mind fled back in time, almost as if guided, to a day when he had stood together with other Earth-wrought and Stonedelvers and Men of the Empire on the Heights of Malador. He had witnessed the astonishing power of the being known as Orhung, the Created, who had been made by the Sorcerer-Kings of the far eastern lands. It was Orhung who had caused the landslide, the filling in of the Hasp, by so doing saving the vast navy of Ottemar Remoon's allies which otherwise would have drowned in the trap set for it by his enemy. Orhung had sacrificed himself and his power in the landslide and had been buried under countless tons of rock, no doubt crushed and destroyed. And here was proof of that!

Carac knew with certainty that the arm he had touched was that of the broken Orhung. No life, no power, attached to it now. It was, Carac knew, as sterile as bone. The shock of having touched such an object began to recede—after all, it could not harm him. In its place came fresh fear, for he knew now what it was that the renegade Stonedelver had carried away. It was the rod of power that Orhung had used. Was it, too, devoid of energy? Carac felt chilled at the enormity of his discovery. If the rod of power was still charged—

Panic was not in his nature, but he moved remarkably quickly, knowing he had to track the Stonedelver. The being's furtiveness meant menace. It could be personal greed that spurred him, but Carac had heard tales of those who served evil and of how they were manipulated by it. If Anakhizer, the enemy in the west, had given the Stonedelver the task of finding the rod, it could mean untold danger to the Empire.

It was not long before Carac again came upon the Stone-delver, who was now moving down yet another fresh tunnel and not one that had been planned by Aumlac's team, moving on with slow but deliberate pace through the packed earth. Carac drew from his belt a short club, a weapon whose size

would have amused many Men, but only those who had not
seen Carac use it.

"Hold your ground," Carac called softly, but his voice
took strength from the earth. The Stonedelver reacted slowly,
almost sluggishly, turning to face the Earthwrought. Carac
was a third of his height. No expression crossed the face of
the Stonedelver and Carac knew with certainty that this creature had had its mind poisoned. It must not be allowed to
leave here with the rod, whatever the cost.

Carac moved forward and the Stonedelver hissed. It had
no weapon other than the rod, but made no attempt to use it.
Instead it bunched its huge fists and prepared to rebuff the
Earthwrought with them. There was no doubt in Carac's mind
that in a normal contest, a Stonedelver would easily better
him, even without a weapon. But this being was unquestion-
ably slow. Carac did not ask for the rod: it would have been
a waste of words. Instead he chose direct attack, hoping to
take the Stonedelver utterly by surprise. His club cracked
against the side of the huge being's right knee and the Stonedelver immediately put out an arm to steady itself on the wall
of earth beside it. But there was no cry of pain.

Carac had glided back, expecting an arm to reach for him.
One blow from that fist would kill him, he knew. The Stonedelver growled, but there was something wrong with it. It
could only follow its prime purpose, or so it seemed. One
hand reached out, but Carac stepped in and swung his club
again. It glanced from the fingers, cracking their bones mercilessly. Grimly, Carac realized he was going to have to kill
this monster. He could not afford pity; he had seen too much
horror in the past, the awful Ferr-Bolgan of the west and the
remorseless will of their master.

As he struck again, Carac saw that little pain registered
with the Stonedelver. It fell to its knees, its bones fractured
by the expert blows of the tiny figure. One blow to the skull,
Carac thought, swift and merciful. Whoever this Stonedelver
is now, he was once one of Aumlac's people and deserves a
clean death. Carac waited for the opportunity, knowing it
would soon come.

Abruptly the earth about him heaved, as if great beasts
burrowed in it. A fall of earth forced Carac back a few paces

and in a moment a whole section of wall had been pushed aside. From out of it came a number of figures. Carac was about to greet them, until something made him retreat further. He thought they were Earthwrought, and so they were, but more than that. From around him now, as if being shaped by the very air of the tunnel, came a score of them. They were indeed Earthwrought, but not of Carac's kind. Their skins were strange to him, for although they were thick and veined, they were very pale, obscenely so, their manes of hair longer and far less dark than usual for their kind. They wore harnesses studded with jewels, something few Earthwrought had time for, and their faces were daubed with scarlet paint, glyphs of an unknown language. To emphasize their uniqueness, they carried not clubs, the traditional Earthwrought weapon, but swords, thin and pointed as the sting of a giant bee. For a moment Carac's confusion obscured their identity: in a clearer moment he might have known them. But he did not doubt they were enemies.

Three of them menaced him with their shining steel. Others set about killing the stricken Stonedelver. They did not do so with relish, but were as efficient as surgeons. There was little blood. One of them took the rod and passed it to the creature that commanded them.

Bemused, Carac swung his club, barely keeping his assailants at bay. He backed down the tunnel to a place where no more than three of them could attack him at once. Thought of the rod had temporarily passed from him as he fought for his life, for he knew these creatures meant to kill him. They were silent, though their ferocious expressions made their intentions clear. Behind them Carac glimpsed their companions making good their retreat as the earth swallowed them. At least, Carac thought, I have no more than three of them to deal with. But a darker thought came with it: they were confident of a killing.

Among his own people, Carac was regarded as an exceptional warrior, and during his sojourn below the mountains of the Slaughterhorn in the northwest he had had to keep his wits about him or fall prey to the hated Ferr-Bolgan, Anakhizer's grim servants. Even so, he rarely met warriors with swords. The three before him were not novices, and although the sword was customarily alien to the Earthwrought, these three were fast and accomplished. They had been selected for that reason, Carac guessed. One of them had sliced through the flesh of his arm before he had seen the move coming. He retaliated by catching the wrist of a second with a difficult back-handed blow. The bone did not break, but the assailant was forced to change hands.

Carac had stepped back to a place where the three attackers could not comfortably press him at once. He had the stamina to fight them for as long as necessary, but his concern was that the main body of them was in swift retreat. The rod of power would be lost and that must not be permitted. One of the attackers lunged a shade too carelessly and Carac brushed the sword aside before spinning his club back and bringing it down on the shin of his opponent. The tunnel echoed to the cry of pain. Carac's elbow shot out and connected perfectly with the temple of the injured Earthwrought, who tumbled into another, deflecting what would have been a deft lunge. Carac had taken a number of bad cuts, but his opponents realized he was not going to be an easy victim. Their doubt began to show. Carac saw it and let out a roar that served two purposes: it was both a challenge and a cry for help. It galled him considerably to have to shout to any fellow who might be listening, but he had little choice. The sound shook the tunnel and the last of the uninjured assailants was momentarily caught unawares, thinking the roof might come down. Carac struck with great speed and agility, his club forcing down through the out-thrust sword, striking flat upon the skull of his opponent. Almost at the same moment Carac was knocked sideways by the rush of one of the others, and he flung his arms around him to prevent the killing strike of steel. Both of them tumbled to the earth, and although Carac prevented the sword from reaching him, he now saw the last assailant waiting for his moment to make the fatal thrust.

Sounds from up the tunnel came down to them all, and presently two of Carac's Earthwrought companions were racing toward them, growling with anger. One of them came too fast and ran straight into steel, but the other had knocked the last of the invaders to his knees for his insolence. Carac rolled free of the being who had held him, and the latter was quickly clubbed.

"Who are these intruders?" cried Gromnar, holding his wounded flesh and wincing in evident agony. For a reply, the intruder on his knees sank forward on to his sword before he could be stopped, killing himself quickly. Carac was on his feet at once, but he saw that all three attackers were now dead.

Gromnar's companion, Haarg, scowled deeply. "But I know the land of these Earthwrought! It is far, far from here."

"Who are they?" snapped Carac, forgetting that he had been rescued from certain death. "They seem familiar."

"Exalted," said Haarg. "If the tales are true, they are from Mount Timeless. But why should they come here? And why kill you?"

Carac spat out a crude curse. "See that Gromnar is tended to. Don't argue! You can't run with a cut like that, Gromnar. Haarg, bring as many of our people as you can. Pick up my trail. I am following a score or more of these Exalted." He said no more, turning and passing the body of the murdered Stonedelver as quickly as he could. Haarg saw the huge corpse, but did not hesitate, helping the badly wounded Gromnar back up the tunnel.

As Carac raced away through the recently made passages of the Exalted Earthwrought, his mind sifted through what facts he knew about them. To most Earthwrought they were legendary, virtually mythological figures, and he had never been convinced of their existence until now. It was said that somewhere in the remote mountain fastnesses of the southeast of Omara there existed communities of Earthwrought who had fled there after the first wars with Man, when the Earthwrought were forced to go below ground to survive. Some of these communities dwelt deep under the mountains and had practically no traffic with the outside world, either above or below ground. Carac had heard of them because his own lands were in the mountains, and rich in rumor. The stories ran that somewhere at the heart of the mountains, where the Exalted held sway, was the fabled Mount Timeless, ruled by the Sublime One. Tales of this mystical being were numerous, fabulous, and Carac believed, exaggerated. He

was said to control his own community of dedicated Earthwrought, the Esoterics, whose word was law in the mountains. They called themselves the Chosen of Omara and were
devoted to the earth and the restoring of its body, the purging
of all evils that had beset it, particularly from the hated Xennidhum, where once the Sorcerer-Kings had held sway. They
were outside the laws of the scattered Earthwise, who were
like priests to the many tribes of Earthwrought below Omara,
and their views, and the views of their ruler, the Sublime
One, were rigid and intractable. The Exalted, it was said,
were their soldiery.

Carac wound his way slowly upward, surprised that the
Exalted were not going deep below. They were able to travel
as easily below ground as Men were above it, yet the party
ahead seemed to be going up into the higher ground above
the shores of the Inner Sea. Furthermore, Carac knew they
were not making for the west, not for the moment. He had
assumed that anyone who would steal the rod of Orhung
would be acting for Anakhizer: the realization that the Exalted could be his allies became suddenly appalling, until he
reflected again on their present course. If they were not intent
on heading to the west, presumably they would seek their
own master in the southeast, the Sublime One. But why
should he seek the rod of power, which Carac knew had been
fashioned and charged by the Sorcerer-Kings?

Before he knew it, he was at a narrow opening which led
to the outside world. The Exalted had broken surface and
were in fact climbing the southern peaks of the Heights of
Malador. Carac paused before following, again smelling the
coming of rain. As if in confirmation, a great flash of light
daubed the peaks above him in garish whiteness, followed by
a tremendous thunderclap. Droplets of rain as big as his
thumb fell, increasing in volume, riddling the slopes in miniature cascades. Behind him he heard the chase, and he
elected to wait for his companions to join him.

Haarg led them breathlessly, his club held ready for the
kill, his face somber, his eyes filled with a fanatical determination. He saw Carac at once. Behind him were a dozen
Earthwrought and one of the giant Stonedelvers, Jungmar.

"Gromnar is dead," said Haarg softly, but the bitterness

was in his words like venom. "The wound could not be closed."

Carac's face twisted in a grimace of suppressed fury. He turned to the storm and at once leapt up on to the rocks beyond. In the flickering light he had seen movement above that marked the flight of the Exalted, and he gestured for those behind him to hurry. The ground churned beneath them, but their feet were very sure and not once did they slip or falter. None of them spoke and the lone Stonedelver read in them the will to avenge their dead friend; it was as powerful a force as that of the raging elements about him, all the more terrible for its silence. The storm had unleashed itself on Medallion with an almost maniacal ferocity, the rain gushing off the slopes. Carac had been right, it would be a severe test for the tunnels at the Hasp.

It took an hour for the pursuit to locate the Exalted. They had not gone to earth, amazingly, for the storm ranted on, but had gathered in a large depression. Some way below Carac and his companions, the Exalted were studying the noisy skies. At first, Carac intended to lead a charge that would catch the enemy unprepared, but he saw almost forty of the Exalted now, and all were armed. He dared not risk leading his party to death, nor could he be responsible for the probable death of Jungmar, the loyal Stonedelver, hunched up beside him in the deluge. Carac knew the huge fellow would attack without question if asked.

"Why are they here?" Jungmar asked.

Carac grunted. "Strange. They are exposed not only to this deluge, but also to Skyrac's brethren." He referred to the huge eagles of the higher peaks.

Jungmar pointed high overhead. Several great shapes were spiralling down, regardless of the storm. "I do not recognize these birds! If birds they are."

Haarg was making himself as inconspicuous as he could against the dripping rocks. "They are not of these islands."

The huge creatures came down, black-winged and fierce-eyed. They were not eagles and were far larger than any bird ever seen before by Carac and his companions. One of them reached the ground near to the Exalted and flapped toward them. An Exalted came to the creature, bent over by the lashing rain, holding out an object that was instantly recognizable. The rod of power. Carac watched with mounting alarm as a curved talon reached out and took the weapon. The beak of the great creature opened, itself hooked like a talon, but no sound emerged. In the half-light, only the eyes were visible, cold and full of malevolence. Within moments the creature was airborne, using a swirl of wind to glide high. As he went with his fellow creatures, the rod seemed to glow for a moment, blue on the black backdrop, but none of Carac's companions spoke. They remained awed by the terrible presence of the sky beings and the black cloak of evil that they spread around them. Now they rose up like leaves, floating away as easily, far above the Inner Sea.

"East and south," murmured Carac.

"Aye," nodded Jungmar. "But to whom?"

Carac stared at him abruptly. "You are the swiftest here. Get word to the city as quickly as you can! The Emperor himself must be told of this. It is the weapon of Orhung that has been purloined."

Jungmar paled visibly. *"Orhung?"*

Carac nodded. "The Created. Quickly, take your message to the Emperor."

Jungmar paused no longer, doing as bidden, and within moments had blurred with the terrain as he sped away.

Haarg was watching the Exalted. "What of them?"

"I think we can do no more than watch them. But as the sky creatures have flown to the south-east, no doubt these will follow."

"To the Sublime One?"

"Rather they do that than go to the west." Carac did not need to mention Anakhizer and those he commanded. He knew that his Earthwrought were eager for positive action, anxious to avenge Gromnar. They were all quite prepared to attack the Exalted force if told to do so. Eventually Carac spoke to them. "We can achieve nothing here now. You must all return to the tunnels. This storm will test them severely. Do your utmost to expedite the working. The Emperor will need the passage to the open sea freed soon."

"Do we not avenge Gromnar?" called a voice.

Carac glared at them, unafraid of a revolt. "Every death

we suffer will be avenged. But not here. I will not waste you in death against so many.''

"What will you do?" called another.

Carac stiffened. "I will watch these intruders and see them off the island. Go now! Quickly. The Stonedelvers will need every pair of hands."

The moment of rebellion was past. With final grimaces at the Exalted far below them, they began to go back. Haarg was the last of them and Carac caught him by the arm.

"See that the work is finished," he told him, and Haarg would have said more, but something in Carac's expression kept him silent. Instead he moved slowly away, still looking back at Carac, who appeared to have come to some grim and secret decision.

Soon afterward, the Exalted began to disappear, absorbed by the earth, as if they had never been. Carac stared at the storm-struck terrain and the still wild sky. Something in the earth moved him deeply and he felt not for the first time the tremendous pull of the land. It seemed to him at that moment that the earth of Omara sang to him, and from the unplumbed depths of the world the chords of all Earth-wrought history swelled. He turned instinctively, to the south-east, understanding that there, beyond the horizons, the cradle of his people would always exercise its magnetism, as surely as any physical force could do. He thought of the wars he had seen and of his dead friends and of Gromnar lately cut down. As he did so, the song filled him and he shared his grief with the storm, alone in this remote highland, and yet part of its bones.

The Exalted had gone under the earth to the east. Carac let the call of the world guide him, and later, with the rain still driving down, he too, took the first steps on his long journey.

2
Elderhold

OGRUND GESTURED with his war club for his three younger companions to prepare themselves. They crouched in the narrow tunnel, eyes fixed on their scarred leader, each eager to begin again the hunt. Their faint body-glow lit the curved walls of the tunnel, picking out its particular shape, the arc made by the passage of the beast they were hunting. Ogrund's face was a cracked maze, his eyes bright fires, and the younger Earthwrought saw in him at times like these the power of the past, his warrior days. They revered anyone who had fought at Xennidhum in the terrible black days of war, but Ogrund even more, for he had come away from that place as leader of the Earthwrought who had been there. None of them knew how that leadership weighed on him. It was a mantle he would rather not have had, for he had been given it after the death of the renowned Ygromm, the Earthwrought who had first befriended Brannog, and who had given his life to save Simon Wargallow of the Deliverers.

Whenever Ogrund thought of Ygromm, his pain was increased by the shadow of the Deliverer, now an ally to the cause and a friend to Brannog. But here in the tunnels, while the hunt was on, Ogrund closed out such grim memories. Ahead of him he could hear the hissing of the nightmare creature they had been pursuing for the last two hours. It was a murkworm, a deep earth dweller, from the north, under the deserts that were the Silences. Many such horrors had fled outwards from the vast desert masses, and although they tended now to live far underground, some of them ventured

16

near the surface, terrorizing what life they found, hunting flesh. Ogrund had responded to a plea from a number of villages where Men and Earthwrought lived in relative harmony along the wooded foothills of the southern ranges in Elderhold. Since the war at Xennidhum, the people of these lands had put aside old quarrels and integrated well. There had always been relationships between the two nations in these forested parts, the tribes of both being scattered. Earthwrought were now accustoming themselves to life above ground, and Men were proving to be far more hospitable than ever before. It was true also that both races had much to achieve together in their efforts to ensure safety from the spawn of Xennidhum. There were numerous towers now along the edges of the Silences, watching for any evil that might try to rise from the deep sinks of those deserts, set there by the almost legendary Brannog, who had been a leader among the warriors who had brought about Xennidhum's fall.

The ground in the tunnel glistened with a thick mucus, as if with the trail of a huge slug and the Earthwrought grimaced at it. Ogrund turned to the youths, a very rare smile on his face, although there was nothing friendly about his look. "Just think about what I've told you. We are the harriers! No heroics and no mad rush for a kill. This thing ahead of us would destroy us all in a moment. I've seen its kind. And what they can do. Just do what you've been taught. Keep the murkworm moving up to the surface."

The youngsters all nodded, masking their dread, but delighted to be so close to the conclusion of this hunt. Ogrund grunted, turning from them. He moved on, then stopped, pointing. In the glow they could see the shape of the murkworm, packed like a grotesque maggot into the tunnel beyond. Its body was pale and blotched, its veins standing out like vines, gleaming with light and blood. The head was not visible, but Ogrund knew that it was wider than the body, with one huge eye and a mouth beneath it that would have frozen most people immobile. That mouth could extend like a giant snake's, trebling in circumference; there were no teeth, but a long, sinuous tongue which moved deceptively quickly, dragging its victims to it. It could take anything up to the size of a horse and once held, the victims were smeared in mucus, shortly to be ingested whole. Only in a deranged realm such as Xennidhum could a creature like this have been spawned.

The surface was little more than twenty feet overhead now, although the murkworm had for the moment ceased making its escape tunnel. Ogrund knew it was daylight outside, hot summer daylight, which this monster would wish to avoid. But there were another two teams of harriers below it somewhere, forcing it upward. They meant to get it above ground, where others awaited it. Ogrund had warned his team that they must hold their ground if the beast tried to turn and strike. There was little room here, but the beast would be even more restricted than they were. It preferred deeper ground and rock, not enjoying the confines of these looser tunnels. If it had tried to enlarge a tunnel here in which to fight more freely, the ceiling would have fallen in on it. The soft upper earth was the fighting ground of the Earthwrought and their mobility in this soil would give them the edge.

Ogrund slipped forward and used his club to probe at the twisting tail of the murkworm. It reacted at once, whipping sideways, but the younger Earthwrought were staggered by Ogrund's speed. Not only was he able to move out of range, but he had followed the blue of the tail and used his club to beat at it in midair. Twice more he did this and the murkworm spasmed forward.

"Spread out!" Ogrund called back. The others did as they were told at once, forming sub-tunnels in a fanning move that would block any sudden turn by the murkworm. But each of them wondered if he could perform even half as superbly as Ogrund, whose use of the club was almost magical. The ground heaved, shaken by a sudden contortion of the beast, and as they looked, they saw the tail end slither out of sight into darkness, moving with frightening speed.

Edging forward, the trio came to Ogrund in another passage, but he pointed upwards. The murkworm had disappeared. From across the fresh opening there came a growing light and moments later another band of Earthwrought joined them in the tunnel.

"It's risen!" Ogrund told them and at once they moved outwards into a new formation. Gradually they began working their way up through the fresh-smelling earth, sensing the open air above them. The murkworm had done as they had wanted. It had fled to the daylight, unable to bear the constant harassment it had been receiving below.

The land here was undulating, rolling southward like a green tide up to the first of the high ranges, its slopes thick with deciduous forest. When the murkworm burst from the earth it was in a clearing, a wide area ringed with trees rich in summer greenery. The creature heaved itself on to the deep grass, shuddering in the unaccustomed glare of the sun, its back glistening like ice. A white membrane slid across its one huge eye and its head bobbed from side to side as it sought a means of escape from this trap of light. The shadows of the deep forest beckoned it.

At first it was not aware of the beings among the trees, but in a moment its discomfort was forgotten as it realized there was food here, and in abundance. Arching its thick but expanding neck, it writhed forward. The Men of Elderhold who had gathered, and who now saw the creature properly for the first time, were struck with awe. Several of them ran quickly away and only the bravest of them held their ground, clutching at their spears until their knuckles showed white. Among them there were Earthwrought, themselves grimly determined to stand their ground as they had been ordered to.

From out of the trees rode a tall figure, his steed foaming, its eyes blazing redly at sight of the monster before it. The murkworm heaved to a standstill, its eye glazed, moon-like. Three gray shapes emerged from the greenery, huge wolves with fangs bared, deep growls rumbling like thunder in their chests. The rider spoke to them and at once they were down on their bellies, sliding forward, devoid of any fear for this abomination from below. The warrior had cut himself a thick shaft of wood and had sharpened it to a precise point; he held it almost casually, but his eyes saw not only the murkworm but also the woods beyond it and those who waited there. Behind him a number of smaller horses came out into the daylight, war ponies, hardy and extremely sturdy, such as were bred in more northerly lands. They had caused much comment when they were first seen in Elderhold, for they carried not Men but Earthwrought, and the latter sat astride them as easily and as comfortably as any Man might have. Each carried the familiar war club, but also a pointed shaft.

Their leader was a Man whose name had already become a legend among the forest villages, spreading like fire from the war at Xennidhum, for this was Brannog, one of the heroes of the war and the Man that some of the Earthwise were calling King Brannog. He had chosen the Earthwrought as his people, the first overman to do so, and he brought, so the stories went, a new era for the people of the earth. With his travelling warriors, his Host, he had set about making the land safe in the aftermath of war.

The murkworm was watching the three wolves, aware of their hunger for it. Brannog was anxious that the creature did not flee underground once more, for if it broke the ring of Earthwrought who were following it and went deep, it would be lost. But he had been gambling on its total lack of fear. The murkworms were not mad, though their brains were small and capable of stealth, and if it were wise enough to wriggle away from the constant goading, it might well flee a massed attack. The timing of the kill would be vital. Brannog must let it attack with confidence. To the amazement of the watchers in the trees, he dismounted. His black steed tossed its mane and cantered back to safer ground.

Behind the murkworm, from out of the churned earth, there now came Ogrund and a dozen of his chosen warriors. They watched Brannog, waiting for his signal and the villagers knew that this was no chance engagement: it had been planned, possibly enacted before. Certainly there were many stories of how Brannog—Wormslayer some had named him—had seen to the death of many of these marauding creatures. Brannog lifted his spear gently and then gave a shout. Many things happened.

Ogrund and his warriors darted forward and struck at the rear of the murkworm, whose eye was firmly fixed on Brannog. The beast shuddered forward, far more quickly than anyone watching would have believed, ignoring everything else but the lone warrior, as if it associated him alone with its pain and inconvenience. Brannog's wolves were up like bolts, leaping forward before the murkworm realized. Their fangs sank into the white flesh of its neck, fixing them there where the gaping mouth could not reach them. The murk-worm continued its irrepressible charge, its tongue now slid-ing out. Brannog knew the awful danger of being taken by that tongue, but he calculated the timing of his movements coldly. When he was ready, he drew back his spear and sent it like a blur of light straight into the eye of the murkworm. The impact snatched the bulbous head round to one side and as it turned, the creature lost it momentum, tumbling over onto a curve of shoulder before spinning and writhing in agony. One of the wolves was flung free, but it landed upright and turned at bay, seeking the chance to follow up with a renewed attack. The other two, unharmed by the crash, held firm, growling loudly.

A gesture from Brannog brought a charge from his mounted warriors, who now lit their short spears and rode past the murkworm, plunging the fire into its soft underbelly. It thrashed about in agony, beating at the sky with its carica-tures of hands, bloated human hands that made it look even more monstrous. Brannog had no sympathy for the beast; it had taken far too many victims for that. Ogrund and his har-riers also came forward, but there was no need for their war clubs. A score of fire spears had set the blasphemy ablaze. In a moment even the wolves had to withdraw from the heat.

Brannog reached Ogrund and he clapped a huge arm around the Earthwrought's shoulders. "Good work again," he laughed, then turned to the harriers. "You chose well. Ygromm would have been proud of you."

Ogrund did no more than nod, his face impassive, but if Brannog was genuinely pleased with his work, he was con-tent. He would never, though, compare himself to his dead friend.

Some of the Earthwrought had been tried for the first time and as Brannog came to them, singling them out, they felt the power of the Man. For one of his own kind, Brannog would have been considered tall and strongly built. The tales were that he had come from the far northwest and had been a fisher of the wild oceans there, shaped by snow-capped mountains and rocky shores. But he was a man of the earth and had proved so many times, never more at home than when with the Earthwrought, below ground or above it. He had, so other stories said, power such as other Men did not have, earth power, and his daughter Sisipher was a sorceress, who could commune with the earth and its creatures better than any Earthwise.

The young Earthwrought felt dwarfed by the huge Man as he grinned at them now. "I know you all must be disappointed at not making the kill yourselves. But you must understand one thing very clearly if you are to be one of my Host. We are a unit. What you did was as important as the blow I struck. Without your acts, the murkworm would be alive yet. So I am pleased with you. I am impressed! That's what you wanted, eh? To impress the legendary King Brannog?" He laughed and they heard in the sound the roar of the mountain wind and the rush of the falls, the rumble of the deep earth. Brannog turned back to Ogrund, who was now scowling in his customary way. "Do we take them with us, Ogrund? We need young hearts if we're to carry this struggle deeper into the forests."

Ogrund grunted and only someone who knew him well, like Brannog, understood that he was also pleased. While Brannog spoke to others of his warriors, he noticed a number of the villagers approaching. He went to them at once.

He pointed to the smoldering murkworm. "I suggest you make sure the creature is fully consumed by the fire. And never make the mistake of trying to cook the flesh of these things for food."

The man who led the villagers was a little older than Brannog, yet he looked haggard and nervous. "Of course. We are only too glad to obey your commands."

Brannog's brows rose in surprise. "Commands? You must be your own men, Landwurd! I don't command you. I was glad to help, but I'm not your king, in spite of what they say about me. These are your lands. We're your guests, no more."

"Yes, but—"

"We've all lived under the shadow of Xennidhum for too long. If you are attacked again, never hesitate to call on the Earthwrought, or indeed on any of the other villages. They stretch back far to the west, right to the new city of Elberon, where Ruan is ruler. So you have allies, I promise you." He took Landwurd's hand and gripped it firmly.

Landwurd was again amazed by the huge figure, who somehow gave the impression of being nine feet tall rather than a mere six. As he took the hand, Landwurd felt the power there, not simply human strength, but something else, as if he had somehow plunged his own hand deep into the earth. Brannog was unlike any other man Landwurd had ever met. There was much of the Earthwrought about him, for his skin was like theirs, thick and more coarse than a man's, far hairier, and his face had an elemental shape to it, intimating at rock and the bones of the land, even of the winds. It was said that Brannog dwelt as much below the earth as above it and partook of its strange fruits, the foods of the smaller people, and even that he could move as they did, through rock and mountain where no ordinary man could go. Such things ought not to be possible, but Landwurd knew that the villages of Elderhold needed such beliefs if they were to climb out of their days of fear.

"Well, I am a poor host!" he suddenly blurted. "Here, Brannog, let me properly introduce my fellows. And then you must come to the village with your Host and we shall celebrate this killing."

Brannog grinned. "Excellent. You'll find, in ten years, that the stories speak of how a dozen monsters were killed this day and of the army of a thousand men who cut them down."

Landwurd smiled politely as his men came forward. He knew that Brannog rarely spoke of his part in the war at Xennidhum—would he describe that as an exaggeration of events, too? Probably, and yet it must have been the most terrifying experience any man could have had.

True to his word, Landwurd saw that the celebrations were thorough that evening. Men from six villages arrived to toast King Brannog and his remarkable company, and Brannog was heartened to see so many Earthwrought from the forest lands among them, evidence that the growing harmony between the two peoples had taken on a new strength here in Elderhold. His own followers, like Ogrund, were also more content than they had previously been, used to the idea of life above the earth and of the company of Men, who had once been called overmen as a term of scorn. Tonight there was laughter as it had never been in the forest, and the songs of the Earthwrought rang out proudly, the Men listening, enrapt, to the wonderful voices, joining them as the night wore on, and dancing to the Earthwrought pipes, the tunes of which were seldom heard beyond the confines of the delvings. In spite of the revels, Brannog found himself thinking of the great change in his life since he had left the fishing village of Sundhaven.

He drank quietly, enjoying the villagers' excellent wine and watching his companions mingling by the fires. In those flames Brannog saw again the torches that had lit the streets of Xennidhum as the army had left it, pursued by the horrors of that place. He shook himself and thought of the year afterward, spent in organizing the construction of many defenses to watch over the Silences for signs of evil, and in making many journeys. The Earthwrought nation had, on the whole, welcomed the news that so-called overmen had fought alongside the smaller Earthwrought and Brannog had met several Earthwise, leaders of the varying Earthwrought tribes. When these had heard of Brannog's friendship and fierce determination to bring their people out to the surface again, they were wary, but those who acted promptly became the inspiration for others. Yet it was an arduous task, for the Earthwrought were scattered far and wide, and there were hints that in parts of the world even the Earthwise beliefs were not held.

Brannog had moved further to the southeast, penetrating lands far from the Delta of the Three Rivers where his friends had been building their new city of Elberon. Brannog had not kept in as close a contact as he would have liked, but the word had come back to him that Ruan Dubhnor ruled now, a more than capable warrior who would surely make the city prosper. And Sisipher, Brannog's daughter, had sent him the three wolves, once Ratillic's beasts, who had also endured Xennidhum. Brannog could not speak to them as his daughter could, for she enjoyed a unique communion with all creatures, but the wolves understood him and his relationship with them caused many an Earthwrought to marvel. Through them, Sisipher had first told her father that she was going across the ocean to Goldenisle, for their old ally, Guile, the heir to the Empire, was being threatened by his enemies.

For a moment Brannog scowled as he thought of Ottemar Remoon, who had called himself Guile to hide his identity for long months. Brannog did not love the man, for Xennidhum had revealed a dark side to him that Brannog found hard to wipe from his mind, however unfair it was to judge him by it. Yet he had sought to make amends and Xennidhum had, after all, marked them all. Brannog recalled how he had received word of Ottemar's abduction. He had not left these lands to go westward. Perhaps I should have done. I should have gone to Ruan's wedding, he thought to himself, knowing that Ruan would have wanted him there when he took the hand of the tempestuous Agetta, daughter of the fierce Strangarth. Somehow, with his growing alliance with the Earthwrought, he did not relish a return to western cities.

I have many ties in the west, he mused. But my course lies before me to the south and east. As long as there are Earthwrought hiding below, afraid of the light, I will seek them out.

He had soon gathered to him a Host of remarkable warriors, their core made up of veterans from Xennidhum, Ogrund's stoutest. To them had come other worthy Earthwrought from numerous tribes, and as the Host ranged about the forest lands, the scourge of Xennidhum's refugees, Brannog had been given the title of king. He had refused it more than once, but as the Earthwrought had insisted on it, he made the title his banner.

"May I sit with you a while?" said a deep voice beside him. Materializing like a wraith beside him was an elderly fellow in a long robe, his balding head shining in the firelight. His name was Kennagh, one of the local sages, a man thought well of by his people. He looked apprehensively at the wolves, but they had fed well and took little notice of him.

"Surely," said Brannog, glad to have his thoughts broken.

"Your Host is remarkable," Kennagh said. "When word came that you were here in the forests, we were afraid."

"Afraid!" said Brannog. "Why should you be?"

Kennagh scratched his head and studied his feet, though

not in embarrassment. "This fusing of tribes, of nations, came swiftly. When the first Earthwrought appeared here some time ago, there were skirmishes. Nothing too fierce, but there was bloodshed. But our common foe united us. We needed a proper bond, a deeper understanding. Even now we have never met the Earthwise of those who have become part of us. He is somewhere out in the forest, like a creature of myth. But he is real, I know that. Your coming may have opened the way for him. It is my hope."

Brannog nodded soberly. "When we fought at Xennidhum, it was a strange company. Deliverers fought beside us."

Kennagh shivered at the reference. "Wargallow himself was there, so I hear."

"Yet you still fear him?"

"We were visited by Deliverers only once. They filled us with dread."

Brannog thought of his own village and of how Wargallow had left his grim mark on it. "My people felt this terror once. But no more. Wargallow is not the avenger he was. Believe me, he is an ally, and much valued." And where is he now? Brannog wondered. I once knew that he pursued his own causes, his own drive for power. And yet, in the ruins of the desert city of Cyrene, he asked me to remove his killing steel, rid him of its curse. I refused him, and made him carry it like a sentence. Should I have been more merciful?

"Aye, well, these are strange times," said Kennagh.

"You'll not be persecuted by Deliverers again."

"It is of unions that I would talk."

Brannog suddenly grinned and put an arm about him. Kennagh felt as though a bear had taken hold of him. "Unions!" Brannog laughed. "Of course! And I need warriors. There are a good few here who would ride with me, eh?"

Kennagh nodded, though something was clearly on his mind. "Aye, you have much to do in Elderhold. Where do you go now?"

For a moment Brannog thought of the west and its troubles, but he turned instead to the dark masses of mountain in the south, obscured by the folds of night. "I've a mind to enter the mountains," he said at last.

Kennagh did not cover his surprise. "May I ask why?"

"Something has been drawing me to them. I have been moving through the forests, cutting down the horrors of Xennidhum where I have found them, but when I reflect, I see that I have been moving ever southwards, looking for a pass."

"Nothing much is known of the mountains—"

"There are Earthwrought there. The legends say that there are many of them, and one great community. If it exists, I must find it." Brannog let out a sudden deep sigh. "I fear, Kennagh, that there is to be another war."

"*War?*" Kennagh gasped, his whole frame shaking. "But with whom? The mountain Earthwrought?"

Brannog shook his head. "No. Something stirs in the far west. Word comes to me that Goldenisle has a new Emperor. Ottomar Remoon, who fought beside us at Xennidhum, has succeeded his mad cousin."

"He covets our lands?"

Brannog smiled. "No, no. He is an ally. But we are all threatened by the darkness in the west. I may have to go to the Emperor with an army, if I can raise one."

Kennagh looked appalled. "But this is terrible news."

"Since the danger grows in power, I am committed." Because my daughter is there, he wanted to say. And if she tells me I must go, I have no right to refuse. Something ties her to the west. Why? When she could have worked here, with her powers, to make my task so much easier. How the Earthwrought would have thronged to her!

"Then my reason for speaking to you is even more strongly founded."

"Oh?"

"It is well known how you have built your Host and how you have joined together Earthwrought of many tribes. And of how they call you king."

"If it unites them, then well enough."

"But you have no men with you, none of your own people. Is there a reason for this?" said Kennagh softly, his anxiety deepening. He would not have enjoyed antagonizing this huge man.

To his relief, Brannog smiled. "Men? No, I have not been avoiding them. It is just that they cannot go where Earth-

wrought go. Where *I* can go. The gifts, the powers that the
Earthwrought have, they somehow share with me. I eat with
them and I take the secret nourishment from the earth itself.
At times I wonder if I am not becoming one of them. I am
not as other men, as you will have seen.'' He laughed gently,
holding out his hands. They were far larger than a man's
hands, made for pushing aside the earth, molding the very
rocks. And in the half-light, Kennagh thought they glowed,
though it must have been the fire. "I was not always this
way. As a youth I fished the deep seas, as far from the shore
as a gull!''

"Yet you ride, and have even taught Earthwrought to ride
with you. It was unheard of until you brought your Host together!''

"Not so. Once, long ago, Earthwrought lived as men live,
and indeed, they *were* men. I have heard their history from the
stones of lost Cyrene. My cause is to bring them up from
the earth and settle them on the surface of Omara. So I teach
them the skills of men, just as they teach me their own skills.''

"It is well that you do so. But since you now spend more
time on the surface, should you not consider having men ride
with you?''

Brannog frowned at the fire, then looked again at the elder.
He chuckled at Kennagh's expression. "You think me in-
sulted? Not at all. You are right. It would be quite reasonable.
Until now, there has been no real need to have men with us.
They would have impeded us.''

"Until now?''

Brannog thought over the elder's words. "You think it is
time I added men to my Host?''

"So many of them want to ride with you. They envy the
Earthwrought. And I vow, they would wish to see this harmony spread. Such enmity as once existed in Elderhold is no
more.''

"Yes, I realize that. It is not so elsewhere. So what would
you have me do?''

"Obviously you choose your own followers—''

"Always. But if you have men here who wish to come with
me, I will inspect them tomorrow, that is if any of them are

fit enough to rise with the sun. By tonight's revels, the evidence is otherwise!''

Kennagh smiled. "Oh, rest assured, there will be men up at dawn.''

"I will speak to Ogrund, my Earthwrought commander. It may take him a while to adjust to the idea, but if I got him onto a horse, I can get him to accept this. Yes, Kennagh, it's a wise action and I'm glad that you've come forward with it.''

"I have one other thing to ask you, although I understand that you may think me interfering—''

"Nonsense! No man ever won a war alone. What is it?''

"There is someone I would like you to meet.'' Kennagh had become serious again and Brannog could sense his nervousness. They rose together, Kennagh stiffly, and Brannog gestured from him to lead the way. He spoke to the wolves, telling them to lie still, and they did not move. Beyond the fires, near one of the village houses, stood a solitary figure, watching the festivities in silence. A sudden crackle of wood from a fire sent up a shower of sparks, and in the bright glow, Brannog saw that it was a dark-haired girl. He drew in his breath, for a moment thinking it was his daughter with her hair shortened. She stepped forward shyly, and he knew then that it was not.

"This is Ruvanna.''

She was, Brannog now saw, not a tall girl, little above the height of an Earthwrought and had a slight build, but with a firmness to her that suggested strength. It was a common feature in Elderhold's women, and yet there was that about her that hinted at Earthwrought parentage, her skin, her broad features. She bowed to him as if he were indeed a king and he felt uncomfortable; her eyes looked down at the ground.

Brannog turned to Kennagh, saying nothing, though his unasked questions were plain enough.

"She wishes to go with you,'' said the elder, his face paling.

Brannog snorted. "I have no wish to offend you or the girl, Kennagh—''

"She has healing powers—''

"So do my Earthwrought—''

"Not like these. She is no ordinary girl. She is one of the newer children."

Brannog studied the girl again. What did Kennagh mean by this?

The elder understood his puzzlement. "Her mother was a village girl and her father was an Earthwrought," he said simply. "There have been several such unions in Elderhold."

Brannog gasped, realizing what it was about Ruvanna that made her familiar. "But that's wonderful!" he said. He went to the girl and lifted her chin. His gaze met one of strong will, grim determination. And something else: was it anger? "So you have healing gifts?"

She nodded.

"And where are her parents now?"

Kennagh spoke softly. "Long since dead. Taken by a murkworm or some other such beast. They lived out in the forests."

Brannog clenched his fists, studying the darkness and not the face of the girl, which yet disturbed him, though he could not think why it should. "Is that so?"

"Will you take her?" said Kennagh.

Brannog listened to the night, his mind far from this place. The music of Earthwrought pipes came again, and underlying it there was other music, but when he tried to hear it clearly, it faded. Ruvanna's nearness reminded him even more of his daughter, whom he had once allowed to leave him, to follow her own life, only to see the peril into which he had plunged her. He had gone after her, and so had begun his new life. The girl before him was no older than Sisipher had been; less, seventeen perhaps. Brannog thought of the west: should he have gone back, to find Sisipher again? Or was he right to expect her to come here? I have other responsibilities!

He glanced briefly at Ruvanna. "It would be unreasonable of me to take you," he said gruffly. "I am sorry." He turned away and the night took him, so that he did not see the flare of anger in the girl's eyes. For a long time she stared at the darkness, unaware that Kennagh had also left her.

3
Ruvanna

SHORTLY AFTER DAWN, as the company of warriors rode out of the village, the sounds of their horses muffled by the grass, Ruvanna watched them from high above, pressed flat to the top of a knoll. The dew was damp and felt cold to her stomach, but she welcomed its embrace, content to be so close to the earth. Sometimes, stretched over it this way, she could feel its pulse and sense the Earthwrought part of her echoing its sighs. Now she could hear each soft hoof-fall as it touched the ground, resonating. She could have closed her eyes and counted off each warrior as he left, those that rode and those that walked, for King Brannog always had his runners with him. But her eyes were wide open, avid for a sight of the Host. She saw it wind away into the trees, going to the south and the far passes that would take it beyond these lands to the higher ranges and then the mountains.

Ruvanna had glimpsed Brannog's huge figure at the front of the column, with Ogrund beside him. As promised, men of the village rode behind them now, together with the full company of Earthwrought companions. There were in all over a hundred warriors, and Ruvanna knew that there were probably twice as many less than three miles away, always keeping within range of their master. Her face flushed when she thought of the king. How dare he refuse me! A girl, he presumes, would be a liability. Or worse, a child! Yes, is that how he thinks of me? I barely reach his chest. But she smiled. She had spent her last day in the village. She would not linger here and when they found her gone, Kennagh would understand what had happened to her. Wherever Brannog took his Earthwrought, Ruvanna would go with them. She had waited for many years to decide on a course to follow, to see how she should use her gifts. As soon as she had seen Brannog and his Host, she had understood.

Before the last of the warriors below had left the village, Ruvanna had slithered backward and slipped away down the back of the knoll to where a tiny brook wandered amongst the rocks there. Using it to cover her trail, she sped away into the woods, fleet as a deer, though far more agile among the reeds and stones. No other creature was more at home in the forest and only the birds moved more quickly. She laughed as she went, something the villagers rarely saw her do, and her musical voice was absorbed by the woods, covered by it.

All that day and the next she followed Brannog southwards, never more than a few hundred yards from the Host, but none of them knew she was there, unless they mistook her sounds for those of a stealthy fox or creature of the woods. If any of the Earthwrought came near, she knew long before they could discover her and she took to the trees or slid under a rock. She became as the breeze, though none felt her stirring.

On the third night, while Brannog's men built a fire, she studied their movements from a rock pile that loomed almost directly above them. Often at night Brannog and his smaller warriors would go under the earth, where it was easiest to keep themselves unseen by any who might be abroad, but since the men of Elderhold had joined them, Brannog had ordered his Earthwrought to spend more time getting used to sleeping aboveground and having a woodfire burning. Ruvanna had heard him telling them, with his usual amusement, that the fire would deter enemies and not bring them slinking in. Ogrund, she noted, was more than a little disgruntled and he seemed to her to be a singularly disagreeable Earthwrought, although his own warriors evidently held him in high regard. No doubt, thought Ruvanna scornfully, he is an Earthwrought given to much blood-letting when it comes to the fighting.

It was while she mentally poured her scorn on the unfortunate Ogrund that she allowed her own defense to slip in a most unaccustomed manner. Behind her, forming a semi-circle that cut off the rock from the rest of the forest, three shapes moved. They were as silent and as phantom-like as the girl had been in her pursuit, and they used the night as if they were made from it. Low on their bellies, inching forward as imperceptibly as shadows, the wolves closed in.

Only when the first of them stepped onto bare rock did Ruvanna turn. She was on her elbows, arching her neck. Her gaze locked with that of the leading wolf and before she could draw another breath she saw the two others shutting off her retreat. Together the wolves dropped, but in a moment they would spring forward. From that distance they would be at her throat without again touching the ground.

GNARAG THE EARTHWISE closed his eyes in meditation. In his chamber, deep below the earthworks of his small tribe, he felt reasonably secure from the complexities of the higher delvings. The lands around him were bare, rocky, too close to the mountains for his comfort, but high enough above the deepest parts of the forest to be free of its countless predators. Earthwrought should live to the north of here, or much further west, where the soil was more loose, more fertile. This place was barren, difficult to make good use of. His people were few, insular. Some of them had tried to persuade him, *him,* the Earthwise! that they should go even further south, to where the great communities of legend were supposed to dwell. He refused, just as he also refused to risk a move to the north and west. Too close to the Silences and the things that crawled out from that abominable place. No, his tribe must remain here, beset by fears and rumors, but not at the mercy of Xennidhum.

There was a loud rap at his door. How dare they! His people grew intolerably lacking in respect. I know I am old and doubtless vulnerable, he admitted, but such a knocking! It is impertinent. I am an Earthwise! Does it mean nothing?

"Enter!" he snapped, raising himself, though he was no longer as tall as he had been, and in fact was shorter than some of his people, who were usually shorter than their Earthwise. His bones ached, too, and most of his white hair had gone.

Two of the tribal leaders came in, both with fixed, sour looks. Gnarag could not remember ever seeing them display a sign of merriment or of contentment with their lots.

"What is it this time?" he grumbled. "Can't you see I am busy?"

"There are strangers coming, Earthwise. Soon they will have entered our delvings," said the first of his visitors, Shirag.

"Entered?" gasped Gnarag, appalled. "Do you need me to tell you this is not permitted?"

"Normally, sir, we would have killed them," said Cannar. "Or at least have sent them on their way. But not these." He glanced at his companion and the two of them said with their eyes that they shared some deeper secret.

"So who are they that they force such indignity upon us?"

"I think, sir, that they are Exalted."

Gnarag shook visibly, banging his staff down into the earth, churning it. "Exalted! Have you been smoking forbidden weeds? Have your imaginations made fools of you?"

"Sir," said Shirag, as reasonably as he could in the face of such derision, "I have some vague knowledge of the legends. These strangers are like no other Earthwrought known to us."

"Do they *claim* to be Exalted?"

"No, sir. But they know of you and say that our tribe has been chosen by their master for a particular task."

"Insufferable nonsense! Where are these impostors?"

Shirag was about to answer when a disturbance behind him made him spin around. Moments later a number of figures crowded into the chamber, much to Gnarag's horror. The Earthwise suddenly looked even more worn, and twice as old. Instinct told him at once that he was indeed facing the supposedly mythical Exalted Earthwrought. Weakly he waved his own warriors away and within a short time he was alone with five of the outsiders.

The first of them pushed forward and glared at Gnarag with something akin to open contempt. "I am Ul-Zaan, from Mount Timeless. You have heard of it?"

Gnarag made no attempt to conceal his pure amazement at being confronted by these extraordinary Earthwrought.

Their skins were repulsively pale, with visible veins and sparse hair, and they wore harnesses studded with, of all things, gems. Their faces were stained, something unheard of among the Earthwrought, the lines were drawn into sigils and glyphs of some language that Gnarag did not recognize. It was quite disgusting.

"Yes, I know the fables," Gnarag murmured.

"Not fables," snorted Ul-Zaan. "Mount Timeless exists."

"Why have you come to me?"

"The Sublime One has chosen your tribe. Be honored."

Gnarag had noticed that Ul-Zaan and his odious companions all wore swords at their belts. Was anything about them normal? "We are, of course, we are. But for what have we been chosen?"

"We have heard stories told on the surface and in the warrens—"

"Warrens?" said Gnarag, as if he had been slapped across the face. Such a word was not used in respect of Earthwrought delvings.

Ul-Zaan ignored the interruption, his voice rising, "—that an overman has come among the forest tribes. From the war at Xennidhum."

"Ah," nodded Gnarag. "I have heard of this barbarian. His name is Brannog."

"He has not been here?"

"Certainly *not!*" snapped Gnarag indignantly. "My people keep to themselves. We don't permit other Earthwrought in here, never mind overmen."

"Which is why you were chosen," nodded Ul-Zaan with what could have passed for a smug grin. "What do you know of this overman?"

"Only what the rumors say. That he fights alongside Earthwrought and goes about destroying the vermin from Xennidhum. That's all very well, of course. But he also encourages Earthwrought to live on the surface, and worse than that, mate with the overmen tribes! For his efforts he is called by certain renegades, King Brannog. The very idea is ludicrous!"

"You do not hold with the Creed of the Earthwise? That

a day will come when Earthwrought and overmen will live together above the earth?''

"Pah! They would enslave us."

"Then you reject this false king?"

"Of course I do."

"That is well for you. But we want him here."

Gnarag looked at the Exalted as if he had just passed a death sentence. *"Here?* Are you insane?''

"Would you question the Sublime One?"

"No, no, but I don't understand—''

"Find a way of inviting Brannog to your warrens. He is not far from here, moving south to the mountains. It is said that he welcomes discourse with an Earthwise. Encourage him. Offer him the incentive of a pact, an alliance."

"Surely you jest! This must be a test. I know I have not been openly supportive of the Sublime One, but—''

"It is to be a trap, you fool!" snorted Ul-Zaan.

Gnarag felt himself whiten with suppressed rage. How *dare* an Earthwrought, Exalted or otherwise, speak to him, *him*, an Earthwise, in such tones.

Ul-Zaan appeared to enjoy the effect that his rudeness was having. "Invite Brannog here, with a few of his Host, particularly those who fought with him at Xennidhum."

"And if he comes?"

"He will, rest assured. When he does, my Exalted will deal with him."

"You mean to kill him?"

Ul-Zaan laughed derisively. "You think I would bring him here for that? No, he's to be taken to the Sublime One."

"For what reason?"

"It is not wise to ask questions about such things. Be honored that your tribe has been chosen."

Gnarag straightened. This might not be so bad. If he could bring the overman here and have him removed by the Exalted, it would be an end to the matter, and the Sublime One would be pleased. "When do you wish me to contact the overman?''

"Select your messengers at once. I will tell them where Brannog is to be found."

* * *

THE WOLVES WERE about to pounce, just as they had pounced on the murkworm and torn at its throat. An instant before they did so, a single word-image formed in each of their minds, like a shout. "Wait!" it said, so imperiously that it could not be denied, solid as a rock face before them. Then, "Listen!," less fiercely. They obeyed, cocking their ears.

"Your master's camp is threatened," came the voice of the girl.

At once all three wolves rose up from their pre-spring crouches and let out warning howls that echoed across the valley below.

Ruvanna turned to look down at the camp, totally unafraid of the wolves, as though they were no more than villagers she knew.

"I can't see the intruders, but there are almost a score of them," she whispered. "Earthwrought from the south. They come offering friendship, but they mean mischief. I can smell it!" She grinned at the wolves, who came to her, bristling but no longer intent on harming her. Their rapt attention was on the camp. As they sat with the girl, watching, anyone who had seen the four shapes in the moonlight would not have guessed that they were not all of the same pack.

In the camp, Ogrund responded to the howling of the wolves as quickly as anyone. Some of the younger Earthwrought and men of Elderhold stood in silence, unsure how to react, but Ogrund was at the ring of guards at the camp perimeter at once.

"Brannog's wolves," he told them, who were unsure, glaring at the dark, half-prepared for an assault. Ogrund did not feel as comfortable with the wolves as Brannog did: Brannog treated them as he would have done pet dogs, though he knew their potential. Ogrund had seen the wolves kill, but he knew they were extraordinarily loyal, and he respected them for it.

"What do they want?"

"It's a warning," said Ogrund stiffly. "Be watchful." He circled the camp, trying to study the dense forest by night. As they moved southward, he was less at ease. The bond that the Earthwrought felt for the earth, the land, was more tenuous here, and although the atmosphere was not one of menace, it yet held its dangers, its unfamiliar coldness.

Other guards hailed him and when he arrived at their vantage point, he saw a number of strange Earthwrought hovering in the trees beyond. They had asked to be allowed to speak to Brannog.

"Why do they come at night?" Ogrund asked himself. "And why the wolf warning?" But the Earthwrought seemed to be friendly, and they were unarmed. Ogrund permitted a small group of them inside the boundary. They were slightly built and lacking in strength, or so it seemed to Ogrund. He was acutely aware of their nervousness, but in the past he had seen much of this when Earthwrought met the Host for the first time. Already Brannog had achieved a legendary status and such apprehension was to be expected.

"Since you come by darkness, Brannog may be asleep," Ogrund told them pointedly. "I am his right hand. What do you seek him for?"

"We are from a small community below the hills, where Gnarag is the Earthwise. He has heard of your cause and of the ambitions of Brannog. Is it true he has become a king among the Earthwrought?"

"It is," nodded Ogrund.

"Then Gnarag would beg the favor of a visit from Brannog. If there is to be a new Earthwrought nation, Gnarag would know of it."

Ogrund nodded again. These audiences were familiar. He understood the fears of his own kind, and their natural reluctance to consider abandoning the seclusion of the earth for the relative dangers of the surface. "I will see if the king is able to receive you."

Brannog was not asleep. He was deep in conversation with two of the men of Elderhold, trying to identify any problems they might meet when they began the quest for higher ground. He waved Ogrund to a seat, but the Earthwrought bowed respectfully and remained on his feet. He had never found the inside of a tent comfortable. Brannog grinned at him. Sometimes he felt that his commander treated him more like a god than a king. One day he would find a way to convince Ogrund that he did not have to prove himself equal to Ygromm, for he knew the ghost of his friend yet haunted poor Ogrund.

Brannog listened to Ogrund's report, then spoke to the men with him. "Do you know anything of this Earthwise, Gnarag?"

The older of the two men, Danoth, a fine warrior in his mid twenties, answered. "There must be at least a dozen scattered Earthwrought communities in the lower hills. Most of them are insular and don't respond to our own Earthwrought allies' attempts to draw them out. There's no trade with them. They have no specific Earthwise, and several minor ones. They may not even be true Earthwise, for certainly their powers are small. I have heard little of Gnarag, and I doubt if he has much power."

"Perhaps if we offer him an alliance," suggested Brannog, "he would become an example to the others. It would show the small communities that I am as much in support of them as I am to the larger ones. Very well, Ogrund, bring me these ambassadors."

Ogrund bowed and was about to leave, when Brannog called him back.

"Was that my wolves I heard?"

Ogrund nodded. "They have not appeared since."

"There was danger in their howling. From what, do you suppose?"

"I will search for them."

Brannog nodded, knowing the wolves would respond.

At that moment, they sat very still, high in the rocks above the camp, waiting for Ruvanna to speak again. They knew their master could be in danger, but they felt the pull of the girl, the need to obey her. They somehow knew that it would benefit Brannog most if they did so.

"I know you're all aching to get back to his side!" she laughed, and they growled ominously, though she pretended not to hear. "Well, you can wait. Whoever has come, has been admitted to the camp. Earthwrought from the hills. Suspicious fellows. We'll wait."

They did exactly as she told them, all watching the camp well into the night until they dozed, half-sleeping but half-alert in the way of their kind. Ruvanna was equal to them in that, and every small sound that came from the camp caused her ears to prick. When dawn broke, the camp stirred, until, with the eastern sky banded with white and pink, Brannog came into view. He had selected a number of Earthwrought and men to travel with him, on foot it seemed. They were to accompany the Earthwrought who had arrived in the night; common sense told Ruvanna that they were yet another tribe who were anxious to come under the king's banner. Yet these ambassadors still filled her with foreboding. Her instincts told her to stand up in front of the entire camp and shout out her fears. Yes, and she knew how Brannog would respond.

In spite of her frustration, she grinned, turning to the wolves. "Soon time to leave. We'll follow your master, but in silence. No one must know where we are—not even your master."

They glared at her, eager to protect Brannog, but still in thrall to the girl. She watched Brannog leave, then swiftly led the wolves from the hill, away into the forest.

Ogrund had not been chosen to go with Brannog, and he was furious. Instead, he was left to see to the bulk of the Host. He consoled himself by considering the high degree of responsibility he had been given. Brannog would not favor me out of kindness or pity, he told himself. Not any more. He is too fine a commander. His army grows. He could not afford to let a fool run it in his absence. I am not Ygromm, but Brannog considers me worthy. I must bend to the task! I must show him that his trust is well founded.

He called to his own immediate commanders. "Form two small search parties! Your best woodsmen. Include men of Elderhold."

"For what do we search?" asked Dramlac, one of Brannog's finest scouts.

"Last night we heard the king's wolves. They have not returned. Find them, or their trail at least. If they have been harmed—"

"By whom, Ogrund? Who would harm such beasts?"

Ogrund scowled at the surrounding forest. "These are strange lands. The wolves were uneasy. They spoke of danger. Find them!"

The scouts raced away at once. One did not argue with Ogrund. He gathered his leaders. "We'll break camp and make our way up the river and to higher ground. It is unlikely we'll be attacked.''

"You suspect a trap?" asked one of the men.

"The Host must always be ready for such things."

The man covered his embarrassment. "Of course."

"I am uneasy," said Ogrund. "Brannog has been met by many envoys since the war, just as he was approached by your own elders. There's no reason to suppose last night's visitors were any different."

"They were evidently frightened," said Danoth. "I think it was our strength of numbers that unnerved them."

Ogrund nodded. "I am sure Brannog would mock my caution, as he often does. But tell your warriors to be vigilant." *Something disturbed those wolves,* he would have added. *And I've a mind to find out what.*

The leaders broke up, organizing their troops efficiently, and soon afterwards the camp began to move out. Ogrund rode up and down the ranks as they left, but each time he gazed ahead, to the south-east, he felt something there drawing him almost inexorably. For a moment the earth seemed to sing to him, joyfully, full of promise, but he shook himself. There were only the ice-topped mountains, the vast peaks of a forgotten wilderness waiting, and their welcome would be anything but warm.

Several miles to the south of them, Ruvanna had perched herself like an eagle high on another rock outcrop, though she had used her unique gifts to blend herself in such a way that no one would have discovered her, not even the most observant of Earthwrought. She had to concentrate very hard now on studying Brannog and his party, for the wolves were becoming increasingly more difficult to control. They had sensed something in these lands, some lurking menace, more dangerous than the Earthwrought of Gnarag's community, and they wanted to hunt it down at once. Ruvanna would not permit this.

She watched from a distance as Brannog and his following went with their escort to a cleared area on one of the many sloping hills above the thickest part of the forest. Once seen, the area marked the entrance to an Earthwrought tunnel system clearly, but Ruvanna knew that the so-called hill-dwelling

Earthwrought did not concern themselves as the forest-dwellers did with camouflage, mainly because there were very few predators roaming above the forest. It was easy for Ruvanna to watch what followed, as Brannog and his chosen companions descended to the system, led by Gnarag's diminutive ambassadors.

Again the wolves wanted to surge down into the valley and up the opposite slopes, but Ruvanna held them. She made them wait for long minutes in silence. Sounds from the forest broke this; the wolves growled softly, teeth bared. Ruvanna then saw another group of Earthwrought moving up the slope, looking about them furtively. The girl drew in her breath in shock, for these were unique in many respects: they were very pale, with light hair, and they wore paint. Exalted Earthwrought? From the mists of legend?

They crawled up the slope and then, following a brief discussion, slipped out of sight into the Earthwrought system. It was all that Ruvanna could do to hold the wolves. She had to allow them to descend the rocks, and she followed them, coaxing them gently, slowing them. They knew, as certainly as she did, that the Exalted meant harm to Brannog. She also knew she dared not follow openly; there would be guards.

What precisely did the Exalted want? If the legends were true, they were servants of the Sublime One, who meant only good to Omara. Yet the whole bearing of the Exalted had been of stealth, of duplicity. Should she return to Ogrund and warn him to come here at once? But was it likely that he, or any of the others with him, would believe her when she said the Exalted Earthwrought were abroad? And if she tried to go back now, she would lose control of the wolves.

She reached the last of the scrub and undergrowth. The curve of open land rose before her, masking the entrance to Gnarag's system. The wolves were flat on their bellies, waiting for the command that would launch them, but Ruvanna elected to skirt the clearing, mentally dragging the wolves with her. Like shadows, they slunk upward until they were beyond the entrance, but over the delvings. Ruvanna put an ear to the ground, listening to the muted sounds that came up to her from below.

Higher up the hillside she scouted around until she found

what she was looking for: a small stream broke from the rocks out of a narrow cleft. Ruvanna was able to wriggle into this opening. It was an alternative way into the system, and soon she and the wolves were inside. She touched the living rock and it was as though it answered her, whispering all its secrets, unveiling the intricacies of its tunnels and fault lines, telling her where the weaknesses were and how they could be widened. Gradually the four intruders dropped lower, going deeper under the earth, closing in on the occupied parts of Gnarag's system. As they went down, Ruvanna felt the air about them trembling: it had its own smell, that of the earth and of decay, but something else also. Fear. Those who dwelt here were afraid, not just of the world beyond their own suffocating realm, but of the recent intrusion. Whatever power their Earthwise had, it was limited, fading. The earth crumbled, dry and neglected. Few things grew in it, and Ruvanna thought of old age and corpses. She drew back from the dour images, but the air of collapse persisted.

She tensed, knowing that she was very close to the diminishing Earthwrought system, and as she sensed the beating of many hearts, she sensed also the presence of the outsiders, the Exalted. Their numbers were ominously vast, as if an army of them permeated these lands, bent on conquest.

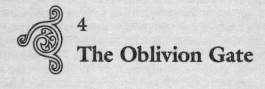

4
The Oblivion Gate

BRANNOG FELT the coldness of the air as he left the sunlight and went down into the tunnels of Gnarag's people. It was an unnatural, unwelcoming cold. He had chosen some of his most reliable Earthwrought to accompany him, although he had no reason to suspect a trap. It had been clear at the camp that Ogrund was suspicious of something and although the grim-faced Earthwrought had not entirely spoken his mind, Brannog was conscious of his fears. Even so, this should be no more than a routine visit. It was not unusual for an Earthwise to remain in his system rather than come to the surface for talks. Brannog knew well enough that each Earthwise was venerated among his tribe, so it would be diplomatic to pay him the courtesy of visiting him. Brannog had to win the confidence of as many of these Earthwise as he could if he were to unite the Earthwrought nation; he had no desire to use a weapon to forge such unity. Yet Gnarag's system was cold and gloomy.

The nervousness of the Earthwrought who had led him here had grown as they descended lower into the tunnels, and Brannog knew that his own Earthwrought were on edge. The place was physically little different from other delvings, although the earth was very dry and the soil far from rich, too full of bare rock and too void of growing things. It needed air. The tunnels were cramped and winding, not well excavated, poorly finished, although Brannog traveled through them as though his body had been transformed by the earth itself into something smaller than it was. He could not account for this power and had long since ceased to marvel at it.

They had been going down slowly, but now the slope became far more pronounced. None of the ambassadors of the system spoke, nor did they look at one another. It was this continuing silence, almost as if the Earthwrought were invaders in their own home, that sharpened Brannog's uncertainty. He glanced at the two leading Earthwrought on either side of him and sensed at once that they had tensed themselves for potential conflict. But why should such an impoverished system wish to trap him? It would have been far more likely that Gnarag would want to hide himself and not become involved with someone like Brannog. The thought solidified in Brannog's mind. Of course! Gnarag would *not* want contact. Brannog glanced at his companions, saying to them with his eyes that they must prepare for foul play.

Tiny steps had been cut into the rock below them, though clumsily and without regard for the rock. They squeezed down the tunnel, narrow by any standards, and came out into a low chamber. It seemed to be the audience chamber of an Earthwise, but it was empty, clogged with dust. There was no raised area at the far end, where one would have expected to see an Earthwise sit in times of decision and discussion. There had been minor falls of rock, now heaped up here and there about the chamber; no one had made any effort to remove them.

Brannog studied the walls of the chamber in the soft glow of Earthwrought light, but he saw cobwebs there and in the dust on the floor there were no signs of footmarks: usually in a gathering place such as this there would be much evidence of use, the floor would be scuffed, and in the air there would be the scent of many bodies. Here everything pointed to abandonment, a forgotten place.

Gently, but with irresistible strength, Brannog took the arm of one of Gnarag's Earthwrought and pulled him to him. Naked terror now washed the face as he looked down into it.

"Where is this place? Where is Gnarag?"

"He will be here!" gasped the Earthwrought, Thengram. A number of his fellows were about to bolt back up the stone steps. They found their way barred as the Host drew out their clubs. But there would be no battle here, for clearly Gnarag's people had no taste for one. They huddled together, deeply afraid.

"I think not," said Brannog, looking around. "This place is without life and has been so for many years. Why have you brought us here?"

The stone itself answered, for as Brannog's words softly echoed from the walls, a great slab dropped noisily onto the steps, sealing off the entrance to the chamber. Dust swirled, a miniature storm, and as the echoes of the falling rock ceased, Brannog's followers ran to the huge rock. It was immovable.

Rothgar, one of the Host, scowled at it angrily. "It fits into its bed perfectly. Strange for such a badly made delving."

"Then spare your strength," called Brannog, "I think you'll find it is locked."

"Then we'll break it apart," growled Rothgar, raising his club. He was even more stocky than his fellows, with exceptionally wide shoulders and brows like battlements. Few of his fellows had ever disputed his decisions.

"It's no use!" cried Thengram. He had fallen to his knees, shaking his head. The Host looked down at him in disgust, for this was a great act of shame in their eyes. Thengram, narrow-trunked and pale, was in startling contrast to the muscular Rothgar. The Earthwrought of this system, the latter muttered, were weak and despicable.

"Where are your spines!" he snapped. "You are like worms! Never before have I seen such a stark, neglected system, devoid of beauty. Have you no pride?"

"It will be our tomb," said Thengram.

"Explain that," said Brannog, though more gently. There was something here that terrified these people more than the stone.

"Brannog spoke truly," said Thengram. "There has been no life here for years. Once this place was a prison."

Rothgar and a number of others were gathering around the kneeling Earthwrought and Brannog could feel their desire to attack him. He stepped in and drew the frightened being up. "A prison, you say?"

"Aye. The walls are of solid rock, as with that fallen door. As with the floor below us. It took a year to carve those steps down into this place, and Earthwrought died in the process. It would take as long to carve your way out. But there is no food, no water."

There were gasps of astonishment, mingled with anger. Brannog held up his hand for silence. He could not believe Gnarag had brought them there to kill them, but he asked the question anyway.

"No. We were told to bring you here. To detain you."

"But not yourselves?" grunted Rothgar. "Surely that was an error!"

"We did not expect this," agreed Thengram. His own people had gathered about him, huddling like children.

"These were Gnarag's orders?" said Brannog. "Why should he wish to detain us?" He could see that the Host were ready to tear their captors apart for this insult.

"It was the others," said one of them. When he was pulled out and thrust before Brannog, he had paled, quaking where he stood. Brannog could hardly believe this was an Earthwrought. He was not used to such weakness in these people. The spirit was as starved as the body.

"Exalted Earthwrought," said another, and at once a silence fell over them all. Rothgar's face screwed up even more in amazement. He looked askance at Brannog. Brannog knew the myths, but he had never encountered anyone before who had met the Exalted Earthwrought.

One of the Host spoke up scornfully. "They are fashioned from dreams!"

"Not so!" cried Thengram. "They are here. A party of them broke into our system and forced an audience with Gnarag. It was their leader, Ul-Zaan, who gave the order for you to be brought here."

Rothgar and his fellows exchanged uneasy looks. Why should Exalted seek them? And why imprison them?

"So we are not to be killed," said Brannog. "What then? Are we to meet these Exalted? For what purpose?" His mind raced. If these mysterious beings were real, it led to all manner of possibilities! The legendary community of the south, the Far Below, could it too, be real?

"We don't know the answers to your questions," said Thengram. As one, his companions bowed their heads, like prisoners who have already been condemned to die.

Brannog motioned his own followers to let them alone. No good would come of tormenting them. He took Rothgar to one side. "I'm sure we would be wasting our efforts in trying to break out of here. You saw the deep rock as we came down. This mountain root stone is very strong, even for you, Rothgar. But have the Host study the walls of this place for any weakness, any fault. Doubtless we will be summoned eventually, but I don't like having terms dictated to me," he grinned. Rothgar gave out the orders at once, glad to have a task to perform, for like his fellows, he loathed inactivity. Gnarag's people sat together, bowed and silent like sheep. As Brannog joined them, squatting on his haunches to talk to them, their nervousness was doubly apparent, particularly as this huge man did not himself appear to be at all frightened.

"You fear these Exalted. But you need not fear me," he told them. "My Host are gruff, short-tempered. But you must understand that they are warriors and have spent most of their lives at war with Omara's many enemies. Have you heard of Xennidhum? I see from your faces that you have. Well, we have been there. Even now we search out the spawn of that place. We are not your enemies. I came here to meet Gnarag, your Earthwise, in the hope that he, too, would accept me as an ally. I still seek such a goal."

There were looks of incredulity among the huddled Earthwrought. One of them leaned closer to Brannog. "Why? Why should an overman seek alliances?"

Brannog explained then, briefly, about his causes, his dreams of bringing the Earthwrought tribes out of the dark. They were rapt by his tale, and he knew that their hearts were for him. But he could not dispel their despondency.

"You are ruled by fear," he told them. "I oppose such fear. Now you understand my beliefs, my purpose in coming to your exhausted lands. You have repaid me by bringing me to this prison. I see why you have done such a thing. But you must tell me more. Who are these Exalted, and what do they want?"

Thengram became the spokesman. "Like you, we did not believe in them, only as the substance of myth. Yet they came and are real enough. They have already killed Shirag and Cannar, two of our leaders, for refusing to accede to their whims."

"Where are they from? Which direction?"

"We think from the south-east. As you go up into the mountains, it is said that there are lost communities of Earthwrought there—"

"The Far Below?"

Thengram and his fellows were nodding, caught like children in the often-spun web of legend. Brannog had filled the air with the hint of magic in naming the mythical community. "Some say it exists," breathed Thengram. "There are wandering Earthwrought who have no fixed homes, who claim to have been to systems which know of the place. If the stories are true, it is huge, like the cities of overmen."

"And the Exalted come from it?"

"No. We know little about them, only that they serve the Sublime One, the Voice of Omara. He dwells in a place known as Mount Timeless."

"A mountain," nodded Brannog. "And he is below it?"

"It is spoken of the Sublime One that he is at one with the earth and the sky and that one day he will come down from Mount Timeless and—" He paused, suddenly afraid of his own vision.

Brannog heard movement behind him. It was Rothgar. "He will come down from Mount Timeless and destroy mankind, raising the Earthwrought nations up from the dark to build their own cities, as they were built in eons past."

Brannog studied Rothgar's distant expression. He had been with Brannog at Cyrene, when they had discovered the lost city under the desert, where it had been buried for centuries. It had once been the cradle of the Earthwrought, before their exodus under the earth.

"Well, then," said the powerful Earthwrought, surprisingly gently, "we shall have to teach these Exalted a new doctrine. Overmen, as you call them, have entered a new age. Our king, whom you see before you, is a Man. Has he come to be your scourge? To drive you deeper into the earth?

And the Host, the warriors who brought Xennidhum to ashes, are we your enemies?

Brannog smiled. "It is hardly surprising, Rothgar, that Gnarag and his people are confused. It cannot be easy for them to accept that the likes of myself are here to befriend them." He rose to his feet.

"What are we to do?" asked Thengram.

"We mean you no harm. Believe that. Now, what is to happen to us? Where are our true captors?"

"They will come."

Brannog nodded. Rothgar's warriors, meanwhile, had been unable to find any weakness in the rock. The trap was complete, so they wasted no more time in attempting to get out. Brannog explained what had happened, and although there was surprise and a little apprehension, most of the Host were eager to meet the beings who had for so long occupied a place in legend only. While they waited, Brannog talked more to Thengram about recent events and of what had transpired in the world outside, which seemed so remote. Rothgar watched his huge ruler, his face grim, but his mind softening. No Earthwrought ever had such patience! And how was it that a being with such strength could exercise such a gentle touch? Ah, but that was an Earthwrought gift, and Brannog Wormslayer drew deeply on Earthwrought gifts. His blood was their blood. He was their pride.

Brannog was still talking when the first sounds were heard. Stone grated on stone, and although all in the chamber looked for movement, it was a while before anyone realized where the noise was coming from. At the far end of the chamber, in the floor, a great slab was being pulled back. Rothgar was first to it, and he saw in the darkness below a flight of broad steps, leading out of sight. There were no brands to light them, and no glow of Earthwrought skin. Up from the deep earth came a strange breeze, carrying with it the smell of ages.

Both groups came to look, and thought they waited, no one emerged from the dark. Brannog looked at Thengram. "Did you know of this?"

Thengram was nonplussed. One of his companions nudged him and whispered to him. His eyes lit up. "Of course! This

is yet another fragment of the legends. Our people have spoken about it sometimes, especially the very old among us. It
must be the Oblivion Gate.''

''Where does it lead to?'' said Rothgar, studying the black
rectangle as if it would emit serpents.

''It is said, to the Holy Roads. And if there are Exalted—''

''Tell us a little more,'' coaxed Brannog. He could see that
the mysteries being revealed here were as fresh to some of
Thengram's people as they were to his own.

''Many legends tell of Mount Timeless and of the Sublime
One. They also speak of his servants, some of which fly from
the mountains, others which go under the earth, using the
forbidden Holy Roads. These are said to be endless, straight
roads that ring Omara, far under the world. They radiate from
Mount Timeless and return to it. Only the Exalted may tread
upon them.''

Brannog was the only one who smiled. ''A path direct to
the Sublime One?''

At his shoulder, Rothgar snorted. ''This is a legend. I smell
something cold and spiteful in those deeps. We have been
brought here to die.''

''By whose hand?'' said Brannog.

''If the Exalted preach war on overmen, they would not welcome you among them, Brannog. Forgive my bluntness—''

Brannog grinned. ''If I have not done so by now, Rothgar,
how is it you are still alive?''

Rothgar laughed at that, shrugging. ''Well, I speak my
mind—''

''I am glad that you do. I think you are right about our
captors. They resent me and probably the Host. But I wish
to meet them. And I would think that this descent, cold
though it may be, is the only way out of this chamber.''
Brannog turned to Thengram and his fellows. ''Well, Thengram! Are you going to remain here in the hope that Gnarag
will have you rescued? Or are you coming with us?''

''You will go down?'' said Thengram, white with fear.

''I think so. I've a mind to see these Holy Roads.''

Thengram consulted his people, some of whom had already drawn back and who were quite content to remain in

the chamber. But most of them were with Thengram. They
had never seen such power in a being before as in Brannog.
He was not an Earthwise, but neither could he be said to be
a true overman. Yet he exuded something, a force that might
inspire faith. His Host were warriors, but could they match
the Exalted?

"We will come with you," said Thengram.

"If you betray us again," said Rothgar, brandishing his
war club, "I will split every skull—"

"No need," said Thengram curtly, the first sign of spirit
he had shown. "You have my word. We will be content to
obey Brannog. That is the understanding."

Brannog nodded, not wishing to waste any more time. He
was the first to begin the descent.

As though in a dream where time disjoints and drifts, they
went down the great stairway, which Gnarag's people evidently had not carved. The illusion of timelessness was main-
tained by the absolute darkness, for apart from the glow of
their own bodies, there was nothing now to break the black
walls on either side. It was as though they were going down
into the ocean's deepest trough, its floor an unguessable distance below them, always out of reach, in some other world.
No one spoke, and even Brannog, renowned for his efforts
to rouse even the tiredest, was silent.

No sound came to them, not even the echo of their own
footfalls, though they were as quiet as spiders. Over them
they felt the weight of the land, colossal, god-like. Brannog
marvelled at the stairs, perfectly cut, yards wide. Who could
have fashioned them? How many other such stairways existed
under Omara? Abruptly he pulled up. At last he had heard
sounds, and turning, he saw by the faces above him that he
had not imagined them. Was it a distant singing, or had it
been music? Deep and sonorous, the breath of a giant.

"An earthsong," whispered someone in the following, and
Brannog was quick to pick up the word.

"What is it?"

The company stood in silence, almost in reverence of the
song, as if Omara herself had spoken to them. "We have
heard a few earthsongs of late," said Thengram. "They slip
into our dreams. Always from the south and east."

"More mysteries," came Rothgar's deep voice. "But since we are dealing in such things, perhaps they are real."

"Something has been drawing us," said Thengram. "We have lost many of our people, mysteriously. Could they have found the Holy Road? Could the Sublime One have called them?"

Brannog might have scoffed at this once, but he had heard the song. Now it had gone, replaced by the solid wall of silence. There had been sorrow in it; is this how Thengram's people had been subdued? He began the descent once more, silent and thoughtful.

Over an hour later they came to the bottom of the immense stair. They tried to look back, but it was as though the sky had descended and with it the darkest night they had yet seen, for only the first few stairs were visible going upwards. Brannog wondered if they would have been able to take in the whole of the stairway without shrinking back from it, humiliated by its size, for it must have been vast beyond thought. What power could have constructed such a thing? On either side of them now stretched a vague grayness, the flat, dusty surface of the Holy Road. To their left it rose slightly, going, they all knew by instinct, to the north-west. It was instinct also that turned them as a body to the right hand path. Like a door to eternity, it beckoned.

As they began the walk, their combined body light at last threw into relief the walls of the Road, which were concave, rising to an angled ceiling. All had been cut from rock, the work of an unfathomable force, for surely even Earthwrought could not have performed such a wonder. There had been powers at work here that were far outside the reasoning of Man or Earthwrought. No hands had hewn this stone. No beast had burrowed and tunnelled here. The rocks, and twisted arches, of the ceiling looked as though they had been cast in fire and molten energy. And the surface of the road was perfectly flat, smooth and polished as glass, save for its gathering dust.

Rothgar spoke softly to Brannog, and his words somehow shocked the deep silence of the road. "This Holy Road, for such it must be, will go on endlessly. We will need food."

It was not usually difficult for the Earthwrought to find sustenance under the earth, but here, in this sterile cavern system, it would not be easy. Nothing could grow here.

Brannog had been thinking around the various problems of the prospective journey until his head swam. "Aye, you'd better send a party to see what can be found." Rothgar went to obey and Brannog considered the Holy Road. *Have I been led here simply to follow this path? If so, why should Thengram's people have been frightened? What does it hold?*

A shout drew his attention, and in a moment he had his answer. Rothgar and a number of the Host came racing back down the road from the left. Behind them torches were glowing, bobbing up and down like eyes in the dark. In their lurid glow could be seen two or more score of armed warriors, shields and swords glinting. These, Brannog now saw, were the promised Exalted, for their characteristics fitted the descriptions Thengram had given him. They carried swords, just as he had been warned. Quickly the intruders had formed a line across the road and they had the look of a force that is readying to march forward to the battle, an imminent one.

Rothgar, an excellent tactician, quickly positioned his own warriors. Thengram's followers took heart, and although unarmed, adopted a positive stance, committed to their new leader, so it seemed. Brannog slipped easily through the ranks and faced the line of Exalted.

"Where is Ul-Zaan?" he said loudly and his voice rang out hugely around the walls of the Holy Road. He had hoped to bring surprise to the stern warriors, but their painted faces were like stone. He saw in them the veteran, the cold, efficient warrior. They waited, unmoved.

Presently another group of Exalted arrived. They approached Brannog and their leader eyed him boldly, his sword grasped, ready for use. "We have a long journey ahead of us," he said. "The Holy Road holds no dangers for us, its guardians. But we will look to your back."

Brannog returned the cold stare. "You presume too much."

Ul-Zaan raised his shaggy brows. "Does this place not intrigue you? Have you no desire to visit Mount Timeless?"

"Perhaps. Where is Gnarag?"

Ul-Zaan snorted. "They tell me you are a king. Why should you concern yourself with an old fool like Gnarag?"

"Has he been harmed?"

The question surprised Ul-Zaan. "Does it matter? But no, he is as he was."

"Where is he?"

"Hiding in his private warrens, far above us."

"I was invited here by him. His ambassadors are here with me now. I assumed he would be here."

"Gnarag acted on my behalf. He has nothing to say to you that could possibly be of interest. Your destiny, king, lies with the Sublime One. Could there be a greater honor?"

Brannog fought the urge to drive his fist into the ugly and smug face of the Exalted commander. He did not need his instinct to tell him that Ul-Zaan had no sympathy for any cause he, Brannog, might have, nor for Gnarag's people. Perhaps the rank of Exalted had made Ul-Zaan important in his own eyes, but it was more than arrogance at work here. There was more than a hint of evil, and though the Host respected the Exalted, already Brannog felt their distrust of them and what they stood for. Brannog understood the ruthlessness in these beings and he recognized its familiarity—it had been the same cold ruthlessness he had associated with the Deliverers until the war of Xennidhum had changed their philosophy. But what was Xennidhum to these painted warriors?

"I would be pleased to meet your leader," he said bluntly to Ul-Zaan. "But your escort is unnecessary. I have business with Gnarag first. Now that I see the way to the Sublime One, I will follow it when I am ready." Brannog felt those behind him ripple as if in a breeze. Like hounds, they were ready to be unleashed, scenting the meat of battle.

Ul-Zaan's countenance writhed, his anger plain. "The Sublime One does not issue requests. You are to come with us, now."

"And if I do not?"

Ul-Zaan turned to his warriors. "I have several hundred more at my disposal, camped not far from here. Must I summon them to strengthen my argument?" He had stepped carefully from the immediate range of Brannog and his followers, and those beside him had closed with him, swords raised.

"Then we are your prisoners?" said Brannog.

"Only if you so choose," snapped Ul-Zaan. "But it is entirely unnecessary."

Rothgar tensed. If Brannog elected to stand and fight, so be it, but would they survive? How important was it for the Sublime One to receive Brannog? he wondered. If it was essential, he would not wish him killed. Even so, Rothgar grunted: Ul-Zaan's vermin could overpower them all easily by sheer numbers. Like rats, they choked the Holy Road.

"Have you an answer?" Ul-Zaan said impatiently.

Brannog had not moved, but now there came an altercation in the far ranks of the Exalted. Swords rang on stone and there were loud shouts, followed by unexpected screams. The Exalted broke ranks and there was a terrible snarling. Ul-Zaan turned and Brannog reacted so swiftly, no one knew what he had done until he had a brawny arm around Ul-Zaan's neck. He lifted the struggling figure from the ground, all but choking him, and the Exalted's sword clattered to the Road. His two aides wanted to stab at Brannog but dared not. Rothgar and Thengram both came forward, Rothgar like the wind; he brained one of the Exalted and Thengram acted in a way that took them all by surprise. He scooped up Ul-Zaan's sword and in a flowing move pinned the breast of the other Exalted, who staggered back, fatally wounded. There had been no more time to debate. They all knew that death walked the Holy Road.

The line of Exalted warriors broke and only now could Brannog see what it was that had so confounded them. Three huge shapes moved among them like fire, tearing at them with great fangs, eyes glowing like coals in the semi-dark. The Exalted were in utter confusion, unable to form ranks and counter the unexpected assault. Many of them had fallen with their throats torn, and others toppled in the crush, trampled on and maimed by their colleagues.

Ul-Zaan tried to speak but could not, barely permitted enough air to breathe by Brannog. The latter roared at Rothgar and his followers to get back on to the stairs where they could best defend themselves, and in moments they had done so. Brannog leapt up with them, only to be followed by the three huge wolves who had wrought so much havoc among the Exalted. Blood matted their huge chests, but they turned, eager to resume the fray. The Exalted were at last gathering themselves, though they were so disorganized that Brannog debated if he should attack them. But he held back, thinking of Ul-Zaan's words of earlier. If there were hundreds more of them near at hand, battle would in the end be futile. But at the same time, flight up the great stair would also be fruitless.

Brannog studied the wolves. How had they come here! They rubbed their huge shoulders against his legs and he laughed at them. Ul-Zaan almost passed out in horror. This overman was *allied* to these monsters!

"They are your own wolves!" cried Rothgar, also recognizing them.

Brannog had no answer: it should have been impossible. He shook Ul-Zaan, placing him on his feet, though the Exalted could not move for terror.

"Call your warriors off," Brannog told him. "Or I will feed you to my wolves and then unleash them on your rabble. I have a dozen more near at hand. Do not doubt it."

Ul-Zaan's mouth opened and closed almost comically, but before any words came out, there was a frightful baying sound from up the road, beyond the gathered Exalted ranks. Brannog was as stunned as they were, for his three wolves were here. As far as he knew, there were no others. But the effect of the dreadful howling was instant, for the Exalted rushed forward, not to the attack, but down the Holy Road, as though a score of wolves were on their heels. Ul-Zaan let out a shriek and leapt from the stairs in pursuit. Brannog's wolves would have brought him to ground in seconds, but Brannog spoke a word to them and they sat quietly. The retreat of the Exalted was noisy and undignified, and they left many wounded behind them, groaning, trying to limp to safety.

Rothgar would have laughed at the sudden flight of the enemy, but his eyes were riveted to the upper road, expecting to see the emergence of the beasts that had given tongue to such ghastly howls. Possibly the shape of the ceiling had magnified and distorted the sounds, but even so, the beasts must be huge. The dust began to settle, and as it cleared, something emerged, shrouded in darkness. But it was alone and it did not lope on four legs.

It was long moments before anyone moved. In the end only Brannog went forward to meet the creature. Rothgar heard him say something, but like the others he was prepared to wait.

"What did Brannog say?" whispered Thengram. "Was it a curse?"

Rothgar clapped an arm about the smaller being and grinned. "I think he said, 'Ruvanna.' "

5
Night Child

OGRUND HAD POSTED his guards and knew that the camp was secure, the Host resting but alert, geared for war if need be. Ogrund himself could not enjoy the luxury of sleep. He had been uneasy about Brannog since the king had left with Gnarag's ambassadors, but he had repeatedly told himself that the visit to the system should be no more than another attempt to win allies. Gnarag, by all accounts a weak Earthwise, should not cause Brannog any difficulties. Yet there was something else that kept Ogrund awake. The howling of Brannog's wolves had heralded danger, but from what? Had it been the ambassadors? Could such poor creatures have caused the wolves to howl in distress? Ogrund heard the echoes of those howls yet and he could not relax for them.

He left his shelter beneath a rock overhang in the forest and wandered quietly through the camp. The men from Elderhold were excellent woodsmen and their perfectly constructed hides blended in with the undergrowth in such a way that only a keen search would detect them. Others had made their resting places high up in the trees, which Earthwrought seldom climbed. Ogrund nodded to himself: Brannog had again shown his better vision, for a number of the Host had not been convinced that Men should be part of the company.

As Ogrund went around the perimeter of the camp, his guards, Men and Earthwrought alike, reported that all was peaceful, both above and below ground. The camp was across the valley from Gnarag's system, but the land over there was asleep, with no hint of movement. Ogrund had sent out a

59

few scouts to watch the land for a radius of three miles around the system, just in case anyone came or went that he should know about.

The camp was lit by a near-full moon, but it looked no more than any other part of the forest. A stranger could have ridden into it and not been aware of it. Ogrund grunted to himself, satisfied, and turned from its perimeter. As he did so, he caught the distant sound, like a shout. He was beside his guards in an instant, his club in his hand.

"A rider," someone breathed and moments later they could all hear the beat of hoofs and the crashing of undergrowth. "He comes in haste."

"And terror," said Ogrund, for it hung like a miasma before them. Out of the darkness the rider now plunged, the horse rearing. It was one of the scouts, his face ghastly with fright. He dismounted in a jumble of limbs, falling to the floor before struggling up. The Earthwrought caught the horse before it could bolt, noting its coat of lather, its terrified eyes. Softly they spoke to it, soothing it.

Ogrund had the rider brought into the safety of the camp, but the Man kept looking back over his shoulder, his eyes rolling like his steed's. Ogrund had water brought and himself sat with the Man. Danoth arrived within moments.

"Imlan! What has happened?" he said.

Finally the heaving chest subsided and Imlan seemed to understand that he was among friends and for the moment out of danger. "They came up the river valley from the north. Dozens of them."

"Earthwrought?" said Ogrund.

Imlan shook his head. "No! They were not Men of any kind either. They were like huge worms, some of them, but I swear they had *arms!* Worse than that murkworm Brannog killed. The light was not good. Their faces—"

"Faces?" repeated Danoth. "This was a trick of the moon—"

"Or a nightmare," said one of the Earthwrought.

"No! I saw them. They came on, ordered and like a procession, or an advance party. It was not these things that so filled me with dread, though even now I shudder to think of them."

Ogrund's eyes fixed Imlan, cold and demanding. His large hands were bunched. "They were no illusion."

Danoth gripped his arm. "From Xennidhum?"

"They must be. What else did you see, Imlan? No matter how vile it was, you must tell us," urged Ogrund.

Imlan nodded, gulping more water as if it were strong mead. "These creatures were like giant maggots, and they were hideous to look upon. I watched them from some high rocks and at first they were not aware of me. As they swarmed past, I saw something else in their midst. It was as tall as a Man, and indeed, I thought it a Man at first! But it was wrapped in a gray robe, the folds swathed about its head so that it could not be seen properly. It had sleeves, so had two arms, and in one hand it carried a long staff, or some such weapon. And it was a master of the things about it, directing them with its staff, just like a shepherd! I had hidden myself well, as I thought, but then that creature turned its hood to me and although I could see no face, I felt that its eyes were upon me." Imlan had gone white, his body shaking as if he had been left out on an ice floe without clothing. "And those eyes! I took to my heels. My horse was already trying to pull free of its tether, and once upon it, I rode like the wind."

"How far?" said Ogrund, his voice barely above a whisper.

Danoth saw his expression. "What is it, Ogrund?"

"Xennidhum's legacy," Ogrund replied bitterly and heads bent forward to catch what he said next. "What he has seen is a Child of the Mound."

The words came down like the promise of ruin, bringing a silence that was broken only by the hoarse breathing of Imlan. Ogrund stood up. So that was what had shaken the wolves!

"It must be killed. At once. Gather the Host. Now!" He had not directed this at anyone in particular, but several of the Host raced away to raise the alarm.

Danoth looked stunned, as did a number of the Earth-wrought. Ogrund knew that the Men had not been at Xennidhum, but to them the creatures of that place must be even more nightmarish. He saw in his own mind the grim dwellers in that city, the legions of madness that had opposed Korbillian's army.

The man of Ternannoc had gone deep down into the citadel to destroy the heart of the Mound, the evil corruption that controlled the black city, and with it, they had supposed, he had destroyed most of the Children. Now that one had appeared here on the surface, Ogrund knew that it was something he had been dreading ever since he had left dead Xennidhum. Just as the spawn of the city wriggled out of the Silences, so had this monster come to the lands of Elderhold.

"Killed?" said Danoth, appalled. "Do we have the power to do this?"

Ogrund grimaced. "Power? It took power to defeat them and their hordes once. And those creatures Imlan has described can die, by club or sword or torch."

"Why is their master here?" asked one of the Earthwrought.

"Flight," suggested Ogrund. "To the southern ranges, where it can lose itself and never be found." Let us pray, he thought, that my guess is true.

Danoth nodded thoughtfully. "Could it have come here for another reason? Is its presence here coincidence?"

Ogrund looked startled. He thought of the nervousness of the ambassadors of Gnarag, the howling of the wolves. "Brannog—"

"Had we better not go to Gnarag's system—"

"Not yet. We must get to this abomination from the north at once. It will never expect to be attacked."

Danoth looked uncertain. Ogrund was in command, but this seemed an abrupt move on his part. It had not taken Danoth long to assess Ogrund's stealth and subtlety, his skill at reading the land about him, something for which the king had undoubtedly chosen him. But dare they risk an all-out attack on something that had unknown power? Surely it would be better to talk to Brannog first.

Ogrund's people were in two minds. If they were told to attack, they would do so. Ogrund had not been chosen to lead them because he was incompetent. His skill, his judgment, his caution, were thought highly of by them all. But a Child of the Mound—there was no other being like it. It would not be as the other vermin they had been hunting down.

Ogrund read all these thoughts in their faces, Men and Earthwrought. Should I do this? I do not do it out of pride! No, I will not prevaricate. "We must move with absolute caution. No horses! Every one of us, Man and Earthwrought, will travel on foot. Imlan, are you well enough to lead the way?"

The white-faced warrior pointed to the north. "Travel down the river valley for less than an hour and you will walk straight into its path."

"Then you need not come," nodded Ogrund. He left them all then, organizing his guards and the watch. Those that were chosen to stay were relieved, though they did not show it. Within minutes almost the entire camp was ready to move out, and once Ogrund was satisfied that he was not spearheading a rabble, he led them out into the forest, fanning them out in a wide arc that ranged from the upper slopes of one valley side to the other. He himself kept to the center of the advance, moving along the river bank, which twisted and dropped, the water fast and white-foamed as it roared northwards. The Host moved at a slow, silent trot that would not have disturbed a hunting cat. Ogrund smoothed over his fears, for they were deep, and he concentrated on his warriors. They filled him with pride, for no better fighting force could exist. Danoth and the Men of Elderhold were superb woodsmen, as accomplished above ground as the Earthwrought were below it. There should be no reason to suppose that they could not destroy this thing from the north.

Imlan's estimate had been accurate. Less than an hour's march down the valley, they heard the enemy below them, where the forest took a sudden dip, sloping steeply away to a widening of the river into a number of pools. As the Host formed a semi-circle around the crest of the slope, the strange murmurings below could be heard. There were no voices, and nothing that hinted at any kind of recognizable speech, no matter how alien, but a vague hissing and growling.

Ogrund sent word to the outer arms of his formation to deploy scouts around the camp of the enemy, measuring its extent. He wondered if the Child of the Mound was above ground. It would make this battle easier, but he wondered why these refugees should not be below the surface anyway. The deep levels had always been their hiding place. What could have brought them up? He paled at the thought of Danoth's earlier words. A rendezvous with

Gnarag's people? To betray Brannog? Ogrund shook his mind free of the thought, waiting.

Whatever minions the Child of the Mound had with it, they were completely under its control, for none of them seemed to have strayed from the central core. This was bad, as it suggested that their master had enough power to restrain them from the sort of mindless journeys they usually made. Ogrund closed his eyes and concentrated his every effort of will, holding his club before him as if he could pour power of his own, power of the earth, into it. Beside him, Danoth watched him, marvelling at the spirit of the small figure, taking heart from its awesome courage.

The word came back swiftly: the Child of the Mound was below, surrounded by its grim followers. There were no guardians and the entire camp was resting. No doubt, Ogrund thought, they consider themselves safe from anything. They use the world's dread to secure themselves. He thought of something Brannog had once said of Xennidhum, that the place was like a disease, a canker, and, just like a plague, it had been avoided for centuries.

"Close the circle," he told his runners. "And give the word that there is to be no fire until I command it." Ogrund knew that there would be a strong temptation for his warriors to light fires, knowing just how afraid these creatures below were of it. But he wanted none of them to escape. He had also warned a strong contingent of his Earthwrought that they must be ready to go below ground if so charged, for some of the creatures would try to escape that way, although the Child of the Mound had chosen its night camp poorly, being so close to the river. It would restrict any subterranean flight.

They began the descent, careful not to disturb loose soil or fallen twigs that would betray their coming. The forest was deciduous, at the height of its growing season, and it was not possible to see through the dense undergrowth for more than a few yards. But at last the Host was above the enemy. Even now their presence had gone undetected, which made Ogrund even more cautious.

The word was passed around the closing circle; it was perilously close to the enemy. "Very well," said Ogrund. "Let us begin."

The command went along the line like fire and now the arrows were ignited. A dreadful cacophony broke out of the camp of the enemy as the forest suddenly seemed to erupt into daylight. A ring of fire spread about it and then the deadly rain had begun. Arrow after arrow was shot into the heart of the enemy, and at once they broke ranks and came screaming up the slopes at Ogrund's warriors. Less committed troops would have fled from the horrors they now saw, for the servants of the Child of the Mound were ghastly. They did indeed have faces, so huge and grossly distorted that they could have been the work of some manic creator. They gaped, spitting and slavering like hounds taken by madness. Their bloated arms clawed out wildly, and even with a dozen fire arrows in them, they came on. But they had no organization, goaded by blind instinct.

The Host met them with club and sword and although it was easy to beat at and strike them, they flailed about so uncontrollably that they claimed many victims. The fire had done its work well, in that it had set alight the heart of the camp, roasting many of the gross creatures in minutes and spreading among them as if a pool of oil had been ignited. The stench was disgusting, the palls of acrid smoke thick and black. But madness reigned as creature after creature tried to rush away from that immense pyre.

The circle of attack held well, in spite of the losses. Slowly it moved in as the rush of the stumbling creatures subsided. Breathing the foul air had become difficult, and Ogrund's warriors were glad of the chance to use the river and its pools to wet cloth and pelt in order to mask the fumes. Ogrund and Danoth almost fell victims to one huge creature as it rose over them, but both rolled away acrobatically, turning to see a dozen of their finest warriors chopping into the beast. As it died, Ogrund took stock. The smoke hid everything more effectively than the night. He looked at Danoth, but neither smiled at their awful work.

"The Child hasn't attacked us," Ogrund grunted. "But we must find it."

A lull came in the battle, broken only by the death agonies of more blazing creatures. They no longer came rushing from the heart of their camp. The Host tightened its formation, watching the smoke. Others tended to the wounded; many Men and Earthwrought had died here. The last of the creatures made their frantic attempt to flee, but they were now chopped down with ease, and after they had given up their lives, a strange silence fell. The smoke parted gradually as dawn began to smolder in the east. Ogrund nodded to Danoth and the ring closed in for the last time.

Beside one of the pools, whose banks were black and charred with the bodies of a dozen fallen creatures, was a rock face, tall and slippery, not an easy climb. High on its crest could be seen a line of bowmen, their fire arrows sending plumes of smoke upwards. Ogrund's warriors had closed right in, and they could see with great joy, that every last one of the creatures had been either gutted or cut to ribbons. Some, Ogrund heard later, had buried themselves, but they had been cornered and destroyed.

Ogrund, however, felt no pride, no joy, for his own fears rode over such emotions. Where was the Child of the Mound? Unless he killed it, none of this carnage meant anything. He had done no more than destroy a plague of vermin. As he stepped through the haze, he saw something at the foot of the rock face, draped in shadow. He moved as close as he dared, with a score of warriors around him. They halted, watching the cloaked thing that was only now limned by the dawn behind Ogrund's shoulder. It was the Child of the Mound, slumped down as if dead. But it moved, dragging itself up like a wounded man. A dozen bows steadied their arrows, waiting for Ogrund to give the command. Still no challenge came from the cloaked being. Its face and eyes were invisible, its arms draped at its side like dead things.

Ogrund nodded. Immediately the arrows sped for their goal, but they never reached it. Somewhere inside the overhang they swerved aside by a fraction, but enough to send them clattering into stone. The Child had not moved. Another dozen arrows were discharged, but they suffered the same fate as the first. Ogrund could feel the eyes of the Host upon him, waiting for his decision. The Child was using its power. How much did it have?

"It's wounded," said Danoth.

Don't give me your pity! Ogrund wanted to cry. "But not to be underestimated," he breathed. "We must not let it get away. This thing can do untold damage." He issued new orders, sending his warriors out to the Host, organizing woodsmen to hew down branches, making stakes of them. "Ring this rock face with the stakes," Ogrund told them. "See that the points angle in at the Child of the Mound. And have fire burning constantly. It may try to break free at any time."

Less than an hour later it was done. The Child had not moved, still hiding in the shadows of the overhang, untouched by the day as it brightened. When the line of stakes was completed, Ogrund inspected it several times before he was satisfied. Then he turned to his messengers, his face grave.

"Send for Brannog," he said. "Go into Gnarag's system if you have to, but find the king. He must come."

Danoth watched as a number of Earthwrought slipped into the trees, wondering at those who had died. Did Ogrund count this as a defeat? He could not read his face, and was far too diplomatic to ask.

Ogrund fixed his gaze on the Child, unwavering. What have I done? he asked himself. I have given up the lives of so many for this. But know this, if you can hear me, spawn of the night: you will not escape me unless you can take us all, aye all. He closed his mind. And waited.

BRANNOG STARED at the girl as though he had been plunged into his own past, somewhere along the road to the nightmares at Xennidhum. But it was Ruvanna and not Sisipher who faced him insouciantly, hands on her hips. He felt a sudden urge to hold her and raise her up before his followers, but he drove the instinct down. Had Ruvanna wrought all this havoc?

"You can tell me how you got here later," he said thickly, confused by his own feelings. "Is there another way out?"

Ruvanna's grin dissolved. She was disappointed, having expected thanks if not praise. Was he angry? She was about to retort, but she saw the wolves behind him, his creatures now. This was no place to fight him. "Yes; quickly. I have made a way. Tell the Host to hurry. There are many more Exalted marching on us from the north along the Holy Road. And there are other dangers behind you. Tell your Host to close up their ears."

"To what?"

"There may be earthsongs. They trap the unwary. Come, quickly!"

As she turned and led the way, hiding her annoyance, Brannog called to his warriors and to Thengram's people, and as one they obeyed him. They saw with amazement that it was a village girl who had rescued them. But where were the other wolves? Rothgar scratched his thick mane of hair, but thought better of pressing for an answer.

A short distance up the Holy Road there was what looked like a minor fall of earth and beyond it in the wall a passageway. It wound up through a fault in the rock like a stream bed, and the Earthwrought easily climbed its incline. The Men found it more difficult, but goaded on by their fear of what might be following, they made the climb eventually. It brought them up into the tunnels of an abandoned part of Gnarag's system, which Thengram recognized, but there were no signs of his people.

"Their shame will not permit them to come out now," he told Brannog. "Though the same shame taints us."

"Then put it aside," said Brannog. "If you are to become part of the Host, you will have other things to concern you. Ruvanna!"

She had been moving on ahead as if in charge of the entire party. As she came back, grinning, he was again reminded of his daughter's spirit and determination. Time fractured: just as he gazed on the past, so did he seem to catch a glimpse of the future, as though it mirrored the strong will of his daughter in this girl.

"If there's a way to the surface, lead us to it," he said impatiently. "I'll waste no more time here. If Gnarag feels any remorse for what he's done, then we'll leave him to endure it. Are there any Exalted above us?"

"I don't think so," she replied, turning to lead the way to daylight.

Rothgar came up beside Brannog, watching the slim back of the girl closely. "How is it that she came to be below? The wolves are obedient to her."

"Kennagh told me she had certain gifts. I've seen such

things before," murmured Brannog, but Rothgar was not aware that he referred to his own daughter.

"Is she to join us? We do not usually take women to war."

"I'll think what to do later," Brannog said. War. How easily the word had come to Rothgar's lips. Must it come to that? Had it not ended at Xennidhum? But there remained so much evil to seek out.

They came to the surface some distance above Gnarag's lair, and saw that the morning was young. Food was found and the warriors used one of the many mountain brooks to refresh themselves. Ruvanna sat apart from them, watching some of them but saying nothing. Brannog deliberately avoided her, though his Host kept eyeing him to see what he would do about her. In the end he went to her. He stood over her, dwarfing her, frowning. She had a great gift, he knew that, for the journey she had made would have been extremely difficult, if not impossible, for many of the Host. Her courage matched that skill, for she had risked a grim death at the hands of the Exalted.

He studied her for a long time and she looked away, intimidated by him. "You must not think me ungrateful," he said softly, and his tone took her by surprise. "But I am a man who has seen the darker side of this world, Ruvanna. You have seen me destroy the thing from Xennidhum, but it was a small thing I did, believe me. I can't expose you to the conflict I take to our enemies. Your people need your gift, helping them to build—"

"I have no people," she said bluntly. "And my gifts aren't to be wasted. You are the king, the leader. You must use me, as a weapon."

Her abruptness, its underlying anger, shocked him. She was a child, and yet she spoke with the confidence, the experience almost, of an adult. "You speak as you do because you have not *seen*," he told her, his voice and mood hardening. "You cannot know what we have to face."

"Then you reject me?"

"No! It is not rejection, foolish girl!" He saw at once that he had used his words clumsily. "Look, Ruvanna, you are as important to your people as my warriors. How can I make you see that?"

He could sense a cutting reply, but a shout interrupted him and he swung round to see Rothgar approaching with a breathless Earthwrought. It was Dramlac, one of the scouts from Ogrund's party. He was smeared with dust and practically exhausted.

"What is it?" said Brannog.

Dramlac saw the wolves, his eyes widening with surprise at finding them here after his fruitless search, but he went on to gasp out his story. Brannog learned then of Ogrund's night journey and of what waited at the end of it. Brannog paled at the telling of the trapping of the Child of the Mound. Ogrund had *challenged* this thing? He gripped Dramlac by the arms, almost pulling him from the ground.

"You are sure this is a Child of the Mound?"

"Ogrund knew it at once," Dramlac nodded.

Brannog set him down apologetically. Was Ogrund insane!

"He feared you might have been trapped," Dramlac said, seeing Brannog's consternation. "He acted in good faith."

But without good sense! But Brannog nodded. "Of course. I should know him better. Are you fit enough to take us back?"

A horse was brought for Dramlac, who was only too glad to be able to lead the party back to Ogrund. Brannog was about to have a last word with Ruvanna, but to his annoyance he saw that she had gone. Perhaps the mention of the Child of the Mound had been enough to convince her that there were better places to be. He leapt up to his own horse, Rothgar beside him, and raced off with the remainder of the Host down the valley, the girl soon forgotten.

When Brannog reached Ogrund, the Earthwrought commander had made good his securing of the Child of the Mound. Brannog commended him on the positioning of the ring of stakes, and there were enough fires blazing to ignite an entire township. Brannog clapped an arm about Ogrund in full view of the Host, his face beaming.

"Well, here's a fine prize, Ogrund!"

Ogrund wanted to gasp with relief at the praise, but he masked his swelling pride. He pointed to the overhang. The Child had not moved, like some dark spider clinging to a rock wall.

"Did we lose many?" said Brannog more soberly, so that only Ogrund heard him.

Ogrund recounted the losses, naming all those that had fallen, even Danoth's Men. "Did I do wrong, sire?"

Brannog shook his head. "If I had been a prisoner and this creature had been lured to me, I would have been destroyed. You did well." They spoke quietly for a while and although Brannog's sorrow at so many deaths was evident, the Host saw that he commended Ogrund.

"I would have destroyed this thing for you," said the Earthwrought. "But I am not sure how much power it holds back."

"I am glad you did not kill it," Brannog grunted, knowing that this would surprise many of his warriors. He turned to them. "Hear me! This has been a famous triumph for the Host. It is indeed a Child of the Mound you have trapped here. You have done well to attempt its execution, but before it dies, there are things we must learn from it."

Thengram and others from his system were staring open mouthed at the shrouded figure in the rocks, and many of the Host were still apprehensive about the being, garbed as it was in legend. Question it? Could Brannog be serious?

"Why is it here?" Brannog called. "Why was it coming up the valley toward us? Was it hunting us, or myself? Or did it follow some other course? Ogrund tells me he thought it might have been a part of Gnarag's deceptions, but that is not so."

Ogrund was relieved to know that Brannog had not been unduly imperilled by Gnarag's people, and when he heard the tale of how Thengram had allied himself to the Host, he was quick to accept him and his followers. He did insist, however, that after this affair he be allowed to go to Gnarag and drag him from his lair, deposing him and setting up a new Earthwise, if one could be found. Brannog let Ogrund bluster, ending the discussion by telling him that he had no wish to be known as a tyrant. If Thengram's late fellows wanted to retain Gnarag as their Earthwise, let them. Anything they had done to snare Brannog for the Exalted had been done out of fear. "If they follow me, it must be because they choose to."

For a long time the camp was gripped by fresh discussions,

and ones in which everyone seemed to have something to
say: no one, not even the king, was certain how to attempt
the questioning of the Child of the Mound. Brannog had the
circle of stakes moved up, right to the edge of the overhang,
and had all the torches brought to it. Still the creature had
not moved, but all were aware that it lived.

Brannog came as close as he dared. "I know that you hear
me!" he shouted, his voice ringing around the overhang, carried to every member of the Host by the rock. "I am Brannog, and I fought with Korbillian at Xennidhum. He slew
many of your kind and we are sworn to slay any of you that
still live. These things you know, Child of Xennidhum."

At last it stirred, its robes moving as if in a breeze. Its
arms lifted a little, but no hands were visible. Its head moved
under the gray hood, but no countenance showed. There were
eyes, though, scarlet as blood, piercing as light. The creature
emitted a low growl that grated along the soul. Brannog's
wolves pulled back, flat to the ground, afraid. The sight of
their fear unnerved Brannog, but he did not show it. Korbillian had possessed immeasurable power which had enabled
him to blast a score of these beings. But how was he, Brannog, to better even one of them?

"Tell us why you are here," he called. His throat had gone dry.
He dare not ride away and leave this thing alive, but it may be the
only course open to him. If he did such a thing, wise though it
may be, what of Ogrund? How could the loyal Earthwrought survive such shame? No, the beast must be faced.

For a while the Child remained silent, its horrible eyes fixing
those of anyone who dared look at it. Then a snarl came from it
and there was a flash of teeth that sent the wolves back further.
The ferocity of the snarl appalled Brannog, as if he faced an elemental power, a feral thing and something not at all human. As
he felt its blast, he knew that he could not overcome it. Strength
of arm would not be enough.

While he waited, trying to decide on his next move, the
warriors behind him parted to allow a slim figure through
their ranks. Brannog paid no attention at first, for like
Ogrund, his eyes were fixed upon the Child. But as he sensed
the figure at his elbows, he looked down. He felt a shiver of

apprehension. Ruvanna stood there, feigning calmness, though staggered at the sight of the creature in the rocks.

"You should not be here," he said softly, trying not to believe that he was somehow powerless to control her.

"Forgive me," she said as softly, still awed by the Child.

"So you have seen it. I would not send my fiercest warriors against this monster," he told her. "Do you understand why I fear for you? For us all? You must leave at once. Do I have to send you back to Kennagh?"

"You wish to question this creature? It has a mind, and listens to every word, every sound in the forest. Such power—"

Brannog stared at her. "You feel it?"

"Oh yes. It is frightful," she whispered. "It knows you are all afraid of it. And how it feasts on that! But it is wounded. The fire took it by surprise and damaged it before it could escape the trap. If your warriors close in on it and attack it with fire, you can kill it, though some of you will die."

"But we'd kill it?"

"Yes. But if you want answers from it—"

He bent to her. "How can you know these things? How can you travel through rock that would tax the strength of the ablest of my Host? How can you command my wolves? Do you read the mind of this creature before us? Where have you learned such talents?"

She shrugged. "I don't know," she answered, a little petulantly. "Is it me or the Child you seek answers from?"

"You've a sharp enough tongue. Have a care that it does not diminish you. And consider carefully—I have no reason to take you into the confidence of the Host, for all your help."

"Then let me show my worth! Use me."

"And how should I do that?"

She nodded to the Child.

He was forced to grin in spite of himself. "Oh, and do you know how to converse with it? Can you demand answers from it?" he said. But the cloud that was his past darkened his mood. Sisipher's gift had been a curse.

Ruvanna, however, smiled as if she had already won a victory of sorts. "Let me show you."

Part Two

THE STEELMASTER

6
Mourndark

HIGH ABOVE THE innermost courtyards of the Direkeep, its principal Deliverers met in the chamber they had set aside for themselves, the most cloistered and private rooms in the fortress, where only a chosen few of their number had been permitted entry since the upheavals that followed the death of Grenndak the Preserver, who had for so long been their ruler. This central chamber was at the very heart of the tower, and its four doors were tonight heavily guarded. Within the chamber six men had gathered. They glanced uneasily at the window, which opened on a churning sky, laced now and then with the glow of distant lightning. As they waited for a final member of their group to join them, they said very little, as if afraid that the grim walls of the citadel would transmit their words to unwelcome listeners. There was an atmosphere of apprehension as charged as the distant air where the storm gathered.

Eirron Lawbrand, the eldest of the group at fifty, was known for his calmness; he was a particularly rational member of the Faithful and since the rebellion had proved himself a diplomatic administrator. Yet he looked now as if recent events had taken something out of him. He seemed tired for once, as if maintaining his coolness with an effort; his fellows were aware of it and it heightened their own tensions. In the distance, the storm rumbled like an ill omen. Lawbrand waved the late arrival to a seat with a patient smile, aware of the strange silence of his companions. Usually by now they would have been talking quietly among themselves, discussing the business of the Direkeep, which they ran in the absence of their new ruler, Simon Wargallow.

These Faithful, who had been absolutely loyal to Wargallow since the very first days he had plotted the downfall of the Preserver, had found the times after the latter's death volatile. Lawbrand had often wondered how they had kept stability in the Direkeep. Initially, no more than a few days after the Preserver had been killed, Wargallow had left with Korbillian's army, marching on the eastern wastes with a thousand Deliverers. In the war there, they had won an appallingly costly victory, and when Wargallow returned to the Direkeep, he had begun his purging of its people with his expected ruthlessness. The Abiding Word, the law of the Preserver, which had governed every move in the life of a Deliverer, was rejected. Lawbrand himself had put the torch to the old writings and records, thus taking his name. Wargallow had stood before a score of great gatherings of his people and had told them, instructed them on pain of expulsion, to cast its doctrines from them. All across Omara, in its remotest places, Deliverers were told of the new way. And the Faithful, the core of private supporters that Wargallow had brilliantly created for years, saw to the strict adherence to the new teachings. Those in the Direkeep who offered resistance, or questioned too hard the death of the Preserver, were either banished, or worse. Many had died, cleanly executed: Wargallow would not tolerate those who fought him and his destruction of the old, merciless ways. For this singlemindedness he was criticized, but not by the Faithful. Wargallow had told them at the outset that the path to a new life would have to be cut through flesh and sinew: from the first they had been committed to it. Wargallow's method had been as merciless and as unremitting as those of Grenndak, but his Faithful never wavered in their cause, like surgeons removing a growth.

It had soon been established that the Preserver's devout followers were, in reality, few, for most of the Deliverers had welcomed the sweeping changes that Wargallow brought. The days of darkness and pain, of cruel, wanton killing, were over, except for those, Wargallow said, who wished to go on as they had been, sacrificing Omarans to the earth, giving their blood to it. But for them, the punishment would be swift. You may be replacing one tyrant with another, Wargallow had told his people (and his enemies had been quick to voice agreement) but too much blood has been spilled in Omara by our people. That will stop, and ironically it may take your blood to stop it.

Now there remained a few remote places in Omara where word of the new regime had not reached, but with very few exceptions the scattered Deliverers accepted the change. Fear had ruled them, and in many cases, Lawbrand knew, it had been terror, for there was corruption among Grenndak's people. If many Deliverers were afraid of Wargallow, it was a different fear, that of guilt and not fear for life, for survival. Those Deliverers who stubbornly opposed Wargallow, or who still nurtured a belief that the Preserver's law should be reinstated were either executed or confined to the Direkeep, awaiting trial. Some had been released, though few wanted that, afraid that their lives beyond the bleak walls would be short, for the Deliverers were an unloved race.

"Is there word?" one of the Faithful asked.

Lawbrand came out of his reverie. He nodded. "From the west. We are soon to receive an emissary from Wargallow."

The news would once have been greeted with excitement, but recently Wargallow's envoys had had little to report that had a direct bearing on events at the Direkeep. Wargallow did not always send a Deliverer, for he had been deeply involved in matters of the western islands for many months. Lawbrand felt that Wargallow had taken great risks in being away from the Direkeep for so long, but it had quickly become clear that there was a great change coming in the west, and one that would likely have consequences for all Omarans. In the eastern lands about the Direkeep, new towns were springing up after the war, and Deliverers were accepted in them, if suspiciously, thanks to the work of their ruler. Many had left the keep to find a new life outside. Those who walked in the shadow of Wargallow were not interfered with.

"As you know," Lawbrand went on, "Ottemar Remoon is now Emperor in Goldenisle. Wargallow remains a close ally to him, and indeed, has taken a major role in helping

him to win his throne. I am sure he will turn his close attention to us now.''

"And not too soon," said Vecta, the youngest of them.
He was no less loyal to Wargallow than any of them, his
devotion being close to the fanatical, but his vision did not
extend far to the west. He seemed, Lawbrand thought, to
have little patience, even with the men of Elberon, the new
city where another of Wargallow's allies, Ruan Dubhnor, was
the ruler. But Lawbrand knew the real matter to which Vecta
alluded, for it was in the minds of all of them gathered there.

"Well," said Lawbrand as calmly as he could, "the emissary has already left Elberon, and can be expected at any
time. He is a Deliverer and comes direct from Wargallow
himself, so no doubt our instructions will be clear."

"Pardon my bluntness," said another of them, Harn
Coldreive. He was a tall, somber man, expressionless and
not given to many words. He had been one of the Six, those
who had carried out the execution of the Preserver, the only
one of them to be part of this company tonight. "This emissary will not be enthusiastically received if he comes with
no more than a report of events, however encouraging. I do
not speak for myself, nor, I am sure, for any of us here,"
and he looked about him almost icily, "but our greater numbers are concerned."

"Aye, there is a restlessness in the Direkeep these days,"
agreed Lawbrand. "Let us hope the emissary restores a little
calm." Meanwhile, he thought, we have to face again the
one problem that we have not been able to resolve. Like a
deeply buried thorn, it pricks our flesh, and when we think
it has worked itself loose, it pricks us again.

"Shall we admit the Steelmaster?" said Vecta, invading
his thoughts.

Lawbrand nodded. The guards beyond the doors were
called. The Steelmaster, Mourndark, Lawbrand knew, would
never be anything other than a problem. He had been the
Preserver's right hand, the gifted surgeon who had presided
over the casting of the purifying steel, the killing steel, which
all Deliverers were given as young men. Their right arms
were removed and the steel of the killing hand replaced it.
Mourndark's work had been his life, the supervising of the

giving of these cruel hands. Wargallow had now decreed that
no more such hands were to be cast and that there were to
be no more amputations, no more mutilations in the name of
the Abiding Word. And Mourndark, shaking with fury, had
cursed the name of Wargallow ever since. He had been im-
prisoned here, though not in some low pit or cell, but in his
own quarters, which were as luxurious as the keep would
allow. His allies were also here in their own fine apartments.
Lawbrand would have had him and his close aides executed
long since, but Wargallow had given strict instructions that
he must not die.

Lawbrand had argued with Wargallow over this, at first
unable to understand the reasoning behind it; after all, Wargallow had quickly disposed of the worst of the dissenters,
so why not the most dangerous of them?

I have to show a degree of compassion, Wargallow had
said. I have to allow my enemies an opportunity to express
their views. I dare not be seen to be cruel, only just. I must
not be another Grenndak.

Lawbrand had spoken to those who had fought with Wargallow at the plateau of Xennidhum. They insisted that he
had changed, mellowed. But Lawbrand remained a little
sceptical. He knew that Wargallow was far too devious, far
too calculating, to act without having first contemplated the
various consequences of his acts. If he kept Mourndark alive,
he had his reasons for doing so.

The door opened and Mourndark entered. He had brushed
aside the two guards, using their fear of him to do so. They
closed the door behind him and he strode into the room,
glaring at the gathered Faithful with more than a flicker of
contempt on his face. He looked to be about Lawbrand's age,
but the latter was certain that he was far older than this, for
his name had appeared in a number of ancient documents
that Lawbrand had burned. Although he had the graying hair
and the facial lines of age, the Steelmaster had the energy
and the movement of a much younger man. His eyes were
cold, the first thing about him that anyone meeting him noticed, eyes that offered no spark of pity or compassion, as
though his fellow men were no more to him than cattle. His
mouth, too, was cold, the lips pursed, with a downward tilt

that suggested not sadness but petulance, irritability. His hair swept back, cropped, heightening the starkness of his face, the arrogance and hauteur. As he stood before his captors, his hands were completely motionless, and like precision tools, they drew the eye, for apart from the women and young children of the keep, he was the only person whose hands were intact, flesh and blood both.

Although the seven men he faced were powerful, men who feared very little in their own grim world, few of them met his eye.

"It has been almost a month since my last audience with you," Mourndark said in a voice that cut just as his instruments had once cut. He made no attempt to disguise his intolerance, his contempt for the Faithful. "In that time you have said nothing to me. My position is unacceptable."

Lawbrand looked at him, his own eyes cold, devoid of the compassion that Wargallow had once spoken of. How could any man feel compassion for this man of ice and steel? "You have no position, no status," he said.

"I am a prisoner here. Yet I have had no trial. Am I not to have one? Or have you already passed sentence on me?"

Lawbrand was nonplussed by the words. *A trial?* Why should he welcome a trial? Surely he knew what the outcome would be.

"And where is Wargallow! I begin to wonder if he is alive. It's been a long time since any of you saw him. I recall Grenndak's death, and how long you kept that a secret, so that you could crawl into his place." He fixed Coldreive with a withering look, the only man who would have dared do so. "Those of the Six that it took to slice down an old man—"

"This is not a debate on the execution—" began Lawbrand.

"Execution? You hide behind the word," said Mourndark. "Call it what it was, murder."

"And how would you name Grenndak's deeds," cut in Coldreive, "if they were not murder?"

Mourndark's face tightened into a mask of anger. He swore under his breath but did not reply.

"We are expecting an emissary," said Lawbrand. "Until

he arrives, we shall make no decisions. He is from the west, where Wargallow is with our allies—"

"Allies? What strange words you use here. We never before had allies. We are the Law—"

"That has changed," said Lawbrand quietly. His companions looked at Mourndark, the man of stone. Most of them, he knew, would have been content to kill him this very day. There was nothing in any of his arguments that could sway them. He was a reminder of the shame of their past, the old days of blood.

"How we have fallen," Mourndark sneered. "Now we dance to every petty king who raises himself."

"When the emissary arrives," began Lawbrand.

"When the emissary arrives," snapped Mourndark, "I demand an audience with him. Let him tell me himself that Wargallow is alive. And let me have a decision. Give me a trial! If I am to be executed, so be it."

Lawbrand's brows raised.

"Yes, I accept that! You may find it strange, but my code of honor, my laws, have not changed. Let me be heard. Execute me, or release me. Send me away from this place."

But they all knew that Wargallow would never permit his release, no matter how far away he was sent. Where Wargallow had enemies, he killed those he could not control.

"Your trial may well be possible," said Lawbrand.

Mourndark came forward and leaned on the bare table, unafraid of them, though most men would have shuddered to be before them. "Let me say this: word has a way of spreading, ripples on a lake. I am not loved, I know that. It has never been my duty to be loved. But since you pride yourselves on your new-found fairness, you had better give me a trial. Your followers will want to see it. They will want an exhibition of your justice. If you do not try me, they will wonder why I am locked away. If I am so evil, so dangerous, will my trial not show this to all who witness it? Will it not be obvious that I am guilty of every crime that you can level at me?" He straightened up with a barking laugh. "Or are you afraid that too many of them will have sympathy for me?"

Surprisingly it was Coldreive who answered. He drew back the folds of his right sleeve and held out his killing steel. The twin blades, curving like opposing sickles, opened slowly and then closed, sharp enough, it seemed, to cut through the very dust motes. "You think," he breathed, "our people love this? You think their dreams are ever free of pain and blood?"

Mourndark looked at the steel as proudly as he would have looked upon his child. But his reply was cut short by Lawbrand.

"There is nothing more to be said, Steelmaster. We must wait for the emissary. If Wargallow commands it, you shall have your trial."

Mourndark's hands moved, the long fingers curling as if around a blade, but he did not retort, instead turning on his heels. He rapped the door, though the guards did not open it until commanded by Lawbrand. Without another look or word, Mourndark left, slamming the door behind him. Beyond the keep there were echoing rumbles of thunder, moving eagerly nearer.

Lawbrand shook his head. "There is nothing left to him but bluff," he said. "But even so, we must resolve this problem soon."

Vecta stiffened. "If there is nothing in the emissary's report that refers to him, as with all the other reports, he should be executed."

Coldreive looked no less stern. "I agree," he said after only a brief silence. Other heads nodded.

Lawbrand's face hardened. He did not rule them as Wargallow did, but he yet commanded their respect for his judgment. "Our path would seem clear. But Wargallow has been most explicit. We are not to kill him."

"Then let us hope," said Coldreive with a chilling air of finality, "that the emissary brings us a positive directive."

Lawbrand's expression was unreadable, but his concern was deep. If as loyal a man as Coldreive, one of the Six, could question Wargallow's strict directives, the unrest was critical.

As they spoke, Mourndark was returned to his rooms by silent Deliverers. They had been told that he was not to die, but Mourndark knew well enough that if he had been foolish enough to try and break free of them, they would hamstring him.

Once in his rooms, which had never been cleared of their

many luxuries, their velvet drapes, their sculpted furnishings, he emitted a string of curses, most of them aimed at Wargallow, whom he felt sure must yet be alive, even though he had charged the Faithful that he could not be. A soft movement behind him made him turn, though not aggressively, for he recognized a girl's footfalls. It was Dennovia, a beautiful girl whom he had brought here and made his companion two years before all this mayhem. Though she had been little more than a child when he had first taken her, he had eschewed other women since finding her. He did not stop her now as she put her lithe arms about him, her fingers brushing at his hair.

"They scorned you," she said softly. She was less tall than he was, with a full figure, her skin a deep gold, her hair as black as night. No one could have denied her great beauty, enhanced by every move that she made, though they were calculated movements. Her eyes, her mouth, would have intoxicated any monarch, no matter how many concubines he might have.

"Wargallow is sending an emissary," he said bluntly.

"Oh, but there have been so many—"

"I cannot abide this waiting any longer," he growled and she drew away, knowing this was not the time to take him to her bed. "I must use this emissary," he said, frowning in thought.

"Do you know how?" She sat beside him on a couch, pouring wine from a gleaming ewer, a relic of better days here.

He accepted the goblet and drank from it automatically, hardly tasting the fine wine. "We have become so used to imprisonment that inactivity is our way of life. We have forgotten how to act! I have so few supporters left in the keep, but there are enough of them."

"You cannot mean to rebel—"

He snorted impatiently. "No. A direct assault on the Faithful would be disastrous. But we can act, demand a voice. A hearing."

"A trial?" Her oval eyes widened in surprise.

"Yes, I could turn that to my advantage. The Faithful don't know how many of my supporters would speak for me."

"Even so, the verdict—"

"Not a pardon, I don't expect that! But to be *released*. Banished. That would suit me. I can achieve nothing here. But in some other kingdom, it would be possible. Wargallow has allied himself to a number of kings, even the Emperor. They must have enemies."

"There is talk of war in the west."

"Quite." He turned his thoughts inward again, finishing his wine and suddenly getting to his feet.

"What will you do?" she asked anxiously, fearing as she had done for a year that their situation was hopeless.

"Wargallow is, for all my hatred of the man, a superb opponent. I have to concede that, otherwise I am beaten to begin with. Nothing he does is by chance. His organization of Grenndak's death was brilliant. And he has been very shrewd in keeping me alive."

Dennovia smiled. "He should have had the sense to kill you."

He laughed. "Yes, it is what I would have done. But he dons the face of compassion. Justice and fair play are his watchwords. Hah! They believe him, who was Grenndak's right hand! But he is using me as proof that he is not the ruthless, cold-blooded murderer that Grenndak was. I have heard how the Deliverers talk of Wargallow. Again, I have to admit that he has performed miracles in winning their loyalty. I did not know how deeply Grenndak was hated. I made many mistakes and that was my greatest."

"And you, my love? How deeply do they hate you?"

Anger flared on that sharp face. But he looked away. She was right. "I never sought their love. Not even their respect."

"Just the power to control them, as Wargallow now controls them."

This time he did release his anger, almost striking her, but he drew back. "It is not that simple!"

She patted the seat beside her. "My love, you don't have to explain these things to *me*. Save them for the trial, if you are to have one."

He sat with her and allowed her to stroke his arm. "But

you should understand, Dennovia. You think I am a greedy man?''

"I understand power," she laughed softly. "It is like a drug. You take a little, a little more, and soon you rely upon it and cannot exist without it."

"Oh, yes. And Grenndak, our Preserver, knew this. None better! Power, he knew, was evil. He had seen it at its worst, working in his own world, turning on his people and those of other worlds, destroying them. So he created the Abiding Word."

"Allowing no power, no gods."

"That is the law we lived by. We preserved the peace of the world. We took away from those who meddled the means to do untold damage. We acted in good faith. For Omara." His voice had dropped almost to a whisper.

"You believe that still." She said this with apparent sincerity, though she knew him too well and recognized the act.

He studied her beautiful face for a moment, then slipped an arm about her. "Yes, I do," he said, as if convinced of it. "It was a harsh law, of course. Grenndak himself was not a lovable master. He himself was corrupt, for he had his own power. Such powers! He sometimes spoke secretly of the journeys he had made before he finally settled in Omara." He abruptly turned from this as if he would guard some secret of his own. "He indulged himself in habits that he would not have wished his followers to emulate, for he did not have the restraint of a god. He had failings, weaknesses, but his ideals were worthy of praise. You might say he was a tyrant. But there are times when the people cannot be allowed to rule themselves. Can you imagine the chaos? The wars?" He stared ahead of him, not seeing her.

Already he is at the trial, she thought, giving them his prepared speeches, his calculated words. "Then you would restore the Abiding Word? Create a new Preserver?" She would play the role of his questioners.

"I must." He turned to her, realizing. "If Wargallow has his way, in a few generations, there will be no more Deliverers. Where power is allowed to exist, and I speak not of the power of rule, but of unnatural power, men will use it.

With it they will do what was done on Grenndak's world, and create what was created at Xennidhum.''

Dennovia inadvertently shivered at the name, for she had heard him speak of it before. Many of the Deliverers who had fought there had perished, and those who had returned had nothing to say of it but that it was a nightmare incarnate.

"My love," she smiled, "you speak as Wargallow speaks."

"What do you mean?"

"Is he not opposed to evil, to dark powers? Did he not risk all when he marched with Korbillian to that place—"

Mourndark rose, sneering contemptuously. "Yes, of course! But why? Purely because he thought he would find power there, power that he could harness and use."

"To do what?"

"Are you so blind! Surely it is obvious what he seeks."

"To consolidate his rule here—"

"Oh, more than that. He has allies in a dozen countries. The very Emperor! Who is what? The cousin of a madman! This new traffic with the west has brought with it a wealth of tales from the Chain about the Remoon House, cursed with madness. The evidence for that runs throughout its history. Ottemar will prove no better. Wargallow knows this. Does he not manipulate the man! Why has he deserted the Direkeep, at a time when it most needed his presence? Why gamble it? Why? For a greater prize."

"The throne?"

"He is not that foolish. Sit upon a throne and at once you are a target, a puppet. He stands behind it now. And mark me, soon he will be sending for an army."

Dennovia was intrigued by the speed of his deliberations. But these were not spontaneous: he had been thinking this over, night after night, giving up sleep to torture himself with Wargallow's ambitions. "An army?"

"You listen now and remember what I say today. Wargallow will call for an army. Then he'll house it in the Chain, yes, on Medallion Island itself! No doubt he'll have it named the 'Royal Guard' or some such grand title. And the Emperor will welcome it with open arms."

Dennovia gasped. "Can Wargallow be that ambitious?"

"You spoke to me now of power. A drug, you said. There is no greater addict than Wargallow."

Her hand reached for his and he allowed her to take it, though his was cold. "Then what are we to do?" she said. "Are we to be prisoners forever? Or do you think Wargallow will ask you to consider peace? Yes! That could be it. If you were to capitulate, then rule here for him—"

His laugh was like a razor's edge. "I am not that naive. No, I have been too much his enemy. When I am no longer useful, I will die—"

She sat up stiffly, her eyes glowing. "Then you must remain useful!"

He smiled at her sudden energy. "I am a knife in his side, girl. I cannot be of use for ever."

She took both of his hands and studied them as she had done many times, marvelling at their perfection. "But you could be."

Mourndark could not believe that she would have thought of something he had not, in spite of her cunning, but he nodded indulgently. "Oh, and do you make plans for me?"

"The steel," she whispered. It was something that terrified, yet paradoxically thrilled her, the killing steel of the Deliverers. She looked again at Mourndark's hands, his perfect hands that had fashioned it. "Wargallow preaches its abolition. He calls it an abomination."

Mourndark's mouth had become a hard line, his eyes cold pools. "It is the symbol of purity."

"There is a way to please him."

"You think so?"

She looked up at him, almost afraid to say what she was thinking. "Free him of it."

He scowled. "I don't understand."

"Reverse the process. Remove his killing steel."

For a long moment he looked at her, knowing that she had said this in spite of her fear of saying it, expecting him to strike her for her blasphemy. But he did not. He walked across the room, speaking quietly.

"It isn't possible. If the steel is cut from a Deliverer, he will die. Slowly and painfully, but he will die. It is as though you are taking away a vital organ. Ironically, it is a death I have often dreamed of bestowing upon Simon Wargallow.''

"Even if you cannot restore his true hand—"

"No. To remove the killing steel would be his death."

She hung her head, lost for a while in her thoughts. She had been trying to suggest this thing to him for some time. Now she had done it, but with a gesture he had dismissed it. "Then we remain at his mercy."

"Perhaps. But while he is so far away, there is hope for us. But we must act soon! My one hope is that the Faithful are assuming those who support me are resigned to defeat. They would not expect a rebellion."

"But as you have said, my love, you cannot challenge them—"

"Everything depends on this emissary."

"Why? It will be just another emissary—"

"I'm sure you're right. More words with which to mollify the Faithful. Good news from the west. But Wargallow will not ask for positive action."

"Yet you desire it!"

"Yes, as do my followers. Unless Wargallow gives the word that I am to be tried, which I welcome, it will be as I have said. And then we will strike. The Faithful do not realize how well prepared my followers are. They think them utterly demoralized."

"But they are so few!"

"Enough to get us away from here." He returned to her side and kissed her lightly, though not tenderly. She had never known him be tender, not with her, not even in moments of passion, and she wondered if one day he might change.

"You will take me with you, won't you?" she said softly into his ear.

"I would not go without you."

She held him tightly, knowing that it was another calculated lie, but without him she would rot here, if they did not execute her first.

7
Emissary

By NIGHTFALL the rain had settled in, a thick, blanketing drizzle after the thunderstorm. The darkness closed down around the Direkeep, its towers remote islands in a sea of pitch. Those who were on watch shivered in their cloaks, hearing nothing but the steady drip of water from eaves and its monotonous flow through the culverts. A few torches flickered under shelter as the night crawled on endlessly.

It was after midnight when the emissary arrived. He rode in with an escort of a dozen men, all of them Deliverers, and he came out of the darkness so abruptly that the guards were taken aback, although they had been told by the bridge that he was coming across. Once inside the keep itself, the emissary dismounted and spoke to his escorts. They ushered their horses away, dissolving like wraiths into the walls. The emissary went with two guards to a stairway that wound its way privately up to the higher towers of the keep. He made it clear that he did not want his presence announced to the entire keep at this hour.

Instead he was shown with deference into a small chamber and although he declined food, he did ask for hot broth. This place had chilled him; he knew it well enough, but its austerity, its starkness offered no comfort. Only when he was alone did he remove his saturated cloak and stand by the fire as it crackled, the flames quickly taking hold on the logs that had been waiting. The emissary rubbed his face as a young man brought the broth, setting it down on the table with a

91

bow. Before he could withdraw, the visitor called him back, closing the door for an unexpected private audience.

"How old are you, boy?" the emissary asked.

"Fourteen, sir." The youth was of medium build and had cropped hair, his eyes darting nervously about the room as if expecting to see something dangerous. The man before him smiled, although behind his kindness there was a hint of chilling strength.

"Let me see your hands," he said.

The boy's face whitened, but he did as asked, trembling. His hands were rough, slightly calloused, for the boy was a hard worker. But both hands were intact. The boy looked away from the right hand of the man, which was of steel, its blades reflecting the flames of the fire.

"Once," said the emissary, "you would have lost this hand." He took the boy's right hand in his own left one. "But those days are past. This is what you would have carried." He held his twin sickled right hand in front of the boy's startled face. "Look at it," he said softly. "And remember it! There were very few of us who did not receive the Preserver's gift. Only the weak or sick did not, and they were not here for very long." He withdrew the killing steel.

The youth had not moved, his chest heaving, his fear obvious.

"Thank you for the broth. And don't fear me, boy. Just you remember this hand and he who gave it to me."

After the boy had gone, the emissary ate his broth slowly, wondering how life in the keep progressed and if its remaining tenants lived less in fear than they once had. If the youth was any yardstick, perhaps not. The Direkeep was a place of dread; too many evil ghosts threaded its corridors, pursuing the innocents who had also died here. The walls spoke of pain, the very rooms of torment.

Mercifully there was a rap at the door. "Enter," said the emissary, deliberately standing by the fire, his back to the door.

Two Deliverers entered, Eirron Lawbrand and Harn Coldreive. "The hour is very late," said Lawbrand. "No doubt you'll want to sleep before coming to our assembly in the morning, but I would appreciate a summary of your report now.''

The emissary did not turn to face him but continued to study the fire. ''You sound perturbed, Eirron. Why should that be?''

Lawbrand knew this man must be a close aide to Wargallow, who would have trusted only one of the more valued Faithful with his messages, but he had not expected to be spoken to in quite such familiar terms. He was about to speak more firmly to the man, when he turned.

Lawbrand's composure slipped for a moment and his mouth opened. ''Simon!''

The emissary came forward, at once embracing his old friend, laughing as he did so. Beside them, Coldreive also looked surprised, and in a moment he, too, had embraced his ruler. There was a rare gleam of warmth in his eyes.

''At last you have returned!'' said Lawbrand. ''You could not have chosen a better moment.''

Wargallow frowned. ''Oh, there is trouble here?''

''It is Mourndark.'' Lawbrand explained and Wargallow listened thoughtfully, not interrupting until his friend had finished.

''Well,'' he said eventually, ''it is as I expected. But you've done well to postpone his execution.''

''I was prepared to carry it out myself,'' said Coldreive.

There was no bitterness in Wargallow's tone. ''I've tested your patience long enough. I had not intended to.''

They talked for a brief while before the two Deliverers left their ruler to sleep. But it was almost two hours before Wargallow did so, his mind churning with Direkeep's past. When he did sleep, exhaustion took him and the dreams fled. He woke just after dawn feeling more refreshed than he had done for many a night.

In the high tower, the seven again met together, and when Wargallow came to them, there was a buzz of pleasure as they greeted each other. He saw not only the strain in their faces, but also the difference between them and the men in Elberon, that new city of hope, and the men of Ottemar's new empire. All had known war and strife, but the Deliverers, those who had been committed to the keep, were the men most marked by their lives. Wargallow's anger at their suffering threatened to rise, but he put it aside. There was so much to do now.

"I have been away for far too long, I am quite aware of that," he told them as they gathered around the long table. "Originally I intended to do no more than visit Elberon to be a guest at Ruan's wedding, then return here. I knew how important it was to consolidate the new government of the Direkeep. But events in the west, which hardly ever concerned us before, have developed to such an extent that we are now very much a part of them, believe me. Just as we became part of the war at Xennidhum, so we are a part of this."

His words brought a cloud with them, for even though no more than two of the men facing him had fought with him at Xennidhum, they all knew what the place had meant. "Surely," said one of them, "you cannot mean that a similar place exists in the west."

"I can't say. But there is great evil abroad. A renegade from Ternannoc, who has already attempted the destruction of Goldenisle. I have seen his work and have fought his servants." He went on to describe the events in which he had become embroiled after reaching Elberon for the wedding he had never attended. He spoke of Ottemar Remoon and of his coming to the throne, and of Eukor Epta, the scheming Administrator who had almost brought disaster upon the Chain, and of Anakhizer, the grim power in the west who meant to unleash upon them all a darkness as final as that of Xennidhum.

"When I rode to Xennidhum," said Wargallow, "it was with mixed feelings. Should I ally myself to the powers that opposed it, or should I use its power to strengthen my position among you? My enemies would say the latter, but I trust you know the truth. I claim no glory, nor am I a model for you or our people. We did it in order to survive, and those of you who were there understand that. We fought shoulder to shoulder with Earthwrought, whom we had been taught to treat as vermin! And we used power, which until then we were sworn to destroy!"

There was agreement. It had been a strange unity, but out

of it had come a new strength, a far more palatable belief. Only the outlaws such as Mourndark wanted to go back to the old ways, jealously trying to guard their own power.

"In the west, new alliances have been formed. If I have been gone for many months, it has been to add to them. We need them. There will be war."

Vecta used the pause to speak. "But is this our war? Goldenisle is so far away. We have so much work to do here—"

"It is indeed our war," nodded Wargallow, no trace of anger in his eyes. He had expected resistance to his words. He took from his shirt a large golden disc, stamped with an eagle. "I am the Emperor's ambassador and I have his seal. I am empowered to act on his behalf." He grinned at their looks of astonishment. "That is not to say I am his servant! Nor are we obliged to take up arms for him. But Anakhizer is an extreme threat. Goldenisle is rebuilding itself, having barely avoided a civil war which would have left it open to Anakhizer's forces. Unless we lend our full support, there is a danger that Goldenisle will fall."

"Forgive me," said Lawbrand, "but Vecta has a point. Your word has been our law—"

"Do not think of me as you did Grenndak!" Wargallow grinned. "I have no wish to be your dictator."

"Of course not," said Lawbrand, "but if this threat is so dire, we would be foolish not to ally ourselves to the Emperor. For our own security. I doubt that any of us here, even Vecta, would argue with that, but we *must* put our own house in order first, and soon."

"How serious is it?"

They spoke then of Mourndark, and of his demands. Wargallow nodded silently, his face impassive. As they detailed a potential rebellion, he stopped them only to ask a few brief questions.

"On my way here," he said after they had concluded, "I came to a decision." He looked at each one of them, and in his eyes now there was a challenge, a look they all knew well. They sensed that he was about to reveal something distasteful, but which he wished to see fulfilled, without dissent. In such a mood, they knew, he was awesome. It had taken such determination, such single-mindedness to plot the fall of Grenndak. No other Deliverer could have done such a thing. "As I rode to you, I passed through new villages, some of them growing to townships, and I was not met by fear. They did not know me, but they knew me for what I was. For once I was not a threat to them and they gave me food and asked for news of the west. And in one place I found the families of several Deliverers, part of the community there." He turned and pointed at the dark stone of the walls. "The fear is here. Locked in."

Lawbrand studied his companions, knowing that whatever Wargallow had decided, it was coming now, however hard it would be for them all.

"The Direkeep must be destroyed," said Wargallow.

Each of them sat back surprised, but now that it had been said, relieved. They tried to envisage the destruction, the pulling down of this place, once a holy of holies, the heart of their world. Wargallow watched them in silence, trying to measure their emotions.

"We have rescinded the Abiding Word. Is there one among you who has reservations about that? Come now, speak out. I'll not bear grudges."

Lawbrand looked stunned. "Simon, you know us better than that! Have we not been your Faithful? Do you doubt us?"

Wargallow sighed and sat back. "No, of course not. But these are testing times for us all." He stiffened, leaning forward. "This place is a symbol of our past, a monument to our evils. I well remember Korbillian's reaction to it. It had been forced up unnaturally, he said, tortured from the earth by powers that should never have been used, powers that gave pain, acute pain, to the very ground. While we remain here, while it stands, it is a requiem to Grenndak and all he stood for. It represents the Abiding Word itself. That is how the world sees it, that is how it was designed! Our future lies *outside*.

"When I rode in last night, it was like entering some vast corpse. All the abused victims of its past were watching me. The rain fell like their blood, so much of it spilled here. I was fed by a youth, whose terror of me stank. This is no place for him, nor for our women and children. Should we dwell in a slaughterhouse?''

They did not argue, nor even answer. He had said what had been in all their minds for many years. He did well to remind them.

Lawbrand spoke for them at last. ''We have cast out the old ways, but in much of Omara we will not be loved. How could we be?''

''I understand that,'' nodded Wargallow. ''Even my allies look upon me if not with distaste, then with doubt. Because of what I have been. But enough of them understand.'' He thought of the magnificent owl, Kirrikree, who had once loathed him, but whom he owed his life. He frowned at his own emotions. ''But they need us, too. Think of that if nothing else.''

Coldreive stood up. ''Then we leave the keep.''

''We will burn it,'' said Wargallow, also rising.

They all looked at one another, waiting to see who would be the first to respond, but none of them broke the silence that followed Wargallow's raw statement.

A loud beating on the door broke the silence. Wargallow raised his brows in an unspoken question to Lawbrand. Lawbrand read something more in Wargallow's expression: was it humor? He rose quickly.

''We are not to be disturbed!'' he called angrily to whoever had had the audacity to knock. The guards there should have known better than to interrupt a meeting with the emissary, even though they had not been told it was Wargallow himself who addressed it.

''I'll wait no longer!'' came a sharp voice beyond the door.

''You'll do your cause no good at all, Steelmaster. Leave us until you are summoned,'' Lawbrand told him.

Wargallow's smile widened. ''Perhaps,'' he said, ''this would be an opportune moment to bring him before us.''

Coldreive stiffened. ''But we should not permit him to dictate to us, sir.''

''I agree entirely,'' said Wargallow.

''Then let me send him away,'' said Lawbrand.

Wargallow's smile had not melted. ''Ah, but if we admit him now, he will think that he has dictated terms to us. Let

him think so. The ground will seem firmer to him. Greater
the shock when it swallows him.''

Lawbrand almost laughed at that. Wargallow had not
changed so much.

"Let him in, Eirron," said the latter, stepping back and to
one side, where he would not be seen from the door.

Lawbrand did as asked and a moment later Mourndark
marched in, stiff and aggressive, a warrior about to defend
both his dignity and his rights. The guards entered with him,
closing the door and bolting it behind them. Both held swords
and clearly Mourndark was not going to be able to threaten
anyone without a swift reprisal. He had not seen Wargallow.

"I know the emissary is here," he said coldly. "You have
closeted yourselves with him for several hours. By now I trust
you have had word from Simon Wargallow. Am I to be given
my hearing before the people of the Direkeep? Or has he
yet again avoided the issue? I warn you, if there is no answer—"

Wargallow moved across the room to where he could be
seen quite clearly. He stood beside a small table on which
there was a tray, a number of wine goblets and a golden
flagon.

"I haven't forgotten you, Steelmaster," he said. "Not a
day of my life passes when I do not think of you." He raised
his killing steel. "How could it, when I carry this?" As he
lowered the steel hand, it struck the edge of the tray. Two of
the goblets jumped, toppling to the floor and rolling noisily
across it.

Mourndark's shock at seeing Wargallow was absolute. His
face had gone white and his hands, usually so controlled,
shook. All his carefully prepared arguments evaporated.

A door behind Wargallow opened unexpectedly and a
young man entered, bearing yet another tray with wine goblets.

"How dare you interrupt us!" shouted Lawbrand. "That
door should be locked!"

There was instant confusion among the men at the table,
who turned to see what this intrusion was. Wargallow swung
round as though he were also taken by surprise. An unlocked
door? The unfortunate youth gaped in utter astonishment, not

having expected to enter anyone's presence, at least, not this formidable company. He stood rigidly, locked by embarrassment.

Mourndark took it all in at once and he acted with alarming speed. He darted past Lawbrand, elbowing him aside, and only the nimblest of moves by Wargallow spared him from being knocked over. Mourndark was at the open door before anyone could stop him. He swung it to behind him with a resounding crash. Vecta was the first of the Deliverers to the door, but before he could open it, a firm hand on his wrist held him back. He turned angrily, steel at the ready, only to face the enigmatic smile of Wargallow.

"Let him go," said the latter.

Coldreive stood beside them. "Do as he says, Vecta. All is not as it seems, is it, sir?"

Wargallow bent down and slid the bolts of the door from within. He turned to the quivering youth with the tray. "You must not blame yourself for this accident, boy. Go back to your quarters, quickly now. Lawbrand, let this boy go. He can hardly be blamed for this." Something in his expression added weight to his command, for command it was, and in a moment the youth had been led away through the other door by one of the guards.

Vecta could bear the suspense of the moment no longer. "But you must surely realize that if Mourndark gets out into the corridors, he may find a way out of the keep altogether! He knows it as well as anyone. He may escape us!"

Wargallow shook his head. "Only for a while. Beyond that door are a number of corridors. They all lead downward, except one, which goes up to the last few floors of this tower. They're empty."

"Are you sure?" said Lawbrand. "You've not been here for so long."

"I came up here last night."

Coldreive smiled at Lawbrand's expression. "I should have guessed by your calmness that there was more to this business," said the latter.

Wargallow indicated the outside corridors. "I have had my own guards placed here earlier, locking every other door except the one that leads upward. You see, I've known for some months that the Steelmaster has been a threat to you. I knew he would seek an audience today, particularly after my brief words with Eirron last night. And I knew that when he saw me, he would try to escape. Now he has only one direction to go in. Upwards. From there he can come down only one way, by the stairs. He is trapped."

Lawbrand's smile changed to a deep frown. "Then you arranged for that boy to enter. It was you who saw to it that the door was open for him. But why? Why this elaborate act? The Steelmaster was already our prisoner.

"I have never thought it would be wise to execute him. Not while he has support. And if we had given him what he sought, his trial, we would have had to banish him. We could have executed him, of course, but his strong defense would have been that we were merely removing a political opponent. I doubt that a decision to execute him would have been unanimous. There would always have been a few who would have pointed to us, possibly in secret, and said, go against them and they will arrange your death. That attitude would weaken our rule."

"Forgive me, Simon," said Lawbrand. "I still do not see. If the Steelmaster is trapped, how has anything changed?"

"I have gambled, it is true, but I think the risk was worth taking. The boy will go below to the kitchens, where he works, and being a youth, especially one who has suddenly become involved in an incident of some excitement, he will talk. He will talk about the Steelmaster's escape, I think. And in the Direkeep, what spreads more than gossip? Or has it changed that much?"

Coldreive nodded. "The word will go out that the Steelmaster has got into the corridors, not that he has been trapped."

"Only we will know that," said Wargallow. "But as far as the rest of the keep knows, the Steelmaster is no longer a prisoner."

"And as such," said Vecta, "he can be hunted and killed on sight."

Wargallow smiled patiently. This young man had much to learn about subtlety, but he did not alienate him by telling him so. "Not quite, Vecta."

While the Deliverers were hearing Wargallow's further plans, the youth, Pol, had hastily carried his unused tray back down to the kitchen area from which he had come. He was still confused by the abrupt events he had just witnessed, and greatly relieved that he had not been punished severely for his part in them. He was quick to find his colleagues, and as soon as he was sure that the head cook was out of earshot, he spoke to them privately.

"A disaster," he whispered and they gathered around, avid for any news. "Wargallow himself has returned!"

"But that's wonderful news, you idiot!" retorted one of his friends. "How can you speak of disaster—"

"Not that! Listen, the Steelmaster was being interrogated. But he's escaped!" gasped Pol.

"Don't be ridiculous, Pol. No one *escapes* in this place!"

"But he's got out into the upper corridors, and who knows the keep better than he does? In no time at all he'll have wormed his way into the walls where no one will find him. Not easily, anyhow."

"Pah, you're making this up," snorted one skeptic. "How could you know this?"

Pol pointed to his tray of wine. "An hour before dawn I was woken up by one of the tower staff. A Deliverer. He told me that the emissary had arrived in the night and I was to take up fresh wine, the best we have, to the assembly. Go on, taste the wine! If that isn't the best we have, you tell me what is. Anyway, at the appointed time, I went up with it, and when I got there, one of the upper guards met me. I thought he would take if off me, but he pointed to one of the doors up there—you know how many there are. 'Wait there,' he said. 'It's not locked.' I tell you, I was stiff with fright. I could hear voices, but not clearly enough to know who it was or what they were saying. Then I got the signal—"

"Signal, what signal?" said another of the wide-eyed boys.

"Oh yes, I forgot. I wasn't to go bursting in on the assembly, I was to wait until they called for me. Well, not actually shouted for me. They would sound a tray."

"Sounds a funny way of doing things."

"Just another ritual, I suppose," muttered another of them,

trying to be knowledgeable and they nodded sagely. The keep was still governed by ritual.

"Anyway," went on Pol, "I went in, and who do you think was in there! My blood ran cold, I tell you." He went on to describe Mourndark's escape, oblivious of how Wargallow's chosen men had made him a party to it.

"What are you apes playing at over there!" roared a voice, and they scattered like leaves in a gale as the huge form of the chief cook came bearing down upon them. Pol found himself facing the full wrath of the man.

"I gather you had an additional duty, Pol. Conducted yourself in the right manner, I trust? Haven't brought us a bad name, eh?"

"No, sir," Pol squawked, his voice almost lost. He dare not tell this brute of a man what had happened. He just prayed that Wargallow's instructions to the Deliverers, that he was not to be blamed, would be adhered to.

"Well, now that you've had your moment of glory, boy, get on with your work here. You're one of us again now."

Pol had never been so relieved to get back to cleaning out the food vats as he was that day, and he said no more of his escapade for some time. Word of it, however, did spread. Wargallow had known that it would do, for in a place like the Direkeep, an enclosed world, any news was eagerly wolfed down by the inhabitants. Pol's colleagues talked to others, and in the telling, the story became slightly altered, but its meat remained the same. Mourndark had slipped his guards and got out into the main structure of the keep. Pol's part in this event, of which his colleagues were greatly jealous, was deliberately omitted from most of the tales they told of it, so that by the time it reached the ears of Dennovia, it was no more than a brief summary. Mourndark had somehow broken free of his captors, choosing the moment they had least expected him to do it, and was loose in the main system of the keep.

While these rumors were spreading throughout the Direkeep, Wargallow was meeting more of its inhabitants, talking in detail to its Deliverers, exchanging news of events in the outside world and of how those who had already left the keep were faring in Omara. He spoke of the towns he had seen and of how he had discovered that there were far more of them. Finally he gathered as many of the keep's principals together as he could and told them of his intentions. He spoke for a long time, and the support for him was stronger, if anything, than before. He had guessed that on his return here the Deliverers would be so relieved to have something positive to do, after all the months of receiving news without instructions, that they would welcome him, and all the more because he had not announced his return.

Lawbrand listened again to him, admiring the way in which he held his people, turning them to his cause, and to that of Omara, which seemed to be in real danger. When the moment arrived for Wargallow to tell them all that he intended to burn down the Direkeep, he was met with loud cheers, and if there were those who regretted his decision, they were not heard in the rejoicing.

"You will find many friends in Omara," Wargallow told them. "And some in unexpected places. This is to be a new age of trust."

Afterward, again with Lawbrand, Wargallow looked tired.

"I can hardly believe what we have achieved here," said Lawbrand. "Perhaps as the keep burns it will strike home to me."

Wargallow nodded. "I sensed their relief, from the first."

Lawbrand looked out at the nearby mountains, watching the eagles wheeling there. They had been coming back in numbers recently, having once fled the eastern menace. "What of our enemies? The Steelmaster's supporters?"

"They must be released. By now most of them will think he is in hiding. I hear that word has gone about very quickly. That boy Pol should be given an estate for his unwitting part in this. Be sure he is not punished."

"He'll hear no more of the matter," Lawbrand assured him. "But is it safe to release the Steelmaster's supporters?

"Yes, but not immediately. After we have burned down the keep. In time, when they are tired of waiting for their master to show himself, they will forget about rebellion. There will always be some who oppose government, whether it is headed by myself or others. I could never hope to control all such rebels. Only those who become a real threat, and without Mourndark, these won't be that, will they?''

''And the Steelmaster?'' said Lawbrand, his voice dropping, though the final piece of the tapestry pulled tightly together in front of him.

''Has Eirron Lawbrand become so naive in my absence?''

''No, I understand.''

''He chose to hide in the upper tower. Let him enjoy the view of the Direkeep in flames. It will probably be the last thing he sees.''

Lawbrand nodded. If this was a new Wargallow, a man who had made allies in a hostile world, a world in which the Deliverers had made of themselves a terror but in which they were no longer so, if this was indeed that new, mellowed Wargallow, then he had not lost his steel edge, the ruthless drive to impose his will. Compassion and mercy he might possess, but his cause had not tarnished, and he would not, Lawbrand knew for certain, turn from that cause while he believed it to be right.

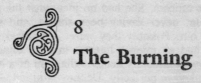

8
The Burning

DENNOVIA WAITED in Mourndark's chambers until nightfall, expecting to be visited by Wargallow's Faithful, who might think Mourndark had returned here in secret if he had found his way around the search parties. She knew better: the Steelmaster wouldn't come here. It would be the last thing he would do. There were other places he would go to for safety, places in the keep that very few knew about, even Wargallow and his most trusted aides.

Satisfied that she would be left alone for the night, Dennovia quit the chambers and wandered the few corridors that formed part of them and connected them to the main core of the keep. All doors to this sector had been locked, making these chambers a prison. All Mourndark's known followers were kept in similar conditions. There was, however, a door set into one of the walls that was another of Mourndark's closely kept secrets, for it led down to a narrow, low-ceilinged room under his main chambers. Dennovia worked the mechanism that opened it and slipped through, closing it so that no one would have known there was a door there.

A single shaft of light cut down from the ceiling where a tiny opening had been set close to one of the lamps of the main chambers, and by this beam Dennovia could see a little flint, taper and oil lamp. Once she had lit this, the shadows fled back. The room was very small and had been cunningly constructed so that no one had ever guessed its existence. Dennovia knew that there were probably many such rooms in the keep, and through them, Mourndark might yet win free of the place. If there were records of such places, it was not known who had them.

Dennovia looked about her, seeing no more than a few chests, draped in sheets thick with dust, and a table piled with old parchments. She had no idea what the parchments might contain, never having been shown, and she did not care to find out. Possibly they were anatomical studies, for Mourndark had an intense interest in such things. On one wall there was a minutely detailed diagram of a human arm, every vein inked in perfectly. Dennovia turned away from it with a shudder. Beside the parchments she saw the gleam of steel, oddly shaped fragments that had been forged far below the keep in its furnaces. The fires were said to be hot beyond imagining, drawn up from the very core of Omara, though she wondered if it was said to frighten away the curious.

She opened the smallest of the trunks, holding her breath as if expecting something to be lurking within, but only the dust rose. Holding the lamp over it, she began to go through its contents; a large leather pouch with a clammy, unwholesome feel to it, more steel fragments, sharp as razors, several thick books. At the bottom was the item she had been searching for, a long and thin wooden box. She felt like a thief as she withdrew it and placed it carefully on the table. She closed the chest and set the lamp down beside the box, looking at it as though not sure that she wanted to follow the course she had set herself. But she did so. Her fingers tripped the catches to the box and in a moment she had turned back its thin lid. Light danced on the contents as if on jewels; but these were no jewels. They were the instruments of the Steelmaster, his greatest treasure, worth more to him than gems, gold, and she knew, more to him than she could ever mean. She would not touch them, but they fascinated her, lured her as a dangerous insect would have.

There were a score of them, some no larger than needles, the largest the size of a knife, and while some had cutting edges that could, she knew, part a human hair at a touch, others were hooked, or ended in minute claws, beautifully fashioned, with moving parts that a skillful hand could manipulate. No one other than the Steelmaster had ever used these instruments, for only he knew the art of the giving of the killing steel. The operation was the most protected mystery in the Direkeep, and should Mourndark perish, the secret would perish with him.

Dennovia had seen the box and what it contained only once before, and as she gazed, half in wonder, half in fear of its contents now, she recalled vividly that first viewing. Mourndark had brought her here. He had not long made her his permanent companion, young though she had been, and that evening they had amused themselves with drugs that had made them light-headed and libidinous. They had made love in the chamber above and then Mourndark had laughed and had brought her down here, like a youth boasting to his friends when drunk. Together, naked, they had come into this dark room, and while she had stood dizzily beyond him, he had opened the chest. He had brought out the box as if he had been holding the most delicate piece of glass and she had giggled as he had pressed his lips to it before laying it on the table.

She watched him as though from another room, for once he had lifted the lid, it was as though he was alone with his instruments. He spoke to them, whispering to them, just as he had been whispering to her, saying things she could not hear, but which sounded like obscenities, words of lust. Then, very slowly, he had picked one of them up and let it rest in the flat of his hand. He ran his fingers along it as infinitely carefully as he had run them across Dennovia's bare flesh, and she saw his maleness harden as he whispered. At last he turned to her, a strange look upon his face, his lips parted in pleasure, and he moved to her with the knife-like instrument. Unable to move, she waited, knowing that if he was going to slide it into her, she would not be able to resist. But he did not: he touched her hair with the steel, showing her the blade, which had cut through her locks like a whisper. Then his free arm caught her waist and he pulled her to him, pressing his mouth down over hers hungrily.

It was only after they had coupled that she realized he had been clutching the steel instrument throughout; there was blood on his hands and on her back. It did not seem to matter whose. Without a word he put away the instruments, just as infinitely carefully. Still in silence he led her back up to the main chamber as though some sacred ritual had been performed. He washed them both, transformed by the act below. For a long time he did not speak and there was no more lovemaking that night. He had never taken her there again.

Now she gazed down at the instruments. They were a part of him, perhaps in a way similar to that in which the killing steel became part of a Deliverer. Although she wanted to touch them, to caress them as he had, she could not, afraid of them. Then, abruptly, she closed the lid. She took a piece of cloth from the table and wrapped it round the box, clutching it to her. Moments later she had doused the lamp and returned to the upstairs room. She put the box in another chest, where many of her silks were kept. It was unlikely that a search would be made of such a chest.

The night passed and she slept intermittently, half hoping that Mourndark would come.

Shortly after dawn there was a tap at one of the side doors. The door opened into a corridor that connected Mourndark's chambers with those of one of his followers. In a moment Dennovia stood by the door. A soft voice called to her from beyond it.

"Any word of him?" she asked.

"None. All of us waited. We are concerned that he has not come to at least one of us."

"Perhaps he has left the Direkeep," she said, praying that it was so.

"He would have got word to us first."

"Yes."

"I must go. The Faithful are abroad. Be wary."

The soft voice was gone, and as Dennovia returned to the room, she felt more lonely and afraid than ever before. Surely he had escaped! He could not still be trapped. But she thought of Wargallow, the man who now held the keep in a grip even more powerful than that of his terrifying predecessor, Grenndak. She knew the extent of Wargallow's cunning, just as Mourndark had known it.

Keys rattled outside the chamber and she jumped back as if she had been struck. The main door swung open and three Deliverers came in without ceremony or deference. They looked about them brazenly, ignoring the girl and her partial nakedness. Quickly she pulled her sleeping silks about her, looking at the three men as they came in, their cloaks dark about them, almost smothering them. Their thoughts would be impenetrable, their loyalty to Wargallow utterly rigid.

"Has your master been here?" said one of them coldly. She knew him to be Vecta, one of Wargallow's most favored Faithful. While Wargallow had been at war in the east, Vecta had shown himself to be a dangerous enemy to Mourndark, and devoted to the cause of rescinding the Abiding Word. There were those who wondered at Wargallow's promotion of such a young man to Eirron Lawbrand's council, but many of the Deliverers were young men, especially after the decimation of their numbers at Xennidhum, and Wargallow clearly thought it politic to promote someone like Vecta, whose influence was well known.

Vecta studied the girl with eyes like steel and a look that cut through those he stared at. He nodded for the others to begin a thorough search and they did so at once, though they did not upset furniture or open chests; their work was not careless, but efficient. They looked at no more than they needed to.

Dennovia stood before Vecta as she would have stood before a warrior who cared no more for her life than for that of a dog. "The Steelmaster? He's not been here since he went before the emissary," she said softly.

Vecta's eyes had taken in every detail of the chamber and came to rest again on her. His cold expression never changed but he studied her closely, as if she might, after all, interest him. She was, he noted inwardly, superbly beautiful, and if he looked too long upon her, she would understand his thoughts.

"You are his consort," he snapped.

"Yes," she said, lifting her chin.

With chilling speed, his right arm came up and the edge of his killing steel rested under her chin, expertly controlled so that it touched but did not cut. She knew that if she moved, her flesh would part.

"Where is he?" said Vecta.

"I have not seen him. Why do you ask me such a question?"

"He has escaped."

Something in her expression of amazement, faultlessly acted, must have melted Vecta's cold heart, she saw, and the killing steel withdrew.

"Escaped?" she echoed. "How could he escape?"

"You pretend you did not know this?" he said curtly. His men had returned, and she saw them shaking their heads, knowing that Mourndark had not been here.

"I did not," she insisted. "How could he?"

"He has been here," Vecta told her, again raising his steel and holding it like a threat before her eyes. "I will cut the truth from you if I have to."

"No, I swear it!" she cried, deciding that she had better feign hysteria in case he did have some sadistic urge he must satisfy. There would be little sympathy for her if he did, she imagined. She dropped to her knees before him, shaking her head and forcing the tears to come. "Spare me! I am no more than his slave. Why should he waste time on me? If he has escaped, he would be a fool to come here. You think he would come for me? I am nothing to him! I am his toy, his chattel! Spare me!" She gripped Vecta's cloak.

He stared down at her, then away. Her beauty disturbed him, just as her distress did, but he must not allow himself to waver. Wargallow's orders had been typically precise. Vecta was to ensure that Dennovia and any other supporters of the Steelmaster were to be convinced that their master had not been executed, but had escaped. An open search, Wargallow said, with the Faithful exhibiting great anxiety, would convince them of the truth of this.

"Get up, girl," Vecta snapped, lifting Dennovia to her feet. She clung to him.

"I've been a prisoner here. Am I to be freed now that Wargallow has returned? Or am I to die?" she breathed, her face inches from his own.

Vecta turned from her. "No, you are not to die. There have been enough deaths in this place. That was Grenndak's way. But we shall find your lover, be sure of it. And he'll answer to Wargallow. The rest of you are to be freed."

Her amazement was genuine. "Freed? To leave the keep?"

Vecta smiled grimly. "We shall all leave it soon enough.

It is to be razed." He pushed her away and motioned his men to him.

Dennovia stared at his back, her mind racing. the Direkeep was to be *razed?* There must be some trick in this. Wargallow—

"Razed?" she called out.

Vecta turned to face her. His smile this time made him handsome. "Our people are leaving. There are better places for us to live than this prison, as you call it. There's nothing here, only evil memories and stones that weep blood."

So that must be it! her mind cried. Mourndark hasn't escaped and this is an elaborate trick! He's trapped here somewhere. Wargallow has him walled in, and this place is to be his pyre.

Again Vecta turned to go, but she ran to him. "Wait! Please don't leave me here now. I've done nothing. I was Mourndark's slave—"

"No one will be left to die," said Vecta. "It is Wargallow's command. See, your doors are no longer locked." At that he left with his companions, and just as he had said, they did not lock the doors, nor even close them. What game are they playing? Dennovia asked herself. But there was no time for deliberation. She had to act quickly.

At once she began preparing what few effects she would take with her, knowing she would have to leave the keep. But before she did go, she had to find a way to speak to Wargallow, if it was possible. Vecta had lied, she was sure. They would kill her, and all Mourndark's followers.

At that moment, early though it was, Wargallow was already preparing his people for the exodus from the keep. Only his closest Faithful remained in the higher chambers with him, making their plans for the destruction of the place that had been their home all their lives. But there were no regrets expressed, even though the outside world would be for most an unknown challenge, no matter what Wargallow had promised them.

The morning passed busily, and as Wargallow walked the corridors of the keep, he saw the spirits of the people soaring, realizing just how tormented an existence they had led. Now, as they got together their belongings, they sang, or shouted gleefully, and there was laughter among the women, a rare sound in this building. The young men, those who had not undergone the grim receiving of the killing steel, were most cheerful, knowing that once they were away from here, then they would truly be free of that curse.

Wargallow walked on alone, although his Faithful watched him, just in case some skulking enemy tried to attack him. Mourndark's followers were still kept in their chambers, in spite of what Dennovia had been told, but Wargallow had said he intended to have them released last of all. He told his council they should be spared, in spite of many protests.

He came now to an abandoned stairway. There were no guards here and had not been for some time. The stairs led upwards, coated with dust. At the top there were two thick doors, both thrown open. Beyond were the austere apartments that had once served Grenndak. The hall was large, its simple stone seats cracked and bare; the fountain no longer worked, broken and neglected. Since the Preserver's death, no one had been allowed here, and in Wargallow's absence, the Faithful had made sure his wishes had been respected. As he walked through the doors now, brushing away the thick webs that had been strung across them, the memories of the place came flooding back to him, and he saw again the being from Ternannoc, the renegade who had fled here to Omara and who had set up the frightful creed of the Abiding Word, the giving of blood.

There were other ghosts here: Korbillian, the huge man in whom power had been invested, power to defeat the ills of the world. He had sacrificed himself at Xennidhum, as so many others had. Ygromm of the Earthwrought, who had unbelievably given his life to save Wargallow, shocking the Deliverer into a real understanding of the earth people. Until Xennidhum, they had been terrorized by the Deliverers, viciously hunted, for they were known to possess power that had been forbidden by Grenndak. Wargallow turned away from these sad ghosts, but one more waited for him by the doors. It was a young girl, with frightened eyes and the slight build of a fourteen year old.

His breath caught at sight of the memory, so many years ago. She had been one of many young girls who had been taken secretly to Grenndak the so-called god, the god who had enjoyed amusing himself with mortal flesh. The Direkeep went in awe of Grenndak's power, his sorcery, and no one dared complain when he called for the girls. No one dared to ask questions if they were not seen again. Wargallow saw the vision before him dissolving, slipping away to oblivion just as the girl had done in life. Fourteen. Grenndak had taken her, and though the young novice Wargallow had searched the keep and had dared to ask forbidden questions, she had not been seen again. He had been extremely careful, having learned even at the age of twelve that acute discretion was essential in the Direkeep. None of those he asked knew that the girl he sought was his sister. Grenndak did not know it, nor ever knew. It had been a secret that only Wargallow and his sister had shared, something they had learned by pure accident, though they had known instinctively that they were bonded by the flesh.

Wargallow looked down at his killing steel. Even this sin against my flesh was nothing to the sin of murder.

He left the chambers, returning to the lower parts of the keep. It was while he was in one of the larger chambers, supervising the preparations for the burning, that the girl Dennovia came to him. She had ventured out of her own quarters, surprised that she was not hampered or questioned by anyone. The young men whistled at her and called out lewd suggestions, made brave by their new freedom and the thought of being outside and away from this realm of shadows. But still her fears did not subside. She could not believe that she was to be spared. Wargallow was known to be a just man and not a cruel one, but how could he let his enemies go free? It had never been his way in the past. If I try to leave the keep myself, she thought, I will be killed, or at least fetched back. Perhaps he plans to burn me with the keep.

It was chance that brought her to the chamber where Wargallow was talking to his craftsmen, men who worked the stone of the keep and saw to its perpetuation. They were deciding on how best to weaken the massive foundations, preparing for the fires that would gut the entire structure and bring it down.

Wargallow heard the altercation as men tried to prevent Dennovia from reaching him. There were many such commotions now, for the people were both excited and anxious, some bordering on panic, though there was no need for it.

"What is wrong here?" said Wargallow calmly, coming to the group of men who held the struggling girl. He recognized Dennovia at once. "Let her stand free."

She was breathing hard, as if she had been running, and though her dark hair was tangled and her eyes were swollen with tears, she yet looked beautiful. Ah, how beautiful! Though she had used her beauty to seduce, just as she had been instructed, and there could be no innocence in such a creature, she would turn an emperor's head. For a moment he thought of Tennebriel, Empress of the Chain now, but the comparison was superficial: both girls were exceptionally beautiful, but there was a voluptuousness to Dennovia, a sexuality that she used with the subtle skill of an artist. A single glance from her would snare many a man.

"You know who I am," she said to him, staring directly into his eyes. They regarded her almost warmly.

His amusement spared him the embarrassment of gaping at her. "Of course, Dennovia. You are the woman of the Steelmaster."

"For which I am to die!"

He frowned. "Who told you this?" The air had gone abruptly cold.

"No one admits it. But do you deny it before these men?" Her cheeks flared in anger.

"Mourndark did not go to you? You don't know where he is?"

"You must believe me!"

He smiled again. "I do."

"Yet still you will have me killed. You cannot pretend—"

He held up his hand for silence, cutting her off. Now as he looked at her, he was forced into making another comparison. His dead sister came back to him. Perhaps if she had been allowed to live, she would have grown up into just such a beauty, though by now she would have been twice Dennovia's age. And what would they have made her? A concubine? He tore his mind from the thought. Must he resort to executing his enemies? He had cause to do so, where Grenndak had had none. Had this girl loved Mourndark? It was unimportant. She had been his slave, as much his victim as his lover. Wargallow had given the young men life without the curse of the steel. Those like Dennovia should be freed also.

"Whether you were the Steelmaster's woman or not, I do not care," he said, hardening his voice to cover the softness brought on by his visit to Grenndak's chambers. "I have no reason to waste your life. Do you still support him? When this place is no more than ashes, will you still seek to raise up a new Preserver?"

She came forward, aware that many eyes were on her, but her hands were visible. If she had tried to use a weapon on Wargallow, his speed would have cut her down in an instant. She came so close to him that only he could hear her words.

"He's to die, isn't he?"

For a moment he said nothing. "Put him from your mind. Everything that this place has been will die with it. Everything."

Her eyes dropped to the floor and she nodded.

"Sire," came a voice behind her. Vecta had entered the room and seen the final exchanges. Wargallow nodded to him.

Vecta drew him to one side, speaking softly. "Your mercy is commended by all and I understand how you mean it to strengthen our new life. But dare you trust her, knowing what she has been?"

"Once outside, she'll be harmless, Vecta. Who would rally to her if she did seek revenge? Let her be. She has served her sentence, if sentence it was."

"Of course, sire. But would it not be better if she went with us, at least for a time—"

Wargallow's expression, more amused than annoyed, forced Vecta to go on quickly with his explanation.

"Until we can be sure she does not have allies among the Steelmaster's followers. I suggest we release her when she is well away from here, in some remote place."

"You would have her as prisoner?"

"Not formally. But let me put my suggestion to her. I think I can win her to it."

"Very well." Wargallow watched Vecta go to the girl, his own expression now unreadable, though the young Deliverer amused him. A more cautious man might not have involved himself in this affair as Vecta had.

"You seem to think," Vecta told the girl, "that we are bent on your execution. It is not true. But consider this, if we were to release you and let you go outside, how long do you think you would live?"

"What do you mean?" she said suspiciously.

"Well, how many of our people know you for what you were? Whether you have been a willing slave or not does not matter. You were the Steelmaster's woman. Once you are outside, you will be in immediate danger."

Dennovia paled, not at his words, but at the thought that there must be further duplicity here. "I do not ask for your protection."

"Even so, it is offered. Ride with us, at my side—"

"As a prisoner!" she scoffed, turning a withering look at the men who were watching. They were all grinning. "Is this your justice?"

"You will be free to leave us, if you wish it. But under my protection, girl, you will be safer than anywhere else," Vecta added quietly.

And I would be close to Wargallow, she thought. Even if he has some twisted scheme I cannot fathom, I will be near him.

Wargallow was speaking again. "The people have been told not to take vengeance on the Steelmaster's sympathizers. But what Vecta tells you is true. They have many grievances. I cannot hope to control them all. You will be safer with us, if you choose to be."

She gave the impression she was not eager to accede, but at last she nodded.

Vecta hid his pleasure and called two of his staff to him, waving them and the girl away as if disposing of no more than additional luggage. When they had gone, he found Wargallow beside him.

"She is very beautiful," Wargallow said enigmatically. But

before Vecta could answer him, he had turned and moved briskly on, issuing new instructions to the masons. But it had been a warning, Vecta knew that. Even so, the girl was superb! He thought of her as he had first seen her in her chambers, half clad, and he had to struggle to tear his mind from that vision.

Wargallow noticed him leave. I may be too tolerant. Once I would have given the girl to the steel. Well, let Vecta look to her now. It may be better to have her where we can watch her.

The burning began after midday. Wargallow's masons had done well to prepare the keep for its funeral, though he wished privately he had had the Stonedelvers here to help him. But the Direkeep was a curse from Grenndak's day—let the Deliverers remove it themselves. Gallons of oil had been brought up from the deep stores and trails of this had been splashed throughout the principal corridors that ran like arteries through the main body of the keep. Fresh tunnels had been dug, and the furnaces below were stoked as they had never been stoked before. The last of the people were taken outside, beyond the bridge that connected the Direkeep to the mountains beyond, and although scores of Deliverers and their families had ridden away to the waiting towns, still there were many who remained to watch this final destruction.

Wargallow and a handful of his skilled masons were left in the keep. Wargallow himself lifted the brand that would begin it. He gestured his masons back and they stood behind him on the bridge of stone. With a last shout of defiance, Wargallow tossed the brand into the prepared pool of oil and watched it flare, then race away down a dozen corridors, taking the flames to the very heart of the keep. The flames that ran below blazed their way through the carefully set timbers that kept aloft some of the main floors, igniting them and sending them crashing, weakening the entire structure. Walls collapsed, floors split apart, until the oil ran down to the deepest furnaces, setting them off so that they exploded far down in the bowels of the earth, creating a fireball that rose like a demon. Like a minor earthquake, the explosions took hold of the keep. In less than an hour the entire outer walls were blossoming with scarlet flame. The bridge charred and cracked, then broke up like sand, dropping away into the great depths below it. Huge chunks of stone peeled off from the keep walls and fell after it.

The watchers on the far slopes drew back at the heat, which was unnaturally fierce. Wargallow did not move, his gaze fixed on the tower of flame before him. He did not smile, nor did he speak and no one came near him. Beside him he felt the glow of his killing steel, heated by the conflagration across the abyss. A great column of smoke had risen up, marking this place for all the world to see, and around it the birds swirled as if in celebration, screaming and screeching their joy.

Dennovia shrank down on the small horse she had been given. She was close to Vecta, but he was as silent as his master. She had hidden her face in her veil, but there were no tears even though she felt sure that Mourndark was in that inferno. How many others had been deliberately trapped there? There was consolation: she had been permitted to bring a small chest away with her, a selection of her favorite clothes and silks. Hidden within them was Mourndark's legacy, his instruments. As the flames roared, she imagined his voice, repeating what he had already told her.

"If you ever have the chance to kill Wargallow, take it. No matter who you use, no matter what means you have to employ, *do it*. Give his blood to the earth. You will have served Omara well if you do this."

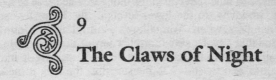

9

The Claws of Night

MOURNDARK RACED up the narrow stairway, knowing that he would have no more than a few moments to outwit his pursuit and find a place to hide. The chances would not be great, he knew, but as soon as he had seen Wargallow, he had known that he could expect no mercy. It had been a shock to see him here. How like him to return to the Direkeep unannounced! He had lost none of his cunning in the year or more he had been away.

As he ran, Mourndark listened, but there was only the sound of his own feet slapping on the cold stone. He went through a low door and slammed it shut, flinging its bolts and pressing his ear to it. Still there was silence. Had Wargallow sent his assassins? They would make no sound and would not be seen until the very end, if they were seen at all. But Mourndark was trained to listen: he heard nothing and the silence underlined the confidence that Wargallow must feel.

Softly Mourndark crossed the disused chamber and exited by another door. A final flight of stairs, barely wide enough to take a man, wound upwards to the apex of the tower, but there seemed little point in going up there and cutting off his only line of retreat. Instead he went down, taking each step with great care, expecting to be confronted by a Deliverer at every turn. The spiral wound down and came to another corridor crossing it. He looked both ways, but the silence closed in.

Of course, he smiled grimly, they have all the time they

need, or so they think. They have merely to lock the doors below and I will be trapped. His grin widened. We shall see.

Satisfied that he was not, after all, being pursued, he made his way to yet another stair which curved down to a corridor choked with dust. Several yards along this he came to a door. It led, he knew, to the lower levels of the keep, by-passing the chambers where Wargallow's Faithful met. Mourndark doubted that anyone save himself knew of this place. He took a small key from a chain inside his shirt, sliding it into the rusty lock and twisting. To his surprise, the lock turned easily, as if well oiled. But the door would not open. He pushed it and then struck it with his shoulder, but it remained closed.

He looked around him, then noticed the floor. It was dusty, threaded with webs, a place where even the rats did not come. But he could see in the poor light that it had been visited recently, for the dust was scuffed. Cursing, he turned back to the door, readying for another assault on it, and it was then that he saw the marks that had been cut into it. The work, he imagined, of a killing hand, and recent. It was a symbol, the private mark of a Deliverer, and he knew it. It was Wargallow's! His enemy had anticipated this move and had had the door bolted from beyond by one of his Faithful, while he had carved this mark. The only escape route back into the keep was impassable.

Mourndark spared himself further efforts at opening the door. He knew Wargallow was too thorough to leave any chance of the door giving way. Instead he hurried back the way he had come, thinking now that the Faithful would have as much time as they needed to capture him. Where could he go to avoid them? He had not previously given any thought to the possibility that the secret doors in the keep could be discovered. How many others had been found by Wargallow's lackeys?

He arrived at the highest room in the tower, and one glance through its single slit of window told him that he was above the turrets of the nearest towers. Quickly he bolted himself in, though he knew that it would be a matter of time before the doors were broken down. Even if he had been able to make himself secure here, he would have starved to death.

He stretched out against a rounded wall, half listening, half thinking. The hours began to pass, but still he heard nothing, no hint that he was being approached. Why not? Wargallow had as much time as he needed, but why should he not have his principal enemy recaptured as quickly as possible? Mourndark smiled. To make me suffer? How ridiculous. Besides, it is not how the man thinks. He does not believe in torture. It is beneath his dignity. A weakness. He acts on his thoughts, planning everything.

The questions had to be left unanswered. He tried instead to think of some way of escaping. He knew that he could not possibly get away down through the tower. Then it would have to be outside. But how? To go down the sheer walls would be impossible, certainly without a rope. He had none and there was nothing here that would serve. The courtyard would be at least two hundred feet below.

As he looked up at the rafters and the conical point of the turret beyond them, a fresh idea occurred to him. I may not be able to escape them, but perhaps I can convince them that I *have* escaped. As the idea took root, his spirit revived. Quickly he got to his feet, reaching up. The lowest of the rafters was beyond his stretching fingers, and though he leapt for it a few times, he could not grasp it. He stepped back to the wall. The room was no more than a dozen feet across, giving him barely enough space for what he intended. He rushed to the opposite wall, running two steps up it and pushing himself out and up. His fingers gripped the central rafter and held. Grunting with effort, he twisted himself up and over the rafter, covering himself in dust and grime as he did so. But he laughed softly. In a moment he had wormed his way up inside the cone of the roof. Overhead he was now separated from the outside by no more than a layer of tiles. He found a loose one and prized it carefully away, laying it down on the beam below him. One by one, he pulled away more of the tiles until he had made a hole large enough to climb through.

He pushed his head and shoulders through it and out into bright daylight. The sun was still high and he took it to be early afternoon. From here, near the apex of the turret, he could see only the blue vault above, and if there were towers nearby, they were some way below him. Carefully now he began bringing up the tiles he had removed. He almost lost one on the slope of the roof, but his fingers caught it before it could slide out of reach. Flat on his stomach, he put the tiles back into the hole, slipping them over the rusting nails into position. It took him over an hour, during which he half expected to hear the door below him broken down. But the silence was fixed. When he had done, the roof looked almost as it had before. From the room below, no one would notice.

It was only now that he took stock of where he was. He slithered up the roof to its point, peering cautiously beyond. This must be one of the tallest towers in the keep. There were other lower ones nearby, but he could not hope to leap to them. He was just as trapped and isolated here as he had been inside. But they may just think he had evaded them. There was nothing else to do now but wait. He could not possibly scale the walls and the very idea of trying made his head reel.

How long can I remain here? he thought. How many days? Provided there were no more storms like the one there had been in the night, he would perhaps last three days. By then any watch on this tower would be relaxed, the search moving elsewhere in the keep. He could go down and take a chance of slipping past them. Three days and nights! But he sharpened his resolve. So be it. He made himself as comfortable as he could on the roof, grateful for the heat of the sun, and closed his eyes, concentrating. He did not sleep, but he exercised his mind in such a way that his body was fully relaxed, his immediate surroundings blotted out as he waited. He was schooled in such control, a master of it, and the remainder of the day passed quickly. He hardly stirred, and if he had been observed, he would have been taken not for one asleep, but for a man dead.

It was the slowly spreading cold of the night that drew him out of his stillness. He knew that he had to perform certain simple exercises to keep himself from stiffening up, and as he sat up, he was in darkness. Like a blanket it had come down, bringing with it a few wisps of shifting mist. He stretched, turning over and going through the practiced exercises. Like many things, they were a legacy of his former master, Grenndak, who had taught him so much.

Afterwards he sat very still, his eyes accustoming to the gloom, trying to find something to fix upon. Instead, it was his ears that rewarded his concentration. Somewhere above him he heard the flapping of wing. An eagle from the mountains, perhaps. There had been a time when all bird life seemed to have deserted the nearby heights, frightened away by the powers in the east that had called Wargallow and his so-called allies to war. But now the birds had returned. Even so, it was not common to hear one at night. Mourndark listened and heard the sounds again, as if the creature had passed far overhead. Yet it had been nearer, he thought again, for it had been loud, a slow, flapping sound, leathery and unlike any eagle.

The air directly above him rushed like a sudden breeze and he ducked down. The bird had passed no more than feet above him! Annoyed, he got to his knees, wondering if this was some sort of nocturnal attack. Could it be an owl? Once he had seen a mountain owl, a huge creature, half as large as a man, but even that would not hunt a man as its prey. A sheep or goat perhaps.

As he strained to see into the darkness and thickening mist, something came down on the other side of the turret. He heard its claws scraping the tiles, but other than that it was silent. The darkness must have given it a false size, for the noise was strangely magnified. He did not know whether to seek it out or to lie low. But no matter how large it was, it could be no match for him, surely. He drew from his belt a short sword which he had cleverly concealed. He inched forward up the roof. I shall have no peace, he thought, until this wretched bird is frightened off.

He reached the apex, only to find himself face to face with the creature. It held its wings out like a huge cloak, pitch against the night, and its neck was long and sinewy, like that of a reptile, as jet as its wings. Its eyes were scarlet, malevolent and livid as hatred, and below them its talon-sharp beak opened in a silent promise of death. Before he could react, the huge head dipped and the beak slashed inches from his chest. He drew back his knife hand by instinct, but as he was about to throw, something gripped him by the shoulders. The pain was agonizing. At once he felt his muscles seizing up, cramping. Seconds later he was dragged from his high place, lifted from the tiles. He would have screamed, but his teeth clamped shut against the pain, blotting out the terror as he was swung outwards by whatever had taken him. It was another of the nightmare flying creatures.

When he began to struggle, kicking his feet, he knew that he was doomed, for his legs touched only air. He heard the steady flap of huge wings above him and felt himself swung sickeningly through the vault of space. Mercifully there was no light to see by.

He had lost his short sword, but now reached back awkwardly to find that a pair of claws dug into his shoulders, their points cutting into his flesh, drawing blood. Like a rabbit taken by an eagle, he had been snatched by whatever grim creature flew over him. Omara could not have spawned such a monster! Unless it was from Xennidhum. The air raced by, and he knew that the keep must already be slipping away, far behind him. They were dropping, possibly to some mountain perch. He tried not to think of the beak he had seen, the curving line of its power that would open him effortlessly.

Mourndark gave up struggling, trying instead to impose the same calmness and concentration of the day on himself, blotting out the shooting pains in his shoulders. The sensation of dropping remained, and he saw a grayness below him that hinted at the land, and a river. He had no idea in which direction he had been carried, but if they had not crossed the mountains, it would probably be the Trannodens, southwest of the Direkeep. He hardly had time to think about it, when the ground came rushing up from beneath him. Seconds later he was released and he let out a cry as he fell.

He landed far more gently than he had anticipated, tumbling into undergrowth that broke his fall. Dizzily he sat up, expecting to be attacked by the creature that had brought him here. Instead he heard it pass overhead, followed by two more of its kind. And in the darkness he still found it impossible to see them clearly. They had voiced no cries, nor did they now. In a moment they seemed to have gone. Mourndark looked around him in wonder. He was free of the keep! He could not have dreamed of such an escape.

As he got to his feet, the pain in his shoulders made him

groan. He fought it as he moved stealthily through the bushes, still waiting for an attack from above. Was this a nest, the den of these creatures? They meant to kill him, they must do. But he found no evidence of a nest, no eggs, no feathers, no droppings. Yet the thought of it helped him to keep from passing out. He got to the edge of the bushes and stepped through them to a hollow. Before him was a grassy bowl and beyond its far rim a dark mass of forest. Protection!

He gazed up into darkness, but for a moment his attackers had swooped away. The sooner he hid himself in the forest, the better his chance of survival. He gritted his teeth against another wave of pain, ducked down and ran. Twisting this way and that, he prayed that the night would shelter him. As he ran up the slope to the forest edge, he pulled up short. Out of the trees and the long grass there now emerged a new danger. A score of warriors had been in hiding. They held their weapons before them, long pikes, and they were ready for the kill. Mourndark turned, but there were others closing off all avenue of retreat. To his dismay he saw now that there were scores of them. He had stumbled into a small army.

WARGALLOW'S PEOPLE HAD begun their exodus from the Direkeep, spreading out as they left the foothills, most of them riding to the west, where they had been promised sanctuary. The families were to be provided for, and many already had contact with relatives in the new city of Elberon and its environs. Wargallow had promised that Ruan Dubhnor, an ally of the new Emperor, would shelter them. Some would build new villages and towns. Wargallow himself intended to return to Goldenisle, knowing that soon Ottemar Remoon would have to go to war with Anakhizer. Wargallow had already briefed his Faithful, telling them he would take a strong army of his own across the sea in ships of Elberon's navy.

Dennovia, always in the shadow of Vecta, did not hear Wargallow speak of these things, but somehow the news always spread through the moving columns. She remembered her late lover's words, hearing him say again that Wargallow would take an army to Goldenisle, and make it a royal guard for the Emperor. Mourndark had known his enemy well.

Dennovia had seen the volcanic flames consume the Dire-keep, and her deepest fears rose up with the fire. He was there, trapped, she was sure of it.

Wargallow had sent messengers ahead to Ruan, telling him that not only would there be a new wave of Deliverers coming to settle in the city and its lands, but that there would be a regiment of them bound for Goldenisle. Ruan had now gathered together regiments of his own, drawn from his warriors and from the lands of his father-in-law, Strangarth. There was also a contingent from the hillmen of the southern lands of Hanool, a people with whom Ruan had recently formed a treaty. In the wake of Xennidhum, many scattered tribes had openly welcomed Ruan's rule, enjoying a security they had never previously known.

Vecta sat astride his horse, watching his leader. Wargallow had insisted that he would be the last to leave, smiling grimly that he would have stayed to watch the final stone fall if he had had the time. The other Faithful, led by Eirron Lawbrand, had gone on ahead to their rendezvous at Elberon, leaving Wargallow, Vecta and a score of prime fighting men to bring up the rear.

"The days of the Preserver are truly ended," said Wargallow as he at last turned his horse from the smoldering ruins, high above them on the mountainside. "These lands are forbidden to us now. Let no one come here again."

Vecta stifled a yawn; he had been awake most of the night, for the keep had burned on brightly for hour after hour. Wargallow, he knew, had not slept. "It was well done," said Vecta. He pointed up at the towering clouds of black smoke which now spread far away to the horizon in the south. "The world will know of this."

"An act of the new faith," said Wargallow. "While the Direkeep stood, there would always be those who doubted us. Even so, there will be now. It will take generations to undo all the ill. Come. I want to get away and find a place to wash the stink of its smoke from me." He urged his horse onward, and Vecta watched him go, calling to his men to follow.

He rode beside Dennovia, the only woman here, and she

watched him from behind her veil, already studying him for a weakness.

"He was there, wasn't he?" she said softly.

Vecta turned away from her, not drawn. "Who can say?" He would have to be wary of her, he knew. She may yet be an enemy, though if he made her his lover, as he intended, he would see that she put the Steelmaster from her mind in time. Trying not to think of her, he followed Wargallow's dust down into the valleys.

Shortly before midday they found a suitable camping place at one of the many tributaries serving the Trannodens, and following the example of their leader they washed themselves clean of dust and of their night's grim work. Dennovia sat away from them, watched by a solitary guard. While Wargallow was here, it would be her only chance to kill him, if one would ever come. But he was constantly protected. Once they reached Elberon, she would be discarded, or what was more likely, given as a slave to some northern tribesman. Wargallow would never allow her to go where she could be a threat to him, even though he had killed Mourndark. That thought stung her again; she could believe nothing else. Yet how was she to avenge him? Through Vecta? She had already discovered that Wargallow thought highly of the younger Deliverer. Did he, perhaps, think of him as he might have a son? Yes, he could be reached through Vecta. Dennovia knew from his eyes that he desired her. No man could hide that from her. Although Vecta had spoken up for her, she knew that it was only to cover his lust. Wargallow would not be deceived either: he would know such things. Ah, but Mourndark had been so right, for Wargallow was a formidable opponent. But Vecta would be her key.

He sat with her as they ate, nodding to the guard, relieving him.

"No doubt you will dismiss me as easily when we reach Elberon," she said casually. "Or is it to be the knife?"

He smiled, watching her, fascinated. Out here, in such a setting as this, it was far easier for him to loosen his guard. "Why should we kill you?"

"I am treated as a prisoner. Your own people, even Wargallow, make time to bathe. By the time we reach Elberon, I will be thick with dust. Your contempt for me is plain.''

Vecta frowned. He had not thought of this. "Of course." He smiled again. "Feel free to bathe."

"In front of a score of you? You see, you think me a common whore. I would rather be filthy."

The smile disappeared at once. "You are right, it is unfair. You should have privacy. Though Wargallow will say that you will flee.''

"Here? Naked? Into a wilderness?"

Vecta laughed gently. "Perhaps not. But if you wish it, I will find you a private pool and stand guard over it for you. The river is cold but clean."

This was precisely what she had hoped for, but she pretended to be scornful. "Two guards would be better."

He snorted. She was no fool. "Either bathe or do not."

After a pause and another grimace of annoyance, she nodded. "Very well."

Vecta spoke quietly to his men and then led the girl up the narrow valley to where a number of pools threaded the rocks. Satisfied that they were far enough upstream to remain undisturbed, Vecta pointed to a deep pool, overhung with branches. "There, privacy enough. I'll conceal myself here, or would you like me to sit where you can see me?"

She smiled at him, but said nothing. Instead of slipping into the bushes, she very slowly removed her cloak, revealing a flowing silk dress beneath. She kept her eyes on his face as she removed this. Beneath it she was naked, and she stretched her limbs deliberately, aware that Vecta's eyes were riveted on her. His mouth opened as he saw her full breasts and the curve of her belly, the curling triangle of dark hair below it. No one could be more desirable, he thought, and he felt himself ache to touch her perfect flesh. For a moment it seemed that he would step towards her, but she twisted round and dived into the water, disappearing beneath its surface like a fish. Mesmerized, he strained his neck for another sight of her.

She is magnificent! he thought, scarcely recovered from the shock of seeing her. She meant to seduce him, he knew that, and he would welcome it. How could he not? But if she meant to turn him against Wargallow, she could not. If he had to pretend disloyalty to have her, he would do so. His men would not come here, being discreet. And Wargallow was in no frantic hurry to get to Elberon, not after the long events of the night.

Dennovia swam for a while, diving and rising as though she had lived in the pool all her life, until at length she stroked leisurely to the shore, where Vecta waited. She rose out of the water before him, a goddess of the river, even more beautiful, the water streaming from her hair and skin, and as she came forward he felt himself moving to her.

As she stepped onto the rocks, she gave a little shiver. "The water is so cold."

At once he opened his cloak to her and put his arms around her. Beneath his sleeve, she felt the hardness of his killing arm and with it a strange, alien thrill. She smiled, raising her face to him, parting her lips in an unmistakable gesture. He bent to her eagerly and put his mouth over hers. He was not experienced in these matters, but her tongue guided his, touching and twisting until his mind felt as if it would snap. But he broke free and pulled her away from the water's edge. "Let us find somewhere less conspicuous."

She nodded, going with him into the low trees. He unclasped his cloak by a bank of thick grass. She stood back from him for a moment, mesmerized by the thought of his right hand, an unbidden vision of Mourndark's secret room flashing on her inner eye. As Vecta was about to remove his shirt, something dropped over his head, light as a butterfly. He hardly noticed it, but in a moment it had jerked tight around his neck, closing off his windpipe. He struggled backward like a landed fish, his face purpling. Dennovia realized, watching in horror as the twine, for she could see now what it was, tightened, cutting the flesh. Vecta was on the ground, struggling like a man who had been poisoned. Dennovia wanted to scream, but could not. Then rough hands took hold of her and her own mouth was covered. She smelled earth.

Unable to see who held her so rigidly, she watched Vecta's final struggles. Minutes later, appallingly, he was dead. From the branches above him, two figures dropped. They turned to her, glaring at her as if they were uninterested in her nakedness, but intent on killing her.

"Where is Wargallow?" said the first of them in a guttural, thick voice. She had hardly understood the words.

She was as stunned by the appearance of the figures as she was by their frightful act. They were two-thirds of her height, yet seemed somehow full grown. They were man-like, but much thicker set, almost deformed, with wide shoulders and ugly, broad faces. Their hair was wild, streaked with dirt, and their hands were disproportionately large, as if they used them for rough work instead of tools and were used to digging, for they were caked with black loam. They even smelled like earth, though their skins were pale, daubed with paint and oil as if in preparation for some ceremony. They also wore jewels, though the stones of these were rough-cut and badly set in their rings. Dennovia had never seen an Earthwrought, but she had heard stories of them. These must be the despicable people from under the earth.

"Where is he?" snarled the spokesman, more beast than man and he raised a long pike that looked every bit as effective as the killing steel of a Deliverer.

"Down in the valley," she answered quickly, guessing they meant to kill her. "Spare me and I'll lead you to him."

"You would betray him so easily?"

"He is my enemy," she said as indignantly as she could. "I was his prisoner."

The ugly figure before her laughed. It made him even more repulsive. "Aye, I'm sure. And was this pig your guard?"

"He was forcing me—"

The Earthwrought all chuckled and she guessed there must be at most, six of them. "Oh, aye," said their leader. "We watched him. You put up a remarkable fight."

She colored, but tossed her head angrily. "Very well, you saw me. But I had to do something! I am a prisoner. I could see he desired me, so I was seducing him."

"She's lying!" grunted a voice behind her. "Slit her gullet and leave her with the other. We'll soon have Wargallow surrounded if he's down there."

The creature facing her came close, his teeth as yellow as those of an old hound. Dennovia would have been glad to expose her beauty to any man, knowing it would put him at a disadvantage. But with these beings she felt only disgust, shame even. "How many?" said the Earthwrought leader.

"No more than a score. I can show you exactly where they are—"

"And if you do, and we gut them all, then what, girl? Will you seduce me, too?"

She could not face him. "I told you, I am their prisoner. I have no love for Simon Wargallow. He has burned my home and killed my own master, who was his enemy."

The Earthwrought's broad face creased in a mass of lines, his thick jaw jutting at her. His head was cocked on one side, eyes narrowed. "Your master? And who was he?"

She hesitated. How much should she tell these people?

The pike pressed into her flesh, a hair's-breadth from drawing blood. "His name?"

"Mourndark," she whispered.

But the pike did not bite home. It withdrew. "Get her clothes. Cover yourself." The Earthwrought snapped, turning away as though she no longer interested him. Someone pushed her and she faced another of them. In a moment a fourth appeared and tossed her the silk dress and her cloak. Quickly she donned them, relieved to be covered once more. She was frantically trying to think why Mourndark's name would have saved her, for it was clear that it had. Yet he had been sworn to searching out the Earthwrought nation, and had exhorted the Deliverers to do so many times in Grenndak's day.

"You know Mourndark?" she asked the Earthwrought leader, but he said nothing.

Instead he pointed down the valley. "Lead us to where the Deliverers are. Slowly and silently. If you try to fool us—"

"I won't. Will you kill them?"

The Earthwrought nodded as if dismissing an act of no consequence. "Except Wargallow. He is wanted."

"By whom?"

"The Sublime One."

Dennovia thought better of asking who that was, never having heard the title before. But if the Deliverers were to die, then he must be an enemy of Wargallow. The Earthwrought must want revenge for the persecutions they had suffered. But was Wargallow not supposed to be their ally now? Mourndark had spat his disgust to Dennovia more than once at this rumor. But if Wargallow had made an alliance with some Earthwrought nations, this must be another tribe who yet loathed him. They spoke his name as if uttering a curse.

They left the glade, and Dennovia did not even glance back at the corpse of Vecta. It was pushed out of sight into the undergrowth.

As they went like phantoms through the trees, Dennovia was aware that many more Earthwrought were gathering, word quickly spreading to them. Once they were sure of Wargallow's position, those who had captured her moved away, up the valley side to a steep slope overlooked by a tall escarpment. Travelling along a narrow path on this slope, closed in by the dense tree cover, they were well above Wargallow's encampment. Dennovia was about to speak, when the leader brought them to a halt. Another party was approaching them, a score more of the Earthwrought. But there was a solitary man with them. Her heart raced at the sight of him as he strode toward her with familiar arrogance.

It was the Steelmaster.

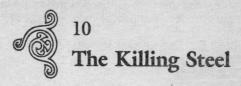

10

The Killing Steel

"WHEN THEY SURROUNDED ME," said Mourndark, "I was certain I'd only escaped the Direkeep to die. Indeed, these Exalted, as they are known, were about to kill me." He had been describing briefly to Dennovia his extraordinary flight from the keep.

"But why did they take you?" she asked, looking around nervously at the gathering of Exalted. The flying creatures that Mourndark had described were nowhere to be seen, for which she was thankful.

"They were studying the Direkeep and found me by chance on the roof. It was Wargallow they wanted, and they took me, thinking I would be able to provide them with information about his whereabouts and a way into the keep. They knew he was here in the east. Their creatures took me to where their main body was camped and I was able to persuade them that Wargallow is my enemy."

"Why do they want him?"

"For the torment he has caused their people," he said softly, so that none of their captors could hear. "Ironically in the Preserver's name."

"But isn't he their ally?"

"Perhaps. But these Exalted are of a high order and serve a great ruler whom they call the Sublime One. He has decreed that Wargallow is to be taken to him. As for the remaining Deliverers, they are to be killed."

She told him of her own escape and of the death of Vecta.

His face clouded as she spoke of the razing of the Dire-keep. "He has *burned* it?"

"I saw it. No more than a few stones remain." She drew back at his frown of fury, but whispered to him. "There was something of yours that I saved. Do you remember that night you took me down to your private room and showed me the chest—"

He gripped her so hard that she gasped. "What are you saying?"

"The instruments—"

"What of them?"

"Safe. I was allowed to bring some belongings with me. Clothes. No one thought to search them. And the instruments are hidden with them. My horse is in the valley, in Wargal-low's camp."

Mourndark's eyes lit up and she felt the shiver that ran through him. His eyes looked away, as though back at the remote keep. Then a smile crossed his lips, though it was evil and spoke of pain and not pleasure. "Then you have done well, Dennovia. Say nothing of them to these crea-tures," he went on softly. "Once we have helped them, we will find a way of freeing ourselves from them."

The commander of the Exalted, Aa-Vulk, was a heavy-set, muscular being, his veins standing out like tiny vines against his pale skin. His face was no less ugly than that of his fel-lows, with an expression that seemed to be fixed, dour and hard. His cheeks were scarred, his eyes dark and full of cold contempt. He looked upon Mourndark and the girl with barely concealed loathing, and though he had told them they would be spared if they aided him, he seemed to have little other than murder in his heart.

He came to them now, ending their brief private conver-sation. "The Deliverers are riding out of their camp," he said simply.

Mourndark looked appalled. "What? But there are no more than a score of them. If you let them ride, you'll lose them!"

Aa-Vulk's scowl deepened. "You do not know our ways. We move more quickly than any horse when it suits us. Under the earth."

This had puzzled Mourndark before, for although he had

been discovered by a vast horde of the Exalted, most of them had quickly gone to earth after his capture. He had traveled with a party of them on foot for a day and a half to get here, but the main group had already been here long before he was.

"But why not attack at once?" he asked Aa-Vulk.

The latter shook his huge head. "We will use darkness. We see better then than by daylight. And the winged ones will come. Let Wargallow go now and make his camp at night later. His men have given up the search for the one we killed."

"Then you have no more use for me," said Mourndark.

Aa-Vulk's face did not change. "I travel with the main force. You and the woman follow, under escort. Until Wargallow is taken."

"And then?"

Aa-Vulk stared at him for a moment, screwed up his nose, then turned away. There was no point in argument.

"They'll kill us," whispered Dennovia, wanting Mourndark to deny it. But he watched Aa-Vulk's broad back in silence.

WARGALLOW'S FACE WAS a cold mask, showing nothing of his thoughts. His men had searched for two hours, but could find no trace of Vecta or the girl. Remarkably there was not even a footprint, not a broken stem of grass to betray that they had ever been up the valley together, though Wargallow knew that they had. As the last report came to him, Wargallow nodded solemnly.

"We can't afford to stay here. Our business in Elberon won't wait any longer. Prepare to ride out."

No one there questioned him. Already the men wondered if Dennovia had somehow killed their companion and taken to the hills. She would never be found in this country, with its thick forests and endless valleys. But how could she possibly have hidden the body, even all trace of a struggle! Perhaps, some of them said to each other out of Wargallow's earshot, the girl had betwitched Vecta so much that he'd agreed to run off with her altogether. It had been clear that he meant to have her. Perhaps, rather than ride to Elberon, discard her, then sail to Goldenisle with Wargallow, Vecta had chosen a different course for his life, with the girl. Probably he would have felt shame at taking for his mate the lover of the Steelmaster, and thus he preferred to ride away privately, some men said. He had been young and it was how young men's blood sometimes ran. Others of the company pointed out that Vecta had not taken a horse. The girl's yet had her belongings strapped to it.

"Should we leave their horses?" Wargallow was asked diplomatically.

He shook his head, but said nothing.

Minutes later they rode from the camp. The remainder of the day passed without incident, and the mood of the men was cheerful, for as they went further from the lands of the Direkeep, their spirits soared, as if they were leaving behind them another life, another time. Vecta and the girl were quickly forgotten, everyone by now convinced that he had run off with the beautiful girl who had shared the couch of the Steelmaster. Everyone except Wargallow.

He never took his eyes from the way ahead, or the sky, or the surrounding land. The mystery of Vecta's disappearance was not solved for him. The girl could not have killed him, and he did not believe she could have seduced him away. Oh, he would have succumbed to lust, no doubt, but he would not have deserted the Deliverers. Wargallow had not made him one of his council unless he was sure of him, and he had been. He had the youth's measure and understood his ambition. The thought of visiting Goldenisle had been far more seductive to him than Dennovia, no matter how exquisitely beautiful she was. So where was Vecta? Wargallow's instinct told him that he was dead. I'm too pessimistic, he told himself. But then, the world crawls with our enemies. The dark images persisted for him, even though the lands through which his party rode were peaceful, seemingly innocent. Had we remained back there, he thought, we would all have died. The thought infuriated him. I should not have been so lax with Vecta. We need such young men.

As the evening became twilight, they camped on a bare knoll that overlooked a shallow valley, although Wargallow would not permit fires to be lit. "We leave before dawn," he said. He had been pushing them harder now, and they sensed his intention to reach Elberon quickly. At this rate they would soon be up with Eirron Lawbrand and the main body of Deliverers, which had left while the Direkeep burned.

Wargallow did not sleep. He wrapped himself up in his cloak and gazed out at the darkness, the trees spread like blotches below. There were two guards at the edge of the encampment, themselves snatching at sleep while they stood watch, thinking this country harmless enough. Certainly it should have been.

When the first beat of wings overhead disturbed the night, the guards took little notice. They knew there might be owls about, or other nocturnal birds, but were not concerned, just as they were not concerned by the occasional call of a hunting animal across the valley.

Wargallow listened, puzzled. Whatever it was that had flown over the camp, it was unusually large. His mind jerked. Large! Vecta and the girl had disappeared, *into thin air.* Had they been snatched by something from the sky? He stared up at the darkness, rising to his feet. He was about to shout a warning, when the beat of wings came again, like a rush of wind, and something huge flapped right over them. One of the guards screamed, the sound abruptly shutting off.

Rushing to him, Wargallow found him spread across the ground. He bent down to speak to him, but the Deliverer's head was a bloody ruin, one side of it ripped open as though by a huge blade. In a moment the aerial creature swooped again, and swords rang out. Wargallow shouted to his men to rise up, and now he could see the outlines of other beings coming up the knoll out of the night. Scores of them.

"It's an attack! Ready yourselves!"

It now became clear that, ironically, the knoll was the worst place they could have chosen for a camp, as they were exposed to whatever it was that swept down from the skies. There seemed to be three or four great birds or flying lizards up there; the light was far too poor to distinguish which. Wargallow called for brands to be lit as claws raked down. The Deliverers had to duck and fight them off almost on their knees. Another of the men screamed as claws gripped him by the neck and wrenched him from the ground. In a moment his bloody corpse tumbled among his fellows. Now the en-

emy on the ground raced in, stabbing with long steel pikes.
Wargallow met steel with steel, using both a flat sword and
his own killing steel. To his horror, he saw that these were
Earthwrought before him, though of a kind he had previously
never seen.

The grim figures fought in absolute silence, stabbing with
their pikes. There were many of them, over a hundred, and
they were excellent fighters. Usually, however, they would
have been no match for the Deliverers, even when the latter
numbered less than a score, for Omara boasted no better
equipped fighting man than a Deliverer. But with the constant
onslaught of the creatures from above, the Deliverers were
doubly exposed. Two of them were run through with the
wicked pikes while fending off a taloned attack.

Wargallow had formed his men into a circle, a wall of
steel, and while one part of this dealt with the attack from
above, the other kept the pikes at bay. For a while the fight
had become a stalemate, but there were now only a dozen of
the Deliverers left alive. The others fought on in horrified
silence, not used to such devastation among their fellows.
Wargallow, who took nothing for granted, was used to death,
though it revolted him no less here than anywhere else.

The Exalted pressed on with their attack. Many of them
fell, for the killing steel of the Deliverers was exceptionally
fast. Yet for each one that fell, another came forward, like a
plague or vermin, with a dozen more behind, fresh and eager
for the kill, maddened by the blood. The Deliverers could
see their dilemma, fighting on with the strength of desperation, their death dancing and snarling before them. There
were a dozen questions they would have asked, even of the
enemy, but so intense was the battle that they kept every
breath in them for the fight. If Wargallow understood what
was happening, he would not say.

Again the creatures in the sky, vast black shapes with long,
sinewy necks and great raking claws, dropped down, talon
and steel ringing together. Wargallow's own killing steel
clashed with a claw, but another found his shoulder and drew
blood. The force of the strike turned him so that he stumbled
into one of the men beside him. In the brief moment of trying
to regain his balance, he was exposed to a second attack from

above and another claw struck him on the back of the head. He was flung forward on to his face, the world spinning. As he tried to rise, a wave of Exalted raced in, their pikes clashing over him with the steel of the defending Deliverers. Wargallow saw in his mind the horrifying stones-that-move, the monoliths of the Mound of Xennidhum, and he recalled in an instant how Ygromm and his Earthwrought had saved him from them. Yet now the Earthwrought sought his blood, and he knew in a moment that they would have it. Blood to earth return.

A mile away from the battle, on another low hill, Mourndark and Dennovia waited with their escort. They had travelled overland all day, hurried on by the tireless Exalted, and when they had reached this place after dark had been surprised to find they had caught up with Wargallow's party. Mourndark was too delighted with the discovery to question the paradox of his day's journey. Now he was anxiously trying to see out into the night. He had been listening to the sounds of battle for some time. Wargallow and his men were hard pressed, and the shapes in the sky dropped and rose, dropped again.

"Deliverers, but they'll never survive this!" Mourndark told the wild-eyed girl triumphantly.

She looked amazed. "Destroyed by these half-men."

"It's those winged monsters. Hear that! Another victim."

A sudden great cry went up from the opposite knoll and it seemed that the Exalted had launched themselves at the last of the defenders, charging them regardless of their own safety. There were more shrieks and screams of pain, a ringing of steel, curses, and at last silence.

Aa-Vulk materialized like a ghost beside Mourndark. He had not involved himself in the fighting and seemed unmoved by the slaughter. "Come with me. It is over." He turned and strode down the hill, followed by his own escort. Mourndark found it hard to keep up with him. Dennovia followed, less eagerly, not wishing to see the carnage that would be on the hill beyond, and yet pulled to it, as Mourndark was.

Torches suddenly flared on the hill of death, limning a great circle of Exalted. There were no Deliverers standing among them. The sky was silent, the creatures there having departed like a storm. Aa-Vulk marched up the hill, passing through his own dead as if they were not there. Mourndark looked at them, however, seeing their number, and he could not repress a feeling of pride that the Deliverers had killed so many of them. Near the top of the hill they were piled in ghastly heaps, blood-spattered and ripped like so many carcasses awaiting the butcher's cutting slab.

Aa-Vulk received the salute of his victorious captains. Here, on top of the knoll, the Deliverers had been killed. Their horses were below in the valley, tethered and safe, though a few had broken free and fled into the night. Mourndark reached Aa-Vulk, breathing heavily from the climb.

"Where is he?" he gasped, eyes eagerly searching.

In answer, two Exalted came forward, dragging with them a single form. It was Wargallow. His cloak was soaked in the blood from his head wound.

"Is he dead?" said Mourndark, his heart racing with pure pleasure at the sight of his enemy.

Aa-Vulk echoed the question tersely and with a withering glance at the Exalted who had dragged Wargallow out, but both shook their heads.

"He lives," growled one of them.

Mourndark frowned, turning to Aa-Vulk. "Why does your ruler want him?"

Aa-Vulk waved the fallen prisoner away. He looked with scorn at the Steelmaster. "It is enough that the Sublime One wants him."

Dennovia had struggled up the knoll, hand over her mouth, trying not to gaze at the sprawled dead, though fascinated by them and their ghastly expressions, the open wounds. She came to Mourndark and groped for his hand, though he hardly noticed her.

"My horse," she whispered.

The implications were not lost on him, however. "Since I have aided you in taking Wargallow, Aa-Vulk, will you not now consider freeing me and the girl?"

"You are not a prisoner," said Aa-Vulk expressionlessly. "But I would prefer it if you travelled with us to the Sublime One."

Mourndark thought of protesting, but held himself in

check. He was alone now, his own supporters at the Direkeep dispersed, his power of little use. The Sublime One, so evidently an enemy of the Deliverers, might be a useful ally. It might prove fortuitous to visit him without resisting.

Mourndark bowed. "It will be a pleasure. Though I would be grateful if the girl and I could ride."

Aa-Vulk studied him critically, as if he would object, but then he nodded. "It is a journey of many days. Very well. Go down and find steeds. And find one for Wargallow. While he is wounded, it will be easiest to take him by horse."

Dennovia hid her relief from Aa-Vulk.

Mourndark took her arm. "Quickly girl! We should leave this place before the wolves come."

As he went down the far bank of the knoll, Aa-Vulk began the placing of his standards, for he intended anyone passing by to know that it had been his Exalted who had triumphed here, and that the Deliverers had died at the hands of the Sublime One. Wargallow may have achieved friendship with certain Earthwrought tribes, but these banners declared all Deliverers to be the enemies of the Sublime One.

In the darkness, Mourndark gripped Dennovia's arm tightly. "Will you know your own horse?" he said coldly.

She winced, trying to pull free. "Of course!"

Silently they came to the grouped horses, all of which chafed nervously, the stench of blood thick in their nostrils. Dennovia felt the chill of panic when she could not at first find her horse, thinking it must be one that had broken free. But Mourndark called to her. He was looking about him: three of the Exalted were close by, though they did not seem unduly suspicious.

"There is a chest here," said Mourndark and Dennovia's eyes widened. It was hers.

"Yes," she breathed.

"Mount up. Ignore the chest."

She did as bidden and he picked out a sturdy horse himself. He cut both loose, steadying them, talking to them quietly. He had not ridden for a long time, but both he and the girl had been schooled in the art of riding, and soon both of the horses were less frightened than they had been.

One of the Exalted stepped forward. "If you've chosen, let the others go free. We've no use for them."

Mourndark did so, retaining one for the stricken Wargallow. He dismounted and led the three horses to a fresh tether, further from the scene of the battle. It was with iron restraint that he prevented himself from going to the chest where Dennovia had told him she had secreted the instruments. But he spoke softly to himself in the blanketing dark.

Aa-Vulk had completed his work on the hill. The body of a Deliverer had been stretched out on a wooden frame and, planted in the ground like some gnarled tree, made an eyeless watcher over the land below.

"We return to Mount Timeless at once," announced Aa-Vulk. Wargallow, still unconscious, was brought forward, and Mourndark watched with relish as he was flung over the back of his horse and strapped to it like so much grain. Mourndark prayed fervently that he would regain consciousness long before they had reached their remote goal.

ALTHOUGH THE CHAMBER WAS VAST, it was almost completely empty. Its walls were of stone, polished as smooth as marble and as reflective as glass, though of a unique kind. They rose up, sloping gently inward to an invisible ceiling drowned in light, far above the floor. Hanging in the vault, trailing down from the bright blue light like fronds below the ocean, were plants, flowerless but rich in multi-hued greens. Below them, in the center of the chamber, was a rectangular block, no more than two feet high and eight long. Stretched on the block was a man robed in a dark cloak which covered him as fully as a blanket. He was hooded, but as he lay face upward the hood had dropped back from his sleeping face. The light seemed to dance and to ripple, bars of it crossing gently, probing, playing across the expressionless features. There was dried blood on the hood, black and incongruous. At first, silence presided, as massive as the walls, but slowly there were strains of music, eddies and swirls that rose and fell sluggishly as though they were currents that drifted throughout the hall as easily and as capriciously as the light.

Into this huge place came a dozen figures, miniaturized by their surroundings. They were as unobtrusive as the music as they gathered about the prone figure. Like wraiths they glided, feet making no sound. They were Earthwrought, though like any Earthwise, they were almost as tall as Men and their faces were like the latter and untypical of the smaller earth dwellers. They wore long white garments with full sleeves, and in the cascade of light from above they shimmered, their faces reflecting the glow.

For a while none of them spoke, content to gaze down upon the figure, which had assumed the rigidity of death, though it was alive. The pulse of its heart reached into the very stone, echoed by it and drawing from it a secret strength like a child nestled in an immeasurable womb. The figures, Esoterics, did not even exchange glances, for they shared the thoughts of each other, their own links with the stone about them more tangible than those of the prone figure.

"All is ready," one of them said, eyes fixed on the sleeping face.

"Yes, we are ready," said another, and the walls whispered back their echoed agreement.

Slowly coalescing in the glow overhead, another shape appeared. It hovered over the group like a golden shadow, its lower limbs no more than wisps of color against the shifting light. The only part of this vision that was sharp was the face, which was neither male nor female, a subtle combination of both. This wore an expression of mild interest but aloofness, as though it looked in upon a scene that was distanced from it and its own sphere of existence.

The Esoterics bent low as a surge of music came and went. Above them the Presence waited, the Eyes of the Sublime One, leader of the Esoterics and Plenipotentiary. It lifted its hands, stretching them out in a gentle movement. Nothing it did was hurried, and in its gestures was a great calmness which rippled outwards from it. The Esoterics straightened, looking again at the prone body before them. When the Plenipotentiary spoke, its voice was like no other voice, soft but strong, clear and musical, as if drawn from the substance of the light around it. The walls amplified its softest breath, its lowest whisper, though never too loud.

"Is this the Man, Wargallow?" it said.

As one, the Esoterics inclined their heads. Before them, the figure did not move, its eyes closed.

"Is this the Man whom the Deliverers have chosen as their ruler, their voice?"

Again the inclination of heads.

"Then it is the Man who has given the blood of our people to the earth. He who has said. Blood from earth and blood to earth return."

"A law," said one of the Esoterics, "which he has rescinded."

"He has destroyed Grenndak, the Preserver," said another.

"And brought down the Direkeep," said a third.

"All these things he has done," said the Plenipotentiary. "Omara has witnessed this." The voice indicated no emotion, no anger, no sympathy. "The Sublime One has felt the agony of the land as the tower fell, and its release from pain."

Two of the Esoterics leaned forward and undid the clasp of cloak that shrouded Wargallow, pulling it back and letting it hang over each side of the stone block. Beneath it, Wargallow wore a dark shirt, the right sleeve buttoned tightly at the wrist. The eyes of the Esoterics turned now to the steel hand, the killing steel.

"The purifying steel," came the voice of the Plenipotentiary, and it drifted closer, its own eyes fixed on the twin curves of steel as they gleamed in the light, striking it like discord. The eyes studied those blades for long moments, seeing not only the unique craftsmanship and the intricate fitting of the parts, but also the many lives sacrificed to that steel. Though the hand was still, it seemed imbued with its own life, as if a single touch would open it like a spider.

"Begin," came the command, and it was as though the mountain had itself issued it.

With extreme care, two of the Esoterics undid the studs at the wrist and pulled back the stuff of the sleeve, but it held. Another of them reached forward with a slim blade and slit the material easily. This was pulled back like skin to reveal the arm as far up as the elbow. As they saw it, the Esoterics let out a combined gasp, their eyes widening. The steel of the hand had been set into a wrist mounting of extreme intricacy, capable of revolving and twisting equally as efficiently as a normal wrist. Beyond the wrist, travelling up into the lower arm, there were strands of metal like wire, duplicating internal arteries, cased in thin, transparent metal. What had shocked the Esoterics was the sight of the flesh that had fused with it, for linking with the wire veins were normal, blood-carrying veins; the metal casing grew into the skin, superbly grafted. It was impossible to detect where true flesh began and metal ended. A closer study revealed that the human veins ran down into the metal wrist.

A further cut was made in the material of the shirt, so that the arm was revealed to the shoulder. Still the sleeping figure had not moved. Its upper arm was almost like a normal arm, except that its veins and arteries stood out clearly. And amongst them, thick and dark like a cord, ran a single artery of steel, the only link with the body. The shoulder was bruised, with a neatly healed scar, a reminder of the talon that had struck it in the recent battle.

One of the Esoterics bent down and probed with his fingertips at the upper arm. It was warm, living flesh. He let his fingers travel down the arm, delicate as a lover's touch; he paused at the elbow, which seemed to be a normal joint. Still it was warm. Even more slowly the fingers slid down to the wrist, and the texture of skin and steel remained the same. The fusion was as difficult to feel as to see. The Esoteric opened his free hand and one of his companions placed a knife in it. With infinite care, the Esoteric made an incision on the upper arm. A trickle of pure blood ran from it, welling and then clotting. The Esoteric moved to the lower arm and made another incision. Again there was blood. He looked up for the first time at the Plenipotentiary.

"Continue," came the command.

The Esoteric hesitated only briefly, then placed the edge of the knife along a wire vein. Once more he cut. And once more, pure blood flowed.

Heads nodded in understanding. The Esoteric took the steel wrist, turning it so that the back of the killing steel was exposed. This was gleaming, just as the extended sickle blades gleamed, steel and not flesh. The edge of the knife tapped at it and the sound carried, metallic and clear. But the Esoteric traced the line of a vein and made his incision. It was a shallow one and at first there was no response. Then a bead of liquid stood out, welling up just as the other cuts had welled. It was darker against the metal than flesh, and the onlookers thought it must be some other fluid. But the Esoteric who had made the cut slid his finger over the place and held it up. It was blood, as pure and red as the other.

"The hand is alive," said the Plenipotentiary. "Like the branch of a tree, or its roots in the earth, it grows. The steel has become one with the flesh."

The Esoterics straightened, again looking at the arm. It lay on Wargallow's chest. Somehow the fusion they had found made the hand even more terrifying, as though, instead of softening the outrage of amputation, the steel had become a blasphemy, an unholy union.

"It is not of the earth," said the voice above them. After a long silence in which even the distant music was still, the voice spoke again. "This Man claims that he is no longer the enemy of the Earthwrought nations. He seeks to atone for his sins against us. The hand of steel is the symbol of those sins. Let him renounce it."

The Esoterics bowed their heads as if in memory of those who had perished at the hands of the Deliverers.

"Renounce, renounce," whispered the walls, carrying their susurrations through the complex hallways of Mount Timeless.

HE WAS AWARE of nothing other than the icy cold. It held him in a glacial grasp, and he gritted his teeth against it, his body shuddering. For a moment he thought he would cry out, but he opened his eyes, thinking he had torn free of a dream. The darkness was absolute, but this was no dream. The cold was receding, as if he had escaped from a pool. He wanted to hug himself, but could not move, too numb. He knew, however, that he was on his back, staring upwards as if at a night sky without stars. There was the illusion of gazing into an invisible distance. Gradually this altered, sight being the first sensation to return to him. There was light, but it was so soft as to be almost non-existent, but by the glow he was able to see, just as he would have seen by star-glow. It was not the sky above him, but a high ceiling. He could not see it clearly, but knew it was there, just as he sensed walls somewhere to the sides of him, though not close. Gradually he felt the hardness under him, the flatness of stone. Something withdrew from it, as if a power in the stone had been pressed to him like an ear. It was a strange bed, if bed it was. His legs, his arms, were yet numb, and he could only move his head a little.

Instead of struggling to restore his circulation, he closed out the cold, which was no longer the torment that had woken him, and tried to dip into memory. For a while the darkness of that pool was as complete as the one of his awakening, but then images swam into view. The knoll, the aerial horrors, the charge of the Exalted. As if to compound his recollections, the back of his head pulsed; the claw of the great bird-thing had struck him unconscious. He had not been killed; he was a prisoner. But the others! So many of them had been slaughtered. All of them? Had any survived?

Perhaps his numbness had been caused by too-tight bonds. He tried to move his legs, but could not, nor could he flex his arms. Why had he not been killed? The attack had been savage and the other Deliverers had been cut down mercilessly. Had a freak blow saved him? The questions could not be answered. Who were the attackers? Who did they serve? They were Earthwrought, yet not of Ygromm's people.

The light improved. It taught him nothing more. He was in a huge chamber, alone. And the walls listened to him.

Again he tried to move his feet, and this time was successful. With a great effort, he moved his left arm. He was not bound, merely stretched out on a slab. Had they left him for dead? Under the earth. But if they had wanted him dead, they would have plunged their pikes into him to be sure of it. But it was foolish to persist with the unanswerable. He concentrated on movement. The numbness, like the initial cold, had drawn back, and only his right arm seemed affected. He used his left to prop himself up on an elbow, twisting his neck to get the stiffness from it.

As he looked down in the gloom, he saw his right arm. He heaved himself into a sitting position, shaking his head.

Slowly he reached across with his left hand, his fingers probing gently, hesitantly.

His arm ended at the elbow.

The killing steel had been removed. He was able to move
his upper right arm now and he saw that it was true, the steel
hand was gone. The remainder of his arm was wrapped in a
soft material, or so he thought, and as he touched it he found
it to be a kind of leaf. For a moment he sat, dazed, unable
to comprehend what was happening to him. But as he thought
of it, the truth crashed into him. They have made an example
of me! The ruler of the Deliverers, bereft of his power. He
almost laughed at that, thinking of the day in the ruined city
of Cyrene when he had told Brannog to strike off his arm.
Brannog had refused, telling him he must carry it like a badge
of shame, which he had done. Yet there was, curiously, no
relief in having it removed. Instead, it came as a shock, striking home now, and he felt the outrage, the horror, just as he
had when he had first received the killing steel. A kind of
madness threatened him, but he fought it back. He must not
let distress overwhelm him; he dare not give way, not here,
wherever it was.

Now that he could move, he swung his legs gently from
the slab and tried to stand. He was very weak, almost over-
balancing, putting out his arms to steady himself. His loss
made itself evident even more fully now, for he tumbled forward, expecting to reach out for support with an arm that
was only partially there. His head rang. Angrily he got to his
feet, looking about him. He was alone still, and there was
no sign of a door. He felt as if he would be sick, but sat back
on the slab until the dizziness passed. There was a curious
musical sound in the air, and he could not be sure if it came
from his surroundings or within him.

It took him a long time to get used to walking, for his
experiences in this place had weakened him and made him
disoriented. Finally he lurched to a wall. He explored its
length, surprised at how warm it was, like flesh. There was
nothing to show where a door could have been and he guessed
that he had worked his way around the circular walls, unless
dizziness had been misleading him. No, he told himself, it
is an oval, and it is sealed.

The effort had drained him. He slumped down, defeated by the wall's stubbornness. He had little alternative but to await his tormentors.

He was almost asleep when they came. He heard no sliding of stone, no tread of feet, but he opened his eyes to find himself looking up at a number or robed figures. They were Earthwrought, he thought, but were almost as tall as a Man. Only a few tell-tale facial characteristics betrayed them for what they were. He eyed them dreamily, unable to rise. A child could take me now, he thought.

"Simon Wargallow,' said one of the Esoterics. It bowed, but not in mockery.

"Did you do this to me?" he said, though it came out as a croak.

"The Sublime One willed it."

The faces that studied him were expressionless. Certainly the eyes had no pity, no remorse for their cruelty. Wargallow forced himself to his feet, his one hand pressed to the wall for support. "His name means nothing to me."

"He is the Voice of Omara."

It was said simply, as though the words would explain everything, but Wargallow frowned.

Another Esoteric addressed him. "He speaks for all the children of Omara."

Wargallow nodded, almost exhausted. "The Earthwrought."

"Those who are not Earthwrought are not truly of Omara."

Here was further irony, Wargallow thought. He had seen Eukor Epta, the Administrator of Goldenisle, attempt to destroy that empire in the name of his brothers of the Blood, the true inheritors of Omara, as he had called them. There must be another outbreak of the same ridiculous obsession in this place. But his smile was cold: there was far too much danger. "So where is this?" he grunted.

"Mount Timeless."

He did not recall it. "Is it in the east, or the west?"

Whether these people were his captors or not, they seemed perfectly inclined to answer his questions. By removing the killing steel, they seemed to have done all that they wished with him, though that seemed a forlorn hope.

"Far to the southeast of Xennidhum," was his answer.

He nodded. The remote mountain ranges. He knew of them. An ideal stronghold for a race of eccentrics. But he realized he should give them credit, for they had reached out far to snare him. And their troops were well organized. Dangerous. How large an army did they have?

"Tell me, what of my men?" he said, though he could not keep the concern from his face, the fear that they had all died in the battle.

"They are all dead," was the blunt reply, delivered without a hint of emotion.

He nodded slowly, his disgust welling. It had been calculated. No mere chance attack. They had other tortures for him to endure yet, that was certain. "And what of me?" He thought of his allies in the west, and of the gathering clouds of war beyond them. He had failed them disastrously. Ottemar would depend upon help from the east, and if Wargallow did not lead the Deliverers, they might not choose to support the Emperor. Eirron knew his wishes, but without Wargallow, what would he do? Many Deliverers felt they had suffered enough war without travelling far to the west in search of another.

"You have suffered enough," said an Esoteric. Nothing else was said, and Wargallow decided to conserve what little strength he had. The Esoterics regarded him briefly, satisfied that he had survived his ordeal, and then they drifted away from him. He sagged down, too tired to try to follow.

He had no idea how far he was from Elberon, or any other possible ally, and just as little idea of what the Sublime One intended to do with him. A sudden stab of pain in his right elbow doubled him up, and as he tried to straighten, he understood just how impoverished he had become. From now on, every step that he took would be an effort, a drain on his will. He would need his anger, his outrage. If that weakened, he was beyond saving.

PART THREE

THE
FAR BELOW

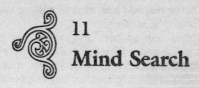

11
Mind Search

RUVANNA FACED the Child of the Mound. It stood, wrapped in the shadows of its hiding place, its features again invisible, and it made no sound, as though it had blended itself with the very rocks around it. Brannog stood beside the girl, one massive hand upon her shoulder. He could feel her tremble beneath his fingers. He was conscious that his followers were gazing intently at the spectacle, utterly absorbed by the contest of wills that already seemed to have begun.

"You cannot know what this creature is," he said softly to the girl.

She stiffened and then slipped easily from his grip. "It will not harm me," she replied, her voice barely reaching him, and before he could do anything to prevent her, she had stepped forward toward the cave. A momentary lethargy took Brannog, and in its grip he was powerless to stop Ruvanna. She went silently and slowly to the underhang of stone, its shadow reaching down almost eagerly for her, and in a moment she was no more than feet from the Child of the Mound. Many spears were raised behind her, and both Men and Earthwrought were ready to leap forward to her defense. Silence clamped down on them all.

Brannog dragged himself out of the inertia and stepped closer to the cave, his heart thundering in his chest. The Child of the Mound abruptly showed its feral teeth, snarling horribly like some elemental being from another plane. But it had moved back, pressed now to the far wall of the cave like a rat caught in a trap. Even so, Ruvanna seemed so small

153

and powerless before its wrath. She stretched out her fingers and it snarled again, its blood-red eyes gleaming, twin points of fire. As she moved closer to it, it slashed at her with its hands, which were like the talons of a huge bird of prey, though they never reached her, always pulling away from her flesh as if it would sear them.

Brannog came behind her, frightened that the creature would lose control and attack the girl. He was about to pull her back when the Child shrank down, its roars subsiding. Ruvanna went to it like a phantom, her hands stretching out to its hood. With a simple movement she slipped it off that dark head, and although the shadows yet smothered it, the onlookers could see now that it was strangely misshapen, unlike a human head, or that of any known beast. The ears were flattened, the brow bulbous, without hair. It was on this expanse of forehead that Ruvanna now placed her hands, and as she did so, the Child went rigid, as if speared. The girl's face became blank, her eyes closing.

Brannog almost stumbled, horrified by what she had done, but it was too late to prevent. The watchers gasped uniformly, spears wavering as they saw this act of extraordinary recklessness: they would have been less impressed if the girl had put her hand into a nest of vipers. Who was she? some of them murmured. Was she insane? Brannog was about to grab Ruvanna and pull her away, and yet he could now see the plight of the Child. Whatever unique power the girl had, she had *subdued* this being. Yet it was impossible! How could she have done such a thing? As he considered it, he stood poised, unable to interfere.

As Ruvanna's hands settled on the warm flesh of the creature before her, she felt an immediate contact that went far beyond that of the body. It was as though she had put her hands into a pool of dreams, a heaving tide of illusion. Its current threatened to tumble her along, but she fought it with her own fierce will, fired by blind instincts that had surfaced from deep places within her. Triggered by the contact, some buried portal had opened, and out of it now flooded a will, a resolve, yet untapped by the girl. The creature growled, but she beat the growls back as if they were physical entities, her hands digging into the flesh. Something else within her, as deeply buried a power as the first, surged up towards the light from its remote underworld. Ruvanna felt herself shaking, like a vessel unable to contain what is surging into it. Her hands, which none of the observers could see clearly, began to feel molten, though there was no pain. Then they were changing shape, reaching down into the head of the Child like the roots of a tiny tree, quickly spreading, wriggling along every artery. Ruvanna was intoxicated by the illusion, if illusion it was, her arms now fused with the creature below her. Like a virulent plague, the roots of her hands had delved down into the very torso of the Child, which writhed and groaned under the tormenting search.

Ruvanna leaned her head back, her eyes closed tightly, lips drawn back from her teeth like a wild beast. From the convulsed body before her she began to drag out its power, its knowledge. Up through the spreading network of roots came more illusions, more thoughts. Whatever secrets the beast had were torn from it now.

Brannog tried to see what was happening, appalled. He could not see Ruvanna's face, only her back, and although her arms were out of sight, he knew that the Child of the Mound was suffering agonies because of her. Dare he interfere? He glanced back for the first time; his followers were silent, as though every tree, every leaf, dared not tremble or disturb whatever act the girl was performing. But that was a Child of the Mound in there! How could she tame it?

Ruvanna's head was singing. Into it now tumbled a dozen seas, whole oceans of knowledge. Like a swimmer desperate to find air, she strove to stay afloat, afraid that her reason would be swept away and dashed on some mental reef. But her own will grew as she foundered, breasting each new wave, each maelstrom, for the depths of the Child's knowledge and memories were extreme. Her arms became scarlet, like those of a worm drawing blood from a victim, and the creature before her cried out, its growls and slaverings reduced now to howls of pain and outrage.

It was this dreadful suffering that snapped Ruvanna back into herself and she glanced down, realizing as she looked what torment she was inflicting. At once she began to withdraw her powers and she felt the retracting of the roots, the return to sanity. When her hands had become again what they were, there was no more than a husk of a creature before her, a quaking animal. To what had she exposed it? She turned away from it in disgust, caught at once in the strong arms of Brannog. Had he seen?

When he saw what she had done to the Child, he gasped in shock, pushing Ruvanna away toward his followers with a shout. He took his sword and with one quick, fierce blow, split its skull as easily as he would have done a dry log. The Child collapsed, no more now than a corpse, withered as that of an old, old man. What could possibly have wrought such a change in a thing of power? Brannog turned away, stunned. Ruvanna was being comforted by a number of Earthwrought, Ogrund among them. But the Men kept well back, understanding these things far less than the earth people. Brannog saw the looks of horror on the faces of Danoth and other Men of the Elderhold. None of them had known what Ruvanna possessed. Did the girl know? Brannog asked himself.

He waited for a while as the girl took a grip on her own spinning emotions. The ordeal had obviously drained her.

"Is it dead?" asked Ogrund.

Brannog nodded, finding that he could not speak.

"Then it can tell us nothing," Ogrund said, plainly disappointed.

Ruvanna raised her head, her face lined with the strain of conflict. "Oh, but it has," she said, and the gathered Host closed in, eager to hear her. She stood clear of those who comforted her, fixing Brannog with the look of an insolent girl once more. Somehow, in spite of what she had done, it was yet how he thought of her. Was that Ruvanna, he asked himself, who beat that creature to its knees?

"What have you done?" he said grimly, though he meant no malice. The Host could see in Brannog the alerted warrior, as if he faced not an ally, but a danger as great as that which had died.

Ruvanna, however, was calmer. "I have drawn from that creature its history, its every secret. *Everything.*" She lifted her hands and inspected them closely, but they were the hands of a young girl, slender and marked only by a young girl's labors. Those around her drew back discreetly, as if afraid to be touched by them, and the Men were tense, unsure how they should react.

Brannog came forward, closing with the girl, though his eyes were on her hands. "Then you'd better tell us."

She nodded, straightening before him proudly, though his power disturbed her far more than the warped power of the creature she had just mastered. His anger, his rage, she could not face. "It was from Xennidhum, as you had guessed."

The Host murmured, eyes turning to the crumpled shadows that were all that remained of the Child of the Mound, some expecting to see it rise.

"The last of the Children of the Mound have left that place, where now there are no more than a few blind beasts lumbering about in the ruins. The jungle has closed in on the city, eating up the ruins. What powers were once housed there are dead, wasted away into the earth. The hosts of beings from the deep earth have gone back down into it, deep, deep below, beyond the minds of Men and Earthwrought. Some of them, like the creatures your Host hunts down, come up to the surface, but less frequently. As a power, Xennidhum is spent."

Brannog nodded, quelling with a glance sporadic cheers from among his followers. "And the Child of the Mound?"

"Like its remaining brethren, it was leaving the citadel of its birth. When Korbillian confronted the last of them, he destroyed most of them, so vast was his power. He unleashed the combined force of the Hierarchs of his world, Ternannoc, and the Children were like ants beneath the heel of a god. Yet they were so puny compared to what they served that not all of them were hunted down and killed."

"So where are they?"

"They have all followed the same path."

Brannog stiffened, the old terrors moving within him like an undercurrent. "To where?"

"The far west. Deep under the earth they went, far down, under the deepest paths made by any migrating Earthwrought. Some went to a land called Teru Manga. Others went beyond that, and west into the forests known as the Deepwalks. It is a realm where no Man or Earthwrought has

ever been, or if he has, he has not returned. There is power
there of a kind that is unknown, even to the Children.''

"Did they go there because they knew they would be sheltered?" said Brannog.

"They were called."

"Called?" Brannog spoke for the entire gathering, every
mind wanting to give voice to his echoed word.

"Anakhizer," said Ruvanna. "Yet another of the fallen
renegades of Ternannoc. A Hierarch."

"Yes," nodded Brannog. "News of him comes regularly
from Elberon and beyond in the west."

"Then you know that Anakhizer plans war on your allies.
He is amassing an army that will be a thousand times stronger
than the one you fought at Xennidhum. And his army will
not be mindless. The Children of the Mound have fled to him
also. And yet there is a cruel irony in their flight." There
was an odd note of sadness in her voice now.

Brannog snorted. "Irony! That vermin such as this should
flock to Anakhizer's darkness? It is precisely the kind of
power they revel in. I see no irony in that!"

Ruvanna scowled. "Then you do not know what these
Children are? How they have evolved?"

Brannog glanced at the fallen Child, his disgust clear.
"These? The Mound corrupted them, turning them to darkness and death. They feed on it as maggots feed on corpses."

"Corrupted them? Oh, yes. But you do not know what
they were?"

Brannog glowered at her, surprised by what he took to be
her concern. "Men of Xennidhum—"

"More than that, Brannog." She walked to the cave, and
this time he made no move to stop her. Beside the broken
body she turned to the Host.

"They are the last of the Sorcerer-Kings."

Brannog, Ogrund and many more looked astonished.
Could such a thing be possible? That such power, such sov-
ereignty over Omara could be so reduced?

"The end of their line," Ruvanna went on. "Weak and
polluted. Did you never wonder what became of them? Centuries of hiding in that poisoned city, exposed to the ravages
of the Mound's power, have brought them to this. So perhaps

now, Brannog, you understand the irony. Those who sought to defeat the darkness and close it out, are now its slaves. Their minds are no longer their own.''

"And the last of them are with Anakhizer, a Hierarch," nodded Brannog. "Welcoming the evil they once fought."

In the long pause following this, Ogrund cleared his throat and spoke. "Will Ruvanna tell us what it was that drew the Child from its course? We are far to the south of the Mound. Why should it come here?"

"It was travelling to the west, far below the earth, when its course was crossed by one of the Holy Roads. As it was passing this, its attention was taken by an earthsong. It knew nothing of the ancient secrets of the Earthwrought, nor of the Sublime One. Thus its curiosity, combined with the lure of the earthsong, brought it south. When it reached these forests, it caught the scent of a hated enemy." Ruvanna looked directly at Brannog. "Those of you who were at Xennidhum are particularly reviled by the Children. You they have marked above all others."

Brannog raised his sword to the sun with a grim laugh. "Then let them come to us!" His Host responded, but in spite of the relief in the shouts, a shadow remained.

Ruvanna did not smile. The things she had seen in the Child of the Mound had left her feeling unclean, as if she had performed a vile act that had left its cloying filth on her. She caught Brannog's eye and at once he called for silence.

"Is there more?" he asked the girl.

"There was confusion in the mind of the Child. As I said, its powers were nothing to what its ancestors had known. Its mind was weak, worked upon by greater powers. When it came here, it was like a ship caught in two tides. The power of the earthsong exerted the greatest pull upon it. In time it would have gone to the very walls of Mount Timeless."

"An accident!" cried Ogrund. "The Sublime One would destroy such an abomination before it came to his walls."

Ruvanna nodded. "Yes, but it was a victim of the earthsong."

"We may all be that," said Brannog. He pointed to the corpse of the Child, calling some of his Earthwrought forward. "Burn that. And any others who are not of the Host.

Then we break camp and leave this place." There was an immediate scurry of activity, the Host being eager to go about its business.

Brannog took Ruvanna to one side. He knew how little he comprehended her, and it was clear, too, that the Men of Elderhold knew hardly more than he did. What had Kennagh known? That she could do the things she had done today? That she was alive with dangerous gifts? Maybe the old man had sensed them.

"Surely," said the girl, with the gleam in her eye that he had seen in earlier meetings, "you will not send me back to the village now?"

"I ought to," he said sternly, but then smiled. "But not yet. There are things we must talk about."

"The Child?"

"Yes. And about yourself—"

She put her fingers on his arm, softly as a kiss. "You mustn't expect too much. What I have, what I can do, are a mystery, Brannog. They shock me, as I can see they do you. Can you understand that?"

To her surprise, he pulled away as though she had slapped his face. But it was not her touch that had stung him. She could not read his mind, but his pain was very clear. "A mystery?" he repeated. "Of course. I know of such things." How can I think of her as a village girl after this? his mind cried out.

She wanted to appease him, to mend whatever tear her acts had made in their relationship. Relationship! she scoffed inwardly. He holds me at arm's length, like a serpent.

Brannog shouted out orders. When he came back to her, his face was set. "You will remain with us for now. I'll decide what is to become of you later."

She had no time to answer. He was among his Host again, directing, planning. Why does he think of me as a burden? Ruvanna wondered. After what I have shown him! How can he think of sending me back? I am stronger than any of his Host! But that thought cooled her. Never before had she tapped the depth of power she had tapped here. What am I! she suddenly asked herself. What is it that sleeps within me?

But she turned from the possible darkness of such a thought, looking again for Brannog. But his Host had absorbed him.

ALTHOUGH UNDERGROUND, Carac knew instinctively that the sun was about to drop below the rim of the world, leaving the foothills and the valleys below the mountains through which he travelled in twilight. He had spent the greater part of the day resting, closer to the surface than he would have liked, but here in the eastern lands he was unsure of himself. My homelands! he thought, and yet I come to their boundaries like a stranger, scurrying and crawling secretly, fearful of blundering into enemies.

It had been a long and arduous journey, and although he had wondered if he should have taken it alone, he clung to the belief that it was right for him. And the earthsong! He had heard its echoes more than once, almost catching it clearly, knowing that if he ever did, it would pull him down to one of the promised Holy Roads. But the old conflict rose up in him afresh. Holy Roads led to Mount Timeless and the Sublime One. But what of the Exalted, stealers of the talisman?

He clambered out of his new chamber and sat up into the rocks of the surface. He was high in the hills to the west of the vast ranges where Mount Timeless was reputed by legend to be. Far below him were the valleys, blackened now with forest, their shadows spreading like midnight rivers up to the lower slopes. Carac studied the skies, but they were empty, save for the remote stars. He had lost the scent of those he pursued, but it had happened before on his long journey from Goldenisle, and he had found it each time.

To his left he saw a sudden gleam of light, near the forest edge. He guessed it to be less than a dozen miles away. Men? Or those he hunted? But the Exalted rarely came to the surface. Whatever business they had with the aerial creatures who had usurped Orhung's rod had been concluded. Carac gave it deep thought. The Emperor has allies in the east, but these lands are far from Ruan's hold.

Eventually it was loneliness as much as anything that prompted him to move toward the light, which he took to be a campfire. He slipped under the earth, moving with great speed and confidence, finding a way where Men would have seen none. Soon he was in the rocks above the fire, looking down to the place where the first forest trees had taken an uncertain hold on the terrain. He saw Men there, and horses, and then, to his surprise, Earthwrought. Why were they not under the earth?

For the first time in long weeks, Carac grinned to himself. Men and Earthwrought together! Then these must be allies, governed by the word of Ruan Dubhnor and his followers, and Brannog, whom some called King. As he studied them, Carac felt movement close at hand. He knew at once that he had been discovered. The camp below was efficiently organized, for it had set Earthwrought to guard its limits, and not Men, who understood the land less.

"Don't crawl about like spiders," Carac growled, knowing he was probably surrounded by a superior force. "Or should I say Stonedelvers? You make far more noise."

In a moment three Earthwrought had closed in on him, their war clubs ready for a strike that would have felled him. "Who speaks of Stonedelvers?" challenged one of them.

"I do" snapped Carac, unabashed.

The Earthwrought studied him. "And who are you?"

"I am Carac, late of the Chain of Goldenisle."

"Who do you serve?"

"The Emperor. Who do *you* serve?"

"Take him below. Ogrund will know what to do."

Carac allowed himself to be escorted down the slope, knowing he would have done the same had he found someone, Earthwrought or not, sniffing about the boundaries of his camp. But he was sure he had come to a place of allies. They knew what he had meant by Stonedelvers, and only a friend could understand that. In a moment he was in the camp, which impressed him with its subtlety. The tents of Men had been erected along with constructions made by his own race, and it seemed that they no longer went under the earth, which puzzled him. There were stories, of course, about King Brannog's dream to bring the Earthwrought out on to the surface, but such a dream would take years to fulfil. Even so, here at least, it was being done.

Ogrund had been asleep, but he bore no ill will to those

who had woken him. They knew what he would have done had they not woken him. He stood before Carac as if he had been presented with a spy, his ugly face crinkled up into a stare that would have cracked stone.

Carac, however, was unmoved, his own face a match for Ogrund's. Like two gargoyles they glared at each other.

"What's this nonsense about serving Ottemar Remoon?" Ogrund snapped at last, fists bunched as if ready to use them.

Carac snorted impatiently, looking away as if already bored with proceedings. "Am I expected to bear the royal seal?"

"Your name?" said Ogrund.

"Carac. Of the Hasp."

"The Hasp? Is that a place, or part of a skirt?"

There were subdued chuckles, but Carac ignored them. His own guards would have been equally as rude to an intruder. "I wouldn't expect such rustics as yourselves to know better, but it's part of Medallion Island. Which is, for your information, part of the Chain of Goldenisle, which in turn—"

"Don't be insolent!" snarled Ogrund.

There was movement behind him and a shadow fell across him. "What is happening here?" came Brannog's voice.

"Some hill dweller has come down from his retreat to give us a lesson in geography," grunted Ogrund. "I was about to prod him back up into his lofty refuge—"

"Indeed!" laughed Carac, feigning indignation. "A fine one to speak of refuge, who lives in this forgotten forest, where war can be no more than a rumor spread by the crows."

Ogrund looked livid. No one had ever dared speak to him in such a way before. He came forward as if about to deliver an even more violent insult but Brannog halted him, chuckling as he did so.

"Quiet, both of you! Who are you, fellow? Where are you from?"

"I am Carac, and I am from—" But Carac did not finish. He now saw Brannog for the first time, and his mouth dropped in awe.

Ogrund threw up his hands in disgust. "An imbecile! Can't even finish a sentence."

"Carac?" said Brannog patiently.

"You are Brannog," said Carac, his voice filling with reverence. Whether it was a trick of the firelight or not, Carac saw before him not a Man, but a Man-sized Earthwrought, a giant, whose eyes and expression were those of his own people, and yet, those of a Man. He had heard of King Brannog, the wanderer, the Man of the earth, the champion. "King Brannog, father of Sisipher," Carac ended, his voice dropping.

"You know her?" said Brannog at once.

"I do, sire. And serve her well, I trust."

"Then you are from Goldenisle?"

Carac nodded, bowing now. "I am most fortunate to have found you."

Brannog looked at Ogrund, suddenly laughing. "Well, Ogrund, we may owe Carac an apology."

Carac shook his head quickly. "No, sire. I ask for none. But I am Carac, who fought under the Slaughterhorn and who stood with the emperor at Goldenisle's seige."

Ogrund stepped up to him, face still creased with a scowl. Suddenly the huge face split in a grin, a rare sight for the company, who laughed to a man. Before Carac could react, Ogrund had gripped his arms. "You have my apology, whether you ask for it or no," said Ogrund. "And you are welcome, Carac of Goldenisle. I am Ogrund, of the Host of Brannog."

"You fought at Xennidhum?"

Ogrund nodded. "I had that honor."

"Then you must accept my own apology for the insults."

They drew apart as quickly as they had come together, both turning, a little embarrassed, to Brannog. He was smiling hugely at them. Experience had taught him to be patient in such matters of Earthwrought protocol.

"Well met, Carac. But tell us, what brings you so far from the Empire?"

Carac wasted no time in describing the events of the night when Orhung's rod had been stolen, and of his determination to follow the Exalted.

When he had finished his tale, he had a large audience, for most of the camp had risen to find out what was happening.

Among the listeners was Ruvanna, though she clung to the shadows, saying nothing.

"But what did you hope to achieve, following alone?" said Ogrund, for now that the apologies had been made between them, they were clearly going to persist with typical Earthwrought banter, Brannog could see that. Brannog did not intervene this time, knowing that it was a mark of each Earthwrought's respect for the other's position. It also signified a growing bond.

"I cannot say," replied Carac.

"Did you think you could trap the entire party and wipe it out?" Ogrund grunted.

Carac gave him a withering look, which was completely wasted, and turned instead to Brannog. "There is more to my journey than pursuit. There is the calling."

Many of the listening Earthwrought straightened like hounds at this allusion, and for a while there were murmurings among them.

"Earthsongs?" said Brannog.

Carac seemed impressed that Brannog should know of such things. "Why, yes, sire."

Brannog nodded. "It is a strange thing, Carac. Many of us have caught their strains. You, too?"

"Even in Goldenisle I heard them. Had I not been in pursuit of the Exalted, yet I may have come here. And my homelands are not far, in Boldernesse."

Brannog pointed through the trees, across the valley to the first of the mountains, now no more than darkness under the sky. "I seek the place of legend, the Far Below."

"In Boldernesse, my people speak of it. Why do you travel there?"

"You understand that there will be war in the west?"

"Anakhizer," nodded Carac. "Aye. The Emperor prepares. Simon Wargallow himself has come to the east to gather his own people."

Brannog's eyes widened. "He has? That is good news. The Deliverers will rally to him. The Host will be easier knowing Wargallow is here. So, just as he gathers his army, so must I gather my own."

Carac looked amazed. "From the Far Below?" Would this proud King dare such a thing?"

"I must try. The Earthwrought must bring forth as great a force as they can. But there are many things that concern me. This calling, this drawing together of the Earthwrought by the Sublime One. Is it to do what I would do myself? To make war on the far west? Or is the war to be against the Empire? What you have told me, about the cruelty of the Exalted and their methods, troubles me. The Exalted that we have seen were hostile to us. There is an evil in them."

Ogrund leaned forward. "Why should the Sublime One seek the rod of the being you called Orhung?"

"It is something we must know," said Brannog.

"Then we have to enter the mountains," said Carac. "But my tribe in Boldernesse, who are hardy, rarely set foot there. There is a bleakness and desolation in them, and they go on, it is said, to the far ends of Omara."

Brannog nodded. "If the Far Below is there, we have to find it, whatever the risk."

12
The Icewrought

CARAC SPOKE LONG into the night to Brannog and his gathered captains. They sat on the earth floor of Brannog's tent, a smoldering fire before them, and Carac talked of the west, of the Empire and of events there. Sitting round the fire, enrapt by his words like children feasting on the stories of a balladeer, the captains of the Host pictured Goldenisle, its characters and its struggles against the night. Ogrund sat with Rothgar, both of them grim-faced and anxious for news, and with them were Danoth and his own right-hand warrior, Rannalgh, both of whom were astounded by Carac's descriptions of the fabulous west. Hardly less awed was Thengram from Gnarag's delvings, whose pride and self-belief grew daily since his release from his former miserable home. In a corner of the tent sat Ruvanna: she had pleaded with Brannog to let her come in and listen. At first he had been adamant that she should go back to the place made for her in the camp, but he had quickly realized that his Earthwrought held her in great esteem (almost as they had Sisipher, he saw with a start) and it seemed foolish to believe that she could be a danger to the Host. He had relented. Better that she hear of things in the west, he told himself.

When Brannog felt that Carac had been questioned enough, he dismissed the gathering, and even then, Ruvanna was the last to leave. She would have asked questions of her own, but a glare from Brannog made her decide to wait until morning. She went out into the cool night, and although the Earth-wrought let her pass with undisguised politeness, the Men

167

were yet wary of her, as if they somehow shared Brannog's
ridiculous suspicions. They were afraid of her, she knew that,
too. Witch, said their minds. It amused her in a way, but
only because it gave her more power. But I do not want to
be set apart. They have always made me so.

A tent had been prepared for her, and although there were
guards, they kept their distance. Once inside it, Ruvanna
stretched out, yawning. It had been a wearying day. And
what marvels Carac had spoken of! She could not sleep. Her
mind danced back to Brannog's tent. Even now he was talking to Carac. She closed her eyes and concentrated. In a
moment it was as though part of her had slipped through the
camp, mist-like, to stand at Brannog's tent flap. Voices, no
more than whispers, came to her. She heightened her concentration until she could hear more clearly. Brannog's rich
tones were unmistakable.

"Then you have not seen my daughter for some weeks?"

Carac, now alone with the king, shook his head uneasily.
"Longer than that, sire. Shortly after the triumph, she went
from us. She had been the constant companion of Ottemar
Remoon and Simon Wargallow until after the battle. Many
Earthwrought were always close to her. Word of her often
came to me and my workers, wherever we labored. And then
we heard nothing."

Brannog wanted to ask a thousand questions, but held them
in check. "But she is in Goldenisle, on Medallion?"

"I will not lie to you, sire."

"Then you have bad news?"

Carac shifted restlessly. He had spoken longer tonight than
he had ever spoken before, usually not being given to discourse and being known for his gruff bluntness. But this Man
had become a king among his people, just as Ottemar had
become the emperor. He must serve him well. "Not bad,
sire. Some of the workers said she had left Medallion. No
one knew where she went, but it was with a strange crew. So
rumor told us."

"Carac, I will offer you no harm if you tell me the truth.
Say all you know of her."

"A sadness was upon her, sire. Even I felt that."

Brannog frowned. "Weariness at the war, do you mean?"

"She did not approve of the marriage of Ottemar to Tennebriel."

"But you told us how she herself proposed it, and how well the match has suited the empire. Has it not made it more secure than it has been for decades? Or is Tennebriel plotting against the Emperor?"

Carac's discomfort was growing. "I am sure she is not, sire. Tennebriel may not love her husband, but she does well by him."

"And Ottemar?"

"He is as a husband should be."

"Then why does my daughter disapprove?"

"She has been through harrowing times, sire, the worst of them in the company of Ottemar, when he took the name, Guile. Such terrors as they shared in Teru Manga and beyond can create deep bonds—"

Brannog's silence told Ruvanna that at last he had understood what poor Carac had been trying to tell him since the beginning, that Sisipher loved the Emperor.

"She loves Guile, that is, Ottemar?" Brannog sounded surprised, but then he laughed gently. "And yet that foolish girl of mine would once have thrust a knife into his vitals at any opportunity."

"Her love is pure, sire. My people felt it, and we share her sadness." Carac said this with an expression on his face that Brannog knew well. Those Earthwrought who served his daughter would die for her without question. She walked among them like a goddess.

"I am rude to laugh, Carac. But she must put such things from her head. The strength of the Empire is vital. So much depends upon it."

"She has put her love aside, sire. By leaving Medallion."

"With whom? This crew, who were they?"

"A Trullhoon, once a pirate Hammavar, led them. Rannovic."

"To where?" said Brannog, his mood changing at once.

"It is thought that they went to the west—"

Brannog stood up. "*The west!* Is she mad! Such recklessness."

"There were survivors of Rockfast's fall. Einnis Amrodin,

some say, fled to the high mountains. Sisipher may have gone in search of him. His wisdom and knowledge are legendary, even among the Earthwrought here. In any war, his help would be inestimable.''

Brannog would have growled his anger, but then he thought of his own life since Xennidhum. Roaming, almost aimlessly, not rallying to Ruan or Guile, as he perhaps should have. They would have had good use for him and his following. And Sisipher would have been nearer at hand. Ah, but she was her own mistress. With surprising powers. She did not need him to stand over her. And he had achieved much here. Yet the doubts crept in.

Ruvanna could not read these thoughts, but something akin to them flashed through her own mind.

Brannog sighed, rubbing his eyes. "Carac, you must excuse me. I have kept you talking far too late. Tomorrow we can speak again.''

"Of course, sire.''

"Tell me—will we find an army in the Far Below? Will they follow us to the west? Or should we turn back now?''

Carac could feel the yearning in the king, the hunger for so many things. It made him ache to share it and he spoke with an effort. "I think we must search, sire. If we find it—''

Brannog grinned abruptly. "Then we shall!''

Ruvanna's mind closed in on itself and she shrank back into her pelts. To be so close to Brannog's anguish, his fear for his daughter, was more of an ordeal for her than anything she had yet endured. His love for the girl was so intense! Woe to anyone who dared speak a word against her! It was Brannog's great strength, Ruvanna knew that instinctively, and yet, she knew also that it was the one weakness he had. In the hands of an enemy, such knowledge could tear him bone from bone. Ah, Brannog, she thought, your heart is vast, and yet is there no room in it for anyone besides your daughter?

As deep night fell, smothering the camp in peace, some of the guards thought they heard music, a soft song from the earth. Yet it was no earthsong, not from the Holy Roads, so deep below. It was no less elusive, but did not call them to it, save to hear its beauty, though it filled them with a strange sadness as if somewhere among them a loneliness cried out.

THE HOST RODE NOW, following the deepening valley of the river, now a bustling stream, up into the lower slopes of the mountain range, and although parties of Earthwrought went ahead to search out the best route to take, still the majority of them travelled overland. Carac, who had never ridden a horse before, found to his amazement that he was able to do so after a few brief lessons from Ogrund and Rothgar. The fact that he was able to form a silent bond with the sturdy hill pony he was given amused him greatly and even his grim expression, which had been privately remarked upon by a number of the Host, softened. Ogrund commented on this, but Carac insisted that his mood had changed for the better because he was in his native east.

"A pity then," muttered Ogrund, "that you cannot be our guide."

This was not entirely fair, for Carac's rough knowledge of the lands here did serve Brannog. Boldernesse itself was some distance to the southwest of them and they rode southeast, but Carac was able to recognize landmarks, certain peaks, and together with Men of southern Elderhold helped to locate the main pass into the mountains. Many tributary streams tumbled down from the great heights as if in a frantic effort to escape them, churning and thrashing, white-foamed and furious, so that keeping to the trails was not easy. The ponies and the Men found the journey more trying than the Earthwrought, though to their amazement, Brannog seemed as nimble as any of the earth people.

Shortly after Carac had agreed with Danoth on the correct valley to follow upwards, he was watching the girl, Ruvanna, and the three great shapes that accompanied her. They were the largest wolves he had ever seen, and he knew that Sisipher could control such beasts and spoke to them, just as she spoke to the revered owls of Kirrikree. Ruvanna seemed to have something of these skills.

"Who is the girl?" Carac asked softly of Thengram as the party threaded its way through the winding pass.

Thengram explained as best he could, although his description of the incident with the Child of the Mound was brief. "Some of the Men fear her," he whispered. "But only because of what she can do."

Carac nodded. He understood fear. She had tamed a Child of the Mound! The stories about these odious creatures had spread to the west, where Carac had shuddered to hear them. Ruvanna had tamed one? Yet she was still set apart from the rest of the Host. Brannog himself was wary of her, Carac could feel as much. Was it because Ruvanna was partly Earthwrought? It was this, Carac knew, that made her beautiful. But he turned his thoughts away, angry with himself. The wolves were Brannog's. Were they a gift to the girl, or her guards?

As the Host journeyed and the days swept by, Carac spent less time with the king. Others came to him for news of the west and he was glad to give it. The lands had indeed softened his heart, he thought, and he even had time for Danoth and his Men. Although Ottemar's men were allies, Carac had spent little time in their company, for both he and they had much to do to rebuild Medallion. But these warriors of Elderhold had become strongly bonded to the Earthwrought. All camps that were made were made together, food was shared, and discussions, plans, were all carried out jointly. And to Carac's utter amazement, the Men had learned some of the Earthwrought songs, and added their voices to them as they rode or when they rested after twilight. Carac began to understand Brannog's dream, and although at first he had wondered about the wisdom of trying to find the Far Below, he now welcomed the idea. Whoever lived there could only be impressed with this fusion of cultures. King Brannog, too, was an extraordinary example of leadership, as much Earthwrought as Man, and capable of Earthwrought skills. The only facet of his character that baffled Carac was his attitude to Ruvanna, for he still seemed to have little time for her, rarely speaking to her and then no more than cursorily. It was clear to Carac, however, that the girl worshipped the huge man. Perhaps Brannog's silence was his way of discouraging this.

It was mid-morning one day when the Host reached a high cleft in the narrowing pass which marked what they agreed must be a branch into the heart of the mountains. The vegetation had thinned away gradually to nothing, the rocks were bare and gray and the snow was about them now, shallow yet but certainly much deeper beyond this pass. The weather had been kind to them and today the sky was cloudless, the sun still hot.

Brannog and Ogrund studied the narrow pass, a gash in the wall of rock ahead, looking for signs of drifting, wondering if there could be any danger of a minor avalanche. Brannog had sent Dramlac and the scouts ahead to test the ground, although Ogrund had warned him that none of them was as skilled in reading snow terrain as he was on true earth. Even Thengram's people, used to bleak landscapes, were wary of the snow.

Dramlac rode back from the defile, face red, an arm waving. "Sire!" he cried unable to contain his excitement!

"What have you found?" shouted Brannog.

Dramlac pulled up so sharply that Brannog thought he would be thrown from his mount, but Dramlac had become a superb horseman. "Sire, we have been met."

"By whom?" said Ogrund, conscious that Carac had nudged his own pony up beside him.

"Unfamiliar Earthwrought. But they may not be hostile. Will you meet them, sire?"

"A trap!" snapped Ogrund.

"I think not," said Dramlac patiently, though he knew Ogrund was his superior.

"Let us see," said Brannog. He goaded his horse through the snow, and at once a small party of his warriors gathered to him, weapons drawn. They rode cautiously through the defile, led by Dramlac, until they came out of its cold shadows into a scooped-out valley no more than a hundred yards across. It had filled up with snow, though it was not deep, and at its far end, below the jutting overhang of stone, the Earthwrought scouts were in conversation with someone higher up in the rocks.

As Brannog and his companions reached the scouts, they gazed up at the rocks, a natural dead end to the valley. An Earthwrought stared down at them, but as Dramlac had said, this was no ordinary Earthwrought. He was far thinner, without the stocky, wide build, and his face was narrow and pointed. His hands, which waved about as he spoke, were tapered, the fingers in direct contrast to the blunt, spatulate fingers of the Earthwrought Brannog knew, for they were thin as icicles, with pointed, sharpened nails. Moreover, the hide of the creature was pure white, tight and groomed, a natural coat and protection, Brannog guessed, against the snows, for clearly this being was in its natural habitat. Its eyes gleamed like ice, slanted and white-browed, but there was an ironic warmth in them.

"Who are you?" called Brannog, his voice rolling around the white walls.

The figure above raised its arm and a shaft of ice gleamed. "I am from the south. Icewrought," it answered in a piping voice.

"I have heard of such beings," whispered Carac. "But only in legends."

"I am Brannog. Will you come down to us and speak? You will not be harmed."

"You are surrounded," came the swift reply, and as those below looked automatically at the rocks above them, they saw that there were scores of the Icewrought looking down at them, each of them armed with ice spears.

"As I thought!" snapped Ogrund. "A trap! We are idiots to have entered it."

Brannog glanced at him and Ogrund turned away, appalled at what he had said. Brannog, however, was grinning. But Ogrund was right, for overconfidence had brought Brannog here. "What do you want of us? There is an army following. A contest of arms would be valueless."

"We have seen your strength," called the Icewrought. "It is what drew us. My spies are better suited to the snows than yours. Are you truly Brannog, whom some call King?"

"He is!" shouted Ogrund, making no attempt to cover his anger.

The Icewrought waved to the ring of warriors around the valley and at once they disappeared, melting into the snow as if they had been no more than an illusion. "I am Korkoris. May I bring my people down to you in peace?"

Brannog raised his brows: he had half expected a fierce

contest, or at least an argument over the pass, for the Ice-wrought held a strong advantage and would have been difficult to dislodge. He waved to Korkoris. "None shall be harmed."

Korkoris disappeared, and Brannog dismissed the mutterings of both Ogrund and Carac, who were in agreement for once. They waited in silence. In a moment, as if he had slipped out of the very stone, Korkoris appeared. He bowed to Brannog, who had dismounted.

"Honor to you, sire," said the Icewrought. "I have come far from my homelands in the ice-fields to find you."

"You knew of me?" said Brannog, surprised.

"The word of the Earthwrought nations spreads far under Omara."

Brannog put out his hand and, startled, Korkoris took it. Brannog felt mild surprise at the warmth in that touch. "Then you and your people are most welcome."

Korkoris's pinched features contracted in a frown. "I would have been glad to bring you better news, sire."

Brannog felt a chill at this, but turned instead to Ogrund. "We will camp here for a time. Gather the captains and bring the Host into the valley. Korkoris, your people are safe with us. Will they join our camp?"

"Gladly," said Korkoris, with an elegant bow. Ogrund scowled at him, but turned and rode off to do as he had been commanded. Carac realized as Ogrund left, how impossible it would have been to forge an army without someone like Brannog to ride roughly over prejudices that would have kept even Earthwrought brothers apart.

Soon afterwards, Brannog's captains had gathered in the open, and sat with Korkoris and his own chief warriors. They were silent, allowing their leader to speak for them. Carac could see that they were very tired, as if they had indeed journeyed far, and possibly too quickly. The remainder of the Icewrought sat behind them, lined up like soldiers awaiting the command to march on, their faces grim, their bodies rigid. With them were some two score of their tiny women-folk, and the children, and even the smallest of these were quiet, as if awaiting their future together to be decided in this hour. The control that Korkoris exercised over them all was extraordinary, for none of them seemed prepared to move without a word from him.

"I have heard of you, King Brannog," he began, "and of what you have done at Xennidhum and since. I have heard also of Goldenisle and of what transpires there. Although we are from the remote ice-fields, we have long ears."

"Why have you left your lands? I can see you have left no one behind you. Is there peril there?" asked Brannog.

"No longer. But there is death, carnage. Great waste of life."

Brannog's followers, many of whom could hear the clear voice, looked appalled by the news.

"Have any of you here," said Korkoris, "met Orhung, the last of the Created?"

Carac felt the stiffness of cold fear. Brannog had turned at once to him, for Carac had spoken long on Orhung's fate. Carac nodded.

"Where is he now?" said Korkoris, and the question was like a shaft of ice.

Brannog nodded to Carac, who answered. "Your message comes too late, son of the ice, for Orhung is no more." Carac described Orhung's passing, the sacrifice he had made at the Hasp.

For the first time, the Icewrought people reacted. Like a wave, their shock ran through them. Korkoris himself looked horrified by what Carac had told him, and his glinting eyes fixed on the snow as if it would offer him consolation. "And the rod of power?"

Carac glanced at Brannog, who again nodded. "Stolen," said Carac.

"By whom?"

"Exalted."

Korkoris jerked upright. Carac's answer had taken him completely aback. "From Mount Timeless?"

"It is a mystery to us," said Brannog. "What do you know of it?"

"Only what the myths tell us. But if it is there, then we have hope."

"Why does the rod interest you?" said Ogrund.

Korkoris looked thoughtful for some time, but then sat

back, talking quietly, though his words were precise, clear. They carried to the entire gathering, though it seemed that he had woven a spell around the company so that if there were any alien ears listening, they could not hear. "My home lands are deep in the ice wastes. To you they would be cruel, hostile lands, just as these mountains behind us are hostile to you, but we breathe the storms and rejoice in the fury of the elements there. Or we did so. Until the events that occurred at the fortress of the Werewatch. We knew of the place, high in the rock walls of the snow range, though we never had cause to visit it. We did not know its full purpose, though our legends told us it had been set there by sorcerers who protected Omara from great evil.

"But one night, out of the very air, like a storm from beyond the world itself, came a force so powerful that the fortress of the Werewatch, so invulnerable, so forbidding, was taken. Its inhabitants were ruthlessly murdered, its stupendous walls torn down, its corpses put to the torch. In utter horror, we went to look upon the carnage, once the invaders had fled. Their work had been swift and terrible. It was many weeks before we learned the true history of events and what was behind them. A few inhabitants had survived, though they did not live long. They were the simple servants of the Created, the beings locked in their undersleep. Those who lived were near to madness and out of pity we slew them. If you know of Orhung, you will have heard from him of that grim night."

"The forces of Anakhizer," nodded Brannog.

"The Werewatch, set there so long ago by the Sorcerer-Kings, were no more," said Korkoris. "All destroyed in a single raid, except for Orhung, who used his wits to flee. But what do you know of the rods of power?"

Brannog studied Carac, hiding his own alarm. "Orhung bore the rod," he said. "We know only of that one."

Carac's mouth opened. "There were others?"

Korkoris nodded. "But of course. Each of the Werewatch had one."

Brannog fought back a sudden wave of nausea at the news. "Then where are they now?"

"When Anakhizer's forces destroyed the fortress, they took the rods of power. All but one of the twenty that exist."

"Twenty," gasped Brannog, his voice almost lost.

"Anakhizer has them?" cried Carac. At once the entire assembly began a noisy discussion, and on every face there was a look of deep dismay.

Brannog quelled the worst of the noise, trying to look calm. "Tell us more of these rods if you can, Korkoris."

The Icewrought leader waited until he had silence. "We have learned, piece by piece, the history of these rods of power. They were forged by the Sorcerer-Kings and given to the Werewatch to use in sealing up the broken places in the walls of Omara, which had been damaged by the working of the Hierarchs of Ternannoc. The rods contain great power, which in turn strengthens itself by drawing on power. Life which is destroyed by the rods is drawn into the rods, stored as power, and used again as power in further work. It is a cycle; the power of the rod cannot be lost. But when all the rods of power are brought together and used as one, their power becomes infinite.

"Orhung carried away with him the only rod to escape the servants of Anakhizer. Now he has the others, and seeks Orhung's rod. Should he find it, he would command all the power of the Sorcerer-Kings of old.

"Just as Korbillian held the power of the Hierarchs," said Brannog so softly to himself that only one of the company heard him. Ruvanna.

Carac interrupted. "The rod goes into the mountains. Can the Sublime One know these things of which you speak?"

"The legends say of him that he knows everything," answered Korkoris. "He communes with Omara, and is its voice. What we know, he knows. Therefore he must know that Anakhizer has the rods. It may be why he had the Exalted steal the rod of Orhung."

"As you say," nodded Carac.

Brannog did not comment on this; there were too many questions yet to be clarified. "What brought you to me, Korkoris?"

"Word of your achievements. It is understood that there will be a great conflict. And we could not remain in our ice homes. If you are gathering an army, then we wish to be a part of it.''

There were a number of isolated cheers at this, but after a moment, many of the Host responded to them, and the sound rose up.

"Your support is welcome," said Brannog. "You pay me much honor by seeking me. My hope is that the people of the Far Below will rally to us also.''

"If you would go deeper into these mountains, you will need our help," Korkoris told him.

Ogrund and Carac were both pleased at this exchange, knowing that the terrain would become far more difficult from here on.

During the minutes that followed, while members of the Host began talking to the people of Korkoris, Ruvanna slipped, almost unnoticed, to the side of Brannog.

"Your pardon," she whispered to him.

He turned, for once smiling at her. "What is it, Ruvanna?''

"Will you ask Korkoris a question for me? Ask him if he has heard earthsongs, or has he felt the calling?''

Brannog studied her for a moment, wondering if there was something she had understood that he had not. "Very well. Ask him.''

"Korkoris, did you come here, to this place, by pure chance, hoping you would find us?''

The Icewrought leaned his head on one side as he looked at her. He took a long time evaluating her, as though he knew her place among these people was important. Earlier he had seen how the wolves kept close to her, obedient as hounds. "We followed whispers of rumor. We knew Brannog was north of us.''

"That is all?" said Ruvanna, eyes fixed on his.

His expression was unreadable. "You think there is more?''

"Well?''

Korkoris felt that she would lift any secrets from him with ease if she chose to. Who could she be? "The music," he said softly and many of his people looked at him. "What is it? I am certain she knows.''

"Calling to you? Drawing you to these mountains?" Ruvanna persisted.

Korkoris nodded. "We have all heard it. It is like a beacon."

"Earthsongs," said Brannog. "Carac heard them as far away as Goldenisle. Now we have heard them. Even the Child of the Mound heard them. And you, Korkoris, from the remotest south. You, too."

"The Sublime One," said Ruvanna. "He calls his people to him. But why?"

Brannog looked up at the snows beyond them. The clouds were coming, dark and laden. But they had to be faced. The west and all its many troubles would have to wait.

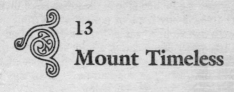

13
Mount Timeless

MOURNDARK STARED at the smooth stone wall before him. His mood was cold, and Dennovia knew better than to try to approach him when he was like this. For days he had been subsiding into his private darkness, frustrated by the inactivity. Here in the comfortable but empty halls of Mount Timeless, they seemed to have been forgotten, left to themselves. Mourndark had said more than once that they were little better off than they had been in the Direkeep.

"Someone must come," Dennovia had said, but he took little notice. At first his mind had been alert, filled with the amazement of discovery, for this lost place, this incredible center of ancient powers, had been a shock to him. Aa-Vulk and his grim Exalted warriors had been a forerunner of something far more awesome: Mourndark knew as soon as he set foot inside the strange walls of this mountain that he was surrounded by a depth of power unguessed at on Omara since the days of the Sorcerer-Kings. And Grenndak had sought to eradicate all power! How would he have dealt with this fortress had he known of its existence? But days of speculation and excitement palled into a long, dull vacuum of isolation. There had been the strains of music and shifts in the light patterns in the walls themselves, but even these had become no more than minor incidents in each day. Dennovia had lost count of the days since they had received a visitor. It had been soon after their arrival. She had been over that exchange a dozen times.

The being had appeared as if it had slipped through the

very wall as though it had been a curtain, so that neither of
the prisoners had been aware of its presence until it stood
close by them.

Mourndark would have spat out his anger, but he controlled it, knowing he had to win the alliance of these people
if he were to have any hope of getting away from them.

The being before him was unlike those who had captured
him, and was taller and wearing a long white robe that swept
to the floor. The face, more a man's than that of the earth
people, was impassive, as if it had never been taught how to
express itself. He bowed, but Mourndark took it to be a
mockery.

"Forgive us if your stay seems long," he said, scrutinizing
the faces before him as though perusing books. "But here on
Mount Timeless we are not used to the measurement of
days."

"Who are you?" said Mourndark.

"I am of the Esoterics. You were brought to us by the
Exalted, our servants."

"And Wargallow? He is here?"

"Secure."

"I presume he is a prisoner? And am I?"

The Esoteric registered no emotion, no shred of impatience. "You are Wargallow's enemies?"

"Has Aa-Vulk not told you as much? I aided him in
capturing Wargallow, for your ruler."

"Yes, that is understood. It is also understood that Wargallow rules the men of steel, the Deliverers. You oppose
this rulership?"

Though Mourndark's expression hinted at as little emotion
as that of the Esoteric, Dennovia knew that he must be aching
to learn more of this place, the power that pulsed through it.

"I oppose it, yes. Wargallow murdered the former ruler."

"The Preserver? Yes. He who made the Abiding Word.
We know of that."

"Wargallow has decreed its annulment."

"That is understood."

"He has become a dictator."

"And what would you have, Mourndark?"

"No more than what is best for my people."

The Esoteric did not react, totally impassive. "Should Wargallow be removed, would you rule in his stead?"

"There would be many who would support me."

"Would you restore your laws?"

"In order to eliminate the abuse of power by those who would harm Omara, yes. It is the way of the Deliverer."

"But they have chosen Wargallow, not you."

"Chosen? Through terror?"

"You would see him deposed?"

"My followers uphold the correct faith."

"That of sacrifice? Of giving blood to the earth?"

"Wargallow's new philosophy is indiscriminate. He does not shed the blood of transgressors for Omara, our god."

"And you would?"

"It is clear to me that there are many forces in Omara which would damage her power, just as the darkness in Xennidhum did."

The Esoteric nodded. "Then you are understood."

"And do I have your support?"

The Esoteric seemed mildly surprised. "Support? No, that is not possible. The Sublime One gives support to Wargallow."

Dennovia saw the hands of the Steelmaster curl like the talons of a hunting bird, but his face remained calm. "You confuse me. I led your servants to Wargallow. I watched them cut his Deliverers down and drag him away. How can your ruler support him? I was spared the killing."

The Esoteric seemed unaware that Mourndark was insulted. "There is to be a war in the far western lands and in the Chain of Goldenisle. Anakhizer is preparing for it even as we speak."

Mourndark's eyes narrowed. "So?"

"The Deliverers oppose Anakhizer. They need unity if they are to be effective in their opposition. Wargallow gives them such unity. The Sublime One wishes to support Wargallow's leadership, as he supports the need for unity among the Deliverers."

"So he's sending him back?" Mourndark tried not to sound incredulous.

"That is so. Soon Wargallow will be returned to lead his people."

Dennovia felt herself stiffen with anger. "That is ridiculous! You've had his men killed in order to bring him here, and now you wish to support him! Do you expect us to believe this nonsense!" she cried.

The Esoteric turned to her blandly. "The Sublime One is appalled by the suffering that the Deliverers have caused the Earthwrought nation in the past. He has, therefore, set his mark upon Wargallow. He knows that your ruler has decreed that there should be no more giving of blood and that the Abiding Word has been outlawed. This pleases the Sublime One, who is merciful."

Dennovia gasped. Then by his own tongue Mourndark had admitted he was an enemy of the Sublime One! This Esoteric had tricked him.

"But why was Wargallow taken by force?" she demanded.

"I have said that the Sublime One has set his mark upon him. He would not have come here willingly for that. The mark is to show Wargallow and all his people that the killing steel is no longer to be used against our nation. Like the Abiding Word, it is outlawed."

Mourndark spoke softly, though his words cut the air like a knife. "And what is this mark?"

"Wargallow's killing steel has been removed. He will be returned to his people without it, so that they will know."

Mourndark looked aghast. "Removed! By whom? How?"

"By Esoterics."

Then you've killed him! Mourndark thought. Nothing you can do with all your powers can change that.

"You are Wargallow's enemies," said the Esoteric. "You would bring disunity and disorder to the Deliverers. Therefore you are not to be released. But the Sublime One is not without compassion. You will not be harmed." He began to withdraw, as though floating.

"Wait!" cried Dennovia, rushing to him, but he was fading, and in a moment gone altogether. Dennovia spun round to face Mourndark, but he was deep in thought. "Prisoners!" she cried, bursting into tears.

Mourndark came to her and, to her surprise, gently stroked

her hair, though his mind was on other things. "A harsh logic," he muttered. "But it may yet serve me."

"How? They know we are Wargallow's enemy."

"The Sublime One has overreached himself. It was clever of him to support Wargallow and allow him to unite our people. Obviously the Sublime One would support anyone who opposes this western threat. But his mistake was in removing Wargallow's killing steel."

"He'll die! You told me—"

Mourndark smiled. "Quite. He'll die. Slowly but inevitably. And the Sublime One will realize then that the Deliverers will never bow to him. There will always be resentment. Unless someone can act as a mediator."

Dennovia took his hands in her own and smiled at them. "Who better to lead the Deliverers than a man without the killing steel?"

"An obvious question," he smiled, raising her fingers to his lips.

WARGALLOW OPENED his eyes. This time he was properly awake and not merely turning over between dreams. He closed his eyes at once, knowing that he was not alone. The room he was in was a narrow one, he had already found out that much. He had been brought here shortly after his strange awakening from the taking of his arm. It throbbed yet, but he clenched himself not so much against the pain but the knowledge. The world moved about him too quickly. He dare not move for fear of being violently ill.

From the gruff voices, it seemed that two captors stood over him. They were Exalted, by their tones, and were disputing how to get him up. He knew he could not feign sleep for long, but he would retain the cloak of exhaustion. It would be easy enough, for his strength flowed back very slowly. He seized at anger, thinking of those of his Faithful who had been cut down. Had any of them survived? Turning gently, he opened his eyes and asked for water.

They brought it, helping him to sip it. Both of them could see how wan he was, unable to sit up without help.

"Should we wait another day?" said the larger of them.

His skin was not painted like other Exalted, but he wore large earrings and a chain about his neck.

"We dare not. The Esoterics want him moved today. We'll have to carry him."

Wargallow groaned as they got him off the bed, setting his feet down but stumbling. He felt the extreme dizziness, his stomach churning as the Exalted half carried him to the low doorway. For a moment he thought he would be ill, the sweat coating his face, but he mastered it and began to try to isolate what strength he had, concentrating inwardly. Outside was a stone corridor lit by the glow of its own walls, part of the Earthwrought mystery that brought warmth as well as light.

He let himself go limp, but there were no grunts of outrage. He looked too ill to be acting. The two Exalted manhandled him up a number of flights of stairs, their footsteps echoing back down the corridor as they went. Ahead of them was another narrow door, not made for Men, but they got Wargallow through it. Once beyond, they let him down and he slumped against a wall. He took a strange comfort from its odd warmth. He pretended to close his eyes, though watched events through slitted lids. The room opened out on to a large balcony without a parapet or rail, a ledge that dropped straight down to the precipice beyond, the sheer edge of the mountain. A spectacular view opened up, with a range of snow-capped mountains disappearing into the distance, linked by cloud and whipping snow, blown by the winds. Elberon was far away now, out of reach. Wargallow used the thought to strengthen his anger, his only weapon.

Another Exalted appeared on the ledge, watching the skies expectantly. He came back to his companions. "Is he ready?"

"Like a sack. But it has to be today."

"Here's the harness. Better get him into it." He gave something to the two Exalted and they returned to Wargallow. Beyond them, through the gaping portal that looked out at the icy peaks, the Deliverer now noticed a number of large shapes swooping amongst some of the nearer crags. This harness must be to strap him to a beast of some kind, and up here, that could only mean an aerial creature. But where would it take him?

"Get him on his feet," said the first of the Exalted, and

he held the harness ready, undoing some of its metal catches. The second Exalted put his hands under Wargallow's armpits and began to lift him. As he did so, Wargallow surged forward on his heels, crashing his forehead up under the nose of the Exalted. The sheer force of the attack drove the Exalted's nose bone up into his brain like a bolt, killing him instantly. He flung back without a sound, and before the second could react, Wargallow was on his feet, grabbing at the harness. He jerked the Exalted to him and in a whipping movement had wrapped the leather straps of the harness around his captive's thick neck. With a rapid twisting motion he tightened the strap and brought his knee up into the Exalted's back. The other Exalted, now on the ledge again, saw what was happening and came running over, screaming abuse and pulling out his short sword.

Wargallow pulled with all his conserved strength, all his hatred, the leather of the harness biting into his victim's neck, choking the life out of him. He lifted his feet from the ground and in moments the third Exalted was upon him. Wargallow swung his struggling victim to and fro, using him as a shield. The swordsman could not find a way through.

"Release him, you fool!" he screamed. "We are not here to harm you!"

There came a shriek from the skies directly beyond the ledge and they knew that the aerial creature was about to land. How many riders would it have? Wargallow's mind cried.

With a last wrench, he ended the life of the kicking Exalted, heaving him forward so that his body almost crashed into the swordsman. He was almost spent, but Wargallow bent down and gripped the sword of the first dead Exalted. He barely had time to raise it to deflect the first blow of the remaining assailant.

"Thrown down the sword! You cannot escape us!"

Wargallow saved every breath that he could. Already his right arm was pulsing with fresh agony, his strength ebbing like wasting blood. But he would not let his enemy see this. Behind him, the aerial creature landed. To Wargallow's relief, there was no one on its back. Its lizard-like neck twisted to and fro as its baleful eyes took in the events in the cham-

ber. HIssing, it tried to force its way in. Wargallow took
advantage of the distraction, concentrating on the last Exalted
and shutting out the sight of the beast. The Exalted was no
match for him as a swordsman and Wargallow drove him
back in a series of ferocious chops and parries.

It became evident from the Exalted's face that he feared
the beast, especially with the smell of blood in the air, for
the pulped nose of the first dead Exalted bled profusely. He
twisted to see where the beast was, and it was his undoing,
for Wargallow struck with the speed of a snake, thrusting the
narrow blade straight into his gut. It was not a clean, quick
kill, but Wargallow withdrew the blade, stepped forward and
finished the Exalted in one merciful stroke. His victim toppled backward into the path of the advancing beast. It howled,
as if in glee, and bent to feed, locking its jaws on the trunk
of the fallen Exalted. For a brief moment Wargallow considered attempting to mount and ride the beast, but it was out
of the question. The blood had maddened it and besides, he
was in no condition to travel.

Instead he moved to the narrow door, hanging on to its
frame to prevent himself collapsing. He was completely
drained. If any others found him, he was helpless. The stairs
were the only exit from this place and he watched them,
listening for the sounds of approaching Exalted. But the only
sounds came from the beast as it devoured its unexpected
meal. Quickly Wargallow went through the door, shutting it
on the scenes of horror. He closed his eyes and drew in a
number of great breaths, fighting off the waves of dizziness
that had started to assail him. To stop now would be fatal.

I must get below, he thought. It is the one place where
these people would not expect me to go. Perhaps the beast
above will tear up all three bodies and make such a spectacle
of it that others will think I perished with them. Perhaps.

As he went down the stairs, stumbling and leaning on the
walls, he listened for any sound. His head swam and he clung
desperately to self-control. After an age he passed the room
where he had slept. There was no one there. The corridor
ran on for a long way before it was met by others and soon
he found himself at the top of a wide stairway that seemed
to go down into a busier part of the building. He dare not go

that way, certain to meet someone if he did. He would be incapable of resistance now. What was this place? A castle? Where was he to go? The only way out would be to find one of his captors, take him by force and find a way off the mountain. But the way he felt now, he could not command a child to obey him.

Voices from below made him stagger back along the narrow corridor. Only when it had curved away and the voices were lost did he stop, his breathing ragged. The walls here were dim, the light poor, and the corridor ended shortly afterward in a flight of very narrow steps that he could barely squeeze down. They were dusty and looked disused, so he decided to try, and found himself following a tight spiral down into the naked rock. Silence closed in like death, and the light grew fainter. How easy it would have been then to give in to sleep. It tried to seduce him, but he knew he would never wake from it if he succumbed to it.

As he wound downward, he heard the sudden soft swelling of music, his head filling with it as if he were at sea on a heaving deck. It was not unpleasant but it had the effect of completely disorienting him, so that for a long time he lost all sense of direction. The waves of pain had ebbed away, and the light pulsed with the music, finally slipping away again. At last there was another corridor, its roof very low, so that his head touched it and he had to stoop. The light improved once more and he slithered down a gradual incline. It was a thirst that assailed him now, driving out the pain in his arm and the dizziness. Down he went, totally bemused, unaware of how far he had come or where he was in relation to the main body of this fortress. He thought he heard voices a number of times, and vague whisperings, but the music swirled over him like a current, washing them away each time. In time he collapsed, and sleep dragged him in.

The pain woke him, for once his ally. He stared at his right arm, the memory of its severance a renewed shock, but he used the pain to force himself to his feet. As he rose, he did hear voices, muted, ahead of him. How far away they were, he could not tell, but he moved on cautiously, sword before him. Its edge was still dark with the dried blood of its victim. Beyond him the corridor broke out into a series of low galleries, and in one of these he made out a group of figures. They were not like his captors had been, and he realized in a moment that they were Earthwrought. They resembled Ygromm's folk, being thick-set and about half the height of a man. Although they sat together, eating, they had tools about them and appeared to have been working on the stone of the rock wall beyond them. Wargallow could not tell what the work itself· was, possibly removing blocks for building. He counted five of the Earthwrought.

Their food and drink tempted him, odd though it would be, but seeing it he knew just how desperate he was for sustenance. Even so, he dared not risk showing himself. He no longer had the strength to fight, and besides, it would be far too easy for one of them to flee down one of the many galleries and raise the alarm. While he deliberated on his next move, he heard approaching footsteps and hid himself in the shadows.

By the wall-glow, he could see the arrival of one of the warrior Earthwrought, who carried a short spear. He stood belligerently before the five Earthwrought and they stood up and bowed to him.

"Don't let me interrupt your meal," grunted the newcomer facetiously.

"Is anything wrong, Gul-Thaan?" asked one of the Earthwrought, his mouth full. The others appeared amused.

"There's been a disturbance in the Heights. A Man."

The Earthwrought looked at one another in genuine surprise. "A man? *Here* on Mount Timeless? How could he have got up into the Heights without being killed?"

"He was brought as a prisoner. They underestimated him. He's broken loose."

Now the Earthwrought exchanged looks of exaggerated amazement, as if they had been told a demon was among them, ready to rend them and dismember them at any moment.

"If you see anything strange, let me know," said Gul-Thaan, ignoring their ridiculous expressions. "Anything."

"Is this Man dangerous?"

"He has already killed three Exalted. He could tear all five of you apart with his one good hand if he came across you. He moved like the wind to get away. He must have done."

"Then we'd better leave and go to our homes at once!" cried one of the Earthwrought with a secret wink at his companions.

"No need!" snapped Gul-Thaan. "You just get on with your work. It's well behind, like everything else these days. They may be incompetent in the Heights, but let's show them how efficient we still are, eh? And keep your eyes and ears open. Got that?"

"Oh yes, Gul-Thaan," they murmured dutifully, their mock-reverence not lost on the listening Wargallow. Gul-Thaan growled something else and then was gone. As soon as his footsteps turned to silence, the Earthwrought began chuckling among themselves like children.

"Five of us with one hand!" snorted one of them. "Is this a Man or a Stonedelver?"

"Better if he were. Then he could get down here and help us with the moving of the stones. Show how efficient we are!" grinned another.

"Aye, did you mark that? Gul-Thaan was a bit unguarded, eh? Talk of incompetence above us! Not the first time we've heard about things going awry. Three Exalted killed? Three? What sort of warriors are they breeding these days?"

"If they're all like Gul-Thaan, it's a wonder a dozen weren't killed," said a third, making a rude gesture in the direction Gul-Thaan had taken, punctuating it with a loud belch.

"Perhaps it wasn't a Man, but a boy."

They laughed and finished their meal, apparently not at all nervous about the prospect of meeting the reported Man. Wargallow wondered at that and their words. Their lack of respect for Gul-Thaan was very marked, and they did not seem to think highly of the Exalted. There was corruption, too. Even so, he could not risk revealing himself to them and appealing to them for help. Instead he waited. In a while they went back to working the stone, and as they labored, Wargallow drifted into a half-sleep, lulled by the clink of chisels and the tap of metal hammers.

It was the silence that woke him again. At once he knew that he was alone, and he scrambled to his feet, disturbed at the prospect. A glance into the gallery told him the Earth-wrought had gone, but then he heard a distant laugh. Quickly he slipped across the gallery, his head ringing to every foot-fall, and followed the sound. It took him a while to locate it, but he did so, at last choosing a corridor and going down it. The Earthwrought were leaving, and he was able to keep his distance but remain not far behind. He had no idea where they would go, but he had decided to follow them anyway. Perhaps they would leave the mountain.

After half an hour's downward journey, the Earthwrought reached a racing underground torrent. There was a narrow stone bridge over it and guarding this were two sleepy-looking Exalted. They sat up with a bored yawn each when they saw the Earthwrought coming and their words were lost in the roar of the torrent. In a moment the Earthwrought were on their way over the bridge, waving cheerily back. Wargallow watched them go from the darkness of the corridor. Again he lifted the sword, drawing on what he knew would be his final reserves of strength.

The Exalted spoke to each other, and one of them moved out of sight. Wargallow waited, undecided, then edged for-ward in the gloom. The guard on the bridge yawned again, rubbing at his eyes. While he looked away from the corri-dor, Wargallow ducked down and ran forward as fast as he could. He was a few yards from the Exalted before he was seen. The warrior drew back his spear, but Wargallow's blade took him in the throat before he could discharge it. Wargal-low stood over him unsteadily, lifting the spear from limp fingers. The other guard was not visible, so Wargallow moved across the bridge, the torrent beneath him roaring as if in anger. He heard a shout and looked back to see the other guard. Quickly he flung the spear, but his aim was wide.

He almost fell as he ran to the far side of the torrent, and as he reached it, the guard's spear clattered in the rocks near him. The Exalted was giving chase, so he turned to meet him, but the guard was wary, pausing on the bridge, knowing that Wargallow was a dangerous quarry. Wargallow could not afford to be held up now. He knew that soon he would col-lapse again, an easy prey. He made to leap back to the bridge and the Exalted turned back. Wargallow flung his short sword and although it clanged off the stone and spat a trail of sparks, the Exalted yelped, losing his footing. In a moment he had plunged into the foam and was carried away with incredible speed.

I should regret your deaths, Wargallow thought. But for those who serve this mountain and its god, I have no mercy.

DEEP WITHIN MOUNT TIMELESS, far from the place where Wargallow had escaped from the Exalted, a chamber of darkness was abruptly filled with rich, green light. Its walls were perfectly circular, its ceiling invisible, hidden in light that flooded from above like the sun. Plants grew here in profusion, rich in perfume, their flowers opening now to drink the rain of light like blessings from a god. Into the chamber, hovering like ethereal spirits of another realm, came a dozen of the Esoterics, their faces serene, their eyes fixed on some inner bliss. They arranged themselves about the tiny pool in the center of the chamber and studied its surface as if it would impart to them limitless knowledge.

In a while a section of the curved walls moved aside like silk, silently. A lone Exalted warrior entered. He wore a sword, his head covered by his helmet, and he bowed stiffly.

"It is here," he said simply.

One of the Esoterics waved condescendingly and the Exalted withdrew at once. Moments later he came back, this time carrying a bundle of cloth. He placed this on the floor beside the pool, bowing low as he did so.

"Open it," came the musical voice of one of the Esoterics.

The Exalted undid the cloth, revealing a short length of metal. He was again dismissed and at once the Esoterics studied the rod, though none of them moved close enough to it to touch it.

"Summon the one from afar."

In union, the Esoterics closed their eyes and in the silence that followed, the air began to stir. The brilliant light flickered as though a storm were coming, and shadows clung to the walls where before there had been none. The water in the pool trembled, ripples spreading from it as if it had been struck by a hand. The Esoterics drifted back, their own faces clouded, for once disturbed. They had seen the presence that was about to come among them before.

The water in the pool rose up like living matter, molding and shaping itself, defying gravity and hanging in the air, a dripping ball. In a moment it had become a vague face, a vast head without true features, save for the open mouth. Eyes and a nose partially shaped themselves, but they seemed to be obscured by thick layers of skin, as if thrusting up against a membrane.

"Who summons Anakhizer?" said the mouth, and the words rumbled like a curse.

Horrified but fascinated, the Esoterics watched as the eyeless head turned this way and that, like a blind man searching for movement.

"We speak for the Sublime One, the Voice of Omara," they told the vision.

The voice dropped, but its words were clear. "Those things that were promised—have they been done?"

"The last rod of the Werewatch is before us."

Light blazed in the hidden eyes of the face and it shone for a moment on Orhung's rod, drinking in its shape.

"The Sublime One communes with Omara," said the Esoterics. "When he wakes from his work, the rod will be brought to you in the west. The Man, Wargallow, has been brought before the Sublime One. He has been made an example of to all the Earthwrought nations. Those among them who called themselves his allies will see how the Sublime One has marked him.

An Esoteric pointed to an alcove in one of the arcs of the wall. In this, dark and silent as a corpse, was the killing steel of Wargallow. "This will be a sign to Wargallow's people, and a sign to our own."

"Have you broken the unity of the Deliverers?" said the voice in the fountain, its anger rising.

"We have not. Wargallow is being returned to them. He will unite them and lead them against you and will stand beside the Emperor and all his allies in the war."

"And the Earthwrought nations?"

"When they see the Sublime One's mark, they will turn

away from Wargallow and the Emperor. Just as Wargallow
unifies his people, so the Sublime One unifies his.''

"If this is so, my bargain with you will be honored.''
Anakhizer's face blazed once more, then it became darkness.
Moments later the sphere of water that had shaped his head
broke and fell back into the pool. The audience was at an
end.

YUTTEGAR PEERED at the body, grunted to himself, and then
waved the burly figure of Tarraneh, his chieftain, into the
tiny chamber. It was dark in here, and hot. Yuttegar's body-
glow reduced to a minimum.

"This is the one we found,'' he said.

"Alive?'' snorted Tarraneh, his Earthwrought features
pulled into a grimace that made him look like an ogre.

"Aye, barely. I've used my poor skills to aid him.''

"This must be the Man they want,'' said Tarraneh, looking down at the dark clothing of the Man before him, prone
on the empty slab. "How many of you know he's here?''

"Only the five of us. What shall we do?''

Tarraneh spat into the dust, wiping his nose noisily. "Lot
of blood on him. Is it his? Murdering pigs.''

Yuttegar shook his head. "He's drawn Exalted blood. They
say he killed three of them.''

"They took his arm?''

"Aye,'' nodded Yuttegar. He had covered it. "And not in
a fight. The work is too intricate.''

Tarraneh swore crudely and spat again. "Exalted! They're
vermin.''

"One of them, Gul-Thaan, said again that there is trouble
in the Heights. For a Man to escape, having killed—''

"May they all rot! We'll wait.''

"This Man will recover.''

"Then we'll hear him. And no one must know he's here.
Keep your four companions away from the mountain for a
while. Take others.''

"It may not matter soon.''

"Oh, why not?'' growled the chieftain, not used to being
disobeyed.

"This Man will come to, but even so, he is dying.''

14
Crevasse

BRANNOG'S LONG JOURNEY into the mountains continued, and although the snow deepened and there were numerous flurries hinting at a blizzard, the worst of the weather held off. The Icewrought brought a strange comfort to the Host, and Brannog thought of Korbillian and the powers he had had. The Icewrought had a symbiosis with the chilling terrain that the Earthwrought understood, and in particular they were able to spread warmth among the travelers, as though they had entered an unspoken pact with the elements that made the journey deeper into the high range no less bearable than a journey across the plains below. Brannog wondered at the timing of the Icewrought arrival, for it had certainly been fortuitous. Korkoris's scouts were pleased to be given the task of acting as the eyes and ears of the advance guard, roaming ahead, searching out the best passes and safest lines to take. The snow and ice held no secrets from them and they were able to predict snow slides and guide the Host away from their paths. Even their tiny children, scampering about with, to Ogrund, infuriating confidence, lent an air of security to the journey.

"Can you say where the Far Below will be found?" Brannog asked Korkoris late one afternoon as the Host prepared to set up camp. "I've been following rumors, advice that it is at the heart of the range, but unless we meet someone or find some definite sign, we could be here for months and find nothing."

Korkoris wiped his needle-like spear, which gleamed like

ice on fire in the late sunlight. "We will find it for you, sire. Already my people learn much from the rock beneath the snow. The Far Below is here, in these mountains. It is indeed deep under them, and from what we have already learned, it is well protected. The rocks are reluctant to yield up their knowledge to us, but we hear their whispers. It will not be easy to enter the Far Below. We will be opposed."

"If we can find its inhabitants, even those who guard it—"

"They will try to confuse us, lead us away. The Far Below is jealously protected."

Brannog shrugged. "Well, first let us find it."

Korkoris bowed and sprang away nimbly to join his people. Brannog could see how well the Icewrought had already used themselves with the Earthwrought. The differences between the two were very marked, but the bond between them was as solid as the rocks, unquestionable, as if it had existed long before they had come together in these snows. There had been a sadness among the Icewrought when they had arrived, possibly, Brannog thought, because they had been forced to leave their ice-fields, but it was lifting now, and his range gave them, at least, great solace.

"They are the true children of Omara," said a soft voice behind Brannog. He turned to see Ruvanna stroking the thick mane of her mountain pony. Her own dark hair shimmered against the white backdrop of snow. Her wolves (yes, I think of them as her wolves now!) were with her, studying the rapidly forming camp below. They had an affinity for her, and he did not challenge her on this.

"And yet they are both its prisoners," Ruvanna added, watching the Icewrought laboring beside the Earthwrought.

Brannog motioned her to him and she nudged the pony so that it came beside his, nuzzling it as if to ask tolerance of his presence.

"Do you feel their sadness?" she asked Brannog.

Her question took him by surprise and he looked down at the camp. It was true, for he had always been aware of the undercurrent of melancholy in his people: it was not lacking the Icewrought. He nodded: he knew the histories well enough.

"It is what binds them," Ruvanna went on. "Wherever there are Earthwrought, or their brethren, such as these people of the ice, there will be an unspoken unity. You are fortunate to have been made a part of them." There was no animosity in her words, only calmness, respect, and something else that Brannog could not fathom.

"And are you not one of them, Ruvanna? You speak now as though you are a stranger. I had been meaning to talk to you before this journey ended. Who are you? How is it you can perform your arts? These powers. The Child of the Mound—"

She shook her head. "That creature was impoverished. Once it may have been powerful—"

"Have you any conception of how powerful—?"

"Oh yes," she shuddered. "I read that in its memory. But when I fought with it, it was weak. I drew on the fresh power of the earth. Xennidhum's decaying corruption is no match for it now."

"Kennagh said you are an orphan, your father an Earthwrought."

"I don't know the truth of it. I recall only the village from my third or fourth year. I have Earthwrought blood, and you can see I do not have the height nor the beauty of your own women—"

"There are many ways to define beauty."

She looked away, stiffening.

Brannog chuckled. "You have your admirers."

She turned to him, but could not meet his smile. "Yes, and there are those who fear me."

"Of course. You have power. Those who do not have it either envy it or shy from it. Some who do not understand it, like Danoth's men, your villagers, fear it." He seemed to tower over her, though for once there was warmth in his voice.

"You disapprove of me, I know that. You did not want me here."

"I fear for you, Ruvanna, that is all. You have shown your teeth, girl, and to me. I think I understand your strength better. You are a girl—"

"Which makes me weak?" she said sharply, eyes widen-
g.

"Once I thought that. But I am a father. Such things make
en protective. Perhaps it is instinct. It is not out of pity I
ve you my concern."

"I don't seek pity, or concern! Accept me as one of your
ost. Do not think of me as—as—an incumbent."

Brannog laughed gently and several heads below turned to
e what had amused him. "Spare me your fury! No one
rries you, do they? I suspect you do not even need that
out pony under you—"

"I need your trust," she cut in.

His laughter ceased at once. "Trust? What do you mean?"

She looked embarrassed, as if she had inadvertently ex-
sed something. "I sense it. I cannot describe what it is,
t you are wary of me. More so than any of Danoth's peo-
e."

He looked at her for a long moment and again she could
t meet his gaze. "It is not you, girl. You have power. I
ve seen such things at work before."

In your daughter! she wanted to shout. Say it!

"I wonder if you know the true depths of your power,"
went on. "There are things in this world that will take
ch power and twist it, without your knowing. It is those
ings I fear. Not you. I am wary, and so should you be."
en he was smiling again. "But you are safe here."

After a while she looked out at the white landscape. "When
e reach the Far Below, will you take me down?"

"I had not planned to."

"Are you ashamed of me?"

He looked shocked. *"Ashamed?* What an absurd ques-
n—"

"A crossbreed. Child of Earthwrought and woman. If I
n to be an example to the dwellers below, a taste of what
ur new Omara holds, then you must be sure that I will
press them." Again she was angry, attacking him with her
ords, challenging him.

"Make an exhibition of you? That's monstrous!"

'It is why the villagers were glad to release me."

"It was you who ran away from them."

"I did not belong with them! I do not belong with any of them."

"Stop this! I understand you if you feel neglected. But you told me you did not seek my pity. In this, you'll not have it! There's work here. There will be war. Like fire it will rage, ignoring those in its path and any bruised feelings they may have. Think of that fire, and nothing else."

"As you do?"

"As I do! Waver from that purpose, and the fire will consume you. Now, get some rest. Soon Korkoris will have found the Far Below." He goaded his horse forward and left her without a backward glance.

Man of ice, she thought bitterly, but as she watched him enter the camp, she relented. A man who could command such love among his people had a heart not of ice, but of fire.

DARKNESS HAD FALLEN and many of the Host were asleep when Ogrund felt a movement at the opening to his own tent. He had made a place for himself in the packed snow inside it, baffled by the warmth it gave, and had quickly fallen into a sleep of exhaustion. However, the snow seemed to dredge up images from below it, as though an army waited there, sharp-speared and eager for blood, and he tossed and turned, waking up, hand reaching for his war club more than once. It came as a relief to him when he actually saw someone at his tent flap. Rothgar called to him softly.

"What is it?" grunted Ogrund.

"They've found it. The Far Below." The big Earthwrought could not keep the excitement from his voice.

Ogrund was on his feet quickly, joining Rothgar on the snow outside. It glowed a soft orange from the central camp fire, where a small party of Earthwrought and Icewrought had gathered. Rothgar and Ogrund went to them, their faces stern, masking their interest.

Carac was already here, and as he saw Ogrund he gave him a smug grin, which the latter ignored. A single Icewrought warrior was whispering to the others, surrounded by them. Ogrund and Carac pushed through the ring of eager listeners. Around them all, the snow seemed to listen.

"It's beyond the southeastern ridge," said the warrior. "I was crossing the great glacier there when I felt it. Only for a moment, then it was gone. So I went down into the body of the glacier, deep, deep, until I found the rock under it. It is a clever way to hide a city."

"A city!" came the whispered echoes of his voice.

"Aye. You are lucky that the Icewrought joined the Host." Ogrund scowled. "Meaning what?" he snorted.

"The Far Below is buried under the very roots of the mountains."

"Then we would have found it," said Carac. "It is mere chance that you did so first—"

"Not so, not so! You would have searched forever. And not found it. It has its cloak, you see. The glacier! There are no entrances to the Far Below, save those covered by the glacier. The only other way into it is under the mountains, and those ways are guarded. Spells and old magic would have sent you around and around until your bones rotted. To be fair, Icewrought would have been similarly confused. I doubt if we would have even got so far under the earth, preferring ice—"

"Be sure of that," nodded Ogrund.

"But the glacier is not guarded. Why should it be? It is like a mountain of ice. For most, it would be impenetrable."

"Did you reach the city?" said Ogrund.

"Yes! At least, its upper limits. I did not see it, the way down was too hard for me. I sensed it, heard the rock speak. Like dreams, it sent me the visions. But I fled them. So vast! Such a place!"

Ogrund allowed the Icewrought to speak on for a while, and then told Korkoris, who had arrived from another nocturnal expedition, the good news. Korkoris quieted his scout and the gathering was dismissed. Ogrund told his own people to keep the peace until the morning. Brannog would be told in good time, but for now he was asleep.

"I see no point in waking him with the news, excellent though it is," Ogrund told his companions. "He needs rest and if we tell him we have found the Far Below, he will want to ride off to it at once."

Dawn had barely insinuated itself over the horizon when

Brannog came out of his tent. Ogrund was already there, dozing at the post where a guard should have been.

"Ogrund!" Brannog roared good-naturedly. The little figure scrambled to its feet as if a host of his enemies were riding down upon him. "What are you doing here? You're a commander, not a guard!"

Ogrund stood before him proudly, his lined face assembling itself into the nearest attempt at a smile it was capable of. "The Far Below," he said breathlessly. "It is found." He went on in his gruff way to describe what the Icewrought had found.

Less than an hour later, the entire Host was ready to ride, with Brannog at its head, impatient to be away. His captains were with him, including Korkoris, and although Brannog noticed Ruvanna, he did not wave her to him. Instead he gave the order to ride on up the pass that would lead them through the southeastern range to the promised glacier.

Although they moved swiftly, it took them until midday of the second day to come through the sharp peaks and stand above the expansive sweep of glittering whiteness that was the glacier. It spread out before them like an ice sea, curving away to the southeast, pouring invisibly slowly through a gap in the peaks there before bending south and onwards to the remote ice-fields of the southern wilderness. Its width measured in miles, but even so, the mountains on its far side reared up, inhospitable and daunting. The Icewrought who had been here had been right: no Man or Earthwrought could possibly have located the Far Below from up here. As the mountains were high, so their roots were deep. Yet how deep was this mighty glacier?

Korkoris began organizing his people at once, and even the women were eager to help in the search. The glacier, they knew, shifted imperceptibly, year by year, but every fractional move adjusted the alignment of the entrances below. The scout admitted that he had found one by pure chance.

Brannog felt an elation filling him. The beauty of the land here, the shimmering ice, like a field of countless diamonds, spoke to something within him and he wanted to sing, to shout out his pleasure. The Earthwrought read his mood and a number of them pulled from their packs their pipes, capering on the snow as they marched, so that soon the crisp air was filled with a peculiar music that spread the wave of euphoria throughout the company. Ruvanna began to sing, softly, but her voice carried outwards and up to the peaks, turning the flights of birds there. The Host joined in with the song, which had only simple words, but words and chords that seemed to stroke into the ice and rock, vibrating from it as if the very earth were an instrument in the hands of a loving musician. As they crossed on to the endless white field of the glacier, Brannog felt himself drowning in the pure pleasure of the moment, knowing that at no time in his life before had he ever experienced this overpowering delight. The music became the universe, drawing into itself every atom of being around it, so that the glacier itself seemed to move and pulse in accord.

Ruvanna, at the heart of the song, stopped abruptly. Gradually all voices stilled. Everyone turned to her as if she had called each name individually. Brannog rode to her at once. She smiled in a kind of triumph. The Icewrought suddenly danced about her, women and children alike, all laughing and tossing up handfuls of snow, bringing down a tiny blizzard of excitement.

"It's here! It's here!" they shouted.

Brannog, his mouth open in a mixture of amazement and annoyance, saw unexpected tears on Ruvanna's cheeks. She nodded to him and he leapt from his mount.

"The Far Below!" he shouted, and his voice carried far out over the glacier. As its echoes died, a great silence rushed in. Now, for a moment, the Host felt very small, dots on a field, isolated, made minute by the sheer endlessness of the ice.

Korkoris leapt up with a cry that made everyone start. "Aye! Deep down below us. The city of legend."

"How do we reach it?" said Brannog and the spell of silence that had for a moment threatened to freeze them all was snapped. Laughter broke out, with a score of garbled conversations.

"Ice power," laughed Korkoris. "We go down through the ice."

"But neither Men nor Earthwrought can travel through ice as you do," said Brannog.

"We will open a way, just as you may have to open a way for us when we reach the stone," grinned Korkoris.

Soon the Host was organized once more. Korkoris took charge, although Ogrund looked a little disgruntled. He could see the sense in this, but his pride flew over him like a banner. Carac hid his amusement poorly. Brannog himself drew back as Korkoris's people formed a long line across the ice. This line, they said, must not be broken. Korkoris fussed over the line for some time, so that both Ogrund and Carac made a number of disparaging remarks about showmanship and pomposity, but Korkoris was not to be denied his moment of ceremony. Eventually the serious business of the day began. The Icewrought were opening a crevasse in the glacier.

They chanted softly over the ice and at last there was a distant groan, a great cracking under the ice as if massive weights of stone were being moved by an army of giants. The chants of the Icewrought were never louder than a murmur of wind, but the power released by them was stupefying to the onlookers. A crack rang out over the ice and a jagged black line ran across it, before the linked Icewrought. They stepped backward a few paces and as they did so, they stretched out their hands, as if pulling the front edge of the crack with them, tugging it and widening it. The darkness of the crack intensified, opening.

Brannog and his people watched like children, dumbfounded by the event. Under them they could feel the ice protesting, groaning like a beast in pain, angered by this interference with its sleep of millennia. Korkoris raised a hand to the sky and his Icewrought fell silent, hands dropping. They panted as if worn out by their exertions, but before them was a black crevasse, some fifty yards long and twenty across.

Ogrund studied its silent darkness with distrust. "What next? Do we leap into it?"

Brannog scowled at him and the Earthwrought looked embarrassed.

Korkoris bowed, smiling with evident pleasure. "It is a long way down to the bedrock."

"Ogrund appears to have observed this," Brannog grinned.
"We will go first," said Korkoris. "We will make the way
fe, though we will use ice webbing. Ogrund will just have
trust us."

"I'm sure he does," nodded Brannog.

The descent began at once, and it was clear that both sides
the crevasse swung dangerously inwards, almost as though
ey were melting before the heat of the afternoon sun. The
ewrought slipped down into the shadows, easily and nim-
y, the drop holding no terrors for them. Like fish diving
to deeper water, they were at home, laughing to them-
lves, the children's joy heartening to those above. Korkoris
gan the arranging of the ice webbing and Brannog mar-
lled at it. The ice people worked at the ice and caused it
melt, run and freeze, creating tiny ladders like frozen
ears, stalactites that hung in growing festoons, piercing the
rkness below, from which no sound came. The ice ladders
ew into a complex latticework, and running down through
e spars of ice, light fell, though it did not melt the ice.
hen Brannog tried the ice rigging, he found it easy to hold,
t as slippery as he would have expected. He went back to
e Host with a grin.

On the surface he began preparing his advance party. He
d no desire to take everyone below, not yet.

"It may well be," he explained to the gathered Host, "that
will be received with hostility. I cannot say how the people
the Far Below will react to my coming. Therefore I will
ke only a few with me at first. The Icewrought will have a
rong advance guard to take us to the bottom of the glacier.
he others will help you to build a camp here."

He then selected Ogrund, Carac, Korkoris and Danoth to
with him. The task of overseeing the Host's encampment
gave to Rothgar, who took pride in the commission. Lastly,
rannog came to Ruvanna.

"Will the wolves be content to wait here without you?"
said.

She did not quite hide her shock, and her heart hammered
if it would betray her. "Of course."

"Then we'll go."

Danoth looked as though he might challenge the girl's

coming with them, but Brannog had clearly made up his mind. The descent began.

It was to be a great test of nerve and courage, for although the Icewrought made light of it, Brannog and the others had to concentrate on the arduous task of lowering themselves down into the strange ice landscape of the inner crevasse. All around them the light scintillated and danced, thrown back from a thousand fractured surfaces, splintered by the contortions of the ice, both natural and Icewrought-fashioned. In places Brannog was able to cling to a sheer wall of ice like a fly, prevented from sliding to oblivion by the steps carved into it for him, and at other times he had to swing out over the abyss, clutching at a long filament of ice that seemed to have taken on the property of living rope under the manipulation of the Icewrought. Their whispers could be heard, echoing like tiny waves on a beach, and when Carac gripped a spar that snapped, they were under him before he could drop, guiding him effortlessly to the safety of a fresh ladderway. The sunlight filtered down in a myriad ways, here magnified by an ice formation, there glanced away into still deeper ice realms, until the sky was no longer overhead and the lips of the crevasse were far from view. Down into the slowly widening maw of the glacier they went, the only light now that of the reflection of their own bodies, soft as candlelight. Neither Ogrund nor his companions had voiced a thought, concentrating hard on the descent, knowing that a fall here meant death.

At last they were clambering across piled shafts of broken ice; they had cut through the glacier to its icy floor. Korkoris stood with his hands on his hips. Beyond him and his people there was a cavern, the ceiling of which was all glittering ice, the underbelly of the glacier. The floor was solid rock, though hard and polished as iron. Yet there was a deep slash in it, as if the stone possessed a crevasse of its own.

"My people will return to the surface to ensure that the others are safe there," said Korkoris. "There may be a storm, or ice winds, and they will need protection. Also the crevasse must be kept open."

"You will come with us, I trust?" said Brannog.

Korkoris bowed. "Naturally, if you wish it."

Brannog nodded to Ogrund. "This is the way down, I nk."

Ogrund was relieved to be out of the crevasse and Korko-'s power. He swaggered to the rocks and bent over the at crack in them, Carac at his side. "Aye, this is the way."

"The rocks are aware of us," said Carac.

"Can you not sense their dismay?" said Ogrund. "It is t as Korkoris's scout told us, they do not guard the way."

"Then lead on," said Brannog. Ruvanna followed him.

Ogrund and Carac began the next stage of the descent, rming their way expertly down into the stone, forging as y went a way for the others. Only Ruvanna found it diffi-lt, though she said nothing. Brannog felt her concern, and mired her for her determination. How like Sisipher she was that! But he turned his mind away from his daughter and ncentrated on the way down. It was true that some strange sitivity clung to the rocks here. Like sleepy guardians un-le to raise the clamor, they were aware of the intrusion. t Ogrund and the others spoke softly to the rocks, telling m that this was no enemy, no violation, but the arrival of ies, of those who loved stone and who fashioned it out of npathy and not for its destruction. Carac sang softly of the nedelvers.

By the gentle body-glow of the Earthwrought, Brannog saw beginnings of a path. They were an incalculable distance low the glacier now, and they could feel the stirrings of far under them yet, as if some huge colony was at work re, layered in stone. The path was recognizable barely, but had been trodden by Earthwrought, its walls cut by them, ssibly to let air in and out of the deep delvings. Strange hoing sounds came up from below, like the rustle of a oterranean wind, or the sighing of a sea that the mountains d risen over.

Ogrund led the way, their passage much easier now, and on they discovered that they were winding down the inner lls of a great circular shaft. This opened like a vent to the art of the world, a fathomless well whose secrets were ob-red by its intense darkness. For hours the party spiraled ound the narrow pathway, minds numbed, locked in stasis their bodies did the work. When they came at last to a cave mouth, they almost went past it. There were still no guards.

Brannog nodded, shrugging off tiredness. The cave seemed worthy of investigation, if only to relieve the mounting monotony of the circular descent. It may be days before they came to the foot of the great shaft. Soon after they had entered the narrow cave they came out onto a ledge that overlooked another vast opening, although as their eyes took it in, they perceived that it was a cavern, but one built on a staggering scale. The light here was murky, mainly due to the distance involved, and as they looked, they saw that its source was the ceiling of rock high above, the curves and cracks of which had the uncanny look of clouds. The stunning distances spread out like the vista seen from a mountain overlooking a jungle, for there were mists here like heat hazes. It was as though they had entered another world, as though, thought Brannog with a shock, they had passed through a rent in the fabric of Omara's skin into another Aspect. No nation, no matter how gifted, could have engineered this fabulous cavern.

"The Far Below," said Ogrund, his jaw slackening as he said it.

"How could we have known it would be so large!" gasped Carac.

Korkoris said nothing, merely shrinking back from the scale of what spread out below them. Ruvanna had inadvertently pressed herself close to Brannog. He put an arm around her slim waist, his face a mask of joy and amazement. They all looked in wonder for many minutes, until at last they turned to one another and began pointing at various things, reveling like children in their discovery. Ruvanna moved away from Brannog self-consciously, but he said nothing, merely staring at the view.

Finally they walked down a fresh path, and ahead of them, sloping away toward the invisible lower cavern, were fields where strange plants grew, saprophytes and other underground vegetation. They helped themselves to some of them, relishing the taste and at once feeling a heady goodness. As they climbed back on to the path, they noticed the first inhabitant of the cavern, working in one of the plantations. It as an Earthwrought, but he was large, tall as an Exalted, ough without the grim visage of that race and lacking the rish tattoos. His arms were particularly powerful. When he w the party advancing, he looked puzzled, though not an- y.

He put down his tool and walked up to them. "Greetings," said, his attention fixed on Brannog and Danoth, though s eyesight seemed poor. His eyes, however, were very large, d Ruvanna wondered if it were the light, which was little tter than twilight on the surface. "I have not seen your like fore. Which part of the city are you from?"

Brannog extended his hand and the Earthwrought was ppy to take it. "I am called Brannog. I am not from the r Below. I am from the surface."

The farmer drew back. "The Beyond? Do you jest? Who e you?"

"It is no jest. Korkoris, come forward." The Icewrought d so and the farmer looked baffled. "This is Korkoris, ruler the southern Icewrought."

The farmer, however, was looking at Ruvanna. "Are you rthwrought?" he said, mystified. He looked at Brannog. And you? In a way you seem to be." He indicated Danoth. But that one is alien to me."

"He is a Man," said Brannog.

The farmer gaped. "An overman? Here, in the Far Be- w?" He turned, as if looking for help. Panic was closing on him, though his wits were a little slow.

"We come in peace," said Brannog. "Will you take us to e city?"

"How did you get here?" the farmer asked, unable to con- in his curiosity.

As briefly as he could, Brannog explained.

The farmer was shaking his head. "It is not possible."

"You must help us," said Ruvanna.

It was going to be difficult to allay the farmer's fears, they ew that, but slowly they persuaded him to take them below. e finally did so, walking ahead of them down the pathway at widened into a crude road. As they went, they saw the ening out of the valley sides, until, rounding a tall shoulder rock, they were met by the most bewildering view of them all, as though the stone had saved it for them, intent on humbling them with its magnitude.

The city of the Far Below had been cut from a cliff face that reached up thousands of feet, lost to view above. Layer on layer of streets and buildings rose up, dug into that wall, the work of centuries. Huge banks of vine hung from the balconies, and elsewhere there were immense clusters of dark green leaves, fed somehow by the artificial light. High above, the buildings were made small by distance, shrouded in misty cloud, while the lower ones were like great warehouses and stores, dropping away to unseen depths. The farmer halted in the middle of the road and pointed up at the towering structure as though it were a god.

"I do not go into the city. I bring my cart to the gates when it is full."

"We are grateful," said Brannog.

As though released from a spell, the farmer trudged back up the road to a low stone wall that led to the fields. In a moment he had clambered over it and was gone, no doubt to forget the strangers. Brannog looked at his mesmerized companions.

"If the inhabitants are to be our allies—," he began, but did not finish the sentence. He had seen Carac's face: he looked as if he, like the farmer, stood before his god.

"I have seen the splendor of Goldenisle," he murmured, "but it is a town beside this miracle." He had put an arm around Ogrund, and he, too, stood in bemused wonder.

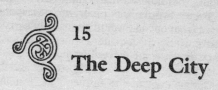

15
The Deep City

As THEY APPROACHED THE CITY, they realized just how enormous it was, towering as it now did over them. Yet strangely, or all its size, it seemed deserted. The air was still, birdless, and from those countless windows and doorways no light shone and there was no hint of movement. But the city was alive, not dead, for all its silence.

"They know we are here," said Ruvanna softly, but her voice carried sharply to all of them. "It's like a single organism. Can you feel its stones breathe?"

Ogrund and Carac were nodding, Korkoris beside them also. "But it means us no harm," said the Icewrought.

They came to a tall gateway, flanked by twin towers, though was open, without guards. The group paused outside, listening. They could hear the play of water, streams that ran own somewhere from the slopes, feeding the city. Other an that there was only the emptiness, as if they were approaching a ruin, or a graveyard. Brannog led them through the gates cautiously; beyond these was a square with a number of narrow roads leading from it, each to a different level the city. The roads twisted and wound, stepped and cobbed, remarkably complex. As the party crossed the square, ey heard the first sounds of life. Sounds of stealth, of gathering, coming from all sides of the square.

"There are scores of them," Ruvanna told Brannog, and her surprise she saw him grin. He raised his hand and the rty stopped, almost in the center of the square.

For a short while longer there was only the silence, but

then figures began to appear. They were well disciplined, their moves military and precise, and by the artificial light, weapons gleamed. The entire square was surrounded by Earthwrought, who now formed tightly packed ranks, bright with spears and swords and other such weapons that the Earthwrought from outside would not usually carry. Ogrund's club looked pitifully inadequate against these tools of war. The gathered Earthwrought were large, their chests banded with muscle, their arms exceptionally strong, and they all had the wide, staring eyes of the farmer that Brannog and his companions had met. Even so, they were peering as if they could hardly see the beings they had surrounded.

"They're not hostile," said Ruvanna. "But they think we are."

Brannog cupped his hands to his mouth, though he need not have done so. His voice carried like thunder to the entire square, ringing back from its walls. "We have come to you openly," he called. "As you can see. We desire no more than to talk to you and your Earthwise."

The ranks around him did not murmur, the wide stares of the Earthwrought fixed, perhaps waiting for some prearranged signal. To attack? Ruvanna's confidence was not shared by the others and even Ogrund and Carac had had their reverence for this place shaken by such a display of power. The Earthwrought who waited had a rugged, determined look to them that suggested they would not be easy to reason with.

Brannog's companions waited for him to speak, though each of them held his weapon tightly, threateningly, as though he would have to use it. Only Ruvanna seemed calm. Brannog's patience was finally rewarded when a figure detached itself from the massed ranks. Dressed in simple green robes, and apparently much older than the soldiery, it had much of the looks of an Earthwise about it. It took no more than a few paces into the square and raised a long staff for silence, a somewhat superfluous gesture.

"We have no Earthwise," came the clear, sharp voice, and Brannog realized with a start that she was a woman. "Not as the Earthwrought of the Beyond have them. Here in the Far Below, there is only the Circle of Preceptors."

"Your rulers?" said Brannog.

"Those whom you might call Earthwise, but who have gone beyond the limits of such powers, to share a higher knowledge. They are our voice and we are accountable to them."

"I would speak to them."

"You trespass."

"I have reason."

"You have broken our primary laws in coming here."

"I say again, I have reason."

Ruvanna and the others could sense a possible argument, but Brannog, who would once have enjoyed a verbal battle, did no more than bow.

"You bear weapons," said the woman.

Brannog did not answer, but went to each of his party and took all weapons. He began to walk toward the woman, but she backed into the ranks behind her at once. Brannog set the weapons down near to them and returned to his companions.

"We dispute nothing with you," he told the woman, but she did not come forward again.

"How did you come here?" was the eventual question. "There is no blood on your weapons. How did you pass our barriers?"

Brannog brought Korkoris forward and at last there were signs of interest on the stern faces of the soldiery. Korkoris spoke for some time of the descent through the glacier and his words had a disturbing effect on his audience. A number of soldiers were seen hurrying away, probably to report the apparent flaw in the city's defenses to higher authorities. After Korkoris had spoken, Brannog talked at length, though he did not say why he had come, nor that he dreamt of finding an army to take to the west. Eventually he told his audience that he would say nothing more, only to their rulers.

"Very well," nodded the woman. She said something to those beside her, and again a number of them exited into the city. "There will be a time for such a meeting soon. While you wait for word of it, we will give you quarters and, if you desire it, food and drink."

"They would be most welcome," said Brannog, with an
other bow.

THEY WERE ESCORTED through the narrow streets of the lowe
city, down several flights of almost vertical steps to a large
building. Inside it they passed through a maze of corridors
until they came to a bare chamber, a room that told them
almost nothing about the city or its people. Ogrund growled
something angrily when the thick wooden door was locked
behind them, but Brannog called for patience. Ruvanna also
told them they would have to be patient, as, she said, they
had committed acts of sacrilege in coming here. Ogrund was
prepared to do as Ruvanna said, and Carac still seemed in
complete awe of the city. Korkoris and Danoth seemed prepared to set aside their own feelings and, like Brannog, be
judged by the laws of the Far Below.

There were no seats or beds here, so the company stretched
itself out on the floor, though it was not cold or uncomfortable and might have been the soft floor of a forest. A number
of young Earthwrought girls brought them food and water,
and though Ogrund pretended to be fierce and ill-tempered,
Ruvanna noticed his pleasure at seeing them. The girls, unlike their warriors, laughed, telling their guests there was
more food if required, but they would say nothing of their
city or its people.

When the meal was over, and none of the party failed to
marvel at its quality, the door was opened. A single Earthwrought guard stood there, filling the doorway with his muscular width. He bowed and entered. He carried no weapon
and held his hands before him to show this, though Brannog
wondered if he needed a weapon with such immense hands.
"I am named Angnor," he said. "You are fortunate. The
Circle will meet for you. Will you follow me?"

"Thank you, Angnor, we will," said Brannog, cutting
short any possible bluntness from Ogrund or Carac, whose
patience with the inhabitants of the city had now almost completely evaporated.

They followed Angnor out along another bare corridor,
into a system of others as simple and uninstructive, until they
reached another door. Angnor unlocked it, and once outside,

n the light once more, they began a long and exhausting
limb, through small walled areas, up endless steps, through
nore chambers and tiny halls, along high, narrow bridges,
oing ever upward until Ogrund muttered something about
eaching the surface before long. Angnor said nothing, never
urning, and his silence gave the impression that he was alone.
le came to a final door, this one in the heart of another dark
all, opening it and gesturing Brannog and his party through.
s the last of them stepped through, Angnor locked it. He
tood with his back to it, folding his huge arms and waiting
atiently as if turned to stone. The chamber in which the
arty stood was circular, its walls like polished marble,
leaming like golden ice. Again, the chamber was empty, its
oor swept clean, smoothly polished and with a series of
mbols running through it like veins. What these meant,
ne of the party knew, but they suggested antiquity and
tual, and the Earthwrought respected them for that. The
rcular wall rose up some twenty feet to darkness that was
 complete it seemed to have been set there like a super-
tural barrier. It was impossible to see into it. However, it
as not to be permanent, for in a moment light broke through
 as if windows high up in a dome had been opened. The
rty saw, silhouetted by the light from above, a ring of on-
okers around the upper level of the chamber walls, though
e faces were hidden in shadow.

"The Circle of Preceptors greets you," said Angnor, his
ice like that of a ghost.

One of the figures above moved and light suddenly flooded
 It was a young Earthwrought, his build slighter than that
 the warriors of the city, though he was larger than Ogrund.
iometimes," he said in a calm, deep voice that suggested
 was older than he looked, "people from the Beyond find
ir way into the Far Below. We are not a hostile nation. We
ve created our own world here and we make no demands
 the world of Omara that is the Beyond. Those who stum-
 into our domain we do not harm, though you will under-
nd that they are never again permitted to leave the Far
low."

"Your pardon," said Brannog as diplomatically as he

could. "But we did not stumble across you. We sought you out deliberately."

There was little reaction on the face of the being above. He waved his hand gently. "So I understand. This is no precedent, of course. Over the years, many have sought the Far Below. To those of the Beyond, it is a legend, usually a fabulous one. We are, to some, an Earthwrought paradise. We make no such claims, but we live in peace, unharrassed by the darker forces that work in the Beyond."

"It is because of such forces that I am here," said Brannog, seizing the opportunity at once.

"You are not Earthwrought. Neither is the girl, although there is much of our race about you both. And you have an overman with you, and an Icewrought. His people are known to us, of course. A strange, strange gathering."

Another of the Circle had stood. He was far older, his face deeply etched and chiseled by age, his white hair sparse, though his eyes gleamed in the light that bathed him. "When Earthwrought reach us, or if one of a brother race does so"—his eyes here fixed on Korkoris—"we absorb them into our society. They usually have no desire to return to the Beyond. But we are liberal only with our own kind. Our laws are very firm, overman." He used the term as a mark of contempt, in spite of a partial attempt to disguise it.

"I understand your reasoning and your laws," said Brannog. "I was fortunate enough to learn something of them and your history in a place far from here in the wastes of the Silences."

"In the deserts?" said the ancient Earthwrought after a pause. Several of his fellows had now risen, eager to be next to speak. Light spread around the balcony and hands were raised. It took a while for stillness to settle, and when it did, Brannog continued to face the elder who had been addressing him.

"In the city of Cyrene," he said. Silence clamped down at once, and with it came darkness.

"I have been there!" shouted Ogrund suddenly. "It's true! The sands have been driven back. Cyrene is free of the desert! Our people toil there even now, bringing water and life back into it."

Brannog put a restraining arm on Ogrund, who subsided, his face like thunder in his own glow.

In due course, another of the Circle stood in the halo of light, a woman of middle years and a soft, patient voice. "We had heard whispers of this miracle."

"Then perhaps you have heard also of the fall of Xennidhum, and of the destruction of the evil that dwelled there?"

"There have been many such rumors over the years, but how could such a place of horror be truly cleansed?" called another of the Circle.

Brannog spoke then of the war, beginning with the gathering of Korbillian's followers and the long, perilous journey to the east. Just as Wargallow had spoken to the Assembly in Goldenisle, Brannog gave a full account of that grim history, of the death of the Preserver, the alliance with the Deliverers, the finding of Cyrene and the eventual overthrow of Xennidhum itself. "So you see," he told the Circle at the end, "it was a strange company. Earthwrought fought beside Deliverers, giving up their lives for each other. Wargallow, who was the instrument of his own ruler, has become a champion of your race as much as his own. Men, whom you still call overmen, the hated name, are riding beside Earthwrought now. And your race dwell on the surface as much as they do below the earth. I do not say perfect harmony exists, but there is a unity there that would surprise you. And I think, gladden you."

"Then you are Brannog Wormslayer," said one of the Circle who had not spoken until now. He was the largest of them, mere inches shorter than Brannog himself, and his face was one that had known hardship, possibly war. He wore a thick mustache and had bushy black brows, his mane of hair braided and tumbling over his shoulders. He had the instant attention of all his colleagues and his eyes glared down, sparkling like ice, his expression formidable, as though he, and he alone, ruled this city.

"I have been called that," said Brannog.

"As you have been called King Brannog."

"That is so."

"By Men and also by Earthwrought."

"As you say."

This surprised the Circle and they began to debate hotly who should speak next. The huge figure banged his fist down on the stone in front of him, signifying that he had not himself finished.

"I hear many tales from the Beyond," he said, his voice silencing every other like an avalanche. "I make a point of gathering them together, although my fellow Preceptors think I waste my time in so doing. They do not admit this openly, but that is for their consciences, not mine. My name is Ulthor. I have many titles, but am known by no one as Ulthor the Patient. Your activities, Brannog, are known to me, if you are indeed the figure of legend you claim to be."

Brannog grinned. "If I am that, it is not my claim," he laughed. "But I have done those things I have said." His smile suddenly vanished. "Yet it is not enough."

"You'd better tell us what you want," said Ulthor.

Brannog then explained to the Circle the dangers in the far west, of how Anakhizer was gathering for a fresh assault on the people of Omara. Then Carac spoke of Goldenisle, and of the new alliances there and of the part played in the war by the Stonedelvers. He refrained from speaking of Orhung and his rod of power, as warned by Brannog. Korkoris followed Carac with a speech of his own about the killing of the Werewatch and of the flight of the Icewrought. When they had all finished speaking, the darkness closed in, more tightly than before, and for a while it was as though the Circle had gone away. But it was there yet.

"When I first met the Earthwrought," said Brannog, "under the mountains of my own homelands, they gave me the name Wormslayer because of what I did. Later they called me friend, and rallied to me, for their Earthwise spoke of a dream his people clung to, that of life on the surface. Life as it was when Cyrene the Beautiful ruled all Omara. Earthwrought have rallied to me, to my Host, because we stand for that ideal. You here in the Far Below have built for yourselves a city of wonders, a magnificence that, for all I know, surpasses the beauty of Cyrene itself. But the Beyond, as you call it, is your true inheritance. Do your ancient teachings not speak of a return to the surface?"

The silence was only brief. "Why should it matter to you?"
called one gruff voice.

Ulthor stood up, eyes blazing. "Why should it matter?"
he repeated in terrible annoyance. "Why should it *matter!*
That question is that to ask one who has taken war to the
darkness in Xennidhum!" He turned to Brannog. "Tell us,
King Brannog, of your plans to become Emperor of the entire
earthwrought nations! Of your dream to conquer all of Omara
and set yourself up as a new supreme ruler." Ulthor turned
to his fellows like a wolf. "Imbecile!" he roared to the one
who had last spoken to Brannog. "Are you capable of rational thought? If this Man had come here to conquer us, is
is how he would do it? With words?"

One of the elders stood up, smoothing down his robes in
dignified, if theatrical fashion. He smiled at Ulthor as
though tolerating an unruly child. "Thank you, Ulthor. Your
point is taken and I see no reason to resort to violence to
conclude the discussion." There was laughter at this, and
Ulthor sat down with a grunt of impatience. His volatility
was well known here. But Brannog was thankful that the huge
earthwrought had more than a little sympathy for his cause.

"Brannog," said the elder, "of course, you are correct in
thinking we have not put the surface from our minds altogether. We have made a good life for our people here, but
you will understand, I trust, that once our survival was severely threatened. After the disasters at Xennidhum and the
chaos caused by the Sorcerer-Kings, we became refugees
from a persecution that threatened to wipe us out. Our, forgive me, hatred of overmen, goes back many centuries. You
must not expect us to ignore it. If you have achieved what
you say you have, we of the Circle must applaud it. But the
way ahead will not be simple. There are those of us here,
such as Ulthor, who think we should already be moving upward again. Opinion here is divided, deeply. The old fears
remain, justifiably so. You tell us that those who were our
enemies are now are allies. Even the Deliverers." He shook
his head. "If this is so, it is a miracle."

"There will be a war," said Brannog. "Whether you ignore it or not. Already my allies are preparing for it. You can
see that I have gathered my Host, and when I journey to the

west, many will join with me. All I ask is that you rally to my ranks. I do not ask for command—send me your own commanders. But if you do not and if the alliance falls before Anakhizer, the deepest sanctuary under Omara will not save you from his coming.''

"Such irony!'' boomed Ulthor. "What, no calls for me to be silent? Can I speak, or will my indiscretion embarrass the Circle?'' He looked back at the tall figure of the elder. "As is regularly my reward.''

The latter smiled. "I think this might be an appropriate time to air this. This is an open meeting. If anyone has an opinion, let us hear it.'' Brannog turned to Ruvanna; she was as puzzled as he was. Ulthor's comment about irony and his indiscretion was intriguing. There was further discussion above, but agreement was quickly reached. The debate would go on.

"Very well,'' said Ulthor, with a wry grin. "You see, Brannog, your talk of raising a force to go back to the surface is not original.''

"Oh? Then others of your race have suggested it?''

"You might say that. We have our own supreme ruler,'' Ulthor went on, but he was unable to keep the scorn from his voice.

"The Sublime One,'' said Brannog, knowing at once.

"You know of him?''

"Aye, and of Mount Timeless and the Exalted who protect it.''

"And do you know of earthsongs?''

"And Holy Roads, aye,'' nodded Brannog.

"Have you heard them?''

"We have.''

"Then perhaps you know that the Sublime One is calling to all his subjects. A Convocation. It goes out across all of Omara.''

"And its purpose?''

"Who knows?'' said Ulthor testily. "It would be logical to assume it is a gathering for war. War upon the surface. Upon overmen and all those who are not of the Earthwrought and their brother races.''

"The true children of Omara," said Ruvanna, and everyone heard her. "The Sublime One accepts no others."

"He is the Voice of Omara," said Ulthor, but he had not dropped his contempt. Was this the indiscretion he had spoken of?

"Tell me," said Brannog, "since this is an arena for your opinions, do you accept him as your ruler? Do you obey him?"

"We are his Preceptors," said one of the elders.

Ulthor banged his fist down once more, and the stone flared with light. "Once I would have obeyed! But I have seen his Exalted, his select warriors. They are cruel, violent creatures. Should we respect such beasts?"

"Ulthor," cautioned one of the elders. "You go too far. Guard your tongue!"

"Let the Sublime One hear me!" Ulthor retorted.

"He will."

"Then I say this for his ears: do not call upon me to follow your Exalted. If I am to go up to the light, it will not be at the heels of those murderers!"

Chaos broke out at this and for a long time it was impossible to make out what anyone was saying. Ulthor had sat down, massive arms folded over his chest, and he gazed ahead of him balefully, refusing to say another word. At last order was restored.

"May I speak again?" Brannog asked. The Circle agreed. "Ulthor has spoken of the Exalted. I, too, can speak of them. I had heard a little of them, from Earthwrought myths, of how they were the chosen warriors of the Sublime One, his protectors, respected by the Earthwrought nations. But they sought to take me, by force, to their master." He elaborated on this, speaking of the Holy Road under Gnarag's hold and of the aggressiveness of the Exalted.

Ulthor grinned. "Well, of course, the Sublime One would not be pleased that a Man, an *overman*, should become a champion of the Earthwrought! No wonder he sent for you! Your stay on Mount Timeless would have been short."

"He would have killed me?"

The elder who had spoken so calmly and tactfully before rose again. "It seems very probable. But we must exercise care. The Sublime One has not shown himself to be a ruthless dictator. He has always acted for the good of his people. His Exalted are extreme, it is true. But what would you counsel, Ulthor? Would you send Brannog to the Sublime One in chains, as a token of our respect for his will?''

Ulthor guffawed rudely.

"Or would you put your own sword into Brannog's hand and let the Sublime One see your support for him?''

Ulthor pointed at Brannog. "This man is an ally! No one here but a blind fool can deny the bravery of his deeds, the fairness of his actions. The old wars between us and overmen may well be a thing of history now. If the Sublime One does not see that, then—''

"Then what?'' said the elder, his voice cutting like a blade.

Ulthor drew in a deep breath and again looked straight ahead of him. "Then it may be time to ask greater questions of ourselves. Of our future as a race.'' His words hung like thunder over the Circle.

"The Sublime One is the Voice of Omara,'' said another voice. "The world speaks through him.''

Ulthor growled. "Aye, and gives us the Exalted, who thrust steel into the bellies of all those who do not obey them. Just as the Deliverers give the blood of their victims. Blood to Omara, aye, but what's the difference? If I am to give my blood to Omara, I will give it when I am ready, and not because the Exalted seek it for their amusement. Do *I* not speak for Omara? Act for her? Have I turned against the earth? Was I not purged, just as you all were?''

Brannog felt a sudden spasm in Ruvanna, who stood very close to him, almost touching him. It was as though Ulthor spoke of something that had struck at her nerves. She was as taut as the wolves would have been.

"No one doubts your loyalty, Ulthor,'' said the elder. "In deed and mind you are proven. But what would you have us do with Brannog?''

"As the Circle, nothing,'' said Ulthor. "Let him be. If, as the Circle, the law and the word of the Sublime One here in the Far Below, we neither chain him nor follow him, we are not committed. If we make no decision, the Sublime One cannot criticize us. So let him go. But let each individual

ar him and make his own decision, for himself. Not as a
eceptor, but as an Earthwrought. Let each of us then face
: Sublime One's reaction.''

"What will you do, Ulthor?" cried several voices.

"What I decide, I decide as Ulthor, and not as a member
the Circle." He took from his neck a golden chain and
read it carefully on the stone in front of him.

Ogrund, who seemed to have been containing his fury with
ounting difficulty, suddenly stepped forward and raised his
t. "Is there only one among you who is not spineless!" he
outed, and even Ulthor looked askance at his expression.
You speak of your own purity! How you have undergone
: ritual of the Purging. Well, then. My master is as loyal
the cause as any of you. He has brought my people through
: darkness of Xennidhum and beyond. Who *dares* to doubt
s purity?"

In the abrupt stillness, Ogrund looked about him, but he
ld up his pride, refusing to step back, or to look at his
aster.

"Your own loyalty sits well upon you," said one of the
lers. "And your words have opened up another way to
."

Ulthor glared at the speaker as if about to retort, but he
d not.

"Brannog seems to be almost as much Earthwrought as he
Man. Perhaps we should then accord him the opportunity
take the ritual of the Purging?"

Ruvanna's hand tightened around Brannog's, as if she had
nsed something dire in what had been said.

"I know very little of this ritual," said Brannog. "Will
u explain it to me?"

"Of course."

Brannog kept very still. This was, he knew, one of the
ost coveted of all Earthwrought mysteries. He had not even
scussed it more than fleetingly with Ogrund, for it was a
ivate, intimate matter. But he knew that every one of his
arthwrought Host had undergone the ritual as a child.

"It is giving of the body to the earth," said the elder.
Though a symbolic giving, you understand. Omara enters
to the body of the Earthwrought, and there is a cleansing

of the mind, a purifying, in which the goodness of the earth, the oneness with Omara is heightened. It is carried throughout life, so that the Earthwrought serve the earth and work for its health. It is the breath of Omara and with it comes the gift of Omara's power.''

Brannog considered this. "And if I undergo this ritual?"

"It will find any darkness within you. Any harm that you offer to Omara or its children, it will burn out of you. It may even destroy you."

Brannog shook his head. "I serve the earth. Let it judge me."

"If he does this," said Ulthor, "and comes from it whole, then let us bring him again before the Circle. To reconsider."

"If you do that," said Brannog, "I shall ask for support, even though it may not be the will of the Sublime One."

Ulthor nodded, his chin on his fist, his eyes studying the Man below him. But in his eyes now there was concern and a cloud across his brow.

PART FOUR

THE SUBLIME ONE

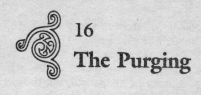

16
The Purging

IN THEIR CHAMBER, which Ogrund now insisted on calling a cell, they debated for many hours the question of Brannog's Purging. Ruvanna was the most against it, declaring it a terrible risk, for Brannog, she said, would be subjected to the unknown. The powers that would flow through him could be dangerous.

"But I have nothing to hide. Even if the Circle learns that we are seeking the rod of Orhung, they will understand why. Our reasons are honest," he insisted.

"You seem to know about the ritual," said Danoth to Ruvanna. "Yet you've not undergone it, girl. Or have you?"

Ruvanna drew back as though afraid of Danoth. "No."

"What do you say?" Danoth asked the Earthwrought.

Carac stood firmly with Brannog. "All Earthwrought undergo the Purging when young. I have never known any of our people to suffer because of it."

"King Brannog," declared Ogrund, "loves the earth as deeply as any of us. It will not harm him."

Ruvanna leaned forward. "The earth, no. But does the Sublime One play a part in this ritual?"

Ogrund and Carac exchanged glances, but it was impossible to read an answer in their grim faces.

"Does your law prevent you from saying?" asked Danoth.

There came a fierce knocking at the door and they all turned to it in surprise, knowing it to be locked from outside. Presently they heard the rattling of keys and the door opened to reveal Ulthor of the Circle. He stepped into the room with a polite bow. Now that he stood beside them, they saw that he was not quite as large as he had seemed at the meeting, except for his girth, but he was easily the largest Earth-wrought any of them had yet met. He retained his nobility, his regality.

"I considered it my duty to speak to you before you underwent the ritual," he told Brannog.

"As Ulthor, or as a member of the Circle?" said Ruvanna.

Ulthor favored her with a scornful glance that would have withered a good many of his people, but the girl stood defiantly before him, undeterred. 'Brannog has not come this far to be killed," she said angrily.

Ogrund and Carac were nodding, surprised at the girl's sudden spirit, but pleased.

"Killed?" snapped Ulthor, his voice rolling around the room. "Why should the ritual do that? Unless he is an enemy of Omara. I think he is not."

"The Purging will show that I am not," said Brannog.

Ruvanna would not be silenced easily. "What part does the Sublime One play in this ritual?" she asked Ulthor.

"Why do you ask?"

"You know why I ask!" she snapped.

"Ruvanna!" said Brannog. "Be silent. I have agreed to undergo the ritual. I have nothing to hide."

'If you pass through this Purging," nodded Ulthor, "and come again before the Circle, I will urge that you are given all the support you require for your crusade. You will know that I am a man of anger, for what I see on Mount Timeless fills me with fury. Corruption festers there. A day does not pass without word of it reaching us. The Exalted are the servants of a system that treats us with contempt. We are not chattels and I cannot believe that Omara would turn from us in the way that the Sublime One has. I know of the Deliverers and of the giving of blood to Omara. I despise the ritual giving. The Exalted are no better in my eyes, and I speak for many of the Far Below when I say that the Exalted are not welcome here. It may be, as your words suggest, that something evil has come into Mount Timeless. If so, I will follow you there and face it, with steel if need be."

He thrust out his hand and Brannog took it, gripping it.
I am not afraid of this test.''

"I can see you are not as other Men, Brannog. Your
rangeness disturbs my race, but it is uncertainty, that is all.
'e know of the ancient dream of a return to the surface, and
though some of us deny the histories, that we are descended
om Men, there is in all of us an instinct to seek the true
ght of the sun.''

Brannog nodded, indicating Ogrund, Carac and Korkoris.
Here is evidence of that.''

"I envy them their life on the surface." Ulthor nodded to
ch briefly, then turned back to Brannog. "You are to go to
e Purging alone, save for one other. You may have a
atcher.''

"What is that?''

"You are permitted to choose one of your companions to
and at your side while you undergo the ritual. The Watcher
to see that none harms you during the ritual, and is per-
itted a single weapon. I will leave you to make your choice.
on you will be summoned." Again Ulthor took Brannog's
nd, then bowed to the remainder of the company before
aving.

They began talking among themselves at once, pleased that
lthor was so obviously a potential ally. Only Brannog and
uvanna were silent, both thinking over the Earthwrought's
ords. Brannog thought himself to be in a cleft; how should
chose his Watcher? Should he make the obvious choice
d take Ruvanna, whose powers were considerable? If he
d so, she would be the one most able to protect him in the
ce of an attack. But from what? Why should he be attacked,
d by what? It was only Ruvanna herself who had spoken
such a thing, or at least, she had implied it. Ogrund would
sume he would be chosen, as Brannog's right hand, his first
ief. To put him aside for Ruvanna, even though Ogrund
eply respected her, would mortify the Earthwrought.

Ruvanna spoke softly to him. "You have no choice, Bran-
g. You must make me your Watcher.''

"Why?'' he said equally as softly. "What are your pow-
s? What is it you've not told me? I know very little of you.

You have the looks of a young girl who few would notice in a village, and yet—''

She colored. ''You still think me a vessel—''

''We may all be that—''

''You cannot risk leaving me. I told you, I don't know what powers are in me, but I will use them for you.'' She gripped his arm. ''For you alone.''

''Try to understand what I do,'' he said, alarmed by the intensity of her gaze. ''This is an Earthwrought ritual. I must honor them—''

''Them? You speak as if they are apart from us. Are we not a part of them?''

''More than ever. But I have to take Ogrund. If I do not, he will never be the same. Since the death of his friend, Ygromm, he has felt himself unworthy to serve me as Ygromm did. It is why he is so fierce with his warriors, why he insists on perfection. If I do not take him now, he will think I have never had the regard for him that he so desperately seeks. You are the stronger, in many ways. If I take him, it will give him strength which you already have.''

''And if you are in danger? How will he save you?''

''I will take that chance.''

''Chance?'' she snapped. The others now realized that their words were heated and they abandoned their own discussion to listen. ''You are in no position to take chances!''

Ogrund came forward. ''You are in dispute?''

Ruvanna turned on him, her eyes blazing and for a moment he wavered, remembering her power. But she softened. ''No, Ogrund. But I—''

''Let us not distress ourselves,'' said Brannog firmly. ''I understand your concern, all of you. But this Purging does not frighten me. I may yet be a Man, but I serve the earth, as we all do. Ogrund, you will be my Watcher.''

Ogrund bowed, hiding his pride. Carac and Korkoris grunted their approval, pleased with the choice, and Ruvanna smiled as if she, too, was pleased, hiding her frustration. It is simply because I am a woman! her mind cried. It is nothing to do with my power. The looks of a girl who few would notice in a village! He rejects my power, and what is left? A child, a thorn in his finger.

When the door opened again, it was to admit a group of Earthwrought. They wore simple, undecorated smocks, and each held a small wand, a sliver of wood. They bowed to Brannog, touching him gently with these wands and repeating over and over a soft chant that meant nothing to him. However, he waited patiently until they seemed ready for him to leave. He nodded to Ogrund, who drew himself as erect as he could and gripped his war club, which had been sent for as the designated weapon. Without another glance at his companions, Brannog left the chamber. The ritual had already begun.

Ruvanna scowled at the door for long minutes after he had gone.

Danoth came to her. "You fear for him?"

"He will dig the dark earth," she said quietly. "He should not think himself so capable of sight."

"If he had refused the ritual, we would have languished here."

Ruvanna did not reply. Instead she went to a corner of the room and slumped down, drawing up her knees and withdrawing into a cocoon of private thoughts. Danoth studied her briefly. What did she seek here? There could be no doubting her gifts, just as there could be no doubting Brannog's suspicion of her. The Earthwrought revered her, though they did not say so openly, not when they read so much doubt in their master. Danoth shook his head: Brannog was unique. He prayed he did not think himself above suffering.

Meanwhile, Brannog followed the little procession of Earthwrought along the twisting streets and pathways, thinking of the girl. Perhaps she was right and he had been foolish to reject her. But it was not a rejection! he argued with himself. How could I abandon Ogrund? And the Circle will be pleased that I have chosen an Earthwrought as my Watcher. Even so, Ruvanna's words persisted and he kept seeing her intense gaze, and felt her fingers on his arm. She had delved into the mind of a Child of the Mound, and had so tormented the being that it had died. What were her powers? Were they hers to control? Again he thought of his daughter and of the dreadful power that had been locked into her, the power to summon up Naar-Iarnoc, guardian of the way to Xennidhum. He had been a Sorcerer-King, just as the Children were the last, debased members of their race. And Ruvanna had

controlled one of them! Could such power as Sisipher had been
given have been placed into Ruvanna? If it had, would she know?

They had arrived at a high level in the city and he had no
more time to dwell on the girl. Beyond a stone portal there
was an open area, circular, that spread out as a wide ledge
overlooking the vast drop. Beyond this flat ledge was the
openness of the immense cavern, which was like the view
from a mountain top, shrouded in the mists of distance.
Looking upward, Brannog could see the ceiling of the cavern, a huge bow, looking even more like a layer of gray cloud,
again as if he were out on the surface of the world. Behind
him the city rose up, tier upon tier, and he gasped at the
thought of how many Earthwrought must live here if all those
countless dwellings were occupied. His speculation was cut
short as he was turned by his escort to the wide circle, the
place of ritual.

In its exact center there was an area that had been scooped
out of the bare stone which had been filled with rich, dark
loam. Around its perimeter had been set small wooden ves-
sels, some of which contained water, others of which contained sand, or stone, or flakes of bark. Between them there
were tiny branches, some freshly cut, the sap still weeping,
and there were little heaps of bright green leaves. From
around the edge of the arena came movement, and Brannog
looked about him to see that a throng was materializing.
These were the Earthwrought, all dressed in simple white
robes, woven from coarse fiber. They carried pieces cut
from the little trees that were so profuse in the Far Below.
With them sat others whom Brannog took to be the members
of the Circle of Preceptors. All of them concentrated on the
ground before them, eyes fixed on the bare rock as if com-
muning with it.

By simple gestures, Brannog's escort indicated that they
wanted him to stretch out in the hollowed bed of earth, and
he did so, nodding assurance to Ogrund, who took his own
place behind Brannog, standing rigid as a menhir, his face a
graven image. I chose well, thought Brannog. His pride is
like a furnace.

The escort withdrew, to be replaced moments later by a
small group of chanting Earthwrought, themselves almost na-

ed, smeared with earth. Each of them sprinkled handfuls of
arth over the prone warrior, but Brannog kept himself mo-
onless. Instinctively his hands dug into the loam beneath
im, and it felt warm, comforting. Here, as he looked up at
le vastness of the space above him, he felt at peace, relaxed.
lready his tension was being drawn from him, and he was
ke a child wrapped in its mother's bed, content and secure.

Inevitably his eyes closed, his body lulled by the soft chant
f the Earthwrought from the perimeter of the circle, which
bbed and flowed like the gentlest of tides. His hands seemed
ɔ sink into the ground, pulling him further to it until he
ɔuld no longer feel it. His mind slipped free of his body,
self earth, though he could use it as a probe to search him-
•lf out. The earth was a vast and measureless body, stretch-
ıg away beneath him, penetrable as an ocean.

From out of the earthdeeps a power came to him, like a
urrent. He felt it embrace him, gentle as a breeze, seeping
ιto him, his every fiber of being. Slowly and with the infinite
atience of the eternal, it searched him, examining him, eval-
ating him. As it did so, his own mind seemed to float about
im, watching, sometimes sharing the experiences and dis-
overies of the search, at other times hidden from them, as
clouds had been drawn around them. Far back into the
epths of his ancestry the probe went, so that he seemed to
ɪvisage an endless chain of Brannogs, rooted long ago in
ɔmara's earth, though their beginnings were too remote to
rasp, at least for him. There were other, more painful things,
ιe sorrows of childhood, the pain of loss, and worst of all, the
assing of his wife. Though he recoiled from it, the power
ιat searched him studied it closely. The entirety of his life,
ιe reaction of his every fiber to its course through time re-
olved in the eye of the watching beholder, so that Xenni-
hum and all that it had been loomed hugely in his vision.
ɪrannog's part in it, and that of his allies, spread out like a
ιultidimensional chart, a huge edifice of conflicting emo-
ions. Brannog lived it again, even more intensely than be-
ɔre. And as he lived it, suffering it, Ogrund stood over him,
ɛeing none of it, but aware that below him his master
ιrobbed with life, unharmed as yet, his body still.

From the turbulence of his thoughts, Brannog turned away,

seeing the gradual ebbing of the earth power that had bathed
and studied him. He felt nothing, only sensed with his mind.
As the power crept back into the earth, so his own body
powers now ventured outwards, searching those immensities
for knowledge. He touched at something that had the solidity
of a mountain, bedrock that went down forever into the heart
of the world, the very soul of Omara. He had rendered up all
knowledge of self: in return he was to be given knowledge.
The balance would determine whether or not he would come
out of the ritual sane, or without his reason, or life.

The contact with Omara was strengthened. For a moment
a feeling of bliss almost drowned him and he felt giddy with
it. But slowly the sharp crags of discord reared through its
waters. Omara was a world of fears yet. The terrible darkness
that had bled into it at Xennidhum and beyond it at other
places, lingered. Pain flooded the earth, and Brannog was
almost scorched by it. His loathing of it, his will to defy it,
spared him the worst of its ravages. He drew on the earth
power, turning it into a shield for himself, and making of it
a weapon of energy.

Omara was all. Omara was god.

The Earthwrought were its children. All life that came from
Omara was its blood. The power of blood was the power of
life, and life was Omara. Nothing else mattered. Everything
that was not Omara was to be reviled, dangerous and destruc-
tive. Omara would die if it were not removed. Omara was
life, all else was as a canker, virulent disease that must be
purged from the body of the world. All power came together
in Omara. All things beyond it must perish.

Again Brannog was plunged into the maelstrom of history,
but this time it was not the reliving of his own personal history, but that of Omara. He saw the working of the Hierarchs
on Ternannoc that had threatened the destruction of so many
of the Aspects of Omara, including the mother world herself.
He saw the canker of its dark power, and understood even
better the words of Korbillian, who himself had chosen the
image of disease to describe what it was that sought to engulf
worlds. And he saw now the vision of Omara, the driving
will to survive that was bringing together its defenses. The
full scope of the war came into sharp, devastating focus.

Anakhizer was no more than a vessel, a man who had umbled on powers beyond his imaginings, and who had oken them. They worked through him now. And they were • longer content to dream in their limbo between Aspects, ifting sublimely, creating for themselves an inner universe, chain of them, that satisfied their every lust. Anakhizer had ught them a different pleasure, that of physical reality. They arned to covet the world in which he dwelled, Omara. They ould devour its life, its blood, its people, and in so doing ould *become* Omara, possessing it as a parasite possesses s host. They were using Anakhizer to formulate their wars •r them, turning nation against nation, readying for the holesale sacrifice. Every life lost, every drop of blood shed, as energy to the powers, not to Omara.

Omara knew this, and knew also that it would be impos- ble to prevent it. The dreaming powers were too vast. With e Sorcerer-Kings and the Hierarchs gone, what power could ithstand them? And yet, there was a way to prevent utter saster. The Earthwrought were the key, the children of mara. They were the only true children of Omara, as were e Stonedelvers and other races who had sprung from the riginal inhabitants of the world, before the coming of the efugees from Ternannoc and other Aspects. In the old wars, lose invaders had ousted the children of Omara, driving them nder the earth and ice, creating by their wars the Earth- rought, children of the dark. Those invaders and their issue, leir descendants, were alien. They had no place in Omara. hey belonged elsewhere.

In his stasis, Brannog felt the first urgency of fear.

Omara must save herself from ruin. There was a way. If ie could allow the powers that threatened her to receive the fe that was not truly Omaran, the intruders, the aliens, then ie dreaming powers could be diverted. The life force that oured into them, the sacrifices, would give them their de- red doorway to reality, yes. But it would not be here, not i Omara. There was a shell, an empty, ravaged Aspect where iey could be housed. The broken Aspect of Ternannoc. De- royed by Korbillian in a staggering act of sacrifice, its ruins aited. Omara would use them.

Omara was all. Omara was god.

It, too, would sacrifice. All things that were not Omaran. They would go to feed the hunger of the old powers, the outsiders. They would sate them. The Earthwrought would inherit their own world and would be again what they were. The circle would have closed, the dreaming powers outside it.

Brannog saw in his terrifying visions the lofty peak of Mount Timeless, rising up from the fangs of the range below it, god-like, omnipresent. Through it, and its holiest of Earthwrought, the Sublime One, Omara spoke to her children. She drew them to her bosom, preparing them for the war that was to come. The war upon the intruders, the aliens. The earthsongs went out, along the Holy Roads, calling, seducing, drawing to the cause the children, those of the earth.

Omara was all. Omara was god.

Before his eyes now, Brannog saw the rod of Orhung, glowing like a bar of molten metal, seething with energy. Unimaginable power had been trapped within it, just as it was trapped in its companion rods, all of which were now in the hands of Anakhizer in the far west. He yearned for the last rod, just as his masters yearned for the body of a world to house them. Once they possessed all the rods, they would become the instruments of sacrifice, for it would be through the rods that the life of Omara was to be devoured. Without them, the act of violation would be difficult, possibly doomed. And yet Omara had chosen to *give* the last of the rods to Anakhizer! Could this be so? This madness? But Brannog saw this with perfect insight. It was true. Omara would do this. Ah, but the price. The price was to be an alliance. The children of the earth were to turn upon their old enemies, the overmen, and all those races who had not sprung from Omara's breast. The Earthwrought were to fight *beside* Anakhizer's forces. Omara would rid herself gladly of those who had ravaged her: Goldenisle would fall, and all the other kingdoms of Man.

Omara was all. Omara was god.

Madness, madness, his mind repeated. Could Omara truly mean this? The Man in him gave vent to a great shout, a cry of anguish that not only echoed across the incalculable distances of his vision, but broke also from his physical lips, so that Ogrund immediately raised his club as if beset by a dozen enemies. He stared about him, horrified that he could do

thing, strike no one. But he could see that the ranks of the
rrounding Earthwrought were bemused also, as though the
out had struck each of them like a clap of thunder.

Brannog's shout was for Man, and for every other being that
nara threatened with annihilation. His horror at what he had
en shown, his wild fury at this insane justice, this purging of a
orld, rose up in him, crashing against the will of Omara, the
hoes reverberating through the onlookers. This must not be!
roared. This is vanity, dishonor, betrayal.

Ruvanna heard this mental cry; it sent her tumbling from
r self-made retreat. Those with her saw her and jumped
ck from her as if she, too, had shrieked out loud. She got
, her eyes wide and staring, though not at her surround-
gs. She was seeing Brannog's vision. Something within her
ced away to join him, to stand beside him and hurl angry
nial at the word of Omara. Her body went rigid and at
ce Carac and Danoth rushed to her and held her, though
ey could do nothing to break her free of whatever held her.
ie was as stiff as a tree, as cold as the dead.

Beyond the perimeter of the circle, the gathered Earth-
rought also heard and understood Brannog's shout for what
was, the voice of all those who had not been born Omara's
ildren. Hear us! they heard him call. Are we not of Omara?
o we not belong to her? Has she not nourished us also?
id we not give our lives up to spare her the agony of Xen-
dhum? Are we any less worthy of saving than you are? You
ho are buried deep under her? Should we go to feed this
irkness that hovers beyond the edge of the world?

For a moment, chaos broke out among the Earthwrought. Their
ncentration, their calmness, had been shattered. Like children
ey milled about, breaking ranks and wandering into the circle
stone, voices raised, arms gesticulating. Ogrund watched them
ardedly, not aware of what had been happening. He held his
ub ready, though. Below him, Brannog shot bolt upright, the
rspiration dripping from his face, his eyes wild.

"Sire!" cried Ogrund, and though full of dread, he knelt
side his master. The ritual was over.

Brannog looked about him, eyes clear now, seeing every
tail of this place, every vein in the living stone. "I am
ell, Ogrund. No harm to me." He saw the confusion among

the Earthwrought, and got unsteadily to his feet. The coldness of dread still clung to him.

Ulthor was the first to push his way through the ring of Earthwrought. He crossed part of the circle and faced Brannog, lifting
a war axe to the heavens. "I hear your cry, Brannog Wormslayer!
Just as I heard the Voice of Omara." He swung his axe and it
whistled in the air. "Such things must not be!"

"The Voice?" said Brannog, suddenly bemused. "You
mean—"

The Earthwrought were coming forward now, having settled themselves. They were again an organized unit and from
out of them came the members of the Circle of Preceptors.
These formed a wedge behind Ulthor, and it was as though
they were reaching out for Brannog.

Ruvanna had been drawn into this like a leaf pulled into a
whirlpool. She felt the closing in of power, the massing
clouds, the will of Omara built into the Circle. As they put
out their hands, talons now, mental claws, reaching hungrily
for Brannog, she opposed them with her own fierce will, an
elemental force drawn from some deep well she could neither
understand nor control. Omara did not relent. The talons
came forward; this was to be the true Purging. Brannog was
to be pulled apart by it, his rebellion torn to pieces.

As it came, Ruvanna unleashed whatever it was that coiled
within her. Like a bolt of fire it smote at every talon, taking
them and snapping them like twigs, inflicting agony. The Circle of Preceptors fell back as one, with screams of pain. Only
Ulthor was unaffected, though he had not put forth power to
strengthen the reach of those talons. He gaped at his fellows,
most of whom were on their knees, like men coming from a
dazed sleep. In a moment their pain had dwindled and they
stood, shaking their heads, bereft of understanding.

In her chamber, Ruvanna went limp and collapsed, Danoth
lifting her as Carac and Korkoris both tried to revive her.

Brannog sensed the withdrawal of something momentous, as if
a threat to his life had been removed. He put an arm about Ogrund,
who still looked for an assailant to do battle with.

"The ritual is over," said Ulthor. "And it does not seem
to have harmed you."

"Was it Omara that sought to destroy me, Ulthor? Was it

Omara who showed me her plan to rid herself of Man? You said something about the Voice of Omara—''

Ulthor looked across the emptiness beyond. "Aye, the Voice. If it is the true Voice."

"And what was it that spared me? I saw those talons, my death in their grip. But something spared me."

Ulthor turned upon the Circle of Preceptors. "I say it was Omara who spared him! Who challenges that?"

"Omara?" gasped one of the Circle. "Then who reached for him?"

"Another will. The will of this Anakhizer, or his masters! It would have blasted Brannog where he stood! But Omara intervened. It was her own conscience, softened by Brannog's plea for his people. Was it not a just plea? Omara thought so. I vow it."

"How can we be sure of this?" said one of the elders, his face the color of chalk.

Ulthor leaned on the haft of his axe and grinned. "Let us put this Voice of Omara, this Sublime One, to the test. Let us go with Brannog to Mount Timeless."

"You would dare defy the Sublime One, the will of Omara?"

"The will! *The will!*" snarled Ulthor. "I echo the shout of Brannog Wormslayer. I cast out the faith of the Sublime One. Just as Omara has. Do not speak to me again of the will of Omara in the same breath as you speak of the Voice of Omara. That Voice is hollow and empty, the Voice of lies and deceit. And betrayal!"

Brannog intervened before Ulthor actually used his war axe on anyone who still wished to take exception to his fiery speech. "The Sublime One has Orhung's rod. He must not be allowed to deliver it into the hands of Anakhizer. Once Anakhizer has it, nothing can be done to prevent the destruction. No pact will be honored and Omara will become the body of whatever those dark powers are that seek to possess it."

Those images had risen up to horrify the Circle. Several of them tried to speak at once, but it was the oldest of them that stilled them. "Our course is no longer clear. All is confusion. What is it that drives us?"

"I cannot say," said Brannog. "Perhaps it is the will of all creatures, the will to survive. I cannot tell you if my own ancestors came from Ternannoc or some other Aspect. Those of my wife were from Ternannoc. Our blood is so mixed, mixed by the centuries. Life is life, and it is all threatened by the powers that Anakhizer serves. They will change Omara. If they take what they desire, what life would remain? What would crawl from their nightmares to flood this world?''

Ulthor faced Brannog, his face grave. "If you had this rod, Brannog, what would you do with it?"

The question hung above them all, potent as thunder. For a long time, Brannog did not answer. "I don't know," he said eventually. "Destroy it, if possible. But I must seek it out."

Ulthor nodded. "We must all do so. We of the Far Below have become too insular, too deeply buried. We should be on the surface, protecting our world! Should we let these so-called outsiders do it for us! Was it us who toppled Xennidhum! No, we buried deeper. Do we fight Anakhizer, or do we let Men do it for us, and in so doing, shame us?"

The gathered Earthwrought heard every word and did not wait for the replies of the Circle. As one they bellowed out their agreement, and Brannog felt a stab of emotion at the thought of such an alliance.

"You must go with Brannog," the elders told Ulthor. "You must go to the Sublime One. Seek the truth."

Ulthor smiled hugely. "Oh, I will."

"Ask the Voice of Omara to speak!" Earthwrought called.

"The Voice?" called Ulthor. "But *I* am the Voice of Omara! And you! And you—all of us. *We* are Omara." He gripped Brannog's hand and laughed again. "You are purged, King Brannog. And so are your people." He lifted Ogrund from the ground and hugged him, the Earthwrought giving vent to their mightiest cheer yet. Ogrund felt himself expanding with a new kind of power, an exultation, and the tears flooded his cheeks.

17
The Living Mountain

"ARE YOU ASLEEP?"

There was no movement beside Dennovia in the soft light of the candles, the shadow time that was like night, but she knew instinctively that Mourndark was awake. Since they had been moved to this larger chamber, he had hardly slept at all. Now, stretched out beside her on the couch, his mind seemed to be going over and over their situation, as though somehow he would discover a way to break out of what had become a spacious prison.

He reached out and stroked her hair, absently, as if caressing a pet. "There are times," he said, "when our hosts pay no attention to us. I wonder how long it will be before they ignore us entirely. Oh, they'll have us fed, and no doubt will provide us with all the other luxuries of this place."

Dennovia sat up, stretching provocatively, the light falling across her breasts, but he did not even glance at her. He had made love to her in this place, but there was a tension in him, knowing that the walls might be absorbing everything. Dennovia, whose senses were ever alert, sharpened by the existence she had lived in the Direkeep, had known from the beginning that they were under observation, like creatures in an experiment, for the Esoterics did have an interest in her and Mourndark, possibly because they expected him to divulge information of some kind. She had managed to convince Mourndark that frequently she felt no such presence, though he was wary.

"We are alone now," Dennovia whispered, leaning over him.

"You think so?" He studied her beautiful face.

"It is like night. Perhaps this mountain sleeps."

He nodded and slipped from the couch. Although he was naked, he felt perfectly comfortable, for part of the luxury of Mount Timeless was its air, constantly like that of a warm summer day. It gave it a uniqueness which Dennovia found fascinating. Nevertheless, Mourndark drew on a robe and belted it. He leaned close to Dennovia, not to kiss her, but to whisper.

"It is safe, I think, to give me what you saved for me."

An inadvertent shudder ran through her. It was the first time since their arrival that he had mentioned the box of instruments. She left the couch. Unlike him, she did not dress, crossing the wide chamber to an alcove where her trunk had been placed by their captors. If anyone had studied the contents, no comment had been made. Dennovia presumed that the Esoterics thought there were clothes in it and nothing more. As she undid the straps, she felt again the apprehension of seeing those cold articles of steel. She turned to him, but his face was a mask of solemnity. He said nothing.

Dennovia listened to the mountain, straining to catch any sound, but there was none. Slowly she opened the trunk and then dug down with her hands through the rich silks until she found what she had put there, the narrow box. She pulled it free as if it were a sleeping animal she did not wish to rouse.

"Give it to me," Mourndark said eagerly and took it. He walked swiftly back to the couch and sat on it, pushing the box under the covers. Dennovia took out of the trunk a silk dress and wrapped it round herself, suddenly conscious of her nakedness as if an intruder had entered the room. She closed the trunk and returned to Mourndark, not sure what he would do. He indicated the couch and she knelt beside him.

"These are our only hope of freedom," he said softly, and now there was a strange expression on his face, one akin to hope.

"But no one ever comes," she whispered. "We never see our food arrive. There are no doors." It was true, for they never caught sight of servants bringing food or water. If there were doors, they were used in secret. Yet whatever they needed was provided. And the food was excellent, the water pure. If they wished to bathe, there was always a warm pool available in another annexe.

"There has to be a door, though I have searched the walls hour by hour."

"You should sleep," she said gently, but she could not bring herself to touch him, knowing those knives were beside him.

"Do you feel these walls?"

She looked around her. "They are unlike the stone of the Direkeep. Not cold. They feel like wood, not stone."

He nodded. "These people of the earth have strange qualities. They created this place. It is like an extension of themselves. Like the killing steel, it is fused with them, their minds. I understand such things."

"Then if we try to get out, the walls will—know?"

A cold smile crossed his lips, picked out precisely by the candle glow. "If the walls are alive, they can feel pain."

She drew back, understanding. The knives! "But won't there be danger in that?"

"Of course," he hissed. "But I'll not rot in this place." He pulled out the box and undid its hasps, and in a moment Dennovia could see him touching the knives there, examining them, gloating over them in the strange, sensual way that he did. His body was taut, his eyes closing in pleasure as though he took far more delight in touching the steel than he did in touching her body. Presently he drew one of the blades from the box. It was long and pointed. He frowned at it as if something were wrong.

"What is it?" she asked, her throat drying up.

"I'm not sure. But the steel has a ring to it. A glow. As if it were alive."

He imagines this, she thought, but dared not say so.

"Something attracts it, as with magnetism." He looked around, but remained puzzled. Then he was staring at Dennovia again. "An experiment. You think we are truly alone for a while?"

"I'm sure they have allotted us a time for privacy." She felt her heart clenching as if it would cease.

"Then come with me." He secreted the blade within his robe. Silently he went over to one of the curving walls, Dennovia behind him. "Feel the wall," he told her.

She did so, running the tips of her fingers along the stone, if stone it was. Again, the warmth intrigued her, the faint suggestion of a distant pulse, as though a vein ran inside it, or a nerve. But the uncanny sensation of being observed was temporarily gone. "Dormant," she told him.

"Bring me the box," he said, ignoring the look of doubt on her face. While she was doing as he had asked her, he pulled out his blade and with it touched the wall. The affinity was not here. In fact, the wall was repulsed by the steel. That was excellent. With infinite care, he pressed the point into the wall. There was no resistance. He waited, half expecting the wall to shudder as a beast would have, but it did not. He drew the blade downward, closely studying the line he had made. In a while it wept, but the liquid was clear, like water.

Dennovia came back to him and set the box down beside him. "What is it?"

"I cannot tell yet."

"Will they know?"

He made an impatient gesture for silence, taking another blade from the set. He worked with delicate care, using several blades, though Dennovia could not see the detail of his work. She kept looking around her, expecting to discover one of the Esoterics watching, but none appeared. The heavy silence remained.

For over an hour Mourndark labored, moving down the wall, testing, probing, a surgeon studying the body of a patient, trying to detect the exact place where he should make his major incision. At last he seemed satisfied. He gave a grunt, the only sound he had made for almost the entire time, and stood back. Dennovia, who had gone back to the couch and was beginning to feel drowsy, jolted awake.

"Well?" she asked.

He did not answer, but a moment later had used the large blade, pushing it deep into the wall as if into muscle. He dragged it down and sideways. Within seconds the wall was trembling like the flanks of a horse, and then a great section of it folded back on itself like skin. Darkness was revealed and a sweet smell. Mourndark called for a candle. Dennovia was instantly beside him. He took the glowing candle and applied its flame to the large aperture he had made. Again the wall shivered and Dennovia gasped. Mourndark laughed softly. He gathered his instruments, wiping them before returning them to their box, which he tucked under his arm.

"Come. There's a passage beyond."

"To where?"

"Stay here if you wish!" he snapped, stepping through.

She hesitated only momentarily, then followed. The walls seemed as if, like flesh, they might close up and suffocate her, their darkness a solid thing, but she was soon free of them and standing in a corridor beyond. Its walls also had the look of well-sculpted stone. Behind her the wall was already closing, a wound healing itself miraculously. Mourndark held up his candle.

"If we meet anyone, try to distract them."

They discovered that the corridor wound around the outside of the chamber where they had been incarcerated. Dennovia dreaded that it might be self-enclosed, but to her relief they found a place where steps led up and away from it, the only other passage. They took this, Mourndark leading. Their shadows danced behind them, the candle flickering as if it might go out.

"They seem to have abandoned this part of the mountain for the night, if it is night," said Dennovia.

As soon as she said it, Mourndark gestured for silence, flattening himself against the wall. She did so, too, and he snuffed out the candle, setting down his box. They both heard soft footfalls and saw ahead of them another light. Coming down the passageway, carrying a small ewer, was a woman, stooped and slight. She had not seen them and was muttering to herself as she came, the words inaudible. She was beside Mourndark before she realized it. His hands came out and grabbed her, one the neck, the other her mouth. Her struggle was brief, and in a moment she gave up, her wide eyes staring at him in shock.

"Is the castle asleep?" he asked, his eyes like knives.

She nodded.

"I'll release your mouth," he told her. "But don't cry out." She needed no further threats.

As he removed his hand, Dennovia took the candle from the woman. The woman spoke in a hoarse, deep voice. "Are you the Man they are searching for?"

Mourndark turned to Dennovia, who shrugged.

The old woman suddenly jerked. "But you can't be. You possess both your hands—"

Mourndark gazed at her with sudden understanding. "Wargallow? They are looking for him? Why?"

"Is he the Man with one hand?" she croaked.

"Yes, where is he?"

"He has escaped. All Mount Timeless searches for him. But it is feared he has left the Body."

"The Body?"

"The inner mountain."

"How could he escape?" growled Mourndark.

"No one knows. But he cannot get away. It is not possible."

Mourndark's face changed. He turned to Dennovia with an evil smile. "They told us he was to be taken back to the Deliverers. Taken back! Yet he has eluded them! Then he'll die, out in the mountains, the fool! Since he's lost his killing steel, even my skills cannot repair him."

"Are you sure?" whispered Dennovia.

"Yes! They could have done no worse had they cut out his heart."

"The Sublime One does not want him harmed," said the old woman.

"Too late," snorted Mourndark. "The Sublime One has killed him. Where is your ruler?"

"It is the time of the Convocation. The Sublime One calls to his children, across all Omara."

Mourndark glanced at Dennovia. "Then he's locked in his work?"

"Just so. Most of the Esoterics are with him, giving power to the Convocation. Those few that can be spared are looking for the Man."

"You serve here; do you ever leave the place? Is there a way out?"

The old woman shook her head, surprised by the question. "No, no. All my life I have been inside, never beyond the Body. I have been honored—"

"But there must be a way down!" He picked up his box with a quick movement.

She tried to struggle free, but fell over the ewer, which shattered and sprayed water. The old woman scrambled away, as if to escape along the passageway, but Mourndark bent down and drove one of his blades between her shoulders, pinning her vitals with an expert thrust. The woman thrashed horribly for a moment, her hands spasming. Dennovia watched in disgust as Mourndark pulled his blade free and cleaned it fastidiously, holding it up to the candlelight to see that the work was done correctly.

Dennovia said nothing, stepping over the motionless body, following the Steelmaster. She tried to push the vision of the cold murder from her eyes as he had wiped away the blood, but it was not so easily done.

They moved on along the passageways for some time, sometimes taking branches, trying to find a way downward, though the way seemed to want to lead them upward. Mourndark said nothing, as though Dennovia was no longer with him, and she wondered if he had made other plans now, plans to uncover as much of the mystery of this place as he could. Its power lured him. His sureness had returned, his confidence, and with it the cunning, the icy will to remove all obstacles in his path. How long, she asked herself once more, before I become such an obstacle?

He held his steel now, sometimes listening to it as if it were a guide, insinuating secrets into his ear. Something in this mountain fastness attracted it, drew it as power drew him. Finding it became as important as escaping.

They came to the first broad passage they had found, stepping up onto its marble floor. Their candle had been discarded, but the walls here had their own light. This passage, with its high, curved ceiling, was lit from somewhere above, decorated with hangings and murals, though their contents

were vague and abstract; they had an uneasy effect if studied
for too long. Mourndark ignored them.

"If we are to get away, we will need help. This entire
mountain is like a fragment of another realm. I am certain it
has been designed to confuse. No one could leave it by
chance."

"Perhaps we'll come across an Esoteric. Some of them
must be about."

The longer they wandered the halls and chambers that
seemed to go on forever about them, the more they began
to suspect they were now trapped in a system that was toying
with them, deliberately leading them this way and that, crossing and recrossing their own tracks. Much of the inner landscape of this part of Mount Timeless was duplicated, halls
looked identical, corridors wound back on themselves.
Mourndark's anger mounted, and Dennovia sensed that it
would break if he did not find some of the solutions he sought
soon. She was beginning to feel perturbed, even threatened,
when he came to a narrow aperture in a wall. He was holding
up his blade, gazing at it as if listening to it. His face changed
as he put his eye to the aperture.

"What do you see?" she asked, sensing his excitement.

He grinned. "This is interesting. See, below us. Another
chamber."

Dennovia looked through the aperture, a long gash that
looked more like a fault than a window. "Exalted," she said.
"They appear to be on guard. But the place is bare. What
are they guarding?"

"I see a dais," he answered. "But no one on it." He took
two more blades from his box, then handed it to her. "Shall
we find out?"

She tried to cover her fear, seeing the gleam in his eye.
What was it about that room that so interested him?

"They are only Exalted," he told her. "Their powers are
small." He went along the hallway, and came to a tall doorway that opened onto the chamber in which the Exalted
stood guard. There were no doors. Carefully Mourndark
looked into the tall chamber: the doorway was not guarded
only the raised dais. He beckoned to Dennovia and she was
by his side at once. By simple gestures he showed her that

he wanted her to wait by this doorway. She nodded, a moment later watching him go down the broad steps. There were four Exalted guards, each like a sentinel at a corner of the dais. As they saw him they swung round, their curved swords immediately dropping in a gesture of challenge. The first of them stepped forward, hideous face screwed up belligerently.

"You are not permitted here," he snarled.

"I have the blessing of the Sublime One. He sent me." Mourndark stepped lightly forward, arms at his side, offering no threat.

The Exalted were not impressed by him. They broke formation and as one came toward him, swords now leveled at his chest.

"Leave at once," said their leader.

Now that they had moved, Mourndark could see behind them; the dais was no higher than his knees and on it rested a single item. It was a short length of steel, a rod. There was no mark upon it, no engraving, and it looked to have no specific purpose. The Exalted were greatly perturbed, as if at any moment they would attack Mourndark.

He turned back and smiled at Dennovia, and she knew he wanted her to ensure no one came in here. She found a place where she could watch the hall. No one was to be seen, and she found the nerve to take out a blade from the box. It hummed in her hand, and for a moment she thought she had seen a flicker of light within it. But she looked up, watching the hall. This venture was insane, but she feared Mourndark more than any of the mountain's inhabitants.

When Mourndark selected the moment to make his play, it came with extraordinary rapidity. He turned slightly away from the Exalted, talking persuasively, though his words did not convert them. He knew this, but it gave him precious seconds in which to prepare. As he turned back to the Exalted, he flicked his left wrist, almost in a wave of contempt. The blade that shot from it had taken its victim in the eye before the others realized what had happened. The stricken Exalted gasped, dropping his sword and groping at his eye, toppling back against the dais. The other three turned to him at once, unaware even now of what had happened.

Mourndark moved forward with blurring speed, his long

blade finding the throat of another victim. By the time this
Exalted had dropped, Mourndark's other blade was in the gut
of a third. He darted back lithely. The Exalted he had struck
were all writhing on the floor. The remaining one stood with
his mouth agape, but his sword was up. With a howl of rage,
he raced at Mourndark, bringing the weapon down in an arc.
Had it landed, it would have cut the intruder from neck to
belly, but Mourndark was far too quick. He stepped aside
easily and whipped his blade across the face of the Exalted.
In a moment the latter was wiping a crimson flow from his
face, blinking as he backed away. He was about to cry out,
when Mourndark's blade, also thrown, caught him under the
chin, cutting off his voice as effectively as a strangler's wire.
Quickly Mourndark picked up a fallen sword and went to
each victim, jabbing at their hearts to complete his grisly
work.

He had already turned from the dead to look at the rod,
when he heard Dennovia rushing toward him.

"Get my blades," he told her. "And clean them."

She backed away from him, appalled by the carnage he
had created with such casual ease. With a feeling of revul-
sion, she pulled the blades from their victims, turning her
head away as she wiped them clean of the thick, pooling
blood.

Mourndark was at the dais, glaring at the rod as though it,
too, would attack him. "What is it?" he asked the air. "I
should know this thing." He bent over it: there was no light
within it, but he detected a sound, a faint hum. He stretched
out his hand over it, not touching it, but it did not feel either
warm or cold. Dare I take it?

Dennovia broke into his thoughts, standing at his elbow
with the three blades. He took them from her and kissed them
in a private ritual that did more to nauseate her than the killings themselves. Mourndark reacted as if he had been stung,
glaring at his blades. They vibrated, and as they did so, he
felt the pull of the rod. So it was this object that had been
drawing them, he realized.

"What is the rod?" asked Dennovia. "Is it important?"

"Four armed guards thought so. Here, in the heart of their

stronghold, where it is most unlikely to find an enemy, still the Sublime One saw fit to put an armed guard on it."

"But what is it? What does it do?"

He stared at the rod, fascinated by it. "We shall find out."

She was putting the blades back into the box, and he made no move to stop her. "We'd better leave—"

"Wait!" he snapped, sensing she was about to go back to the steps. He gripped her by the arm and pulled her to him. Their eyes locked and she knew then that, for some reason, he meant to harm her. There was no love in his eyes, and now, more than ever before, she knew that he had never loved her, could never love another being. It was not in him. He craved power, as an addict. There was no room in his heart for anything else.

"Pick up the rod," he said in a voice so low that she almost missed the words, though the lust in his voice thickened it.

She made to tear her hand away, but he would not release it. His grip was tightening, cutting off the flow of blood to her fingers. He forced her hand down toward the rod. "Pick it up!" he breathed.

"No! Don't make me do it!"

With a jerk, he thrust her hand onto the rod, his eyes narrowing as he studied her reaction, his face inches from hers, watching for a sign of agony. Her fingers closed automatically on the rod, drawn to it, but she felt no pain.

"It's just a piece of steel," she said faintly, but something deep within her cried out that it was so much more.

Mourndark looked down, seeing her unharmed. Then he thrust his mouth at hers, his free arm pulling her to him. She wanted to struggle free, repulsed by his kiss, as if raped by him. But in a moment he had pushed her off anyway, though not before he had snatched the rod from her hand. He stood with it held out in front of him. He felt nothing. It was as she had said, just steel, a simple rod.

Dennovia fell back, looking up at him with fresh terror. For an instant she thought of the knives, of trying to kill him here and begging for mercy from the Esoterics. But there was a shout from the steps behind her. Into the chamber drifted three of the mysterious figures. Their faces, usually so serene, were ghastly: they had seen Mourndark standing by the dais with the rod. Each of the Esoterics looked at the rod as if it were a precious object about to be smashed by a lunatic.

Mourndark saw their concern at once and held the rod up, brandishing it like a weapon. "Keep your distance!" he snarled.

They went rigid, prepared to obey him. As Mourndark's grip tightened on the rod, he felt it warming to his touch. From the box where his blades were kept, there came a faint hum, and the rod came alive. There *was* power locked inside it, he realized. This must be some vital relic of the Earth-wrought nation.

The first of the Esoterics had seen the slain Exalted, unable to disguise his shock. "What is it that you want?"

"I have what I want," said Mourndark.

"Return the rod of power to the dais and you will be given anything you ask for. You have only to name it. And you will be given your freedom. If you do not, the wrath of the Sublime One will be unleashed upon you—"

"I think not. He is far too busy. I understand that he is at the Convocation. Your halls are empty, your companions locked in their working. Save your breath and don't deny it."

"Who has told you these things?"

"Can you deny it?" Mourndark cried, waving the rod threateningly.

The effect on the Esoterics was instant and they nodded to him, aghast. "Yes, yes. You must not interrupt the Convocation. The Sublime One is in communion with Omara herself. He speaks to the earth, the core. Tell us what you desire."

"I will know more about this rod. I know it has power," he told them. "And I will use it. But what is it? Who made it? *Who?*"

"It is the rod of Orhung, last of the Werewatch."

"I know nothing of either. Explain."

The Esoterics looked to one another for guidance. They knew that this madman could destroy them all with the power in the rod, and they had to believe that he knew how to use it. But what else dare they tell him? "It is a sacred relic," said their spokesman. "From Omara's far past. The Sorcerer-Kings used it to ward off their enemies."

"The Sorcerer-Kings," mused Mourndark. "Enemies? From where?"

The Esoterics gaped like fish.

Mourndark's lips curled in a parody of a smile. "From beyond Omara? From Ternannoc, and other ruptured Aspects?"

"As you say—"

"And why should the Sublime One desire such a tool of power? What enemies does he intend to scatter with it?"

"The Sublime One will destroy all those who are enemies to the Earthwrought nation. But the rod is a deterrent, a threat, no more. You, Mourndark, understand such things, for you created the Deliverers."

"And persecuted your people for their use of power," he smiled coldly. "So now you would use this to, what? Deter us from so doing again? Or would you make proper use of it?"

He glanced at the rod, knowing there was far more history attached to this dull-looking object than he could possibly have imagined.

Dennovia saw the empty expression on his face, but she felt a cold hand of dread clutching for her.

As Mourndark felt the rod, turning it in his hands, he realized it had begun to pulse, as if it, too, sensed something deeper within itself. Like the arm of a Deliverer, it received images, commands from his brain. These things were no mystery to him. He laughed suddenly, a grating sound, pointing with the rod at the leader of the Esoterics and at once a bolt of light flared from its end. It sizzled across the chamber and struck the chest of the Esoteric. He blew apart as if hit by a thunderbolt, and in the dazzling glare, his companions were flung backward like dolls. They smashed into the steps behind them. Mourndark swept the rod from side to side and in a second had made ashes of all three.

Dennovia crawled away, whimpering at this depth of cruelty. Mourndark, sobered by her pitiful figure, lowered the rod. It lost its heat instantaneously. It had become again a length of inanimate metal. But stored within it now was the life force of those it had obliterated. Mourndark knew that as surely as if the rod had spoken to him. Indeed, he felt that his dialogue with it had hardly begun.

"Come, come, Dennovia," he said, going to her. "Here is a key. It will open the walls of our prison and take us out."

"Throw it away," she whispered, her eyes fixed upon it.

He laughed, ignoring her words. She got to her feet, inadvertently clutching his box of blades to her bosom. But it was as though she could hear them whispering, eager to be close to their master, and that monstrous object he now carried. Mourndark touched her hair condescendingly, but all warmth she had felt for him was gone. He had taken a new lover, one he would worship for as long as he drew breath. To him, Dennovia had become no better than the dust beneath his feet.

The long night was coming.

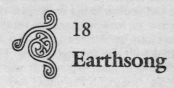

18
Earthsong

THERE WERE FLURRIES of snow, gusting about the Host as it made its way over the icy waste of the glacier. Brannog rode now with Ulthor at his side, together with his captains of the Host. Korkoris of the Icewrought had organized his people on the flanks of the army, for army it had become, and they used their own unspoken powers to drive away the sting in the weather. No one in the Host complained of the cold, and the wind seemed almost to rise up over them, flowing away like a swift current that has been diverted. Without the uncanny skills of the Icewrought, the Host would have fallen to the harsh exposure of this white emptiness. As it was, it moved on in relative comfort, covering the powdery ground easily and without incident, the miles falling away behind them. Ulthor had called together a vast host of his own, and there were several thousand loyal Earthwrought from the Far Below in Brannog's Host now. They had come back up through the glacier, mingling with Brannog's people willingly, almost as if they, like Ulthor, had been waiting for years for some sign from above them that the day would come when they could leave the deeps of the earth. At first the natural daylight of the surface, the searing glare of the sun on snow, had stunned them, but they had quickly adjusted. As they marched, their hearts warmed and although they knew they marched to a conflict with the unknown, they were in good voice. Brannog's Host was glad of them, and even Ogrund's hitherto sour face broke out in the occasional smile as if, for once, he was content with life. Ruvanna felt the

255

tremendous energy of the beings about her, the banner of
hope that was now held aloft, but within her, no longer deep,
was a shadow, a thought that ahead of them there would be
a storm that would test the mettle of them all, and her most
of all. Brannog had spoken to her once since the ritual Purging, but she knew he was reluctant to speak of what had
happened. Thankfully he did not know that she had intervened, had shared with him the nightmares of revelation and
had used power to beat back whatever it was that had tried
to destroy him. She had had little control over the things that
had possessed her, but what disturbed her most was the fact
that for all her sharing of power with Brannog, he yet seemed
apart from her, almost beyond her reach. It was a gulf she
could not bear to contemplate.

Three days beyond the glacier they came through a narrow
pass that brought them to another high valley. It dropped
away sharply, then rose up in a sequence of massive peaks,
gray-flanked and forbidding, topped with pure white. Korkoris pointed to a single mountain that stood out behind them,
towering over them with the possessiveness of a god. Its peaks
were swathed in clouds: they writhed, hiding it jealously.
From here it looked impossible to reach, let alone scale. Not
one of the Host failed to gape at its majesty, its regal omni-
science. Mount Timeless. It defied them with its very presence.

Brannog was scanning the range ahead, searching for a
pass through it, when an altercation broke out on the slopes
below him. He could see a number of figures, struggling as
if in conflict. He urged his pony forward. As he and his
leading party came upon the group, they saw that it consisted
of a number of his Host, mainly Icewrought, who held a
wriggling stranger, a large Earthwrought, though one of an
unfamiliar tribe. Brannog gestured for him to be released and
he faced him.

The Earthwrought looked shocked at the sight of such a
huge Man, standing over him, with so many companions.
Behind him there were many more.

"Who are you?" gasped the late prisoner.

"I am Brannog, from the Elderhold in the north. Som

call me Wormslayer." Brannog used the name because it had evoked most response during his travels.

This Earthwrought, however, seemed not to be familiar with it. "I am Huttilik. I see there are many Earthwrought with you, yet you are an overman."

Ulthor snorted, speaking up before either Ogrund or Carac could respond angrily, which they had been about to do. "I am Ulthor, of the Far Below. You have heard of it, I take it, Huttilik?"

"Why, of course! My uncle, Yuttegar, knows someone whose brother has been there—"

"I am of the Circle of Preceptors. What village are you from?"

"It is below us," said Huttilik, far more awed by Ulthor than he was by Brannog, though it amused Brannog that this should be so, especially as it so infuriated Ogrund and Carac. Brannog decided in his own mind that in future, Ulthor was to be a major key to the door of Earthwrought unity.

"Is this the Convocation?" said Huttilik, staring about him at the many strange faces. Why, there were more overmen here! And the woman, who was she? Not Earthwrought, and yet she had some of their features. Ice people, too—they were known. Horses! Such a gathering!

"Yes," said Brannog quickly before any of his captains could reply. "We are bound for Mount Timeless. The Sublime One calls, does he not?"

Huttilik's face became a scowl, but he quickly forced a smile. "Yes, of course," he said sheepishly. But Brannog had understood.

"You do not approve?"

"The Sublime One is the Voice of Omara."

Ruvanna was beside Huttilik before anyone could stop her. "But Brannog is correct, is he not? You and your people do not approve. You would have answered the earthsongs long ago if you had. Brannog does not approve either. We are here to challenge the Voice of the Sublime One." She knew that Ogrund and Ulthor in particular would be content to let her speak for them, but also knew that Brannog would likely be furious with her for having taken this on herself. But she had read Huttilik better than any of them.

He hesitated no more than a moment. Then he clenched his fists and screwed up his features in an expression of ill-repressed rage. "It is the Exalted! They treat us like beasts. Many of the delvings in these lands are forced to give up Earthwrought to go to the workings under Mount Timeless. To quarry the stone, laboring at the mountain, delving, repairing. Once the Exalted had the honor of doing such work, but now they have given themselves airs. They consider themselves above such things! Above them! Exalted! Pah, they are vermin!"

"Well said," called Carac. "From what I have seen of them, you are correct. And Ogrund here has no love of them, eh, Ogrund?"

Ogrund growled confirmation, though his scowl remained fixed on Huttilik.

"They are murderers," said the latter. "Our people have died before now, forced to work too hard. Can you imagine that? Earthwrought killed by stone?"

Those who heard this were audibly appalled.

Huttilik suddenly stared hard at Brannog. "You say you have come to challenge the Sublime One. Are you the first?"

"First?"

"Overman?"

"Why do you ask? Have you seen others?"

"One other."

Brannog frowned in thought. Another man? Here, in this wilderness?

"By some miracle he escaped from Mount Timeless," said Huttilik. "But his time is near."

"Dying?" said Brannog. "Who is he?"

"He has hardly spoken. He was found by some of our stone workers. He is in the village. Can you save him? The Exalted must have made cruel sport of him, for they took off his hand."

Brannog looked to his companions and at Ruvanna, but none of them ventured an explanation. "Will you take us to him, Huttilik? I promise you that your people will be quite safe. If necessary I will come alone."

"Sire!" protested Ogrund.

"I think you should take a few of us with you," grinned Ulthor. "If you'll forgive me." He winked at Ogrund.

Huttilik bowed. "I'll take you all, since you are no allies of the Exalted. If you're going to carry war to them, my people will want to join you!"

Without further ado, Huttilik began the descent, gliding over the snowy terrain as easily as Korkoris's Icewrought, and the Host followed him more slowly. When he glanced back occasionally, his eyes bulged to see such a great company and he wondered if, at last, the Exalted were going to be given a lesson in manners they richly deserved. As long as the village chiefs didn't berate him for bringing the company down on them, particularly as it contained and was led by, of all things, an overman!

To her surprise, Ruvanna was motioned forward, to ride beside Brannog. She felt the eyes of the Host, burning into her back.

"You sensed Huttilik's hatred of the Exalted?" Brannog asked her.

"Like a firebrand."

"And this man they have found. Who can he be?"

She raised her brows. "I can't see such distances, any more than I can look into the future." As soon as she had said it, she wished she had not, for his face clouded and he turned from her as though dismissing her. Why was he so sensitive about it?

Huttilik had gone ahead to alert the delvings, which had been cut into an exposed rock-face; they were a compromise between life on the surface and delvings underground. No sooner had Huttilik delivered his message to the inhabitants than several score of them were peering out of their tunnels. They were wary, however, and Brannog could see that they would have fought if they had had to. He gave the order for the Host to camp at a distance, then dismounted and went forward with his captains and Ruvanna. Huttilik reappeared with a number of armed Earthwrought. Their weapons were made of bone, cut and sharpened as if taken from the corpse of some large mammal. The exchanges were brief but polite.

"There is a man here," said Brannog. "I would like to see him."

No one disapproved and he was taken at once to the tunnel system. Ogrund was first to stand at Brannog's shoulder and Ulthor also insisted on accompanying him. They went below, at length reaching a narrow chamber. To their surprise, a fire burned in a crude hearth, the logs crackling and the flames throwing out a roseate glow. On a rough bed at the far end of the chamber there was an inert figure, covered by a pelt. It appeared to be asleep.

Brannog approached, then gasped when he saw the face. He dropped to his knees. It was Simon Wargallow, although the face was so pale and haggard he was hardly recognizable. "Wargallow," he breathed, but the Deliverer was unconscious. Slowly Brannog pulled back the covers, again gasping at what was revealed. Wargallow's right arm was swathed in leaves, but even so it was obvious that his hand, his killing steel, had been cut away at the elbow. A wave of horror and nausea swept over Brannog. The steel had been a curse, but to have had it removed! He could hardly breathe without an effort, and in those brief moments of shock he seemed to relive all those events which he and Wargallow had been through. Wargallow, whom once he would have cut down, but who now drew from him a sudden surge of pity, and with it, molten fury. He turned to his watching companions, face livid.

"Bring the girl!" he yelled, his voice booming in the enclosed chamber.

Ogrund reacted at once. As he ran up the passage, he fought to keep his own emotions in check. Wargallow! For whom Ygromm had died. A Deliverer. But he said nothing, fetching Ruvanna as quickly as he could.

She stood beside Brannog, aware of his anguish.

"When Kennagh first took me to you, he called you a healer. He said you had certain skills," he said to her. It was almost a challenge.

"Yes," she nodded, but his words filled her with dread, for she knew what they meant.

"This man is Simon Wargallow. I cannot imagine how he came to be here in the east. You see what they have done to him?"

She nodded in silence.

"Can you save his life?"

She knelt down beside Brannog, shocked by the pain in his eyes. She studied Wargallow closely. His heart beat strongly yet, and his brow was warm. "Leave me," she said softly but with a finality that Brannog understood. He rose and ushered the others outside. He looked back as he went and for a brief moment the cries and shrieks of Xennidhum's fall were in his ears.

Ruvanna undid the leaves that bound Wargallow's arm. The work that had been done, the amputation, had been done expertly. Very little blood seemed to have been lost, but the veins that remained were oddly discolored. To her amazement, Ruvanna discovered that some were unlike human veins, and there were parts of the flesh that were hard and cold, almost like a skin of metal. She listened again to the heart. For an hour she touched Wargallow's body, his head, chanting over him, calling upon secret things in her own mind, spells that had been there when she was born, linking herself to the soil of the room's floor. Some of the earth she took and molded, pressing it to Wargallow's skin, touching his ruined arm a dozen times.

When at last she had finished, she knelt back, drained, unsure if she had succeeded. Brannog found her slumped, muttering softly. At another time he might have felt compassion for her.

"Well?" he said. Wargallow's face did not seem so pale, though he still had the look of a man near death.

"What's left of the arm is strange. I can reach his flesh, his bones. But when his people made his arm, they used strange elements. And arts that I simply cannot duplicate. I fear for him."

"Will he live?"

She looked up at Brannog, seeing the vastness of his concern. "Death was coming for him. I have pushed it back. But it will come seeking him again. I can delay its coming. Does he—mean much to you?"

The pain probed Brannog unmercifully, the more acute because it was so unexpected. He had not known just how strong his bond with this man was. "Once I hated him, as we all did. Atrocities were committed in his name. But what

he was, he had been made, just as his arm had been made.
The detail of his life he had never shared. But I suspect his
life was far darker than anything we could have imagined. At
Xennidhum he fell under the shadow of one of the stones-
that-move, frightful, unnatural beings that obeyed only the
madness of the Mound. Ygromm, who was the leader of my
Earthwrought, gave his life to save Wargallow. Since then,
Wargallow has been as strong an ally as Omara could wish
for. I found this hard to believe, but my own daughter, who
once felt only terror when Wargallow was near her, has sent
me word often that Wargallow has served the Emperor loy-
ally. Do you know, he once asked me to strike off his killing
hand!'' He turned away. After a moment he had recovered a
little of himself, and his anger. ''Is there nothing you can
do!''

''I will try—''

Wargallow's eyes suddenly opened, focusing on the wall
over him. He turned his head slowly and saw the girl. ''Some
water,'' he said. Ruvanna went at once to a jar.

Brannog leaned over the Deliverer. ''Wargallow,'' he said.
''Do you know me?''

Wargallow saw the great face looming over him, and for a
moment he studied it, seeing the changes in it, the rugged-
ness, the subtle alteration of its features, its coloring, the
thickness of hair and brow. And the hint at powers. ''Brannog.''

''Who did this to you?''

Wargallow took the water from Ruvanna and insisted on
sitting up. Brannog automatically put an arm about his shoulders and helped him.

''Events have become very confused in my mind,'' said
Wargallow. ''For some reason I was trapped and abducted.
Taken to Mount Timeless. You know of it?''

''Yes, and of its ruler.''

''His Esoterics removed my arm, but they didn't seem to
intend my death. I cannot guess what they had in mind. I
couldn't risk them using me in some way, probably to torment the Deliverers, or force them into acts to serve their
master. Somehow I got free of them, but my strength fails

me, Brannog. Even here, with the help of the Earthwrought who found me. I'd be dead already if not for them.''

"You are in even safer hands now," Brannog assured him.

"They hate the Exalted! Only that saved me.''

"I've an army behind me. We march on Mount Timeless. As soon as you're fit to come with us.''

"Oh, I'll ride, I promise you. Just give me a day or two. But what do you hope to achieve?'' Although he was yet bemused, Wargallow understood the danger in Brannog's intent.

"Somehow the Sublime One has found Orhung's rod of power. It is not inert and is to be used in a plan that will unite the Earthwrought nations against the Emperor, and ally them to Anakhizer.''

"The rod?'' said Wargallow, puzzled. "But how?''

Brannog explained what had happened in greater detail.

"Then at last I see how I was to have been used,'' nodded Wargallow at the end of it. "They would have sent me back! To unite my people and join Ottemar and all his other allies.''

"To go to the sacrifice. But the Sublime One did not expect his own people to revolt against such a plan.'' Again Brannog enlarged upon events, and as he did so, Wargallow took strength from his words, sitting up and nodding, his mind working as quickly as it ever had. Ruvanna was amazed at his powers of recovery.

She sat in the shadows, but Wargallow looked at her as if he had heard her. "And the girl? Who is she? I felt her touch me. She went far below the skin.''

Brannog beckoned Ruvanna forward. She came, a little afraid now. Wargallow's reputation sat on him like the mantle of a king.

"She is Ruvanna,'' said Brannog gruffly. "She's—well, a girl of remarkable powers.'' He softened and grinned at her. "Child of Earthwrought and woman. There are many such unions now. She and those like her will be the new hope.''

Ruvanna glanced at him, thinking that perhaps he was mocking her, but his sincerity surprised her.

"You have looked deep inside me, I think,'' said Wargallow, and she could not meet his gaze. "That is as it may be, but tell me, did you see my death?''

She did not answer and it was enough for him.

"I understand discretion," he said.

"Since the Sublime One wounded you," cut in Brannog, "we will hold him to account. We ride to him as soon as you are able."

"Give me some food. I feel hungry again. Your healer has given me an appetite. And mercifully, the pain has gone. It was that which sapped my strength."

Ruvanna would have objected to being called a healer, but she saw Brannog's face and let it pass. Instead she left them. Brannog helped Wargallow to his feet, for the Deliverer insisted on standing. He was dizzy at first, but had soon taken his first few stumbling steps.

"Brannog, my life may well be running away. I can feel the slow drip of strength from me, even though your girl has worked hard to prevent it. Don't be hard on her."

"Is it so bad?"

"I think so. But I must come with you to Mount Timeless. The Earthwrought who are loyal to you must be made to see that the Deliverers are their allies."

"They know it already."

"Nevertheless, all Earthwrought must see it. I will go with you."

Brannog gave him words of encouragement, but a shadow crept over the big man, stealthy as the night. His fury wanted to break free, but not yet. "Of course you shall come. Eat your fill. Then, if you're up to it, I'll introduce you to some remarkable companions."

Wargallow nodded. For a brief moment he thought of Aumlac and the Stonedelvers, whom Brannog had not seen. His thought darkened as he wondered if he would set eyes on them, and on Goldenisle, again. It seemed a forlorn hope, and the loss dug into him like the point of a spear.

Ruvanna went into the Earthwrought delvings and began preparing special food for Wargallow. The Earthwrought women immediately recognized her skill with herbs and other plants and were eager to help her. As she pulped the food, Ruvanna thought again of Brannog's concern. If Wargallow died, and it seemed inevitable, Brannog would be distraught. He did not know it, but Ruvanna did. How strange that his feelings for the Deliverer were so powerful. His thoughts confirmed that he had once wanted Wargallow dead. But now he saw Wargallow as a symbol, a weapon against the threat of annihilation. And Wargallow's plight had damaged Brannog's belief in his own power. Brannog was no boaster, Ruvanna knew that, and he was not arrogant, nor did he take anyone for granted. But he had belief in himself as a ruler. To see Wargallow dying had shaken Brannog's faith in himself. It had placed before him his own vulnerability. But how, oh how, could she help Wargallow? What could she do to prolong his life? No sacrifice is too small, she told herself. Brannog must be strong, must not falter. Without his strength, his belief, we are all doomed.

As she took the food to the chamber, she began a deep search of her mind, stumbling blindly along corridors that, until now, she had not thought to tread, nor dared. As she did so, she became withdrawn, silent, so that as she gave the plate to Brannog, he asked her if she was well, but she ignored him. Instead she went away and he watched her go, a flicker of concern in his eyes. But he turned back to his friend, forgetting Ruvanna in his haste to help him.

Wargallow's appetite seemed to increase as he ate. "This is excellent," he said, and he smiled. "An intriguing creature, that girl."

"There are things about her that I fear," said Brannog. "I believe she is loyal to us, don't mistake me. But I recall too vividly my own daughter and the deceits practiced on her by the Sorcerer-Kings. How they used her line, my wife—"

"You never speak of her," said Wargallow. "Perhaps you should. Such pain can only be eased if it is brought out. I am beginning to realize that."

Brannog grunted ambiguously. "We each keep our past in its tomb. One day we'll open them. But not yet. There is too much to do."

"Indeed."

"And besides, I want to hear about that grinning buffoon who now calls himself Emperor!"

Wargallow laughed, his spirits strengthening. "Guile! He was well named, though no one dares call him that now. He is Ottemar Remoon." His expression became more serious.

"He's changed, Brannog. It is not the fool we once knew who sits upon the throne of Empire."

"This war has changed us all."

"Well," said the Deliverer, with a hint of embarrassment which Brannog found unusual in the man, "you'd better see to a horse for me. I can gossip just as easily as we ride."

WHEN BRANNOG LEFT Huttilik's delvings, his Host had been swelled yet again, for a good many of Tarraneh's warriors had scores they were eager to settle. Having now heard the full tale of the Host, Tarraneh himself was anxious to be a part of it, gladly swearing allegiance to its King. He was able to guide Brannog through the upper passes to the final barriers that spread like the white skirts of Mount Timeless.

Wargallow had recovered much of his strength, and if he felt pain still, made light of it. Brannog wondered if, after all, Ruvanna had been able to work some special cure over him. Now as they traveled, he was pleased to listen to the Deliverer's tales of the west and of how Eukor Epta's plan to ruin the Empire had been thwarted.

Up and across the snow slopes they went and even though the great peaks soared over them, they were of good heart. As usual, the Icewrought took the flanks and used their skill to ward off the worst of any cold, although the sky had become a blue vault, the sun glistening off the snows. For two days they moved upward, until Ruvanna heard the distant chanting. At first she thought she was imagining it; beside her the three wolves padded along, unaware. But gradually she knew it for what it was, an earthsong. She could sense the changing mood of the Host as all of it began to hear the song. Coming from all around them, sent by Mount Timeless, it began to swell, to captivate.

"Brannog!" she cried urgently. "We are being lured. We dare not follow the earthsong here. If we do, we'll be powerless. It would lead us to disaster."

Brannog shook himself, realizing that he had been reacting to the earthsong without knowing it. The Host was slowing and many of the Earthwrought were thinking of the earth and of delving down in search of the Holy Road that must be somewhere far beneath them. "The pull of the song is far stronger here," said Brannog. "How do we resist it?"

"You must tell the Host to sing its own song," said Ruvanna.

"Sing?" echoed Brannog, for once looking helpless.

"Ogrund, Korkoris, Ulthor!" cried Ruvanna. "There are marching songs, battle songs of your people. Quickly—lead the singing now, or we will be drawn below. We must enter Mount Timeless from above."

Hesitantly at first the Earthwrought agreed on and then started singing a rich, sonorous marching song. Brannog encouraged the Host to join in, and soon the entire company, including Danoth's Men, had taken it up. Even though the latter did not understand all the words and struggled with the odd rhythms, they caught the spirit. Wargallow also sang, brokenly, but could not resist a shake of the head at Brannog, who himself had a very fine voice.

"Here's a fine sight for you," he said, leaning across to Wargallow.

"Keep singing!" Wargallow replied, and they moved on up the snows, their song echoing around the dramatic slopes ahead of them. They were on Mount Timeless, intending to climb to firmer ground among its wind-cleared rocks so they could enter it from the most unexpected of angles.

Ruvanna herself sang now, and something in her voice, in her own song, which differed from that of the Host, wrapped them in a blanket of immunity from the swells that drifted up from beneath them like a miasma. What song she sang, she did not know, only that its power came into her and used her like an instrument to perfect its music. Though her eyes were open, she saw nothing, only the dancing rhythm of her own song. Beside her the wolves cringed, moving away from her, afraid of the power that filled the air about her, invisible but vast as a storm wind. As they loped up the steep bank of snow, they let out a sudden howl, their snouts pointed up at the buttresses of whiteness above, as if something malign stood there.

Their howls caught the attention of one of the Icewrought who was on the extreme flank of the Host, and instinctively he looked to the place where the wolves' attention was fixed.

At once he saw the danger: at any moment there would be
an avalanche. He found a protruding rock and leapt on to it,
cupping his hands and giving a shrieking sequence of notes.
Immediately his own people stopped singing and turned, as
one, to him. He pointed and with extraordinary speed the
Icewrought, led by Korkoris, raced to the front of the Host.

"Avalanche," said Korkoris to Brannog. "The mountain
hears our song and is angered. This is our reward."

Brannog growled and beside him Wargallow was trying to
prevent the ponies from bolting, for they knew what was
coming. Brannog thought of Korbillian, and of how he could
control such things, but here, what could they do? Had he
led the Host to this?

Korkoris, however, was darting about with the agility of a
spider. He issued instructions and even Ogrund, Ulthor and
Carac obeyed him quickly, listening to his words and passing
them on. The Host rapidly formed itself into a diamond
shape, digging itself into the snow, while the Icewrought went
to the front of the diamond and, as a body, made themselves
a spear shape. No sooner had they done so, than a great
cracking and booming sounded from almost overhead. In a
moment there came a great rush of white madness, and the
avalanche was unleashed, as though cast at them by an infuriated mountain. Rolling clouds boiled up, as though foam
gushed into an icy pool, and the first heavy wave of snow
tore down the mountainside like the fist of a god.

In seconds it had reached the Icewrought, engulfing them.
Brannog felt his heart shuddering in his chest and pressed
himself as deep into the snow as he could. The far sound of
music was washed away by the force of the snow, like raw
thunder beyond him. He shivered, expecting its impact to
smash him back down the mountain, washing the entire Host
to its doom. But the impact never came. Instead there was a
roaring overhead, a sound unlike anything he had ever heard
before. It was a sound of unsurpassed terror and in it was the
threat of ten thousand deaths. Wargallow, too, had ducked
down, his mind almost bursting with the sound above him,
his back like ice, awaiting the moment when it would be
broken and pulped.

Slowly the roaring diminished. When the silence came, i

was stark. No earthsong seeped up from under the ice. The mountain was still, its anger spent for a while. Brannog raised his head, amazed by what he saw. No one was harmed, for the snow had struck the arrowhead formation of the Icewrought and passed on either side. Korkoris stood up, looking back to see that his charges were safe. He grinned, capering and raising on high his spear of ice. He shouted out something in a strange tongue, an ancient incantation, Brannog assumed.

Brannog leapt across the snow, which seemed oddly thin, and embraced Korkoris, lifting him from the ground like a bear. Korkoris laughed and the Icewrought cheered. In a moment the sound had been taken up by the entire Host and they knew then that not a single life had been lost.

Wargallow watched in amazement. Ah, Brannog, who could have foreseen this? How would Ottemar and your daughter react to it? If you ever sail into Medallion's inner waters, what a welcome there will be for you.

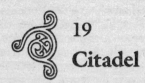

19
Citadel

THE DAY WAS SHORT; there was no dusk. Night fell quickly and heavily. Up on Mount Timeless the Host found shelter under the tall ice slopes, and again the Icewrought exercised their power, drawing it up from the rocks under the snow, gathering around the Host and watching over it. Even their children were able to add to the protective workings. Fires were lit in the camp, for although it was not cold, they were comforting on this dismal mountain, and the Host talked cheerfully, morale high. Ulthor's people took every opportunity to talk to Ogrund's and Danoth's and Carac moved about, learning as much as he could. He would have spoken to Wargallow, but the Deliverer sat with Brannog, and they seemed immersed in private conversations.

Brannog could see that Wargallow was tired now, and was again beginning to weaken. The Deliverer had pulled his cloak tightly about him: he did not mention his arm. Ruvanna brought food to him and he ate it with relish. She had a supply of mushrooms that she had brought from Huttilik's village and prepared them carefully, aware that Brannog watched her now, perhaps to see that she was doing as much as she could for his friend.

As Wargallow ate, she asked Brannog, "May I speak to you?"

"Of course. Sit with us."

She did so, and both men saw by her face that she was wary of something. "This mountain is rich in power," she told them. "It confuses the mind with its working. We must get to its heart as quickly as we can or it will blind us all.

270

with madness, even the Icewrought. They did well to divert its avalanche, but if the mountain unleashes its full anger on us, we will not be able to withstand it. I am surprised it has not already done so."

"It must be the Convocation," said Wargallow. "Much of the Sublime One's power is being used for that. But what do you suggest?"

"I've tried to penetrate the power below. It is linked to the Sublime One, the mountain being controlled by his will. The heart of the mountain is called the Body. The Convocation goes out from there, and as you say, Wargallow, it draws on much power."

Brannog was nodding. "Then we've timed our arrival well."

"Something else. The Esoterics are also involved in the Convocation. It is nearly completed. The Esoterics are needed by the Sublime One to aid him in the focusing of his earth-songs. Mount Timeless is well defended, but mostly by Exalted. They are warriors, as we know, but they have no power other than the strength of their arm."

"How many of them are there?" said Wargallow, at once the military commander, his entire attention focused on the coming assault.

"I cannot tell. But there are a great many. An army. They have been recalled. Mount Timeless is thronging with them. But as you see, it is night, and like most other creatures they sleep. Even as we speak."

"You think we should attack now?" said Wargallow.

Brannog had not been looking at him but at the girl, wondering if there could be any chance that this was a trap. Time and time again she had demonstrated her power and had used it for him and his Host. She must be an ally. But dare he risk everything on a word from her?

"It is not for me to say," Ruvanna answered the Deliverer. "But the attack must be soon."

Brannog's eyes narrowed. "Once we are inside, what then? Should we find the Sublime One and destroy him while he is locked in his working?"

The idea did not appal her. "It may not be easy to do that,

even though he's distracted. You think him evil enough to warrant execution?''

Wargallow snorted. ''If you are asking me that, girl, Brannog will tell you my answer. Ottemar Remoon might have spared Eukor Epta, the poison at the heart of his Empire. I killed him, or if you wish to be diplomatic, executed him. What the Sublime One plans is genocide.''

''But if there was a way to defeat him and yet control him,'' said Ruvanna, though she saw Brannog's suspicions at once. ''Do you still doubt my loyalty?'' She did not wait for an answer. ''I am loyal only to Omara. Before you, before anything else.''

''That is as it should be,'' said Brannog, but there was an edge to his voice that stung her.

''How could we control the Sublime One?'' said Wargallow.

''This rod of power—''

''What of it?'' said Brannog, too curtly.

''I have sensed its presence. Like a fire in the night, it glows from afar. Even here I can feel its latent power. There is so much that it could do. If the Sublime One should attempt to wield it—''

''He has promised it to Anakhizer,'' said Brannog.

''Yes, but he may be tempted to use it on us—''

''If we seize the rod,'' said Wargallow, ''can we use it? To control the Sublime One as you say?''

Ruvanna nodded solemnly. ''I think so.''

''And you could find it?''

''Yes.''

''Then it must be our goal,'' said Wargallow, sitting back He looked to Brannog for an objection, but the big man was staring hard at the girl. ''We are fortunate indeed, Ruvanna to have you with us,'' Wargallow added. He was smiling a her, finishing the water she had brought for him, but some how his expression filled her with a fresh fear. Did he, too distrust her? Could she convince none of them that she mean only to help them? Her anger would have flared, but for a instant she felt what they must have felt, seeing herself an her shadowed powers as they must. They had been throug so much already; their doubts were not so unreasonable.

She found an excuse to leave them and went out to the wolves which leapt up as she came and talked softly to them. To her surprise she found that Brannog had joined her. The wolves gave him an equally warm reception and he fondled them as though they were puppies. They licked at his huge hands.

"Do you see a change in him?" he asked Ruvanna.

"A little. I can't arrest it forever."

"How long?" The question came at her like a shaft.

"A month, perhaps."

He turned away, cursing under his breath.

"Brannog—"

He swung back to her, eyes ablaze in the firelight, and he looked more than ever like an Earthwrought, twice as large and twice as powerful.

"Brannog, I've searched, within me. If I could save him—"

He softened and put a hand out to touch her sleeve. "Forgive me, girl. Anger rules me now. As it has done more than once before. I use it to forge my strength, though it's not an easy steed to ride. I have seen too many good men destroyed. Far too many."

She wanted to hold him, to promise him every shred of power she possessed, but dared not move. "My power—" she began.

He broke from his reverie, gazing down on her. "Yes?"

"I've tried to understand it. Its dimensions. When I subdued the Child of the Mound, I was forced to control its mind. It was like a dark pit, filled with confusion. Its powers were deformed, almost useless. But I glimpsed things there. I tried to gather them. Some of its secrets I have stored. It is part of the process."

He frowned. She was not inventing this. He could see her attempt to concentrate, to understand what it was that moved inside her mind. "Go on."

"It would take many, many days to sift it all, and it would be a dangerous task. But I have a point at which to begin. The rod."

"But what would the Child know? Ah, wait, though. The rods were created by the Sorcerer-Kings—"

"Yes. I have been trying to learn something more of the rods. I went back into that dark pit and found something of their history. The metal from which the rods are cast is not of Omara.''

Brannog looked surprised. "What are you saying? From Ternannoc?"

"No, from another Aspect. The history is confused. I have no name for the Aspect. Trying to piece the memory of the Child together is like trying to hear one voice in the shouting of an army. But I know that the metal came from elsewhere. And I know also that the Sorcerer-Kings used the powers of that other place to forge the rods, and invest them with power. It was a dying Aspect, destroyed like so many in the working of the Hierarchs of Ternannoc. The rulers of the dying Aspect wanted to help the Sorcerer-Kings ward off the black power that had destroyed them, so they were glad to create the rods for Xennidhum. These rulers were called the Seraphs, the givers of light.''

Brannog guessed that there was far more to this history, one that Ruvanna wanted to give to him. She had closed her eyes as if searching the lost Aspect for the truths of its past. This was no deceit.

"Those long-lost rulers are no more. Only the rods they made have survived them, except for one. I think that is what was buried in the mind of the Child. The images are not clear, but it seems that one of the Seraphs came to Omara. His Aspect was one of water, threaded with strange islands I cannot describe. But as the Aspect perished, the survivor came to Omara. He was helped? I cannot see. But the Child's mind has no record of the Seraph's death. I think it may still be alive.''

"Do you know where?"

"Beyond the eastern edge of this continent. Out in the sea. It is a water dweller.''

Brannog was about to frame another question when he heard voices. Ulthor and Ogrund were approaching, calling out to Brannog as they did so. Brannog waved cheerfully and touched Ruvanna's arm lightly. "We'll speak more of this. For the moment there is other work. You may be right about our having to enter Mount Timeless tonight.''

She nodded and watched him go and because of the warmth he had at last exuded, the wrench was harder to bear. Her mind went back to the lost Seraph. It would have power. Should it be sought out? To what end? But already she knew.

Power to set back Wargallow's death even further. But what time was there? If she built up Brannog's hopes for his friend, what would he do? Turn from his cause here? How deep was his concern for Wargallow? Should I wait?

The wolves licked at her and she smiled at them, whispering. "Am I loyal to Omara first, or should I serve Brannog before her?" In the camp she could hear the fresh excitement of the Host. The talk now was of battle.

Brannog and Wargallow were with the captains. They were all eager to begin the assault, none wishing to remain on the outer slopes of the mountain. Wargallow told Brannog that there was no better time to unleash an army than when it was as hungry as the Host was now. "But use the girl," he added.

"Ruvanna?"

"Who knows better than you what powers these girls have?" It was not said unkindly.

"You're right, but—"

"She's loyal, Brannog. She's far more than that."

"What do you mean?"

Wargallow looked at him for a moment, but then shook his head with a wry grin. "Never mind. But we need her with us. Korkoris and Ulthor will prize a way in, but she'll find the rod."

Ulthor's thick arm encircled the shoulders of the tinier Icewrought. "That we will! Give us the word, Brannog Wormslayer. There's the scent of Exalted blood in the wind. Let them feel the anger of the Faithbreaker!" So had Ulthor named himself, and so was he called.

Soon the Host was ready, every member of it alert, awake to the task. Wargallow had been right. There would be no better time to carry the assault forward. They began the final climb, the Icewrought searching out each crack in the ice, the Earthwrought studying the bleak rocks. They were already very high up on the mountainside, and although the night winds raced in as if manipulated by vaster powers, the Host was untouched by them. A place was found which Korkoris promised would yield a way into Mount Timeless, a fault in the rocks that could be made to penetrate deep into its hostile walls. Ulthor grunted his approval and Ogrund nodded eagerly. Brannog could see that he in particular had

a deep regard for the big Earthwrought from the Far Below
and had relinquished to him the command; Ogrund had not
said as much, but Ulthor had that effect on those around him.
Brannog was pleased, for it took much of the strain from
Ogrund, who yet worried about his own worthiness. Also it
enabled Brannog to concentrate on Wargallow. But for Ulthor, Ogrund would have found Wargallow less easy to tolerate, Brannog thought.

The way was opened. It became a deep cleft, a dark gash
into which the Host filtered, one by one, orderly and silent.
Deep, deep into the rock it went, lit by the faint glow of the
Earthwrought and the crystal light of the people of Korkoris.
Wargallow was uncomfortable in such an enclosed place, and
he marvelled that Brannog moved here as much at home as
an earthworm, his eyes seeing everything, reading every vein
in the rock. How the man had changed! Why, he was truly
more Earthwrought than man. The girl, too, Ruvanna, was
an extraordinary creature. It was as though her mind inter-
acted with the rock as they passed through it, both giving
and receiving messages. And such a contrast to the high-bred
women of Ottemar's court!

Ruvanna could hear the distant beat of the heart of Mount Timeless. "We must go upward," she said at last. "The Body is the
high part of the mountain. It opens out to the sky. The Sublime
One does not hide himself down in the deep earth. He draws
power from the wind as much as from the rock."

"Dreaming of the surface," said Ulthor. "Just as we did."

"I did not mean to insult—"

"No insult to me, Ruvanna! We belong where we can see
the sky. Up!"

They wound up through narrow places, cracks in the stone,
and time had no meaning. Night had conquered the world, as
though daylight would not come again. For an age the Host
climbed steadily, its going muffled, and only Wargallow and the
Men made any sound, unable to be as silent as the rest of the
Host, who moved with the stealth of spirits. They came to a
wider place where they paused for something to refresh them.

"There are sentinels," said Ruvanna, "but most of the
Esoterics are with the Sublime One. The Convocation has
ceased for a short while, but only until daylight. The Sublime

One is drawing upon more power and his Esoterics are helping to feed it to him.''

''And the rod?'' said Wargallow.

''It's there, somewhere. I feel it yet. But the power within it frightens me.''

The rod, the rod, thought Ogrund. Is it all the Deliverer can think of? To think that our King is unsure of Ruvanna, and yet he puts his faith in a Man who once took pleasure in hunting us down into the earth!

They moved on, at last breaking out into a tunnel that was neither dusty nor forgotten. They sensed that the Exalted had been here recently. They must be in the outer regions of the Body. As they began the circling, moving around the tunnel complex, they heard footfalls ahead of them. The alarm had been raised at last: the Exalted knew that the walls of their mountain had been breached. A dozen of them abruptly appeared, brandishing their swords as if expecting an attack. Brannog guessed that they must have been aware of the Host beginning its ascent of the mountain. He wasted no time in hailing the Exalted. It was Ulthor who pushed to the fore, preparing to strike the first blow with his axe. There was a brief moment of silence, of calm, and then the Exalted rushed forward. They were confident, unused to fierce opposition, but as they broke like a wave on the front rank of the Host, they were cut down mercilessly, every one of them. Ogrund, Carac and Korkoris each took out an Exalted and Ulthor sliced his axe through two of the enemy before they could respond.

Wargallow was forced to move back, only now aware just how handicapped he was by the loss of his arm. Ruvanna drew him to one side as another score of Exalted came racing up a side tunnel. They were met by Brannog and his followers in a howl of frantic activity. Again the Host crashed into their enemies with a ferocity that took the exalted completely by surprise. But in the second encounter, Earthwrought lives were lost.

''I don't like this,'' Wargallow breathed, close to Ruvanna's ear. ''This could go on indefinitely. How many of these Exalted are there? And how far is it to our goal? Brannog fights like three men; I have seen him before now. But even he cannot go to the heart of this place if it is stuffed with defenders. We don't have a Korbillian to drive them aside.''

If it was a question to test her own power, she did not answer, trying instead to see how Brannog was faring. But she need not have feared for him. He had cut down three more Exalted and with his captains had beaten off the next wave of Exalted. He called the Host on and they poured forward, carrying Ruvanna and Wargallow with them along the tunnel in a living stream.

There were more groups of Exalted to clash with, and although more Earthwrought fell, the Exalted were able to do no more than hold back the tide of invaders for a brief period, most of them either falling or fleeing. Eventually the Host broke through into a larger series of chambers, and here the fighting was more violent, with scores more drawn into the conflict. The Men were glad of the room, and Danoth and his companions cut a bloody swathe through the Exalted who opposed them. Wargallow was careful to keep Ruvanna away from the worst of the fighting. The Host thrust back another great wave of Exalted, and then found itself on a wide pavement which curved away around the inner rim of the Body. Looking out over the parapet of this area, they saw the true formation of Mount Timeless.

The heart of the mountain was hollowed out, like the inside of a dead volcano, and high above them the upper mouth of the rim formed a circle of teeth against the sky, like a closing trap. Up from the central floor of this vast inner gulf rose another massive spire of rock, the upper crags of which were fashioned strangely into a parody of buildings, a deformed castle. There seemed to be no way across to this soaring edifice. Wargallow leaned on the parapet and craned his neck. The drop was sheer, bottomless. But as he looked along the curve of the wall, he saw a bridge, a single span of rock, arching across to the central spire, which must be the Body. He grinned to himself, thinking of the Direkeep and its lone bridge, which had kept all intruders at bay for years without number.

For the moment the battle seemed to have died down and Brannog came to Wargallow and Ruvanna. "That must be our goal," he said, pointing to the slender bridge. "The Exalted have fled to it. They will defend it and the gates beyond it in their droves. We must be vastly outnumbered."

Ruvanna nodded at the central spire. "The Heights, they call that place. The rod is there. As is the Sublime One."

Ulthor, his chest heaving, blood dripping from his axe, laughed grimly. "It's only a matter of time before we get across. We're cutting them down like wheat, no matter their numbers."

"But how much time do we have?" said Brannog. "Once the Convocation is truly completed, what of the Sublime One?"

"We must win the rod," said Ruvanna. "We could not have known the scale of the powers at work here."

"Then we must fight our way over quickly," said Brannog.

She nodded thoughtfully. "There may be another way for some of us. See, up there." She pointed and they followed her finger to see dark shapes flying high above the upper spires of the castle. Dawn had broken in the outside world and thin, orange light picked out the rim of the mountain, a circular halo.

Carac gasped. "I have seen those creatures! They fetched the rod from Goldenisle. The Exalted met them."

"Are they large enough to carry riders?" said Ulthor.

Carac snorted with disgust. "They would pull us to pieces with their beaks, or tear us to nothing with their talons."

"But," said Wargallow, "I was being prepared for one of them. A harness was brought. I recall it now—"

"They can be controlled," said Ruvanna. She pointed to the wolves, which had returned from their kills in the chamber. "Just as the wolves can."

"*You* can control them?" said Ulthor, astounded.

Wargallow grinned. "I have seen such power in a woman."

Brannog scowled at him. "You seem to forget Xennidhum, my friend. There we had an even larger army to carry up to the plateau. There were the dome plants, but it was as it is here. The Host cannot fly."

Ruvanna cut in. "No, but a few of us could—"

"As at Xennidhum," Wargallow said to Brannog, still smiling.

"If I could find the rod—" said Ruvanna.

"It is bound to be protected," said Brannog. "The Exalted must know its value! It would take the Host to prize it from them."

"At least let me see!"

"She's right," said Wargallow. "A small party could get across and go in without being detected. I'm prepared to go with her."

"Don't be a fool," snorted Brannog. "You can't fight."

"I killed three of them to get out of that place," Wargallow replied, but his smile had not faded.

"And I," said Ruvanna, her own eyes sparkling, "am hardly without power, am I?"

"You must lead the Host," Ulthor told Brannog. "And I will stand with you. If we launch a full offensive, it'll take the entire Exalted force to keep us at bay! Besides, I've no stomach for an aerial journey."

"Nor I," said Korkoris. "Spare me that!"

Brannog looked to Ogrund, who stood to attention at once, demanding to go by his very demeanour. Brannog nodded to him. "And you, Carac?"

"Of course. Someone's got to look after this oaf." He clapped an arm around Ogrund, who looked at him as if he would brain him on the spot. But he was secretly delighted that Carac would be with him.

"Danoth," Brannog said to the Man of Elderhold. "You are needed to control your warriors. But will Rannalgh go?"

"I will, gladly," said the scout, and Danoth nodded.

"Who else?" Brannog mused.

"It will be enough," said Ruvanna.

"Five of you? It seems pitifully few."

"They won't be expecting us."

"Quite," said Wargallow.

"But where are your flying creatures?" said Ulthor. "Do you expect to snap your fingers at them and have them perch on the wall for you?"

Ruvanna stared at him reproachfully, but Ulthor would not flinch. "Move back from the wall, all of you," Ruvanna insisted, and after a moment they had all done so. She leapt up onto the flat parapet and raised her hands, ignoring the horrific drop before her. Immediately Brannog was looking along the wall and road to see if there was any sign of the Exalted offensive, but they had all retreated to the bridge in the distance.

Already they could be seen massing there, readying for a determined defense that was going to be murderous to break.

Ruvanna called out strangely to the brightening vaults overhead and in a while a great shape began floating down toward her. At first it seemed that it must sweep her from her precarious perch, but it veered away, to be joined by other shapes. The creatures were ferocious, with huge, hooked beaks and claws that indeed looked capable of pulling a man apart. Ulthor and his companions needed no second bidding to stand well back. But five of the beasts had come in answer to Ruvanna's undoubted power.

"What are they?" said Brannog.

"Creatures of the Sublime One. They are from another age, part of the mystery that clings to Mount Timeless. Their minds are very simple, but they are fiercely obedient. It is an easy thing to speak to them. They think I speak to them for their master and will obey me. Even the Exalted can control them. In a moment the five who cross can mount. They will not harm us."

The creatures glided to the wall. They were twice as large as a man, with elongated wings that folded up as they landed. Ruvanna climbed fearlessly onto the back of the first and called out to the others. Wargallow was the first of them to mount.

Once it was clear that Wargallow and the girl would not be attacked by the creatures, Ogrund took his mount, as did Carac, and Rannalgh was the last. They all took a grip on the necks of their beasts, and in a moment Ruvanna swept up into the air. The others followed in a flurry of wings. Quickly they were airborne and high above the Host. Brannog gaped after them, but could not help a grin as Wargallow nodded almost casually. It was only as the figures grew small that Brannog felt a sudden cold stab: he may never see any of them again.

"Are they mad?" said Ulthor, his face as grim now as Ogrund's had ever been.

"Ruvanna will protect them," Brannog said automatically. "She has great power. I knew it at the Purging."

Brannog would have questioned him further, but Ulthor was already shouting fresh instructions to his warriors. "We'd better get across that bridge," he told Brannog with a wave of his axe. Brannog nodded, calling out to the Host. They responded eagerly, licking their wounds and moving forward. Brannog's wolves were beside him, their fangs bared at their enemies in the distance.

High overhead, curving upward on the thermals of the inner mountain, Ruvanna and her companions soared close to the black spires of the Body. Light shone from some of the slitted windows, green and scarlet as though other powers danced within, and the roar of air about them grew in volume as though the mountain resented their flight. Wargallow clung with his one arm to the neck of the beast; it felt cold beneath him, treacherous, yet it obeyed the unspoken commands of the girl. She was close beside him.

"If you find a way in, set us down!" he called.

They rose as one above the upper towers, still far down inside the scooped-out central cone of Mount Timeless; the outer walls hung over them like frozen clouds. Daylight poured in now, splashing on the jagged points of rock that stabbed up at it from the trunk of the citadel. As the creatures flew directly over it, their riders saw the inner Body, amazed as its heart was revealed. The core of the citadel was also hollow, a deep shaft, and from it came a thick beam of light and heat. As the birds were goaded by Ruvanna toward it, they shuddered, adjusting in mid-air as if caught in a strong wind. A wave of song rose up with the light and Ruvanna was forced to guide the birds away from the light's beam.

"We cannot enter the beam and descend!" shouted Wargallow above the growing noise. "It'll kill the birds!"

"The light comes from the Sublime One," Ruvanna called back. "He is at the base of it."

"We have to get to the towers. Find a stair!"

Ruvanna nodded. Further speech was impossible, for the sound now swelled awesomely, the song of the gods, volcanic and thunderous. Ruvanna managed to get her bird down to one of the higher rocks. She chose the outer facing slope of the citadel, away from the powerful light and sound, and soon the others had followed her. Once the riders had all dismounted, the birds were allowed to take off, and they made at once for the outer daylight, their screams of terror drowned out by the sound from below them.

When Ruvanna reached Wargallow, he looked suddenly drained, his face white. He clutched his ruined arm as if it gave him great agony.

"It will pass," he insisted. "It comes in waves. Hurry! We must get below."

She helped him to his feet and they joined the others, threading around the lower part of the tower before they could climb, spider-like, up to a ridge in the stonework. Light spilled over it in a green wave, and the roar of sound buffeted them anew.

Ruvanna shook her head; they could not go that way.

Carac pointed to the jet black rock on which they stood and by gestures made them understand that it was impenetrable. Ogrund nodded agreement.

"Window?" Wargallow mouthed, and again the climb began, sideways now. They had seen a dark window, not daring to attempt entry into one of those outpourings of light, but it was a tortuous crossing. The Earthwrought kept close to Wargallow, partly carrying him. His face had become ashen, his lips a bloodless gash. Carac could hardly believe that he still had the will to keep moving.

Ogrund made the dark sill first and dragged himself onto it like a dying insect. But he rolled over and dropped into the room beyond. A moment later he had helped Carac in. Ruvanna followed and Rannalgh helped the Earthwrought get Wargallow to safety. When they were all in the room, a dismal, empty cave, they sank down, their ears ringing, their strength sapped. Ruvanna feared for Wargallow. He would not be able to drive himself much further.

Rannalgh was leaning from the window, pointing far downward. "The bridge! Brannog's crossing it. Such a battle!"

All of them save Wargallow craned their necks to see. Below them they saw the mingled Host and Exalted, bodies falling from the chaos of battle into the black embrace of the abyss. It was impossible to judge which side held an advantage, but Ruvanna could see that it would be a bloody and slow affair. The time it would buy her would cost them dear.

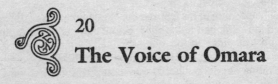

20
The Voice of Omara

A LOW DOOR LED from the disused chamber. It was not locked. Ogrund opened it cautiously, but no light spilled in from the corridor beyond. He nodded to the others and went out. They followed him. Wargallow had recovered some of his strength, but he moved slowly, his face screwed up against the pain. Each step he took was like a wound. Ruvanna tried to decide which way they should go. There were stairs ahead, twisting down into the gut of the rock like the trail of a worm. They had to go down in the near dark, so it was a slow descent, though no one barred their way. Silence had mercifully become their companion.

When they reached another door, they found it locked, but Ogrund used his club to break the lock, Carac ready to attack anyone who might be beyond, and Rannalgh holding his own sword ready for a killing thrust. The wood of the door splintered and the door swung outward, but no one rushed to see who these intruders might be. Still the stairway spiralled down into the shadows, until there was another door, also locked. Again Ogrund broke its lock and again no one came. The stairs stopped at a corridor, this much wider than the one they had been following, and it sloped to the right, into the center of the citadel. From its polished marble floor, it looked to be regularly used, and there were glowing lamps at intervals along it.

"Do you sense the rod?" whispered Wargallow.

"Only vaguely," said Ruvanna. "Since we've entered the citadel, things are distorted. I cannot guess how far down we have come, nor how long it has taken us. The forces at work here are outside nature. I am not sure what controls them. But the rod is here somewhere.''

Beyond the corridor there were numerous intersections cut into the black rock. Some went upward, some curved away on a level, and others became stairways to yet lower levels. All hinted at immense distances. It was impossible to judge which one to take. Finally Ruvanna's instinct led her downward, and in an abandoned chamber they found one of the Esoterics. Stretched across a slab of black stone, he was dead, the front of his tunic soaked with blood. Ogrund examined him, turning away with a look of pure disgust.

''No sword did this,'' he said. ''His flesh has been scorched.''

Mystified, they moved on and at the junction of another passageway found the corpses of three more of the Esoterics. All of them had been badly charred, and one was headless. Ruvanna drew back at the sight of him. ''The rod!'' she whispered. ''It was used to do this.''

Wargallow's eyes narrowed, closing out his pain for a moment. ''But these are the Sublime One's most high servants. Who could have done this? Surely Brannog could not have broken through.''

''There is terrible evil at work here,'' breathed Ruvanna, unable to conceal her terror.

''Could Anakhizer's servants have arrived?'' said Wargallow, looking about him as if he would see the source of the dreadful killings.

''I don't know,'' said Ruvanna. ''But why should he destroy the Esoterics? The Sublime One has already promised him support.''

They crept lower and now found themselves in a part of the citadel that must be the center of Esoteric activity. Plants grew in carefully nurtured profusion, tiny fountains played, and gentle light broke through from unseen sources above, though not the screaming light of the core of the citadel. Wargallow recognized the walls, the lofty ceilings. In such a place he had lost his arm. But there were more Esoteric corpses and on one wall a huge black stain, as if fire had been directed at it. Ruvanna went to the mark and touched it with her fingers. She withdrew them, wincing.

"The rod?" said Ogrund and she nodded.

"Here!" called Carac, and when they joined him in yet another tall chamber, he was pointing to a pair of huge doors, etched with strange glyphs that stood out like knots in the wood. Ruvanna went hesitantly to the doors. She pressed her ear to them. Her eyes widened.

"I hear them, singing," she said. "Esoterics. They're gathered."

"The Convocation," said Ogrund.

Wargallow faced the doors, gathering his last reserves of strength. The doors mocked him with their vast height, but he pointed to them. "You must break them down."

Rannalgh barred the way. "The Sublime One may be beyond! There are but five of us! Five!"

Carac looked at Wargallow. "Whoever wields the rod may also be there."

Wargallow shook his head. "A killer of Esoterics? No, that must be their sanctuary. Ruvanna, if you have the power, break down the door."

"The rod is not there," she said. "But the Sublime One is. I can feel him."

"We should await Brannog," said Ogrund. "What could we gain by blundering in? Rannalgh is right."

Wargallow leaned on the door, suddenly tired. Of course, it was ludicrous to go in as they were. Why was his thinking so clouded? "The rod has been taken? How far? Is it still in the citadel, Ruvanna?"

Ruvanna looked all about her, like a blind person trying to guide herself by sound. Her eyes went upward. "Sometimes it seems to be above us, and at others below."

"Then we must split up," said Wargallow.

"To achieve what!" snapped Ogrund. "What can two or three of us do if we meet the thief? You have seen what he can do!"

Wargallow drew in a deep breath and gritted his teeth against a fresh attack of pain. "We have to find the rod."

Ogrund would have retorted, but the sound from beyond

the great doors cut off. Silence swallowed them, its intensity stunning.

Rannalgh pointed to the doors. "It's stopped."

"The singing is over," said Carac.

Ruvanna put her ear to the doors. "Then the Sublime One must be awake. The Convocation is over."

BRANNOG HELD his wolves in check. Their great chests heaved, flecked with the blood of their victims, and Brannog, too, drew in gulps of air, his arm heavy with killing. Ulthor wiped mingled blood and sweat from his face and a dozen others in the first rank were glad of a respite. Yards away, across the bridge, the gathered Exalted stood, their faces haggard, their swords down, waiting. The fighting had been terrible, close-packed and furious. Countless victims had fallen into the void, many of them Exalted. But Brannog had lost valued companions, though this was not the moment to mourn them. The Exalted could see, however, that the Host meant to smite them aside, whatever the cost. As with all battles, there had come a point when the outcome was known. The Host could not be held.

Brannog pointed with his bloody sword. "Open the doors to your citadel. I have not come to harm your master. Nor will I harm the Esoterics. But I will have an audience."

There was a long pause, during which silence came like a wave on both sides. It was broken by the moans of the wounded and the coughing of the exhausted. Between Brannog and the gates there were still countless scores of the Exalted, but they all listened to him now.

A single Exalted came forward. It was Aa-Vulk, their commander. "What do you want with our master if it is not to attack? You have an army at your back."

"The Sublime One plans war," replied Brannog. "You hear the Convocation, and how the Earthwrought of all nations are called to arms. But there is a common foe, and it is not Mankind! I have come to teach the Sublime One that Man is your ally."

"Aye, with steel and force!" was Aa-Vulk's angry reply.

"I will place my steel in his hand, as a weapon for him to use," shouted Brannog. "There are warriors here from the lands of ice, and from the Far Below. All willing to fight for the Sublime One. But not against Men. Your true enemy lies in the far west, beyond the Deepwalks.''

Aa-Vulk spat and would have called out a denial, but there were a number of arguments breaking out behind him. ''Silence!'' he screamed, but he was shouted down. Suddenly a shaft thrust from the packed front ranks of the Exalted, running Aa-Vulk clean through. He sagged to his knees, and two of his warriors rushed to him, smiting him and pushing him over the edge of the span, laughing as his body twisted over and over, to be welcomed by the dark below.

''The battle is over!'' shouted another of the Exalted. ''Cease fighting, Brannog, and you can have your audience.''

''Throw your arms after your leader,'' shouted Ulthor, and the Exalted began to argue again.

''None of you shall be harmed,'' Brannog told them.

At last they were ready to capitulate. ''We will do so, but your wolves must remain outside the citadel.''

Brannog nodded, talking softly to the great beasts. ''Very well.''

There was more agitated discussion, but the Exalted tossed away their weapons and the gates to the citadel were opened. Ulthor stood close to Brannog as they entered, ready to defend him against treachery. But as they saw the depleted numbers of the Exalted, they knew just how dispirited they were. Dozens of them had been dragged back inside, wounded and maimed. They had no stomach left for a fight and were relieved to have survived the affair on the bridge. Brannog's Host, itself reduced, moved into the citadel, not eager to fight on, but prepared to do so if it had to.

''Take us to the Sublime One, at once,'' said Brannog to the Exalted leaders.

''Careful, sire,'' said Ulthor. ''We have no more than our wits to bargain with.''

Brannog leaned closer to him. ''More than that if Ruvanna finds what she came for.''

''You would use it?''

''As a threat. No more than that if I could help it.''

They followed the self-elected delegation of Exalted, descending a broad flight of stairs that dropped gradually into an eerie brightness. Sonorous music came from beyond, but there was no sign of the Esoterics. The Exalted were uncomfortable, surprised by this, and the unasked questions on their faces made Brannog wonder what was amiss. They arrived at a wide chamber which had the stench of death clinging to it. There was blood on the floor and the walls were charred. Several Esoterics had been slain, their crumpled bodies seemingly having been subjected to great force. The Exalted saw them and dashed away into the corridors before they could be stopped.

"Leave them," Brannog told Korkoris, who was about to take a detachment of Icewrought and give chase. Brannog studied the fallen Esoterics. "Who has done this?" he said, amazed.

"Ruvanna?" Ulthor whispered.

"I cannot believe it," said Brannog equally softly. "Unless their lives were in great peril. We must find them."

They left the chamber of death and came to another, beyond which were two huge wooden doors. These had been flung open and light streamed out, thick and viscous as a liquid.

"The music," said Ulthor. "It has ceased."

The Host drew back from the wall of light, wary of it. Brannog shielded his eyes and tried to peer into it, but it was overpowering. He stood in the great doorway with Ulthor and Korkoris, the Host edging forward, committed to following.

"They're here!" gasped Korkoris. "Ruvanna and the others!" He pointed, now able to discern five silhouettes in the chamber beyond, their shadows streaming out behind them like lines of black energy. But neither Brannog nor his companions could enter: the light was like a wall.

Before them, in the chamber, the five figures were absolutely still, their muscles clamped, their senses almost suspended. Wargallow felt no pain: there was only a void, bright but endless, empty. He was no longer aware of his companions, nor were they aware of him or one another. They were trapped in the moment, locked rigidly.

Ruvanna had led them through into this chamber when its doors had opened. The music had ceased, but she knew that inestimable power confronted her. The Voice of Omara, its living embodiment, the Sublime One. Her own senses were not numbed; her own power throbbed into life. She, alone, saw through the abyss of light into the chamber. It was the largest she had ever seen, beyond imagining, its remote walls lost in a haze as though she had stepped into a subterranean subworld within the shell of Omara. And before her was a huge column of light that went upward to the sky itself and down into whatever furnaces powered this world. Spreading away from this column, like the spokes of a wheel, were the Holy Roads, wide paths that led out under the earth to every point of the compass. Light streamed down them, so that their far horizons could be seen, mocking logic. Even now Ruvanna could hear the far away reverberations of sound as the earthsongs sped down those Roads, calling to the children of Omara. And just as she heard the vanishing music, so she heard the coming of the Earthwrought, their myriad tread, for they had answered the Convocation, no matter how far away they were. Moving to the edge of distance, they came along the Roads, thousands of them, raising their own voices in song. Here, in this measureless place, they would bow to the Sublime One, eager to carry war with them in his name, and against whom he chose.

Ruvanna closed with the light. It had fallen silent and its intensity had waned. Within it there was a single being, no larger than herself, a gray shape that coalesced and pulled from the light its own substance, like layers of vitality. It sat on a simple throne cut from a slab of black stone, and it wore the humblest of garments. Ruvanna moved toward it, knowing the veil of light would not harm her. Then she saw the face of the Sublime One and almost stumbled. It was that of a woman.

Her features were perfection, her body that of a divinity; it seemed to exude light. She had eyes that shone and pierced the heart. She raised a hand, langorously, her smile ambiguous. "I knew you would find me," she said, and her voice was pure music, rippling on the air. Ruvanna felt herself dizzied by it, as though by strong perfume. She must fight this, she knew, or succumb to the powers here, and bend before it. None of the others could help her now; they were like stone.

"You see my children answering my call," said the Sublime One, standing up now, lithe as a jungle cat, her hair like a cascade of gold. "All your attempts to hold them back have failed." She smiled with glowing confidence, as though with one sweep of her perfect hand she could wipe away a world.

"I mean them no harm," said Ruvanna, and after the voice of the golden woman, her own voice sounded brittle, cold.

"Yet you have destroyed my servants with cruel fire."

Ruvanna gasped. "What? You mean the rod?"

Still that face of exquisite beauty smiled at her. "Of course—"

"Don't you know who it was?"

A suggestion of a frown moved on the face of the Sublime One. "Why do you pretend confusion?"

Ruvanna looked about her in desperation. Whoever had the rod must be loose. But where? "It was not us. We came here to steal it, to prevent you from fulfilling your pact with Anakhizer."

"So that you could avoid the destiny of your kind?"

"Then you meant it? To sacrifice us all?"

"Omara will live. The vile power that seeks her blood will be turned aside. Your kind will be the means to that end."

"But if Anakhizer's servants have the rod, why are they destroying your servants, the Esoterics?"

Again the Sublime One frowned, this time with deeper uncertainty. "He does not have the rod. Not yet. It is you who have purloined it."

Ruvanna laughed, but it was a sharp bark, mirthless. "This is foolish! You say I have the rod, and I say you have it. Neither of us has it. So where is it? Can you not see into your own citadel?"

A sudden look of fury shook the Sublime One, and although it changed her beauty, contorting it into a refinement of anger, of sheer will, it took nothing from her splendor. She moved slowly, hands raised as she surveyed the remote hordes of Earthwrought who came nearer down the Holy Roads, the sound of their singing clear on the air. "Nothing can be changed! It has begun. Omara has spoken!"

Something inside Ruvanna recoiled at that, and she felt a sudden stab of pain, a bursting of light. All the powers that

she had ever glimpsed, tapped, now surged. Omara! Casting
out its adopted offspring? Ruvanna saw again the visions of
Brannog's Purging, the shared secrets. Omara had sent them.
But no! It had been the Sublime One, speaking as the Voice
of Omara. The very thought shattered a last inner barrier,
and Ruvanna staggered as if a dam had burst, flooding her
with new knowledge so vast and so deep that she could not
contain it. She flailed about like one drowning, the images
about her tossing her like waves, the waters riddled with rap-
ids, sharp fangs of thought that threatened to break her with
madness. But she drove her own will like a wedge into them,
dragging out cohesion, understanding. Grinding up the lies.

And Omara spoke to her.

It was not the beautiful, fanatical creature before her, the
Sublime One, that spoke, but a softer, deeper voice, from far
within.

Ruvanna had unlocked this voice when she had understood
the truth. The Sublime One had tried to use the Circle of
Preceptors to destroy Brannog, but Omara had saved him,
through Ruvanna. The sacrifice, the giving up of the aliens,
the outsiders, was the Sublime One's will. She had been in-
fused with the power of Omara, the living will of the world,
its embodiment, and spoke for all the Earthwrought nations.
But the centuries had corrupted her. Her loyalty had become
a fanatical faith, a drive for survival that was blind, deaf.
Fashioned over so much time, it had become a sword, and
the hand that wielded the sword swung it without true vision.

Omara had at last understood this. And had questioned the
acts of the Sublime One.

"Who am I?" Ruvanna whispered to the awesome gulf of
power. "And what do I carry? Brannog feared me because
of it. You can hide it from us no longer."

The answer came, wrapped in the eddies of time. Ruvanna
had been the child of a young village girl who had loved and
been loved by an Earthwrought from the forests of Elderhold.
They had lived together, apart from the villages, until one
day the Earthwrought had been killed in a hunting accident.
His young mate, stricken with grief, took her own life, her
blood running into the earth of the forest. The infant daughter
was left to crawl alone among the lost paths of Elderhold.

Omara tasted the blood and heard the cries of the child, the creature who was part Earthwrought, part Woman, her blood mixed, alien yet of Omara. There were many such hybrids in the world, and they could not be ignored. Omara put power into the child, to study how it felt and thought. With this power, the infant had found its way to a village. And as the years had gone by, Omara fed on Ruvanna.

Ruvanna knew that the time of the testing had come, just as Brannog had faced his Purging. The Sublime One stood before Ruvanna, the embodiment of Earthwrought power, the raw, untamed spirit of Omara, the animal hunger for survival, the talons. Ruvanna must test that power with that which she had been given. But how to use it? Would she, like the Sublime One, use it to sacrifice her enemies? Put the Sublime One and all her followers to the sword? Or should it be mercy, union?

Ruvanna gasped as if a door had opened to allow in a blast of winter. The Sublime One watched her with growing interest, but without a trace of fear.

"If you have come to me for mercy," said the Sublime One, "you have had a wasted journey. This force that uses Anakhizer, this power from outside the Aspects of Omara, lusts for physical being. It can only achieve it through the taking of life, raw power. It would have devoured *all* life in Omara to *become* Omara. I will change that, divert its purpose. I will give it life, but not Omara. I will give it Ternannoc! There it will enclose itself, the gates to Omara shut to it forever. So you see, how can I spare you and your kind? How can I fail my children?"

"Enclosed," nodded Ruvanna. "Just as you are enclosed in your Body. A timeless world beyond which you cannot see. For which you cannot speak."

The Sublime One seemed unmoved.

"If you did, you would see who has come to challenge your right to speak for Omara. King Brannog, a Man, leads them. His Host is made up of Earthwrought, Icewrought, Ulthor's followers from the Far Below. And more. Stonedelvers in the West. Men come with him. They defy your decree. And they will not be denied a voice."

"I do not hear them," said the Sublime One with utter disdain.

"*I* will be that voice!" said Ruvanna and the echoes of her own words sounded inside her. Was *this* why she was here? To speak out for Omara, to be its conscience?

"How dare your presume!" snarled the Sublime One, wheeling, fingers extended, but as she did so, her face suffused with pain and she staggered, leaning on her throne.

Ruvanna stepped forward, unable to prevent herself. "What's wrong?"

"My Esoterics. So few of them left. Dead." As the Sublime One collapsed, falling into the throne, face screwed up in agony, her thoughts gushed out, unbidden and unprotected. The Esoterics were her body, extensions of her being, her power. And the rod had been destroying them. The Sublime One was *wounded*. For the moment she could not use her power, only in an attempt to regenerate her strength. But as she tried, her control slithered away, and a transformation began. Ruvanna had to stand back from it as the shape before her changed. The beautiful girl bloated, her arms thickening, her face stretching as the bones beneath it grew, and the entire body convulsed, its size trebling. In a matter of minutes it was over. The Sublime One had lost the guise she had chosen for herself, the guise she had sought to use to mock the Men who were coming to challenge her. Ruvanna saw the Sublime One as she was. An Earthwrought of immense build, too vast to move, a creature whose age defied calculation. Like a gigantic spider sitting at the heart of its fatal web of power, she sat astride the throne, eyes sunk deep in her huge face.

How easily I could kill her, Ruvanna realized. It was Omara who was showing her this. A simple blow would end it. The Sublime One is defenseless! This is the true test. But it went deeper yet, and Ruvanna felt herself sway as the truth hit her with the force of a physical blow. Omara had passed her own judgment. It had studied this conflict of ideals. And it had chosen. Ruvanna not only had the opportunity to destroy the Sublime One, *she could replace her.* Become the new Voice of Omara.

She looked about her, terrified. The Host stood at the door

to the chamber, immobile as sculpture. Brannog, Ulthor, Wargallow, all statuesque and oblivious. And still the Earth-wrought were marching down the Holy Roads, countless, all ready to meet their ruler, to obey her will. Carry the war to the west. Ruvanna was transfixed by the realization of what she could do. The power offered to her now made her weak.

The light in the column had faded to a gentle glow, its power dimmed. Omara waited. As it did so, the frozen figures came to life. Wargallow lurched and dropped to one knee. It was to him that Brannog ran first. He put his arm around the Deliverer and got him to his feet, staring helplessly at Ruvanna. She looked equally helpless.

"The rod," said Wargallow through his pain. "Where is it?"

His words stunned her. She had almost forgotten it! For all the power that had been wavering here in this chamber, for all the searching of ideals, there was still the rod. Who had it?

Ruvanna closed her eyes and tried to search the stone around her for some clue. Within moments she had sensed the rod, somewhere high above them. It blazed like a living brand, through rock and earth. Ruvanna used Omara's power to locate it.

"You see it!" cried Brannog, realizing.

She nodded. "Yes. Up there."

Ulthor was beside them, glaring at the huge figure of the Sublime One. She watched them as if drugged, hardly moving. "Can that be the Voice of Omara? That parody?"

"The rod has done that to her," said Ruvanna. "It has been killing the Esoterics, her life force."

"Then she'll listen to us?" persisted Ulthor.

"She has," said Ruvanna and felt a renewed wave of fear at what she had learned. To become the Voice—but she could not contemplate it. There was too much in that, it filled the mind, crushed it. "The rod! We have to regain the rod. If not, Anakhizer will destroy us all."

"Search for it, quickly," said Wargallow. "Leave me here, but find the rod."

Ruvanna nodded and led Brannog and those who would go up the stairs beyond the doors. The Host followed in as or-

ganized a fashion as they could. Only one figure did not go
with them. It was Ogrund. He came to the side of Wargallow,
his war club in his hand.

"I fought with you at Xennidhum," he said, his face grim.

"I remember you, Ogrund," said Wargallow, his lips
white. "And Ygromm. I have seen his death a hundred
times."

"And I. Why did he die for you?"

Wargallow looked at him, though without fear. "And have
you hated me since that day?"

Ogrund's hand tightened on his war club. "Your survival
was no consolation to me."

Does he mean to kill me? Wargallow suddenly wondered.
Has he kept his hatred of me so silent all this time? "Ygromm
did not throw his life away for me. He did it for Brannog."

Ogrund scowled. "For the cause?"

"We were an army, Ogrund. Ygromm was not the only
one who died—"

"You think so little of his sacrifice?"

"*No!* Do you?"

Ogrund stiffened. I cannot kill this Man.

"Go with your master, Ogrund. Find the rod."

But Ogrund squatted down, shaking his head. The silence
closed in around them.

In the corridors far above them, the hunt went on noisily,
with dozens of chambers searched. There was much chaos
uncovered, and more bloody deaths. Whoever had the rod
was using it ruthlessly and with absolute abandon.

Carac suddenly tugged at the arm of Ruvanna. "Mistress!
We were foolish not to think of it—the birds! It must be."

"Of course!" Ruvanna cried and Brannog looked puzzled.
"The thief is making for the birds. How else could he escape
from here?"

"You controlled them before," said Brannog. "Can you
do it again?"

Ruvanna answered by closing her eyes in concentration. In
a moment she was making strange, low sounds. Her eyes
opened, but she stared at something invisible. "I see him,"
she said. "A man and one other. A girl. They are on the

parapet, high above. But the birds have heard me. They will not come to him.''

"Then we have him!" said Brannog, and Ulthor gave a shout of triumph.

"Be careful," said Ruvanna. "He has the rod." As she said it, she winced.

"What is it?" said Carac, instantly steadying her.

"It is nothing," she lied. But she had felt another's pain. It was Wargallow. He had to have attention, and quickly. "Brannog," she said. "Go up there with great care. You cannot miss the tower and its occupants. I have to go back—"

"Back?"

"It's Wargallow."

Brannog faced her, a rare fear in his eyes. The guilt at having left him threatened him. "How long?"

"You must let me go to him. If not, he won't survive the day."

"Then go! Tell him I'll bring him the rod!" Brannog forced a laugh, moving away quickly, and the Host followed him.

Ruvanna went back, the way down seemingly far longer than the climb had been. When she finally reached the Sublime One's chamber, Ogrund stood up. Wargallow saw her and nodded to her, his eyes misty with pain. At once she bent to him, clasping his damaged arm to her breast and muttering something to herself. Wargallow felt the easing of the pain at once. He closed his eyes, unconscious.

"Is he dead?" said Ogrund.

Ruvanna shook her head. "No. Not for a long while yet. I will give him strength."

"I thought his death would give me pleasure," confessed Ogrund.

She looked at him sharply.

"But when he dies, my master will mourn him as he has mourned no other."

Ah, but there you are wrong, dear Ogrund, thought Ruvanna. There is one he mourns yet. "He's an ally, Ogrund. Whatever happened before. Guard his life as you guard mine."

"Mistress—"

"We are one. You must do it."

Ogrund nodded. It was as Wargallow had said.

Ruvanna looked at the Sublime One, having almost forgotten her. Would she recover, if allowed to? If Ruvanna did not accept her mantle, what then? If I do not become the Voice. And I may not. Omara forgive me, but there is another path I may have to travel.

PART FIVE

BAY OF SORROWS

21

The Rod

"KEEP MOVING! HURRY!" Mourndark called from the steps above Dennovia. Although he held the glowing rod firmly, there was a hint of desperation about him. Dennovia responded at once, jerking as though he had touched her with that fire. Since the first killings below, she had been trembling with an inner fear that she tried not to let him see. He had moved about Mount Timeless with a fresh anger, brutally using the power of the rod, destroying everyone he found, laughing at their death agonies. He had searched for the Sublime One, intent on delivering the death blow there, too, but somehow the mountain had foiled him with its dislocation of time and space. Although Mourndark seemed to be closing in on the ruler of this place, he could not find him. Dennovia became more appalled by each act of violence, and took no pleasure from the senseless slaughter. With her disgust, her inner fury also welled. Mourndark had been afraid to touch the rod until he knew it was safe. If it had not been, she would have been the first to die. She was nothing to him, and knew it now. He almost despised her: he had his weapon, and with it could do untold damage. What could stand in his way, what could withstand the irresistible?

She followed him upward, the stairs spiraling to the top of another of the countless towers. As she went, she clutched to her the box of instruments, though they were of no comfort to her. She acted from instinct, trying to be inconspicuous, not wanting his attention for a moment, but as he reached the top of the stairway, he swung round. He had no patience with her tiredness and looked at her now with contempt, almost disdain, as if he was annoyed with himself for ever having possessed her.

"I'll waste no more time on this empty rock. There is a simple way off it." He motioned for her to join him, impatient to leave. They had come out onto the flat top of the tower, where there were a few steps leading up to a wall surrounding it. Part of the wall had no parapet, a landing place for the great birds of the tower. A sound nearby made them both turn and Dennovia felt her belly contract in expectation of another killing. Mourndark raised the rod, seeing one of the Esoterics approaching.

"This is a forbidden place," said the latter, his normally serene face puzzled.

"Bring the birds," said Mourndark coldly. "Or I'll use this." He turned and unleashed a bolt of power that slapped into a wall and turned it to a smoldering, charred gash.

The Esoteric gasped, staring at the rod in utter disbelief.

"Bring the birds! You have the power to do it," snarled Mourndark. "And then you can take us away from your holy mountain."

"What have you done?" said the Esoteric, suddenly looking down, as though he could see into the rock and the horrors there.

Mourndark unleashed another bolt and reduced more of the wall to ruin. "Hurry!"

The Esoteric went quickly to the open parapet and raised his arms. Dennovia watched him anxiously. She turned to Mourndark. "Leave me here," she said. "You have no use for me now."

He glared at her as if he would strike her. "Hold close my blades. Press them close to your heart."

The Esoteric looked at them, his face distraught.

"What is it?" snapped Mourndark, striding to him.

"They will not answer me. I have called them. Usually they obey and come. But it is as though another will, stronger than mine, holds them off. The Sublime One—"

Mourndark laughed. "Is that so? Then I'll burn my way down until I find your ruler—"

"Please! You cannot—"

Mourndark pointed the rod at the Esoteric and Dennovia turned away, dreading the flash of power, the stench of burnt flesh. But Mourndark did not use the rod yet. "I'll reduce you, limb by limb, if you don't bring the birds. You have the power. Don't try to deceive me."

The Esoteric returned to the parapet. Mourndark grabbed Dennovia, pulling her with him. They stood below the Esoteric as he again raised his arms and attempted to bring the birds. But there was silence in the sky, and no movement.

"They have departed," said the Esoteric at last.

"Very well," breathed Mourndark, and he ended the life of the Esoteric as he had ended the lives of so many others. Dennovia twisted to one side, dropping to her knees. She felt exhaustion dragging at her, her body shaking. Suddenly it seemed cold up here and she felt exposed, as if her own death crept slowly, gloatingly toward her. Was Mourndark mad? she wondered. Had the power in the rod twisted his mind so much that he had become a slave to it? But she knew his lusts, his restless craving. The rod was only an outlet to those things that had always gnawed away inside him. He was fulfilling desires he had nurtured all his life.

He stood over her, not seeing her, directing his frustration elsewhere, his eyes studying the skies, willing the birds to return, though he knew they would not. Very well, he would go back into the citadel and burn his way out of it.

While he had been exhorting the Esoteric to search for the birds, Brannog and his companions were moving upward in search of him, although they were unaware of who the man was who carried the rod. They went upward cautiously, keeping as silent as the stone about them, so that no one would have guessed that so many of them were moving, or even breathing. Ruvanna had told them the way, and Mount Timeless did nothing to confuse them, instead helping them to find their goal.

On the spiral stairs, Brannog paused. "This is the tower. He is above us." They took a tighter hold on their weapons as Brannog climbed upward like a cat.

He heard a sudden flare of sound, the walls flashing for a moment and knew that the rod had been used, possibly in another killing. Brannog motioned his forces to either side of him, signalling them to fan out and surround the top of the tower, moving along its upper wall. They did so at once. Brannog took the right-hand side of the wall, crawling along the battlements, ducking down so that he would not be seen. It took no more than a few moments for his Host to be in place, in a formation that overlooked the level top of the tower. Through broken stones in the low wall, they could look down and see the one they had pursued.

The tall Steelmaster was standing beside a young woman of exceptional beauty, although her hair was disheveled and her face streaked with tears. She was on her knees, as if the man had beaten her. Behind them were the remains of another victim, smoke curling above it. Brannog studied the man, the mask of iron cruelty that was his face, but he did not recognize him. He held the rod, and it glowed with a rich, vibrant scarlet, as if it had been filled with the blood of all those it had destroyed. The power within it was vast, Brannog knew this instinctively. It almost seemed to reach out for him and stab at his thoughts.

Korkoris was beside him, belly to the ground. "That rod has power beyond his control. How are we to deprive him of it?" he whispered.

"I don't know," said Brannog. Now that he had seen, he had no ready answer.

Ulthor's face loomed over the shoulder of the Icewrought. "We can rush him from all sides. He'll never kill us all. Some of us will get through."

"We can do it as a last resort," said Brannog. "I want as few deaths as possible."

"This is no time for sentiment, Brannog!"

"We will wait," said Brannog, with finality.

Ulthor growled impatiently, fingering his axe, but he bit back a retort. He tried to peer through a gap in the wall, and as he did so, a rock loosened itself and before Ulthor could retrieve it, it had slipped beyond his grasp. In a moment it clattered on the courtyard below.

Mourndark turned to it at once, his rod extended. "Who's there! Show yourself, or I'll turn the entire wall to ashes."

Brannog could see Ulthor's horror, but also that the brave Earthwrought was going to do something dramatic and hope less. As Ulthor stood up, so did Brannog, and all around the wall his companions did likewise. Mourndark pivoted, taking in the entire gathering. As he did so, he grinned.

"Well, well. A pretty trap. But it will do you no good."

"If you use the rod," called Brannog, "you'll kill some of us. But you'll die with us. Who are you? And what business do you have here?"

Mourndark snorted, "Are you the commander of this rabble?"

"I am Brannog."

Mourndark had leveled the rod at the chest of the huge man above him. "I know your name from somewhere."

"I am from the western shores."

"You are a Man, but you have the look of one of the earth people. You obviously enjoy their company. Bring them down from the wall. All of them."

Brannog nodded to his companions, and they began to file down to the flat top of the tower, the entire company facing Mourndark in silence. They had gently fanned out.

"Mount Timeless is full of surprises," said the Steelmaster. "What possible use could you be to the Sublime One?"

Ulthor had, by using no more than his eyes, signaled to Brannog and other key Earthwrought that they must risk everything in an attack on this man. Brannog had signaled agreement, but the signal must come from him.

"We came to the Convocation," he said. "The entire Earthwrought nation is being gathered."

Mourndark's face glowed as he studied the rod. "Is that so? Ah, yes, the war with the west. The one you call Anakhizer."

Brannog frowned. "Are you not his servant?"

Mourndark read the surprise on the big man's face. "You thought I was? No, I serve no one. Once I had a master, but he was killed."

For a moment there was a stir of hope within Brannog. "Then if you are no ally to Anakhizer, are you his enemy?"

"Possibly. I know very little about him, or his plans. I have been a prisoner for some time. Since—ah, but I *do* remember your name, Brannog." Mourndark smiled, but there was evil in it.

"A prisoner?" said Brannog. "Where? Here?"

"I was incarcerated in the Direkeep. By your ally, Bran-nog. Brannog, who fought at Xennidhum, of which I have heard so much."

"The Direkeep," Brannog echoed softly. Who *was* this man?

"I doubt if you know me, Brannog. Wargallow will have seen to that. I am Mourndark, the Steelmaster."

Brannog nodded slowly. "Yes, I know of you." The cre-ator of the Deliverers. A man Wargallow trusted less than a viper.

"It has done Wargallow no good in the end. By now I imagine he must be dead."

Brannog kept very still. What did Mourndark know? "You have killed him?"

"You misunderstood me," Mourndark laughed. "No, I have not set eyes on him since he came here. But your ruler, the Sublime One, struck off his killing steel. Had he asked me, I could have told him such a blow would be fatal."

Brannog felt the blood draining from his face. "Why is that?"

"There's no way back for Wargallow. Even I, the Steel-master, who know more about the body than any other, could not save him. The damage is irreparable. The Sublime One unwittingly pronounced a death sentence." Mourndark said it with relish, enjoying the anguish of the man before him. "And besides, why should I save Wargallow? If I had found him, I would have prolonged his suffering, not ended it."

A look passed between Ulthor and Brannog then, and as it did so, Dennovia saw it, guessing what was about to hap-pen. There would be more death, wholesale slaughter. These people had no idea what Mourndark carried. Everything in the girl that had ever shied from the Steelmaster's contempt rose up in protest.

"No!" she screamed as the rod rose, and at the same moment she flung the box she carried with as much of her remaining strength as she could at Mourndark. The edge of the box cracked against his shins and he flung up his arms in reaction. Pain raced through him at the blow, shocking his nerves. His fingers opened like a sprung trap and the rod of power tumbled through the air, a bar of livid light. The box of blades snapped open as it struck his shins and the bright instruments sparkled as they rained across the steps, each of them reflecting the light of the rod as it whirled through the air. They seemed to vibrate as though answering its call.

No one moved, all poised like hawks awaiting a signal. Eyes watched the rod as it turned end over end, leaving behind it a curious trail of scarlet light. It struck the stone floor, sparks dancing from it, and rolled to the top of a stair. For what seemed a long moment, no one moved to collect it, as if all were afraid of it. Then it dropped from sight, and they heard it roll down several steps, finally coming to a halt some way below.

Mourndark, who had bent at the knees, now leapt forward, ignoring his pain. Ulthor was in his path and Mourndark grappled with him, getting an arm around the Earthwrought's neck. As Ulthor struggled, about to break the hold with sheer strength, Mourndark had reached down and lifted one of his blades. He held it at Ulthor's throat.

"If you value him, keep still," said Mourndark. Even Dennovia kept back from him now, as though it was her own throat that felt the touch of the steel.

Ulthor fought for speech. "The rod," he gasped. "Get the rod." The rest was choked off as Mourndark tightened his grip, his arms remarkably powerful. He moved forward, pushing Ulthor before him in spite of his efforts to break free. Every other eye was on Brannog, waiting. They would not sacrifice Ulthor unless Brannog gave the sign.

But Brannog did not move. He knew that none of the Host would do so until he did. Ulthor's eyes pleaded with him to let Mourndark take his life, a bloody trade for the rod. Brannog remained immobile. Mourndark came to the top stair, searching for the fallen rod. Ulthor could not break the tightening grip.

From the darkness on the stair there came a bright glow, and for a moment it seemed as if the fallen rod had answered a call, for it appeared to rise up. But it was being carried from below. Someone else had been first to it. As the figure emerged into the light, hidden from everyone by Mourndark, the Steelmaster let out an audible gasp. His grip relaxed on

Ulthor for a moment, and the hand that held the knife at the Earthwrought's throat fell. Ulthor reached like a released spring, swinging free. He brought his hand down on Mourndark's wrist and twisted it viciously. The blade fell with a clatter on the stone. Before Mourndark could respond, he had been thrown to the floor, with Ulthor pinning him, ready to deliver a blow to the skull that would have killed him instantly.

Mourndark looked up as the figure stepped from the dark, holding the rod of power in its left hand. The rod was no more than a few inches from Mourndark's eyes. He gazed past it at his enemy, Wargallow.

Brannog and his followers were yet rooted, as though Wargallow was a ghost. Mourndark tried to speak, but could not, his mouth dry.

"Steelmaster," said Wargallow, though his voice was tired.

"Kill me swiftly," said Mourndark at last, through clenched teeth. "You should have done it long ago."

"You are probably right," said Wargallow. "Mercy is the prerogative of the weak."

There was a soft touch on his arm and he saw Ruvanna beside him. "Give me the rod," she said.

Wargallow looked down at it, knowing that one touch of it to Mourndark's flesh would end him. But he handed it to Ruvanna, relieved to be free of it.

Ulthor looked to Brannog. "I can make this very swift, and clean, though this creature hardly deserves it."

It looked as though Brannog would nod agreement, but Ruvanna stayed him. "No. Spare him."

Ulthor glared at her. Ogrund was behind her. "*Spare* him? I am with Wargallow. Mercy is out of place here. Have you not seen the havoc this man has wrought?"

"We may need him," said Ruvanna simply.

Ulthor's eyes appealed to Brannog. "There is no hurry," said the latter, trying to read Ruvanna's face. "Secure him."

Ulthor nodded to Dennovia. "And the girl?"

Brannog did not even look at her. She had pulled her knees up under her and sat in a tiny ball, her hair almost covering her face. "Have her watched, but not tied. We owe her that much. Ruvanna, Wargallow, we have to talk." He motioned them to the parapet.

"How is your arm?" he asked Wargallow when they were out of earshot of the Host.

Wargallow forced a grin. "Ruvanna has worked another of her spells on it. I'll see Goldenisle yet."

"Good," said Brannog, not wishing to dwell on the matter. He turned to Ruvanna. "This Steelmaster, why should we need him?"

Ruvanna sighed and looked out over the drop to the far walls of the outer mountain. "The Sublime One is very weak. Mourndark almost destroyed her, though he did not find her. By killing the Esoterics, he reduced her power. She will recover some of that power, but can never be what she was."

"Then we should waste no more time here," said Wargallow. "The rod must go where it will be safest, in Goldenisle."

Ruvanna's mind was in turmoil. I cannot tell them the truth—that I could become the Voice of Omara, take this gift that Omara offers me. If I am to do it, it must be now. Omara will no longer support the Sublime One, nor return to her the power to control the Earthwrought destiny. If I accept the role of Voice, that power would come to me. If I refuse to accept, Omara will remove my powers. The Earthwrought destiny will be in their own hands. There will be no Voice, unless it is heard in the combined voices of Ulthor, Brannog and other leaders.

"Ruvanna," said Brannog, a little impatiently. "You have not answered me. Why should we need the Steelmaster?" He pointed to where Mourndark had been bound with leather thongs. Ogrund stood over him.

"You recall I told you how I had sifted the secrets that were deep in the mind of the Child of the Mound?"

Brannog nodded, but frowned. She seemed to be reaching her point by a circuitous route.

"I spoke of a survivor of the water Aspect, the Aspect where the rods were created by the Seraphs for the Sorcerer-Kings. I have tried to open my mind to this survivor. He lives yet, in the Bay of Sorrows."

"I've not heard of this place," said Brannog. Wargallow did not comment, prepared to listen.

"It's far to the east. And he is there. When the Sorcerer-Kings made their first tentative journeys into other Aspects, before the time of the Sealing, they met other beings of great power, such as the Seraphs. It was these who made the rods for them, later, when the troubles began. But others visited the Seraphs when the working had damaged so many walls between Aspects. The Hierarchs of Ternannoc fetched up in many places. Some came here. One of them reached the water world of the Seraphs. He learned the secret of working the metals there, and when that world began to die, polluted by the working that had gone so tragically amiss, he came here. With him he brought the survivor."

"In exchange for his secrets," Brannog guessed.

"Yes."

"Who was this Hierarch?"

Ruvanna nodded to Wargallow. "You know that."

"Grenndak," said Wargallow. "Who created the Deliverers."

"Yes," said Ruvanna. "Grenndak taught his servant, the Steelmaster, how to fashion the killing steel. And how to give it to the men who became Deliverers. The Steelmaster was the only one with the genius to turn Grenndak's knowledge into an art, a skill."

"This explains the power," said Wargallow. "For power it was."

"But of what use is this knowledge?" said Brannog.

"The survivor is alive yet. I can find him. And commune with him. I have the power to do what no other can."

"To what end?" persisted Brannog.

"He gave the Preserver the knowledge of how to create the killing steel, how to make it a living part of the Deliverers."

Wargallow grunted. "Living, aye. As alive as the rest of me."

"*Metal?*" said Brannog.

"It is why I am dying."

Ruvanna filled the silence quickly. "But it may be that the

survivor possesses the knowledge of how the damage can be repaired."

"It is not possible," said Wargallow coldly. "You dream, girl."

"And," Ruvanna went on, ignoring him, "we have the Steelmaster. His skills. His genius."

Wargallow laughed mirthlessly. "You think he would help me? Repair me? Brannog, this is foolish talk! We must get to Goldenisle with all speed. We have to prepare its defense. Anakhizer cannot be much longer in beginning his war. Word of what has happened here will soon reach him—"

"Wait," said Brannog, his eyes locked with those of Ruvanna. For a moment it was as if the two of them were alone here. "You are saying that if we find this Seraph, we may be able to save Wargallow?"

"It is not practical!" said Wargallow.

"The survivor is alive, in the Bay of Sorrows. I can find him," promised Ruvanna.

"How long?" said Brannog.

Ruvanna looked away. "The sea is vast. But he's there. And we have the birds."

Wargallow shook his head. "I am moved by your concern, Ruvanna. But Mourndark would rather die than help me."

"We'll see," said Ruvanna.

"What will happen if we leave the Sublime One alive? Or are we to kill her? There are few who would say no—" Brannog began.

"It will be a long time before she has power enough to control the Earthwrought, if at all. There is a better one for the task," Ruvanna grinned, and her eyes went to Ulthor, who was talking to his warriors below. "None of the Earthwrought is more eloquent than Ulthor when it comes to a speech, especially a call to arms. Who better to address the Convocation?"

Ulthor heard the last of her remarks and came forward, raising his axe. "You speak of Ulthor the Faithbreaker! I'll stand by my new name. It will be an honor. And let me put an end to the Sublime One, publicly! A quick, clean execution."

"No," said Ruvanna. "You would offend Omara deeply.

Omara has shown mercy. Unlike Wargallow, my belief is that mercy is the prerogative of the strong.''

Wargallow could not help smiling at the girl's nerve. "Why did Omara abandon the Sublime One?''

Ruvanna was caught unawares by his question. ''Abandon?''

''We were in her power.''

''But Mourndark's slaughter weakened her.''

''But what of the will of Omara? Was her intention not to sacrifice all those not of the Earthwrought nations? Was the Sublime One not speaking Omara's will?''

Can he see into my mind? Ruvanna thought, the cold fear of such a possibility making her unable to answer for a moment.

''Ruvanna,'' said Brannog softly. ''It was not Omara who intended to deliver us to the dark.''

''No, no,'' stammered the girl. ''Omara understands us better. Our coming here, our protest, has shown her that.''

''Then perhaps,'' said Wargallow, ''Omara is deliberating.''

Brannog and Ulthor both stared at him. He had sounded almost flippant. What had he sensed? Was something amiss?

''If we've shown Omara that we're capable of fighting for our survival,'' Wargallow went on, ''and for her survival, surely we can expect a little compassion.''

Ulthor's frown deepened. ''We reject the Sublime One as the Voice of Omara. Do you think Omara has another voice?''

''She must have a will, a force that works for her own survival. If Omara is truly considering how to use her powers, we have to act, and quickly, before the choice is taken from us. That rod has immense power. Connected with those that Anakhizer has, it could yet bring ruin to us all, every nation, whatever its history. But what else can the rod do? Why did Orhung carry it for so long? I have often asked myself this, if Orhung had not used it to bring down the landslide that saved Goldenisle, what would he have done with it? He never made that clear to me, for all the time he spent close to me.''

Brannog and the others were all staring at him, but none of them interrupted him.

"Could the rod, perhaps, be used to control the others?"

Brannog looked askance at Ruvanna, but she was locked up in thoughts of her own.

"I think," added Wargallow, "that we must get it to Goldenisle, and quickly. We do not know what Omara will do."

At last Ruvanna spoke. "The power that seeks to possess Omara can be deflected, using the rod. But it would be through sacrifice, war. Omara cannot avoid war. Whoever is sacrificed!"

"Unless," said Brannog, "war can be prevented."

"Which seems impossible," said Wargallow.

"I agree," said Brannog, and Ulthor was nodding.

"But if the rod could be used to control the others," said Wargallow, "then it could be turned upon Anakhizer and his forces. Let *them* feed the old powers."

Brannog considered. "It's an ambitious plan, Wargallow. How could it be put into effect?"

"Now that we have the rod, it is time to design a plan."

Ulthor suddenly laughed, a great booming sound that turned the heads of all the Earthwrought below. "You're a man after my own heart, Wargallow. Aye, let these alien powers have their sacrifice, but it will not be our people."

Wargallow nodded. "You had better reconsider your thoughts about hunting ghosts in the Bay of Sorrows. The rod must go to Goldenisle, at once!"

"That's well enough," agreed Brannog. "It can be taken there very quickly. There is armed escort enough to take a dozen such rods to safety. But you and I and Ruvanna and Mourndark can search out this survivor—"

"You should go with the rod," Wargallow said softly.

But Ruvanna sighed. "If we do agree to search for the survivor, we have to take the rod with us."

Brannog shot her a look of instant suspicion. "Why?"

"It is the only thing that lends power enough to keep—"

Brannog stood close to her, his anger close to the surface. How many more secrets had she kept from them? "To keep what, girl?" he said quietly but icily.

"To keep Wargallow alive."

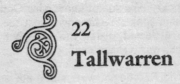

22
Tallwarren

BRANNOG STOOD ALONE on the wall overlooking the mountain. It was almost time to leave, and the Host was rested. In the silence, Brannog had given much thought to what had to be done. The decision had been left to him, although he knew that Ruvanna and Wargallow were yet opposed to each other. It seemed incredible that Wargallow should be so ready to give up any chance of survival, for Brannog had seen the ferocity with which he had fought in the past. Was this a true dedication to Omara? A final cleansing of any guilt that clung to him for the things he had done in the name of the Preserver? Or did he merely lack the will to go on, drained by the events of the last two years of his life? Perhaps the loss of his killing steel had done this to him, robbed him of his own steel will. Brannog had already decided that Wargallow was capable of loyalty to Omara; he had demonstrated it with frightening intensity since his conversion to the cause. A combination of circumstances, then.

And Ruvanna. The enigma. Brannog could not decide how he felt about the girl. Girl! She had become a woman in a few short weeks. But something had happened on this mountain that she had not disclosed, he was sure of it. Oh, she would not betray them, he was certain. She meant to champion Omara, the Earthwrought, Mankind. It was noble of her to want to save Wargallow, but why? It could be a fool's errand, a wasted journey that could so easily jeopardize the entire venture. The rod must return to Goldenisle. The only safe way was for it to go at once, in the keeping of the entire

Host. Yet Ruvanna was adamant that they try to help Wargallow. Did she have some other motive?

I must try, of course. The man I once hunted, whom I would have killed. Now I am considering these colossal risks to save his life. Would he do the same for me? But that is not important.

"Brannog," came a deep voice. It was Ulthor. "Your pardon."

"Of course. I am well rested."

"There is no more time. Already many of the Earth-wrought are gathering beneath us in those vast halls. The Sublime One sleeps, or so it seems."

"Then go down to them, Ulthor Faithbreaker, and tell them of the coming war in the west. Tell them of Goldenisle and of Elberon and of all the nations of Man, and of the Stone-delvers and Icewrought, and of your own nation. Tell them that it is the will of Omara that they raise their weapons and prepare."

"For the war?"

"We must prevent it if we can. But we must be ready. I fear, my friend, that it will come to war."

"And you, sire? Have you decided?"

"I must go to the Bay of Sorrows, and from there on to Goldenisle. After that, probably the far west." Brannog and Ulthor came down from the wall. All his commanders were waiting for him.

Wargallow stood with difficulty, like a man who had been without sleep for days. "Well?"

"Ulthor will address the Convocation. Then he will lead it, and the Host, in my name. West, to Elberon. I expect you all to obey Ulthor in everything."

No one demurred.

"Ogrund!" Brannog called. The Earthwrought was before him in an instant. "You will come with me. We leave for the Bay of Sorrows. Your charge will be the Steelmaster. Carac. You will come also, and ride with Wargallow."

Korkoris came forward expectantly and Brannog's hand fell on his tiny shoulder. "No, Korkoris. You must take your people with Ulthor. And Danoth, take the Men of Elderhold. We'll not be long in coming to you." He turned at last to

Ruvanna. She held up the rod, which was now its former dull color.

"Must I carry it?" Brannog asked her.

"You must." She turned to where Dennovia still sat in silence. "I will bring the girl."

"Will she be of use?" said Brannog.

"She will be safer with us." Ruvanna gave Brannog the rod. "We each have a charge. Here is yours."

Wargallow had no energy left with which to argue, and presently the company said its last goodbyes, the Earth-wrought hugging one another and wishing those who would go with Brannog well. Ruvanna stepped up onto the wall and raised her arms, calling to the huge birds. Four of them swept down from the open skies, dropping onto the ledge as lightly as a breeze. Ogrund and Carac stared at them in undisguised horror, but Ruvanna spoke to the creatures, instantly paci-fying them.

Mourndark had not spoken since his defeat, his mind closed in on itself. He was tied and secured to the back of one of the birds, and eventually Ogrund mastered his nerves and sat behind him, war club across his knees. Ruvanna grinned at him and supervised Wargallow's mounting up. The Deliverer was almost asleep on his feet, and once he had been secured, he slumped forward. Carac sat behind him, holding him with a free hand. Mourndark's instruments had been gathered up and replaced in their box. Ruvanna took this to Dennovia.

"Here," she told her. "Carry these for us. They may yet undo all that has been done."

Dennovia looked up. It was the first time she had done so since she had attacked Mourndark. Her eyes fastened on the hated box and it seemed that she must refuse it, but when she saw Ruvanna's face, she held out her hands meekly.

"Should we trust her with them?" Brannog asked Ruvanna softly.

"I think so. She has betrayed Mourndark. In her heart there is a deep loathing for him and the terrible things he has made her do. She must have seen much evil in the Direkeep, but nothing like the destruction she has witnessed here. She knows that the blades are a part of Mourndark. While she carries them, she has power over him. She needs that much.''

Dennovia clutched the box to her as if it were a young baby, and went to the back of her mount. She offered no resistance and said nothing. Ruvanna mounted behind her, watching as Brannog himself mounted the last of the birds. They were quiescent, waiting as patiently as steeds, and with a final wave to Ulthor and the captains below, Ruvanna led the flight upward. Within moments the tower had become a minute spire far below the birds. They circled once, hearing the cheers rising up from below.

''Will Ulthor master the Convocation?'' Brannog called to Ruvanna.

''Of course!'' she laughed, her face lighting up. ''And you would not have left him if you thought otherwise. But you could have no better general. Omara will read his heart: she has already done so. There is only love there, Brannog. Worship. He will not betray Omara, nor she him.'' And if we find the Seraph, Brannog, I will give you what you desire, the life of your friend. There will be no more Voice of Omara. Only its people.

She concentrated on steering the birds with a part of her mind, trying to search the land below with another. They came up out of the huge chimney of Mount Timeless into a day that was cloudy, threatening rain. Gray clouds scudded in from the northeast, where they were heading, and with them came a dampness, a chill and a hint of foreboding. Carac and Ogrund were rigid, legs locked about their aerial chargers, their terrors of flight not yet subsiding, but as they looked down and saw the immensity of the landscape below them, their amazement got the better of their terror. Peaks rose up at them, icy and white, and swirls of snow were dragged from their heights like sheets by the winds. Deep valleys and sweeps of glacier opened up under them and the range spread out as far as the eye could see, swallowed by distant banks of cloud.

Ruvanna could already feel the pull of the sea, far away. As though he shared this mystery, Brannog sensed it, as if its currents worked on his memory, the days of youth he had spent on his vessel, striving to find shoals in the deep waters

of the western ocean. Yet his heart was somehow not glad-
dened by the thought that he would find the sea again. This
place toward which they flew was well named, Bay of Sorrows. Already something drifted on the air from far away, a
desolation, a melancholy that permeated the upper airs like
a mist. And they tasted salt, though in it there was an element
of decay and decline.

All day they flew on, numbed by the flight, each withdrawing into his thoughts, bodies almost forgotten, so that they
passed into a kind of dream, where the dips and swells of the
flight were like sudden changes in imagination, veering away
from the darker edge of nightmare. The sun fell away somewhere over their shoulders, plummeting, and for a brief while
the last of the high peaks were splashed in orange fire, their
bases lost in pools of night.

The mountains and foothills were behind them when Ruvanna began to realize the birds were becoming extremely
agitated. They knew what was ahead; the thought of the sea
terrified them. Ruvanna would not be able to force them over
it and control the four of them. During twilight, she landed
them. They came down near a wide river estuary, where sand
flats had already turned slate gray, loud with the sounds of
resting gulls. The skylines were flat, the country dull and
featureless.

"The birds won't fly over the sea," Ruvanna told Brannog
after she had dismounted.

He looked angry for a moment, but then tiredness got the
better of him. "No? Then perhaps we should go back without
any more delay."

She looked about her. There were a few trees here, bent
by a prevailing wind into a curiously slanted shape. Dennovia
sat beneath one, her face calm, as if she had done no more
than get off a boat. Carac helped Wargallow to shelter and
the Deliverer was soon asleep, wrapped in a blanket that
Carac had brought. Ogrund pushed Mourndark to another of
the trees and tied him to it securely. He met with no resistance. The Steelmaster had not uttered a sound on the journey
and his eyes were dull, his expression vacant. He seemed to
see nothing and Ogrund wondered if part of him had died

or if part of his mind had snapped under the strain of his defeat.

"If we are to go back," said Ruvanna, "we must fly now. The birds will not linger here. If I hold them, they'll become angry, dangerous."

Brannog grimaced. "How far is the sea? I can smell it—"

"Two miles down the estuary."

"And the Seraph's island?"

"I can reach it."

Brannog looked at Carac. "We can go under the sea to it—"

Ruvanna shook her head. "No! The earth is too polluted. It would kill the Earthwrought if they tried to dig."

"Then this is madness," Brannog hissed. "We cannot fly back now. We're all exhausted."

"I cannot hold the birds—"

"Then let them fly!" he growled, moving away. "Get some sleep." He went to attend to Wargallow.

Ruvanna watched him for only a moment, tears of frustration in her eyes. Then she turned to the birds and let them go, watching them flap off noisily into the deepening gloom. She heard a sound and thought Brannog had come back, but she found Dennovia at her shoulder, a head taller than her. She had combed her hair and wiped away the dust from her face. Even in the dark she was beautiful and Ruvanna felt herself clenching as she compared herself.

"Will they return?" said Dennovia.

"No. We travel on without them."

"Where is this place you seek?"

"In the sea. An island. In the morning I will find it."

"Mourndark will never help you. He would rather die. Since he held the rod of power—"

"I have glimpsed his mind," said Ruvanna. "It held a strange charm for you once."

Dennovia did not flare as Ruvanna thought she might. She glanced at the box of instruments she had set down by a tree. "Do you look into all our minds? I wonder what we would find in yours."

To Dennovia's surprise, Ruvanna smiled. "Selfishness," she said.

"I don't understand."

"Did you love Mourndark?"

Dennovia looked away. "No. But, yes, I thought so, once."

"Or did you love what he stood for? His power?"

"It doesn't matter," said Dennovia coldly.

"Love is selfish. Mourndark loves only power. He covets it and sacrifices everything for it."

"Oh yes," nodded Dennovia bitterly. "But you have your causes. Do you not sacrifice everything for them?"

The question took Ruvanna unawares. "I?"

"Omara. Earthwrought. Men. Your causes. Yet you put them aside, risk everything by coming to this wilderness. To save the Deliverer. Is it because you love Wargallow?"

Ruvanna almost laughed. "Wargallow?" She shook her head. "You think that?"

"What use is he? Why risk so much to save him? Only love could be so selfish."

"Brannog needs him. They have fought many times together, and—"

Dennovia smiled, holding her head. She had become again the regal girl who had once held such an esteemed position in the Direkeep. "Brannog needs him. So you do this for Brannog."

Ruvanna looked away. "If Wargallow dies, Brannog will be in despair. It will be a torment to him."

"Men die. There is war, disease. Does Wargallow mean so much to Brannog?"

"You were right when you said you don't understand. Wargallow is a symbol of what has happened in Omara. A triumph of justice over cruelty, corrupt thinking. Brannog hated him once, and wanted him dead, but he saw in him the change, the symbol of what must be if Omara is to survive. It goes deeper. Those who endured Xennidhum together are always bonded."

"So you would save Wargallow for Brannog's sake, and for Omara's. But most of all, I think, for your own. Selfishness, as you told me."

Ruvanna gazed at her as if she would retort, but her expression softened. "So you do understand." To her surprise, Dennovia rested her fingers on her arm, soft as silk. There was no malice in the girl as she walked silently away, leaving Ruvanna to turn inward, to her own pool of sorrows.

The journey had worn them all out. Soon they slept, though Ogrund insisted on keeping watch. Carac relieved him, and between them they kept guard throughout the night. In the morning the day was chill, clouds rolling in thickly from the sea as though it sought to obscure its secrets from them. Grayness clung to everything and drizzle seeped down, soaking them in spite of the Earthwroughts' attempts to prevent it. They all took some comfort from the rod, which Brannog kept at his belt, though he was uncomfortable with it, longing for the day when he could pass it on to someone better suited to wield it. Who would that be? he wondered. Ottemar Remoon? Again and again he confused himself with doubts as to how Anakhizer's threat should be dealt with. They needed a Korbillian, someone who could lead them with a resolve and a power like a furnace. Brannog had the resolve, but the power of the rod was not for him to bear to war.

They broke camp, trudging along the flat banks of the estuary. In the fog it seemed that their journey would be laboriously endless.

Brannog spoke softly to Ruvanna. "I did not expect this. We cannot afford to move so slowly." He nodded back toward Wargallow, who was now being carried by Ogrund and Carac. "Is the island close to land?"

"There's a village ahead," she answered. "We'll need a boat."

He saw the determination in her eyes, though she was tired, the weight of the journey wearing her down. "Ruvanna, this search has become a thing of desperation."

She nodded, tears welling in her eyes. "Yes. But the survivor is out there. He is."

"Perhaps you should try to recall the birds—"

"Not yet. The village—"

"We have nothing with which to pay for a boat! Are we to steal it?"

She had no answer. It was as though she was lost in the

night, groping for a safe passage through it. Her sudden hopelessness at last struck him, but he felt no anger, only a wave of compassion. Her plight revealed her to him for once as a frail, vulnerable girl.

"Ruvanna, you were right to think of saving Wargallow. I would have given whatever was needed to save him myself. But now I think we must consider our other responsibilities." He studied the mist. It had closed in like a fist.

"He'll die," she whispered.

He put an arm about her. "Then at least we'll bury him with dignity. Since there is a village, we'll go there. Whoever dwells there will surely not deny us the right to give him to the earth."

She looked up at him suddenly. "But they may yet give us a boat—"

He would have shaken his head, but at that moment he found himself staring into the gaze of Mourndark, and Brannog saw in the eyes of the Steelmaster a cold light, a callous gleam, the flicker of triumph. Then it had gone.

"We'll see," he told Ruvanna. "Quickly now."

They went along the narrow path for a further hour, until Ruvanna's sense of place brought them to the outskirts of the village. It was built largely on long stilts, running out as it did into the estuary to a sand bar where a tiny fishing fleet had been moored. The tide was very low and the buildings were like huge herons in the mist, silent and patient, listening for a hint of movement. Water sighed in the distance, and an occasional gull called, but otherwise the village hardly breathed.

Ruvanna gripped Brannog's arm, and he felt the chill in her fingers. "There's no one here!" she gasped, but she spoke out of fear, not glee.

Brannog studied the first buildings. They were rotten, their plank walls broken by the wind and rain, a sense of decay reeking from them. Some had collapsed, others were dark with weed; the shreds of sea mist that clung to them were like cerements. Roofs gaped, floors sagged, the jetties leaning, some buried in the sand like old bones.

"It is a place of the dead," said Carac, his eyes narrowing as if to shut out the vision of ruin. He pointed to a sign that had fallen down, propped carelessly against the side of a shed by the wind. Its faded lettering said, "Tallwarren." "I've heard of it," said Carac. "As a child, I heard tales of this sea and of how it drove the fishermen away from its shores. The fishers of Tallwarren stayed until the end."

"What happened?" said Brannog.

"The sea kills," said Carac. "Something in it."

"The Seraph," said Ruvanna. "His own world died and he came here. But he has had to change the sea to sustain himself."

"The sea kills," said Carac again.

As if answering him, a breeze sprang up and with a mournful voice haunted the buildings. The deep sense of misery threatened to engulf the watchers, but Brannog raised his voice angrily. "Then if this is a dead place, I'll not fear it, nor its empty voices."

"Can we cross the sea?" Ruvanna asked Carac.

"If there is a boat."

Brannog grunted, annoyed by the mood that assailed them, and walked deliberately into Tallwarren. He had to tread with care, for many of the walkways underfoot were rotting, their mildewed wood soft and treacherous, but he picked his way along them, going out toward the sea. The stink of the mud, combined with the peculiar smell of the sea, like rotting fish, nauseated him, and he tore a strip from his garment to wear as a mask. Below him, on the mud flats, were the scattered hulks of boats, most of them ruined. Some jutted up despairingly from the deep mud, already being sucked, tide by tide, into oblivion. Others, overturned, revealed gaping holes, blind eyes, while others had simply disintegrated.

While Brannog searched, his companions found a relatively dry shack and huddled in it, eating a little food and waiting. Neither Carac nor Ogrund could bring himself to join Brannog on the walkways and both secretly wished that no suitable craft would be found. Dennovia alone seemed untroubled by the place. She was mopping Wargallow's brow while he slept on, his heart beating faintly. Mourndark was immobile, his eyes again expressionless.

"Brannog is right," said Dennovia. "The dead cannot harm us."

"Perhaps you do not feel them," said Ruvanna, almost to herself.

"I've lived close to death for far too long," said Dennovia. "Tell me, if we survive this strange quest, what am I to expect?"

Ruvanna snapped from her gloomy mood and tried to smile. "You? No harm. Your freedom."

"To go where? I've lived my life inside the Direkeep. How should I fare out in Omara? It seems a hostile place."

Ruvanna shook her head. "You have seen only its evils."

Dennovia nodded. "Possibly. I should like to see Goldenisle. I have heard tales of its opulence. What is it like? Decadent, I expect."

"I've never been there," said Ruvanna sharply.

Dennovia laughed. The girl of power was easily embarrassed.

An hour later, Brannog returned, thick with mud to his thighs, its stink clinging to him. He was breathing heavily, but grinned widely. "I've found what we need. The tide will take her out, but not yet awhile. Come and see, all of you."

There were no protests. Tallwarren had worked its spell over them all. Carac and Ogrund each took Wargallow and supported him, carrying him, and Brannog kept a watchful eye on Mourndark, though he seemed to have fallen back into immobility, apart from his automatic, plodding walk. Dennovia still held his knives, but she walked beside Ruvanna, her own mood less dark. Brannog was aware more than once of her eyes upon him. The mist and gloominess had done nothing to detract from her beauty, and Brannog knew how such a woman could use beauty as a weapon. Given the opportunity, Dennovia might be dangerous.

Dennovia saw the Earthwrought struggling to keep Wargallow on his feet. If he does recover, she wondered, how will he react to me? Perhaps he has forgotten that it was I who seduced Vecta away from his camp. If he recalls that, he'll want to question me hard.

They had come to the ailing heart of Tallwarren, where some of its larger buildings, once stores, had survived the worst ravages of the years. A number of jetties had broken up, their stilts buckling, now prodding like spears at the mist.

What had once been a quayside was choked with craft, tangled together like fish netted in weed. They reeked like corpses.

Brannog pointed to the end of a long jetty, itself intact, though encrusted with weed and clams below the water level. The tide was returning, already washing over the sand bars, and as it came it brought fresh waves of despair, as if it could be a physical thing. But there was a boat, once a proud fishing vessel, chained to the jetty. It began its dance on the black waters as the tide swirled about it. Ruvanna could see Brannog's hopes rise: here was a sea, an element he understood well, no matter how polluted. He had rooted himself in the earth, but the sea was in his blood.

"Can you sail her?" said Ruvanna.

"She's mercifully sound, with a strong hull," Brannog replied. "These sails are no use, but I've found others unused and dry." He saw the looks of horror on the faces of Carac and Ogrund.

"Can we not wait here for you, sire?" said Ogrund, his features already paled by the thought of taking to the sea.

Brannog would have smiled, but read the distress of the Earthwrought. "Is that what you wish?"

Ogrund grimaced, but shook his head. "It is what I wish, but not what can be."

"I'll need you to help me sail the ship," Brannog told him, but it did nothing to strengthen Ogrund's resolve, nor Carac's.

While the tide crawled in, Brannog organized the collecting of the sails, laboriously dragging them from their abandoned warehouse. They were patched and ancient, but usable. By the time he was satisfied that they had been rigged and tied, the craft was partially afloat. Its stern, however, was firmly embedded in the mud that silted up the harbor.

"We must get her off before the tide turns," said Brannog.

"It looks impossible," said Dennovia.

Ruvanna snorted, as if dismissing the other girl. "How do we free her, Brannog?"

"Get everyone in the bow," he replied. "And move as much weight there as you can." He dashed away and pulled from the remains of another building a long pole. The wood

was seasoned and had not rotted. Brannog watched as Carac
and Ogrund got Wargallow to the prow, and Mourndark was
herded by Ruvanna and Dennovia. There was no revolt in
the latter, in fact she seemed pleased to be given a task.
When Ruvanna began dragging old netting to the ship's bow,
Dennovia was quick to help. Brannog climbed with care down
a crumbling iron ladder to water level and rammed his pole
hard under the stern of the boat. He clung to the ladder and
used a shoulder to heave against his makeshift lever, timing
the waves and acting with them. There was some response,
but the craft would not swing free. Full tide was nearing.

"Ogrund, Carac!" he roared, and they came to him, staring down apprehensively. They hated being off the land, but
he could not afford sympathy now. "When I heave on this
pole, throw your weight against its end." They understood
what he meant at once, and as the next wave shouldered its
way in to the harbor, all three of them tried to lever the hull
free of the mud. Again the craft moved, but not enough to
float free.

Ruvanna could just make out their exertions from the prow.
She realized that Brannog could not free the craft, for all his
efforts. Dennovia, panting from her own efforts, saw by Ruvanna's expression that the attempt was doomed, and with it
the quest. "Is there nothing we can do?" she said.

Where is my power now? thought Ruvanna. She closed her
mind to the awful mood of despair, the cloying misery of
Tallwarren and this most dismal of seas. As she did so, a
shock of realization ran through her. The suffering of the
village had remained here, almost as a physical presence. It
worked on those who visited it, trawling them like fish with
its gloom and despair. In this, there was a perverse power.
If I could use it—

She tried, drawing on what Omara had given her, pouring
it into her concept of the village. Giving a form to that pain,
molding it. She began a soft song, strange words and ca-
dences, and she used it to dig down into the land, the sand
and the mud, dredging it up from the harbor bed.

Carac and Ogrund felt it first, the stirring of the earth. In
horror they pulled back from their task, leaving Brannog to
stare incredulously at their expressions. Their eyes were fixed

on the sea. They read into its swirls the movement of something other than currents and the tide. Brannog swung round. The waters below the boat churned. Dark shapes twisted under the hull. Sharks? Too dark, black as mud.

Ruvanna shaped them, giving bizarre life to the mud itself, like a potter squeezing at clay, and as she did so she deflected Tallwarren's ghostly powers into her work. The boat shuddered. Brannog saw, though he could not guess at what had moved it. He clambered up the ladder, abandoning his long pole. Carac and Ogrund were like stone, transfixed. Brannog had to push them along the jetty.

"Move! The boat is freeing itself!" he shouted. He lifted the last of the mooring chains and carried it over his shoulder as easily as a rope. The two Earthwrought scrambled over the gangplank onto the ship, and Brannog followed as nimbly as though he were on land. He tossed down the chain and rushed to the stern. As he did so, he felt it judder free of the mud. He leaned out over the rail, looking down. The water churned, black as oil; in it there were a number of beings, fashioned from silt, featureless, their thick, misshapen arms pressed to the hull. Brannog thought that something much larger was moving under the ship, as though the mud flat undulated. He turned away.

Dennovia had come to him. "It's her," she said. "She's doing it!" Her beautiful face was pale, her eyes wide. Brannog ignored her and began adjusting the sails, not wanting to miss the opportunity to catch the tide. The boat swept forward, eager now, in a moment passing the end of the rotting jetty and nosing out into open water.

Ruvanna sat down, eyes closed, her strange sculpting over. It had drained her, but as she gulped in lungfuls of cold air, her strength returned. She managed to grin at Ogrund as he stood over her.

"I will not ask what you have done," he said solemnly. "But are you well?"

"Of course!" she smiled, standing. "And so now is Tallwarren." She pointed back at the receding fishing village, huge cranes in the morning mist. The shadows closed around it, but the depressing cloud that had threatened to suffocate the company had been lifted. Ruvanna knew that she had freed whatever miserable spirits had haunted the village. Now only its bones remained.

Her smile faded. Within herself she felt the ebbing away of some of her own powers. What Omara had given her, she was taking back. She began to understand her own destiny better. Since she had not become the Voice, a human outlet for Omara, her powers would not last. How soon they might fade, she could not guess. Long enough, she prayed, for her to find the survivor. And commune with him.

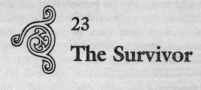

23
The Survivor

RUVANNA STOOD at the prow of the ship, stiff as a figurehead, her eyes scanning the peaks and troughs of the sea. It was rough, the craft tossed like a leaf, though Brannog steered her with absolute authority, his instinctive skill, not used for so long, coming back to him. He measured the wind and rode the waves with ease, though this Bay of Sorrows was the strangest sea he had ever been upon. The water was almost a livid green, growing darker as the ship moved out into the heart of the Bay, now thirty, forty leagues from the shore. The wind seemed to come at them from all directions, as though it had its own mind and sought to confuse any mariner that passed. But there were no other ships, and Brannog doubted that any had sailed here for many a long year. The sky dropped down on them, a rumpled blanket of grays and blacks, always threatening a storm. Rain fell heavily, then broke off to become thick drizzle, and it never ceased. If the company had been miserable in Tallwarren, only Brannog was beyond that now. But he wondered to himself if perhaps he had become a little mad, pursuing a cause that took him so far from the lands to which he should have been speeding.

Carac and Ogrund, both terrified of the sea, had been violently ill, hiding themselves away amidships, covering themselves, closing their eyes and minds, though the callousness of the sea found them out. Wargallow was wrapped in thick blankets and he slept on, while Dennovia watched over him, herself pale, though not as ill as the Earthwrought. She felt pity for them, but was unable to move for fear that the motion of the ship would bring the awful sickness upon her also. Mourndark had been tied to the base of a mast. If he saw or felt anything, he had closed himself off from it. His head was bowed and he only moved when the boat pitched.

Ruvanna could sense the far presence of the survivor. She knew the direction, and each time the ship threatened to veer away from it, she shouted back to Brannog and he made whatever adjustment was necessary, throwing his great strength against the wind and sea, sometimes roaring his anger at it, though afterward he laughed. But he thought to himself that the quest must be ended soon. They were far across an uncharted sea and Ruvanna acted from blind instinct rather than knowledge.

As the spray swept over him and the sea boiled up, tossing a curtain of spume over the rail, Brannog looked back. The land had slipped out of sight and no island or headland broke the vast expanse of green and white now. But something moved at the stern of the boat, several shapes. There had been no hint of life, no sea birds, and these were not birds either. They were garbed in shadow, featureless, their movements obscured by the extreme slowness with which they moved. It was as though they slid. They had come up from behind the boat, or from below it. Brannog had no time to shout. Ruvanna had already broken away from her fixed vigil and she struggled down the pitching craft to stand with him.

"What are these things?" he called above the wind.

She was looking at the shapes in horror. They were over the rail, eight or nine of them, and they were dark gray, fashioned, it seemed, from the mud of the sand bars, the silt of the sea bottom. Their outlines were those of men, but their heads were no more than rounded masses, their eyes, nose and mouth no more than rough guesses, the beginnings of features. Ruvanna did not answer Brannog, but she had no need to. He could see what they were. *She* had created them, drawn them up from the mud to move the boat free of it. And they had not been left behind.

"Elementals," she said. "I put power into them."

"Then remove it."

"I cannot. They are a part of me." She seemed dazed, as though she had only just realized what she had done.

"Then they mean no harm?"

"No. Leave them." She turned away abruptly and went back to the prow, ignoring Brannog's look. He studied the motionless shapes, but they seemed prepared to remain where they were. Their effect, however, was unsettling, like the threat of attack, and though Brannog turned from them and back to his task, he sensed them.

Ruvanna felt a numbing cold inside her. She was responsible for the grim elementals. Like faithful hounds, they would dog her footsteps, moving when told to do so. She dare not destroy them, for they were her burden. But unless she did destroy them, they would always be near. It was the price for their being. She studied the sea. She could see chunks of weed and rotted wood passing them, carried by the restless tide. Out here, far from any land, the water had become more oily, viscous and deep green as if it poured into Omara from another realm, a shattered haven where the survivor and his kind once thrived. But in this sea now there was only death, for no Omaran fish could live in these waters. There were things floating in it, things that she could not understand, as if they were part of something greater, chunks of torn flesh, remnants of a corpse beyond imagining. But it was her own mind, she told herself, giving distorted form to the floating debris of the ocean.

Behind her, Dennovia had sensed a change in the sea. Its color was bizarre, a shade of green that looked wrong for water. She had never been near the sea before this trip, but something told her that this was not right. The sky was a troubled gray, but the sea did not reflect it as it should. It held its own strange color. And whatever it was that bobbed on its surface was not normal. More and more she thought of death and decay, of floating corpses, and the slaughter of battle. She left Wargallow and stumbled back to where Brannog fought for control of the craft.

"Better to stay where you were!" he called above the din and Dennovia realized as he shouted that the wind was rising, heaping up the sea for an even greater offensive.

"Can the ship survive this?"

"Aye!" He grinned at her and her eyes suddenly fell on the shapes at the stern. Her mouth dropped, but if she screamed, the first crash of thunder smothered it. Brannog put an arm around her and pulled her to him. She gripped him at once, terrified.

"They are not dangerous," he shouted in her ear. "Our only enemy here is this sea."

"It stinks of death! Are these not its children?"

Before he could answer, the ship was taken by a wave and slammed into another that crossed it. Like an angry god, the sea was determined to put an end to their progress. Brannog almost toppled over with the girl, but he steadied them both. "Help me with this!" He gripped the helm and she did as he told her, throwing what strength she had into the battle. The ship righted, wallowing, but rode another huge wave. Dennovia only glanced back once, expecting to see the shapes gone, smashed into the raging spray behind, but they were unmoved, clinging like limpets to a rock.

Ruvanna knew the storm was about to unleash its fury on them. She knew also that the survivor was somewhere ahead, filling her mind now. Alive, dreaming his own tormented dreams. "Lord of waters," she said to him, arrowing the words outwards, drawing on her powers, "put aside this storm. We will find you. The storm will not hinder us." But she knew that no matter how much of Omara she drew on, this was elsewhere. There was no safe passage, no surety. Disaster stood at their elbow, eager to claim them. The boat shuddered to another awesome blow, and Ruvanna almost lost her hold on the rail.

As the ship rolled, Mourndark's bonds tightened and suddenly snapped. Like a stone released from its bed, he rolled across the deck, fetching up against a pile of netting that saved him a broken limb. From his brief sanctuary, he looked up at the middle of the craft. Brannog and Dennovia fought with the wheel together. The other girl was not to be seen, presumably in the bow. And the two dogs of the earth were in hiding, possibly even dead, killed by an element that tortured them. Mourndark had not been seen; the others were far too busy fighting the storm. It seemed likely that it would kill them all for their stupidity in coming here. What a nightmare realm!

Yet he was free, if only for a moment. And where was

Wargallow? He looked around, shielding his eyes from the whipping surf, the sting of the salt which threatened to blind him. Ah, the blankets and oilskins there! That would be him, and as good as dead from the look of him. How could these idiots believe they could save him by bringing him *here,* to this realm of madness? Mourndark had heard it all, from his moment of defeat, although he had feigned otherwise. He had been waiting, trying to find a time to make an assault on freedom. Here, in this doomed craft, he could never escape, but chance had snapped his bonds. If he could recapture the rod, who could say what else he could achieve?

Something slid and struck his thigh. Turning, he grinned again. It was the box containing his instruments. He took it, holding it lovingly as if a lost child had been restored to him. Carefully he took out the longest of the knives. He closed the lid, securing it, and slipped the box under the netting. Should I plunge this blade into Wargallow's heart? But he grinned. No, too simple, too kind. Let him go down to death slowly. I want him revived, so that he'll know what it is that calls for him. I want to stand over him when that realization comes.

He rolled away, into cover, still not seen by Brannog and Dennovia. He thought of his lover. Ah, but how quickly she would betray him. She had her own pretty skin to think of. She would use the only weapon she had, her intoxicating beauty. Brannog would be the obvious target for her. She had more nerve than most of her kind, Mourndark knew that. Even now she displayed it, masking her terror, grappling with the wheel, standing beside Brannog. Her efforts would be of no use to him, but he would be impressed, no doubt. And if the storm ever died and the ship rode calmly, she would draw him to her bed with ease. The big man would be unable to resist her, her arts. How quickly she would enslave him. But not if I reach her, Mourndark thought. Since this ship plots a course to eternity, I'll destroy them all first. Dennovia will be the first one to feel the knife.

He found it difficult to move up the ship, so dreadfully was it tossing now, but at least he could do so unobserved. Brannog could spare no time for anything but his concentration on the wheel. Dennovia was weak, at the point of collapse, but she clung to the wheel as if it were her life. Her will and

tenacity surprised Brannog. She should have had a better life,
he thought, but he veered from such thoughts, working frantically to keep the prow of the ship from disaster. Where was
Ruvanna! Surely not still in the bow!

The survivor had acknowledged her, if he had not answered her. Ruvanna felt the distant stirring of a mind, a
huge mind, and now a part of it raced up from its lost abyss
to meet her own thoughts. The survivor felt the coming of
the ship. Ruvanna clung to that, guiding the prow with her
own power, calling on all of it. Whatever Omara had put into
her, she would use, no matter what the cost.

Mourndark had managed to pass the two figures at the
helm. He was almost exhausted, soaked through, his arms
and legs bruised and weakened so that he wondered if he
could go on. He was tempted to give in, to fall where he was
and let the next wash take him overboard. But he forced a
grin. Not yet! Not with the rod so near at hand. He crawled
to a vantage point not far behind Brannog. Kill him first, the
knives were saying to him. They had all joined voices to
whisper to him, as they often did. Like lovers they spoke to
him, beguiling him. How could he deny them? Yes, kill Brannog. Then the rest would be so easily done. Hah! If I had
the strength, I would take Dennovia, have her before the
storm. And then administer the final stroke. I will place her
with Wargallow and let them die slowly, together.

He pulled the knife from his sleeve. I dare not rush to him.
It is only a few feet now, but the ship heaves like the very
sea itself. A throw? But he did not like the idea. He was
adept, but this storm posed too many problems. Too easy to
strike a bone, the killing thrust deflected. Brannog must die
at once. Mourndark was too weak to struggle with him.

He crept forward. Dennovia had slipped to her knees,
hanging on to Brannog, her arms about his knees, her hair
and clothes plastered to her. Mourndark studied her, realizing that Brannog would not be able to break free of her easily.
A sudden rush then. That would be enough. One perfect
thrust, and he would die. Mourndark drew in a breath, readying his arm. His hands were absolutely steady, as though he
were in a silent chamber about to perform surgery. The splen-

dor of the act bouyed him and he felt himself slide into the numbness of control.

When the moment came, he surged forward, the knife mere feet from his victim's back. As it began the last plunge downward, Dennovia opened her eyes, screaming soundlessly, for the wind tore the sound away. Mourndark felt himself clamped by a terrible force, his arms held rigid, his neck, his legs, his trunk all gripped. He could not move, nerveless. His instrument of death fell, the point striking the deck so that it went deep. Brannog whirled, his eyes falling on the quivering blade, knowing at once that it had been meant for him.

Mourndark was behind him, but the elementals had him, three of them gripping him like a doll, their thick fingers wrapped about his arms, his neck. His eyes bulged as though the beings would squeeze the life from him. Dennovia cringed, but Brannog got her to her feet, one hand still on the wheel. They both looked at the elementals, unable to speak.

The storm raced away, as if it had no need to watch the spectacle below it, and the sea abruptly gave up its attempt to swallow the ship. Brannog turned to it, staggered. How could this be? But at once he saw Ruvanna coming to him. She was smiling, but as soon as she reached the wheel, her smile disappeared. Brannog thought it was the sight of the elementals and the limp figure they held. But Ruvanna had seen Dennovia, hugged like a lover to Brannog's chest.

"The men of mud," Brannog said, no longer needing to shout. His hands were no longer on the wheel. "Have you done this?"

Ruvanna shook herself free of the shock. "What? No—"

"Then they must have acted for you," said Brannog.

"Release him!" Ruvanna told the elementals and at once Mourndark crumpled to the deck. He looked to be unconscious, dead possibly. Ruvanna bent to him at once, discovering that he was yet alive.

Brannog and Dennovia stared at the elementals. They had all gathered, waiting like slaves. Brannog knew they were exactly that, slaves to Ruvanna's will.

"Have they killed him?" said Dennovia.

Ruvanna glared at her, then looked away. "No. They know I want him alive. For the island." She indicated to the elementals that she wanted Mourndark taken back to the mast and watched. With slow, ponderous movements, they did as she had silently commanded them.

Dennovia shuddered as they went.

"If you're cold," said Ruvanna, "you'd better cover yourself with a blanket." She turned away and returned to the prow.

Brannog studied her as she went, not noticing Dennovia going back to her own post. In a moment there was another movement at his elbow. Ogrund stood there, his big face pasty, his eyes red and sore. He had never looked more miserable. Brannog clapped an arm around him at once. "Cheer up, old friend! The storm has passed." Brannog studied the sky as he said it. It had been an ominously abrupt ending to the storm, not the usual way of things. "Where's Carac?"

Ogrund tried to speak, but could not do so, but he indicated with a nod of his head. There were other nets heaped up, and Carac could be seen emerging like a crushed spider.

"The island is not far," said Brannog. "Soon we can land." He took the wheel. "If you're well enough, go down and watch over Wargallow."

Ogrund nodded, but stiffened as he saw the elementals for the first time. "What are these monsters?" he gasped.

"They serve us," said Brannog, his humor dissolving. "They do nothing unless Ruvanna wills it. Ignore them."

Ogrund again nodded, helping Carac to his feet and the two of them had strength for nothing else than to go and sit beside Wargallow. Brannog held the wheel, but somehow it seemed as if the ship now moved of its own volition. Or Ruvanna's.

While he thought of her, she was gazing in fury at the calmer seas ahead of them. *The whore!* her mind snarled. Her net is cast, and cast for Brannog. Is he so stupid as to believe she sought to help him? Clinging to him, half naked! And he did not cast her off. He allowed her to grip him.

Who comes in anger?

The voice struck her with the force of a blow, and she

closed her mind as if she had been caught naked. The island! The survivor was there. Awake.

Awake, aye, awake.

Ruvanna almost reeled at the intensity of the voice inside her. But she tried to calm herself, to put aside her own needs. "I am Ruvanna, of Omara. It was I who woke you."

The sea ahead was level, open and empty. Its color had changed to light green, though there were banks of strange weed floating in it, and other stranger shapes that could not be identified. *It was not my purpose to pry into your thoughts. But they came at me like thunder. Jealousy is an emotion shaped in fire. Yet it has served your purpose. It has awoken me, though I had no wish to be disturbed.*

Ruvanna felt herself mentally blushing, but she quickly put all thought of Dennovia from her mind. "You are the survivor, from the water world. The master of metals."

You understand me? What I am?

"Where are you?"

You are near me. Your present course will bring you to me. Since your craft has, by some miracle, survived the storm set to protect me from such an intrusion, I will let you come to me. Your powers intrigue me. The voice fell silent and Ruvanna could not raise it again. Instead, she looked ahead of her, watching the horizon, where wisps of green mist danced and curled.

She did not hear Brannog as he came to her side, but as she turned, she could not meet his gaze.

"The ship does not need a pilot now," he told her. "The survivor has discovered us, I think."

"Yes," was all she said.

He sensed her coldness toward him, baffled by it, but decided that this was no time to pursue it. Instead he studied the horizon. Soon his keen eyes had seen the smudge that was the island. He pointed.

The ship sped on, the smudge darkening, the mists unveiling it like a gift. There were no birds circling it, no sign of life. Although the sea shifted, thick and oily, it moved with a minimum of sound. Brannog felt sure they must have slipped through a gate into another realm. Was there yet a rent in the fabric of Omara's walls? Was this what Korbillian had meant when he had talked of such things? No sea of Omara, no expanse of water, could be so extraordinary. What were these things that floated by? They were like the dead, never glimpsed fully, as though they were only the extremities of something vaster that floated below.

"This cannot be Omara," he said.

"It is," Ruvanna told him. "But changed immensely by the power of the Seraph. His world died long, long ago. But the Preserver, Grenndak, had him brought here in exchange for his secrets. What power the survivor has, he uses to alter and distort the sea about him, to make it as his own world once was. He tried to keep us away, as he repels everything Omaran. The sea would kill us."

Brannog frowned. "It has done everything but drown us. Are we not tainted by it?"

"Omara has protected us from it."

Through you, he did not say, but knew it to be the truth.

And again my powers are diminished, she thought, but did not tell him. "The survivor will receive us. He is alert to us."

To her annoyance, Dennovia joined them. She had combed her hair and wrapped herself in a fresh blanket, though its shabbiness did nothing to reduce the impact of her beauty. "This change is sudden," she observed.

"It is the survivor's doing," said Brannog. "Are we welcome, Ruvanna?"

"He is not hostile to us. He only set the storms to guard himself and to keep intruders from harm. He is not a being of malice. In fact, he has done much to help Omara. The metal secrets that he gave to the Sorcerer-Kings, the rods of power."

Brannog gasped, his hand at once going to his side. But the rod was there, a cold length of metal, all glow gone from it. It seemed to have lost all the power it once had.

"Dormant," said Ruvanna, seeing his consternation. "Don't be deceived by it."

"Will the survivor help us?"

"When we reach the island, we will know." Ruvanna watched the island as they drew closer to it. Like the curious sea, it was like no other island they had seen. It seemed to be overgrown with a peculiar kind of growth, a thick weed or moss, or combination of the two, with rich green streaks in it, flowing down to the water in banks of tangled, vine-like profusion. The island rose up smoothly in an unbroken curve, no sign of rock poking through its dense cover, and even now there were no gulls, no hint of a bird or other life. Like impenetrable roots, the growths obscured everything.

"I see nowhere to land," said Brannog. "I wonder if we can moor to this vegetation. Or clamber up it. It looks as sleek as a seal's hide."

"Climb to where?" said Dennovia dubiously.

"We must go ashore," insisted Ruvanna tersely.

Brannog understood that she had no time for Dennovia. He found this odd, for before the sea voyage she had been in several conversations with the girl, as if their shared plight might bring them closer together. But it was not so now. Ruvanna's attitude had changed sharply, as if she had only scorn for Dennovia. And Dennovia was aware of it, though if anything, it seemed to amuse her. She was an unusual creature, Brannog mused. But of course, having been little better than a slave in the Direkeep, she would know no better.

The ship nestled closer to the island, coming under its shadow. The dense greenery rose up, cliffs of it, and it was impossible to see into it more than a few feet, almost as though the entire island was composed of nothing else. Great knotted boughs, if wood they were, curled into the sea. At least, Brannog decided, they would give them a place to moor.

"We'll tie up here," he told Ruvanna. "Unless you know where the survivor can be found."

"Not yet."

"This is ridiculous," said Dennovia suddenly. "How are we to ascend? Why not sail around the island? Is there no other way onto it?"

Ruvanna turned on her angrily. "Are you in charge of this expedition? Have you suddenly risen to lead us? You forget yourself!"

Brannog kept between the two girls. "Be sensible! We have

not crossed the sea to argue like children. Dennovia is not a prisoner, Ruvanna.''

''No, that is quite evident!''

Brannog scowled at her. ''What are you talking about?''

Ruvanna turned to the island. Her lips closed in a tight line. Abruptly she reeled, hands going to her head.

Put away your fire! the voice roared to her.

''Ruvanna!'' cried Brannog, reaching for her. Dennovia was also at her side. Ruvanna shook her head, eyes brimming with tears.

''Who has done this?'' said Brannog, looking up at the island.

''It is the survivor,'' said a voice behind them, and they all turned to see Carac and Ogrund standing there. ''He is awake and listening,'' said Ogrund.

''A little wary of us,'' added Carac. ''Though he should not be.''

''Can you speak to him?'' said Brannog, knowing their skill in such things.

''Not as Ruvanna can,'' said Carac. ''But we understand him. He wants us to go to him.''

''There is no easy way up to the island,'' said Ruvanna, now recovered.

''What of Wargallow?'' said Brannog. ''He cannot be revived, and even if he were, he is very weak.''

''The elementals will carry him,'' said Ruvanna. She had composed herself, ignoring Dennovia altogether. ''Ogrund, Carac. You had better help Mourndark to climb. He is by no means dormant. While you slept on the voyage, he tried to attack us.''

''Slept!'' gasped Ogrund. ''Mistress, we did not sleep.''

''You know they were ill,'' said Brannog, displeased. ''The sea is no place for them. Or had that slipped your mind?''

Ruvanna said nothing to him, merely pointing to Mourndark. ''Bring his instruments. There is one by the wheel. Fetch it.''

Ogrund did so at once.

As the climb began, Brannog looked back to see the elementals, still as gray and half-formed as they had looked in the dimness of the storm, laboriously carrying Wargallow.

They did not seem capable of such work, but in their ungainly way they climbed, as if no task would be too much for them. Ruvanna did not even look at them, as if they were an embarrassment to her, an extension of herself that she viewed as bitterly as she would have a physical imperfection.

Carac, Ogrund and Mourndark climbed easily enough, the two Earthwrought openly delighted to be off the ship. When Mourndark struggled, they goaded him on quietly. Ruvanna had taken the lead, moving nimbly, leaving Dennovia deliberately to climb with difficulty. Brannog, she thought, would no doubt help her, glad to have an opportunity to put his arms about her, and how ready she was to allow him! She could almost feel the girl's hot breath at his ear, the touch of her lips on his skin. She slipped on a wet branch, but had recovered before anyone could help, furious with herself for letting them see.

They were nearing the summit. Ruvanna was concentrating on the climb, forcing the terrible images of Dennovia and Brannog from her mind, when a sudden awareness began to steal into her. She felt the life of the island, its awakening pulse, its heartbeat, just as she felt the earth power in Omara. But the island was more than alive. As the shock reached her, she paused to cling to the vegetation.

Brannog could see her above him and wondered if all was well with her. She had become almost feverish in her will to succeed on this quest. "What is it?" he called.

Suddenly she laughed, hanging precariously with one hand. "We've found him! The survivor. He's here."

"Where? Above you?"

"We're holding him. The island *is* the survivor."

24
Judgment Isle

BRANNOG STARED at the fronds he was gripping for support.
What did Ruvanna mean, the island was the survivor? That
it was a living entity, a being? He met the gaze of Dennovia,
who shook her head at him. There was no time to question
Ruvanna, for she had clambered on upward, quickly disappearing over the crest of the green cliff. The others followed,
and once they had crested it, they were able to rest. The
vegetation swept away from them down to their right, hiding
that part of the island, while on their left it rose up steeply,
apparently to a pinnacle. Brannog calculated that the island
was at most a mile across, possibly two miles long.

Ruvanna had already moved on, impatient to reach her
goal. She was following what looked like a path in the greenery, which here was so matted as to form a thick carpet underfoot, tangled and mossy. The vegetation never grew higher
than bush level, and there did not seem to be any trees. As
far as Brannog could make out, the vegetation was all of the
same type, its only variation in its rich greens, some as bright
as the sea had been, some darker than pine needles. He wondered if the sea had taken its color from this place, some
strange discharge, needed in the water to sustain the alien
island.

The party had recovered from the climb and Brannog gave
the word to follow Ruvanna.

"Are you certain she knows what she's seeking?" said
Dennovia softly. "There's a wildness about her I don't understand."

"It must be the storm," said Brannog. "Her powers mystify me, but she used them in the storm. Each time she does so, she is weakened. But she understands this place better than we do. We must be guided by her and be patient."

"Of course," she smiled, keeping close to him.

A short while later they saw Ruvanna, standing on a small ridge, looking out at something, silent and statuesque. Brannog was the first to reach her, and as he did so he sucked in his breath. The island's secret was spread before him.

"The survivor," said Ruvanna.

The island was not just a mountain of vegetation. Here the rocks began, if rocks they were, for, as with the vegetation, they were unlike anything Omaran. The stone was a strange hue, shot through with tiny veins, flesh-like and smooth. It curved across to a ridge and then downward toward the water. Somewhere below there must be a cliff that sank into the sea itself. Vegetation on the rock was sparse, as though reluctant to grow on it, while on the higher reaches of the island it tumbled over the heights. What took Brannog's breath was the fact that the stone had a live feel to it, even more so than Omaran stone, as if it were a thick skin stretched over vital organs. He had heard sailors' tales of remote islands that moved, bursting into molten fires as volcanoes, but this was very different. He could feel life under him.

Carac and Ogrund were at his back, their expressions almost amusing, they were so surprised. Ruvanna glanced at them, nodding as if some secret had passed between them.

"There's nothing here!" protested Dennovia. "Just rocks! Have we come all this way to look at rocks?"

"You are incapable of seeing beyond your own body," said Ruvanna.

Carac frowned at Dennovia. "You do not see him?"

"See who?" she replied irritably.

"There, and there, and there," said Carac. He pointed to varying outlines, and Ruvanna was smiling, nodding.

Brannog suddenly grunted. Only now did he see the true shape of the formation himself. They were standing in the wrong place to view it properly, but as he craned his neck and turned his eyes this way and that, he found the shape. It was a gigantic carving, a sculpted face. The ridge ahead of them looked as if it could be the nose of the carving, and below it was the curve of its top lip. Before them was a depression in the stone that must be an eye, the eyelid drawn over it, polished smooth by the winds of centuries.

"The face of the survivor," he said. "Carved here by the last of his people," he said.

"Carved?" said Ruvanna, with more than a trace of scorn.

Ogrund took Brannog's arm. "It is alive. It is the survivor."

Brannog scowled. "This? But it is an island, vast."

"It is the head of the survivor," said Ruvanna with a note of triumph. "Sustained by the sea."

Dennovia gasped, subtly moving closer to Brannog so that she could hold on to him, but he moved a few steps to prevent her.

"Come with me," said Ruvanna, going downward and the party had little alternative but to obey. She led them onward, traversing the edge of the stone, not once stepping out onto it. None of the others did so either, afraid that if they did they might invoke some dire curse or penalty. Lower they went, coming at last to a rise that opened to a small, flat area, before falling away some fifty feet below to the sea. Ruvanna turned and pointed upward.

The face loomed over them, gigantic, unmistakable. If it had been carved, it would have been the work of utter genius, for the rock was worked in staggering detail, every line and every curve etched in, each growth upon it set with agonizing precision. No one on Omara could have made such a work, unless it was the Sorcerer-Kings at the height of their powers. The entire party were in absolute awe of the face, even Mourndark, who looked shaken by it. Only the elementals remained as they had been, waiting silently with their unconscious burden. Above them the face, sleeping, looked up at the open sky, the vegetation of the island now seen to be a forest of hair, sweeping back from the crown and down its sides, framing it, falling into the sea.

As they watched those features, so ancient, so alien to their own kind, the face moved.

It was not an exaggerated movement, and it was impossible to say which part of it had moved, but the watchers sensed it. In that all-consuming silence the slight movement was highlighted. Others followed. Without warning, two gray eyes gazed down at them, eyes which suddenly glowed with the richest of green depths, like wells into the very ocean. Curiously, light seemed to rise up from those deeps, bathing the onlookers. Dennovia's nails bit into her hands and she shook with fear. Mourndark, beside her, felt naked, stripped of his every thought, his mind wide open to whatever this monstrous presence intended. Even Brannog felt a churning in his gut that he had not felt since the worst of Xennidhum. It was not evil he faced now, but power beyond his wildest imagining. The sheer scope of it, the thought that this was a living creature, its *head*, threatened him with panic. How could such a thing live? What type of world must it have inhabited? And then he thought of the destruction of that world, the powers that must have been unleashed to have achieved such a destruction.

Only Ruvanna looked unmoved. She stood brazenly under the gaze of the twin eyes.

So you are the children of Omara, said the voice, reaching inside all of them.

"Some of us are not," Ruvanna called and her voice struck the rocks of the great face and was amplified by it, as if she had shouted.

Refugees then, like myself.

"We are all victims of the work of the Hierarchs of Ternannoc," Ruvanna told the face. No one else wished to address the face, allowing the girl to speak for them.

And what brings you before Seraph Zoigon?

"The same thing that brought Grenndak to you."

There was a prolonged silence. *Grenndak? The seeker after powers? Ah, but it was ever thus. Power. Secrets. Mysteries. You complicate life. And what happens when you have powers? You destroy.*

"Omara is threatened."

By whom? Has Grenndak abused the powers I gave him? Have you come to set that right by demanding more of the same? I have few powers left now. I relinquished most of them in my own search for peace. Omara is slowly winning back her sea from me, and rightly so, for I stole it. The sea around me is losing its power to sustain me. In time it will cleanse itself of me and what I have done to survive here. There will be no more of my storms. If I have harmed your world by hiding in it, I am truly sorry.

"You earned your sanctuary," said Ruvanna. "No one would deny you that. The Sorcerer-Kings made good use of your powers. The rods that you cast for their Werewatch would have kept the ancient evils at bay."

Are you saying that they failed?

"Not at first. The Werewatch carried them and used them to seal up the tears in Omara's fabric made by the working of the Hierarchs of Ternannoc. But the rods have fallen into the hands of evil."

I gave warning of such a thing. While the rods exist, they are a threat, just as they can be a blessing. This is your world. You are its children, refugees or otherwise. You must shape Omara's destiny. I have done enough.

"You helped the Sorcerer-Kings. And you also gave power to Grenndak. You taught him the use of metal, power over it that no other creature but you had. Grenndak, a renegade from Ternannoc. A Hierarch!"

He sought to atone for what his people had done. The Hierarchs destroyed many worlds, including my own. Grenndak wanted to prevent it happening here. I cannot deny that I acted from self-pity. I came here, knowing that I would bring harm to the sea, but I have not caused irreparable damage. I have said that the sea will soon mend, and when it does, I shall perish. Omara will have extracted her revenge. That is just. I have had centuries of life, of dreaming. It is enough.

"Do you know what Grenndak did with the powers you gave him, the secrets of metal?" Ruvanna told him then, gave him the history of the Deliverers and of the Abiding Word of the Direkeep, the warping of the Preserver's mind, the torment of Omara's people under his grim laws.

So, came the voice, saddened by the tale, *this is how his dreams ended. He meant to be a champion. There was no evil in him when he brought me here. Fear, perhaps. Is that what has changed him?*

"The Abiding Word has been revoked. The Deliverers are the last of their kind—"

"She deceives you!" snarled Mourndark, pushing forward.

Brannog gripped his arm until he winced. "Silence, or I'll choke the life from you—"

Peace! roared the voice, and they all staggered before it. *I will hear all of you.*

Mourndark shrugged free of Brannog, turning to the face of the Seraph with a look of glee. "You heard from the girl of Simon Wargallow. He sought rulership for himself. Just as the Werewatch purged Omara of evil, so did the Deliverers. You have said how power corrupts. That was the work of the Deliverers, to prevent such corruption!"

Then you would restore them?

"Omara will not survive without them."

With you to lead them?

Mourndark's smug expression brought a shiver to Ruvanna, but she dare not prevent him having his say before the Seraph.

"Do you recall your visit from Grenndak, Seraph Zoigon?" asked Mourndark. "How he pleaded with you to help him undo the terrible errors made by his fellow Hierarchs? How he would use your gifts to secure Omara from doom?"

Though it was long ago, I recall it. It was not an easy bargain to strike. Grenndak was persuasive, his logic good. And I wanted sanctuary. Grenndak had the power to bring me here—

"You were worthy of saving," smiled Mourndark. "You could so easily have annihilated Grenndak, a Hierarch himself, for what they had done to your world. You acted in good faith."

I claim no honor for what I did.

"Do you recall that Grenndak had a number of companions with him? His most trusted retainers?"

Brannog stiffened as though an icy wind had swept across the island. What was Mourndark coming to?

I did not speak to any of them, but I recall them.

"I was the first of them. Grenndak's right hand. I am a surgeon. I learned from Grenndak, for it was I that he trusted with your secrets. It was *I* who showed him how to utilize them. There is no one else who has that skill.''

It is clear to me that you are the enemy of the others, said the voice. *Why have they brought you before me?*

Mourndark was about to formulate a glib answer, when Ruvanna cut him short. ''As he says, he is the only man with the skill to perform the metal surgery, the giving of the killing steel.'' She motioned her elementals forward and silently they brought Wargallow, laying him down on the thick vegetation like an offering.

Who is this man? He is dying.

''He is Wargallow.'' Ruvanna explained what had occurred at Mount Timeless and of how the Sublime One had intended Wargallow to go back to his people as a symbol, a sign to all Earthwrought that the Deliverers were their enemies.

Then you wish me to save this man, said the Seraph when Ruvanna had finished. *To repair his arm.*

Ruvanna nodded. ''That is our only reason for coming to you. We do not seek power for ourselves. Only the Steel-master does that. He would become a new Grenndak, though far worse!''

''Seraph Zoigon, that is unreasonable,'' said Mourndark coldly. ''I seek justice, no more. To reclaim what you gave to my master, who was murdered by Wargallow.''

You have all wasted your journey. I have told you my powers are waning. I could do something for the man, but not save his life. I am moved by your concern for him. If you truly sought me for his benefit, it is a noble thing—

''But you will have the power,'' said Ruvanna, turning to Brannog. ''Give me the rod.''

He had hidden it inside his shirt for the climb. He had no hesitation in giving it to her. She held it aloft. It was dull, seemingly lifeless, but the light in the eyes of the Seraph flared as he saw it, as it did in Mourndark's eyes.

One of the rods! came the voice, and those before him were rocked by the force of his surprise.

''You created it,'' said Ruvanna.

Not alone. But the Seraphim did so.

''It has power.''

Yes. And I see a power there now that shocks me. For what

purpose has this rod been used? The powers within it are awesome. It has been used to drain life, to suck power into it. But from where?

Ruvanna pointed the rod deliberately at Mourndark and he drew back, trying to keep from its range. But no light sprang from it. "Mourndark found the rod. And you see how he used it. Not to heal wounds, but to create them. The Esoterics, the body of the Sublime One. He turned them to ashes."

You must take great care! What you hold is a weapon of incalculable power. My best advice to you is to cast it into the deepest part of the ocean. Sail out to the east, beyond my seas. Cast it away.

Ruvanna shook her head. "I did not bring it here for that. I brought it for you. You lack power. Then take it. Use it! Save Wargallow."

There was an appalling silence. The eyes of the Seraph closed and it seemed as if he had abandoned them, horrified, perhaps, by what Ruvanna had demanded. But at last the eyes opened again, and this time there was pain in them, a deep anguish.

You do not realize what you do.

"Can the rod be used to save him?" persisted Ruvanna.

Yes! the voice cried. *But don't you see? The temptation. That power could save me, give renewed life to me. How many more centuries would it give me?*

Ruvanna looked at the rod. "No. You won't use it for that. Not any more. Enough is enough."

After another long pause, the voice spoke. *Why do you want to save this man? One man among so many. From what you tell me of your world beyond my sea, he is not loved. He is not a great leader.*

Brannog put an arm about Ruvanna and she thought then that the truth must surely come out. "I will tell you that," said Brannog to the face. "Of all of us and of all the Men and Earthwrought I have known, none is more deserving of life than Simon Wargallow. He was once a man of darkness, a creature of Grenndak, just as Mourndark is now. but he discovered that darkness in himself. He is changed. He is no paragon, and those of us who know him and his will still question his methods. He shows no mercy to the dark and tells us we are fools to tolerate it at all. Even so, Omara needs him. It is strange, but he is the proof that the way to peace need not be through violence. If you can save him, do so." He looked away, embarrassed by his own words.

The Seraph appeared to be silent once more, but it had chosen to speak to Ruvanna alone. *Is that why you do this? Because Omara needs Wargallow?*

She flinched, unable to hide her thoughts, though she could not speak them aloud. *You know why I have come here*, she answered, so that only the Seraph could hear.

You gave up enormous power to come and ask for what Brannog desires. Do not think I have not seen that. Does he know how deeply you love him?

Since he does not care, I will never tell him!

Then I will not presume to. What is in your minds I can read easily. It is why I will not support any of Mourndark's insane desires. But all your thoughts are private. But you must think, Ruvanna. Consider this: power carries consequences. We may choose it or reject it. Whichever choice we make, there will be a reckoning. I could so easily take the rod and use its power for myself.

But you won't.

No, I will not take it. Omara will benefit better if I do not. This is not altruism, you understand, for I am just a being who is tired of the fight for survival. Giving up the rod will be a small price for me to pay! But you, too, have given up power. You, I see now, could have taken everything Omara has to offer you. You could have become the Voice of Omara. Yet you have rejected it. Will Omara benefit more from your choice? Or from your act of selfishness? Because you value love more than the power you would have had?

Who is to say I would have used the power wisely?

That is too easy an excuse. You must weigh the responsibility that was offered to you, and your own wisdom.

I have made my choice! I want Wargallow saved.

And if I save him, do you think Brannog will love you because of it? Is that the real prize you seek?

There were tears in her eyes as she looked up at the face. To the others, it seemed as though nothing had passed between them. They waited, motionless as the elementals.

Yes, I want his love! But it is not why I did it. If I had known he still would not love me, I would yet have chosen to save Wargallow for him.

Then I am answered. And so are you. Your love, you see, is not so selfish as you seem to think it is.

What will you do?

I can give Wargallow life. Make him whole again. I will need the power of the rod, and the Steelmaster's skill. But you must know that in his heart there is only hatred. For Wargallow most of all.

Then I will use force! I will give him to the elementals—

Again there was silence and Ruvanna wondered if the Seraph had changed his mind. But he spoke to her privately once more. *Would you use force on Brannog to make him love you?*

Of course not!

It is the same thing. You have the power to impose your will on any of the others. You think it wrong to force a man to love something, and yet you would force Mourndark to do what he least wishes to.

I understand you, but if Mourndark refuses to help, what other course is there? It is no more than he would expect! And it is how Wargallow—

Would act. Yes, I know that, from Brannog's words. Wargallow is an extremist. No sacrifice is too great for him, not if it will provide him with success. It is a dangerous path to walk. However, I admire his cause, and his sense of justice. I have read it in his mind.

And Mourndark? Ruvanna asked in desperation.

We all have our price, said the Seraph ruefully. *Even I was bought.*

Ruvanna knew that the Seraph had said all that he would do for the moment. She turned her attention to Mourndark. Her cheeks were flushed; he stared at her venomously, as if he had decided she had already betrayed him.

"Mourndark," she said. "The rod is lost to us."

He stared at it, frowning.

"I will give it to the Seraph," she told him.

"Wait!" said Brannog. "We cannot dispose of it. Use it to help Wargallow, but it must go to Goldenisle—"

Ruvanna pulled away from him angrily. "Then take it!"

She held it out. "Sail now, at once. But leave Wargallow here. And me."

Brannog looked shocked. "You have spoken to the survivor?"

"Yes. The rod can save Wargallow."

Mourndark's lips curled in a contemptuous sneer. "And Zoigon; is that it?" He looked up at the face. The eyes had closed. "And he accuses me of greed!"

"Well, Brannog?" said Ruvanna.

He stared at the unconscious Deliverer, knowing what Wargallow wanted. He would have sacrificed himself without a second thought. If Brannog agreed to losing the rod to save him, Wargallow would never forgive him. Everything pointed to Wargallow being abandoned. Brannog closed his eyes. I cannot do this.

Brannog, came the voice within. The Seraph spoke to him alone, as it had done to Ruvanna. *I will save him and restore him. But the rod will not be lost. You must say nothing to the others, however.*

Brannog fought to mask his reaction to this. What game was the Seraph playing with them? But he pointed to Wargallow. "If he can be saved, then spare him."

"You are a fool!" snarled Mourndark, but he dared not attack.

Ruvanna shook her head at him. "The rod is lost. Is that all you desire? Is there nothing else that would satisfy you?"

He glared at her, not comprehending. "What do you mean, girl? What do you expect of me? Should I ask for mercy?"

"No. But you expect to die?"

"I am your enemy. All of you. Even that whore, who would thrust my own knife into me! Wouldn't you?" he laughed scornfully at Dennovia. "But why should I expect better from any of you?"

"I cannot believe that you wish to die," said Ruvanna. Mourndark did not answer her. "Well, do you?"

"The island has clouded your mind. You think I will say yes? Of course I have no wish to die. I would prefer to see you all toss yourselves from the cliffs! Is there a point to your absurd questions?"

"I wish to strike a bargain with you. A life for a life."

"I see. Mine."

"Quite so. Your life for Wargallow's."

Mourndark's frown deepened. "Then it is true," he murmured. "You and the Seraph cannot save him unless I help. It *is* the reason you brought me here!" His frown became a terrible smile of triumph.

Brannog swore, but Ruvanna touched his arm. "Well, Mourndark, what is it to be?"

"You think I will believe you? That you'll spare me? To what end? Leave me here on this dying island? Or have my throat cut later when you are safely away?"

Ruvanna shook her head. "No. You'll be taken back to the mainland and freed. I will see that you are protected."

"Hah! By whom?" But as he said it, he turned to the elementals. They were like stones, gray and silent. "By *these?*"

"They are my will," said Ruvanna. "If I tell them to protect you, they will."

"And later, when you tell them to kill me—"

"No. I'll recall them."

He considered this for a while, then finally nodded, but a wolfish grin lit his face. "Very well. But there are a number of conditions. Since the elementals do all that you command of them, you must tell them this. As soon as they reach the mainland, they are to obey me. And me alone."

His words shocked her, but she nodded. "I accept. But if you try to use them to harm me, or any of us, or for any evil—"

"No. I'll be more than glad to be free of you."

"What else do you want?" snapped Brannog.

"My instruments. I must have them."

"On the mainland," said Ruvanna. "Only then."

"Agreed."

"That is all?" said Brannog.

"Almost." Mourndark laughed and held out his hand to Dennovia. "I could not go without my beloved Dennovia." His voice was thick with derision and Dennovia paled.

She clung to Brannog. "Don't let him touch me," she said. This time Ruvanna stepped to her defense.

"Dennovia goes her own way, Steelmaster. She has suffered enough indignity through you."

"You refuse me? Then you had better strike me down and be done with it. Come! Use your powers. I am ready." Like a cornered wolf, Mourndark stood at bay, his hands before him like claws.

"Insane," muttered Brannog.

Ruvanna raised the rod and stepped to Mourndark, and she looked as if she truly meant to turn him to ash. But she felt her hand gripped from behind. She turned to beat off Brannog, thinking it must be him, but she met instead the imperious gaze of Dennovia.

"Not that way," said the girl. "Put aside the rod."

"Let him die," hissed Ruvanna.

"And undo all that you have done? No." Dennovia walked toward Mourndark. "I will go with him. I have nowhere else to go."

Mourndark gazed at her strangely, then laughed. "She has answered you, earth woman! We have our bargain."

Ruvanna was close by Brannog's side. His face was a mask of perplexity. "If you want her," said Ruvanna under her breath, "I'll save her."

"Want her?" he gasped.

"Your desire is clear—"

"You presume too much," Brannog snorted. "Mourndark! Listen to me. You have your bargain. Your life, your freedom, protection. But I will tell you this. I am King Brannog. My eyes and my ears see and hear across this world. There is nowhere you can go that I won't know of. If you touch her, if you go near her without her approval, everything is canceled between us."

Mourndark merely laughed. "As you wish."

Brannog glared up at the Seraph's great face. "What must we do?" he asked Ruvanna.

She also turned to the face. The eyes opened once more and observed her. "I have Wargallow, the rod and the Steelmaster," she said.

Lift up the fallen Wargallow. Let your earth beings bring him into me.

At this, the stone lips parted, opening to reveal a dark

cavern, the inside of which was like the very deeps of space, though starless. The entire party stood back from this gulf, apart from the elementals.

Bring him to me. Place the rod in his hand.

Mourndark watched sourly as the elementals lifted Wargallow, his frown darkening as the rod of power was put in Wargallow's left hand, the white fingers wrapping around it, the rod on his chest.

"I'll need my knives," said Mourndark to Ruvanna, and she gave them to him. He clutched them to his chest like a child with a precious toy.

Yes, bring the knives of your trade. They were cast from the same metal as the rod.

Mourndark nodded with an almost reverential glee and watched the elementals as they stood at the lip of the cavern.

"Go on," prompted Ruvanna.

For a moment Mourndark looked as though he might reject all that had been agreed, but he mustered his courage and with a final, contemptuous laugh, followed.

Dennovia hung back, but he seemed to have forgotten her already.

"What of us?" Brannog asked Ruvanna.

"We must wait here," she said. "We are all at the mercy of Seraph Zoigon now."

Brannog nodded, wondering how much of a temptation the rod of power would be to it.

25

The Power

OGRUND AND CARAC, who seemed more exhausted by their ordeal on the sea than any of the others, had settled themselves in a sheltered place not far from the base of the great face, and they fell into a deep sleep, the first they had permitted themselves for many nights. Here, at last, they felt safe, sure that the island offered no harm to any of them. Ruvanna stood over them for a moment, satisfied that they were recovering from what, she knew, had been a dire experience for them; the Earthwrought rarely ventured near the sea, let alone upon it. Too long a journey could have killed them, though she had given them something of her power, and would not have permitted them to die. Even so, she had not expected the journey to have been such a drain on their strength. It was only in the relative peace of the island she was able to consider it.

Brannog also felt exhausted, but would not allow himself to relax. He studied the great face. It seemed to sleep, more like carved stone than ever, the eyes closed, the features stiff. It was difficult to believe that this being had spoken to them. An hour had passed since Wargallow and Mourndark had disappeared into it, their exit followed by a deep silence. Brannog turned to the girls. Dennovia sat on the ground, looking not at the face, but out to sea.

"What made you do this?" he asked her, unable to contain the question that had been chafing at him.

She did not look at him, merely shaking her head. "I understand Mourndark better than you, although I cannot pretend to know him. When he told you he wouldn't agree to your demands, he meant it. He would rather have died than be forced."

"But why should he insist on taking you with him?" said Brannog.

She smiled sourly. "Not because he has any feeling for me! I thought once he might have. But since Mount Timeless I have learned how foolish I was to expect such a thing. No, it was done out of spite. I cheated him, caused him to lose the rod of power. That was the object of his love."

"Then he will seek to be revenged on you."

"Oh yes. Already that has begun. By denying me my freedom. He does not want me, not as before, so my days with him will not be easy—"

"Then why?"

Ruvanna, who had been listening to the exchange, made an exasperated sound. "You understand so little," she told Brannog. "We would have lost Wargallow if Mourndark hadn't agreed. Dennovia realized that. We owe her everything."

Brannog was nonplussed, looking away. So Dennovia had made her own sacrifice. And here was Ruvanna, supporting her. Not long ago she was ready to denounce her, perhaps even kill her, judging by her fury. These women were impossible to fathom.

Ruvanna had walked away, finding a place where she, too, could rest. Solitude offered the best solace here on the island.

Dennovia glanced after her. "This voyage has cost her more deeply than it has me."

"Why do you say that?"

"She has given up much to achieve her goal. Can you not feel that?"

Brannog looked no less bemused. "There are great powers in her, and a skill to achieve things beyond even the strongest of the Earthwrought. She woke this island—"

"But those powers are diminishing, Brannog."

"She's exhausted."

"We all are. But Ruvanna has almost used up her powers."

"How do you know that?" he said, slightly irritably.

"I'm a woman. I understand Ruvanna. And her anger, her jealousy."

"Jealousy?"

Dennovia shook her head again, gazing out to sea. "To me it is written clearly on her face, in every glance. She has been jealous of me from the moment she first saw me. Other women have reacted to me this way. I was chosen for my beauty. Do you not think me beautiful?"

"Of course."

"Then I am a threat."

"I can see that you would use your beauty as a kind of power—"

"I have no other."

"Few men could resist you."

She looked at him, her eyes gleaming, her smile rich in knowledge. "No man could," she laughed. "Not even you, Brannog."

He scowled, uncomfortable. "You think not?"

"Never mind. But Ruvanna knows it. And so she came to hate me for a while. She saw my arms about you—"

"You were in peril, we all were! You acted from a need for preservation—"

She laughed, the sound melodic, almost alluring. Brannog looked at Ruvanna, but she was lost in her own thoughts, out of earshot.

"Did you not think me overfamiliar?" said Dennovia. "Be honest."

He did not look at her. "The truth is, I thought you saw in me a chance to free yourself of your past."

"Oh, so you understood that much at least!" she clapped her hands. "You surprise me."

"Why?"

"You see so little. Yes, I wanted to use you, and it would have been easy, be sure of that. I have no powers, no magical abilities, but what I do is powerful in its way. But I wanted to show you something else. I wanted you to see Ruvanna's anger. At first I wanted to do it because I am cruel. Mourndark taught me how to be cruel, although it may be something within me. My life in the Direkeep would have appalled you. Yet I took pleasure from it when I could knowing no other way of life. I wanted to enjoy Ruvanna's pain.''

"At first?''

"Yes, at first. But I relented. I wanted you to see her jealousy.''

"Why torment her if you had relented?''

She looked at him with a puzzled expression. "Do you understand nothing?'' She spoke harshly, surprising herself, and Brannog drew back. "She has rejected everything to come here and attempt to save your friend. Why? Why has she done that, Brannog?''

"She knew the island, that there was a chance—''

"Yes. But even Wargallow insisted that the rod should go back to the west. You took an appalling risk in coming here. Ruvanna knew more than anyone else what was at stake. She forfeited her own power to come here. And all that she could have been.''

"What do you mean? What would she have been?''

"Ask her! Ask her why she sacrificed it.''

Brannog's confusion churned like a pool. He was like a man groping for a rope that would pull him out of it and set him down on the shore of clarity.

"For *you*, Brannog. She did it for you.''

He gaped at her.

"You wanted Wargallow saved. She knew that you would have given everything to save him, whatever your reasons. And because of that, she was prepared to pursue that cause above all others. When I knew that, and when I saw Mourndark threaten to deny her her goal after all she had suffered to achieve it, then I knew the meaning of jealousy. I envied her the power to love.''

"You prevented Mourndark's death and our failure.''

"I am amazed that you have not read all this for yourself. But as you have not, or if you have hidden it from yourself, then it is time you were told.''

Again Brannog glanced at Ruvanna. She appeared to be asleep. Hidden from myself, he thought. He was about to speak to Dennovia, but she waved him away as if dismissing a tedious courtier. He was too tired to argue and left her to gaze up at the great face. Its mouth was slightly open, but there was no movement of those perfectly chiseled lips.

Brannog's feelings were no clearer, chaotic. At last the tiredness cramped him. This was not the time to follow trails of logic, of clarity. He sat on the thick mat of vegetation and closed his eyes, but sleep evaded him, and a thousand demented images closed in on him. The intense silence of the island folded them all, and soon they had become statues, as if carved from the same strange stone as the face of Zoigon.

BRANNOG'S TURMOIL, his waking dreams, coalesced into a single form. It moved from darkness, towering over him, and from it a face glared, the eyes fiery, full of loathing. It was Mourndark.

He alone had emerged from the mouth of the Seraph. His hands were at his side; at first he could not move them. As Brannog's full concentration returned, he realized Mourndark was no threat, just drained of energy, like a man who had been without sleep for days. Mourndark staggered, but would not allow himself the indignity of a fall. He no longer carried his blades, but Brannog saw the blood on his hands and shirt.

Dennovia and Ruvanna came quickly. They watched as Mourndark made to speak, but no words came yet.

"Is he alive?" said Ruvanna softly.

"Yes," said Mourndark at last, though his tone was full of bitterness.

"Restored?" said Brannog.

"My work here is over, my debt paid," said Mourndark coldly. He looked at his hands, scowling at them as though he would never use them again, as though they had betrayed him. Then, without another glance at the others, he lurched away.

"Leave him," said Brannog. He was stepping toward the open mouth. "Zoigon!" he called, and the word echoed back from the cavern of darkness. But there was no movement, and no reply.

"I'll go in," said Ruvanna.

"No," said Brannog at once, but she smiled at him.

"I have to. It's safer for me."

"We cannot trust Mourndark—"

"He's beaten, Brannog," said Dennovia. "Whatever happened in there, it finished him. There is no trap."

"The island is dying," said Ruvanna. "It has been for many years. But this last act has accelerated its dying. If Wargallow is alive, I'll bring him out." Before Brannog could dissent, she had gone through the open mouth into the dark. Brannog would have followed, but Dennovia restrained him.

"Let her go. Zoigon will not harm her. She still has power, and we do not."

"If she does not return quickly, I will follow."

Dennovia smiled at him in a strange way, but he tried to ignore her.

Beyond the gate, Ruvanna felt the dark close in at once, stifling. She fought it, pushing it back. As she did so, she felt the pulse of the Seraph.

I live yet, came its faint voice, as if from far, far below her. *But like you, I am tired. This was the hardest working of them all.*

"Where is he?"

Below.

She moved down into the oppressive dark, unable to feel anything beneath her, although she walked unimpeded and did not fall. Blind instinct was all that she had left, her senses negated by the vacuum in which she moved. She carried her will like a torch, determined that she would not be foiled, not now. She knew that her own powers, given to her by Omara, had been used up almost to the full. When this was over, what would remain? Would she have even as much as an Earthwrought child? If she lived. But she tossed the thought away as if it were a threat to her progress.

Her journey was interminable, but at last there was light of a kind. Green and pallid, it hovered ahead and below her. She seemed to drift down to it. She could see the various shapes of this inner world. There were thick roots and tendrils, as if she had stumbled into the burrow of a large animal. She looked down and gasped, for the floor of the chamber was rich not in soil, but in mire. She recognized it and its sea-like smell at once: the elementals! They had been altered, broken up and spread like a carpet.

Omaran mud, Omaran goodness, said the voice. *It was needed for the working.*

Ruvanna moved across it, aware that there was very little life left in the mire. It was a burden she would no longer carry, an absolution of her guilt. There was a body before her, stretched out on the soil. It was wrapped in darkness, a cloak that had been woven from the very inner night of this place.

"Wargallow," she said, but his face was yet ashen, reposing in death, or so it seemed.

He lives. Give him your power. Mine is almost spent. The voice had become very weak.

Ruvanna stiffened. Was this to be a life for a life, hers for that of Wargallow? But there was no answering voice. She stared at the motionless Deliverer.

In a while, she began to sing. Her pure voice filled the chamber, finding its remote walls, its corridors, as if the entire island would swell with it. And as she sang, the perfect melody floating around and up and beyond, she felt Omara's power flooding out of her, more of it than she could have dreamed of. Like a living stream it swept across the chamber, imbuing the soil, the mire, and the body of Wargallow with a fresh, pulsing energy. Wargallow did not stir, but his face was no longer pale.

Ruvanna felt herself overtaken by an enormous lassitude. The power still came, but she knew that it would, after all, draw out her life with it. Yet it would revive Wargallow. Soon. The song faded, her eyes closed, and the darkness beyond the world closed in hungrily.

From out of it, hands clawed at her. They caught her and dragged her upward. A different, floating sensation took her. She heard a cry of anguish—was it the remote voice of Brannog?—and the last notes of her song died. The fight was over. The dark had won. Oblivion claimed her.

"See to him!" yelled Brannog in the enclosed space. He had struggled here as fast as he dared, falling more than once, his ears ringing to the sound of that agonizingly beautiful song. There was something in it that spoke of grief, a lament, of death. Dennovia had come with him, unable to keep her balance. But as they had come at last to Ruvanna and snatched her, Dennovia almost fell over the body of Wargallow. She looked down at him to see that he was moving. She tugged at his shoulder and his eyes opened.

Silence raced in on them, but a glance told her that Brannog had already begun the difficult return to the surface, as if he had abandoned the Deliverer. He carried Ruvanna close to his chest as if she were his child.

Wargallow tried to form a word, but the effort was too great.

"Get up!" screamed Dennovia, terrified that the earth would close in on them, walling them up forever. She slapped Wargallow across the face, and something in her terror must have reached him, for he began a labored movement. He got to his knees, still wrapped like an insect in his dark cloak. With Dennovia's frantic help, he got to his feet.

With infinite, painful slowness, they began the pursuit of Brannog.

The song had woken Ogrund and Carac, and as Brannog came out into the sunlight, the Earthwrought held out their arms and relieved him of his burden. They stretched Ruvanna out on the carpet of vegetation, touching her face and whispering to her. Brannog knelt over her, his chest heaving.

"Is she alive?" he gasped. She had felt so frail, so cold, as he carried her.

Neither Carac nor Ogrund spoke. They busied themselves in their ritual. Brannog felt his chest constrict. *Ruvanna!* She could not die, not now, not after this. He watched, oblivious to the movement behind him.

Dennovia had emerged from the mouth of the Seraph, and as she did so, she collapsed, utterly spent, covering her face with her hands. Her body shook and she hugged herself, otherwise not moving. The darkness of the mouth stirred for a last time. It was Mourndark who was the first to see what emerged.

Framed by the alien darkness, it was Simon Wargallow, his body wrapped in the cloak provided for him by the Seraph. Only his face was visible; it wore a perplexed frown, like a man emerging from a long fever with only half his memory. He stood without moving, looking down at the prostrate form of Ruvanna and the three beings bent over it.

Mourndark shuddered, as if he had looked into the eyes of his own death. No one noticed him; in a moment he had slipped over the edge of the vegetation and was lost to view. No one gave him a thought.

Brannog shook Ogrund's shoulder. "You must save her!"

When the two Earthwrought straightened, suddenly diminutive, both had tears in their eyes. "She is alive," said Ogrund. "But we cannot save her. She has given everything." His eyes suddenly widened as he saw the huge shape that rose over them all.

Brannog turned, his own eyes moist. Wargallow stood there like a man risen from the grave. "She is not dead," he said.

"What have you done to her?" said Brannog, anger coiling within him.

Wargallow shook his head. "I have been in a strange land. There were nightmares, clashing powers."

"You've killed her!" snarled Ogrund, getting to his feet. For a moment it seemed that he would hurl himself at Wargallow, but Brannog restrained him. He could feel the livid fury of the Earthwrought. Wargallow remained dazed, looking down at himself as if aware of something that had been eluding him. He freed his left hand and pulled aside the cloak. His body was intact, his right arm wrapped in thin leaves which reached from beyond his elbow down to a full length of arm and hand.

"My arm," he breathed, staring at the leaves as if seeing the impossible.

Brannog gazed at it, nodding. "Restored, just as promised. But we did not know what it would cost." He held his own anger in check, watching as Wargallow began to undo the leaves that bound his repaired arm. As they fell away, dull metal glowed in the sunlight.

Carac and Ogrund fell back, shocked. What had once been the killing steel had been remade, refashioned. Mourndark had performed his art with a new degree of staggering precision. The curved sickles, the cutting edges, were gone. In place of them was a hand, a human hand, perfectly made, though cast in the secret metals of the Seraph. Wargallow lifted the arm, testing it, moving it. It responded perfectly, perfectly grafted to him, as much a part of him as his own flesh. But as it moved, Wargallow felt a sudden stab of dreadful understanding.

"What has happened?" he gasped.

"It is faultless," murmured Brannog.

Wargallow shook his head. His face had become pale once more, his horror apparent. "This cannot be!"

"What do you mean?" said Brannog, suddenly alarmed.

"Where did the Seraph mine this metal?"

Brannog shrugged. "From within himself. It was his power—"

Wargallow held up the hand, concentrating on it. As he did so, it turned a pale blue, pulsing with an inner light. Brannog recognized it at once.

"The rod!" he gasped. "Zoigon has used the rod!"

I told you it would not be lost, came the voice, and all heard it. They turned to the face. The eyes merely flickered, not opening.

"I cannot carry this!" shouted Wargallow, so sharply that Dennovia gazed up at him. When she saw the hand, she drew back.

Zoigon did not answer. Wargallow's voice fell. "I cannot carry it," he said quietly to Brannog.

"After what we have come through," said Brannog, "you have no choice."

"You have no conception of what power lies within this monstrous thing," Wargallow told him.

Ogrund pushed past Brannog and stood directly before Wargallow, bristling with anger. "Our mistress has forfeited her life to give you that power! Far better we had left you to die! You will carry it!" His own hands clenched, the veins in his thick neck standing out. Carac was beside him, equally as stiff with fury.

Wargallow was horrified by their hatred. His people would never be free of that; the past could never be erased. He had no anger to match theirs. He nodded slowly, lowering the arm. "So be it."

Dennovia was on her feet, and she found the strength to come to Ruvanna. She bit her lip when she saw her.

Wargallow gently moved her aside and bent over Ruvanna. He looked up at Brannog, who seemed like a general who had lost a war, ruined by defeat. Ruvanna had, after all, meant much to him.

"I cannot begin to understand what I am to do with this new-found power," said Wargallow. "So much has gone into the making of this hand. From the Seraph and from Omara itself."

"Omara?" said Brannog, surprised.

"Through Ruvanna. Some of the dreams return to me. Ruvanna drew from Omara. Omara gave her power and would have given her far more had she chosen to take it. And the rod, the arm, is not merely a weapon for destruction."

They watched as he listened to Ruvanna's heart. She was alive, but barely. Even Carac and Ogrund grudgingly let him study her. He finished his examination. "I can do one thing. I may save her, or hasten her death. But before night arrives, she will die anyway."

Brannog scowled at the closed eyes of the Seraph. "Will Zoigon not save her?"

Wargallow shook his head. "He is no more alive than she is. He, too, will be dead by nightfall. And we dare not stay here until then."

"What can you do?" said Brannog.

Wargallow held out his steel hand. "This may save her."

There was a long silence. Neither Carac nor Ogrund moved, their eyes fixed on Ruvanna. Dennovia looked upon the steel as if it were a serpent.

Brannog answered. "Then use it."

"And if I kill her?" said Wargallow.

Ogrund's frown tightened. "Then your powers will not save you, Deliverer."

"Then," replied Brannog thickly, "she will be at rest. Do it!"

"Very well. Move back."

Carac, Ogrund and Dennovia did as bidden, but Brannog demurred. Instead he knelt down beside Ruvanna and lifted her head, gently placing it in his lap.

"Brannog," said Wargallow. "If this fails—"

"Then you must place us in the earth together."

Wargallow knew from the big man's eyes that he meant this and would not be moved from it. He nodded. In a moment he had lifted Ruvanna's hands as gently as Brannog had raised her head, putting them together on her chest with his left hand. Then, with great care, he touched the hands with the steel fingertips of his new hand. The blue glow paled to white, then became scarlet. Wargallow felt the surge of power, and to his shock was able to control it, to direct it. He stumbled back. Ruvanna had not moved, nor reacted.

Brannog looked askance at him, but he shook his head. "I dare do no more," said Wargallow. Still Ruvanna did not stir. Brannog bent to her heart. He could hear its beat, unchanged, faint.

Long moments dragged by. Dennovia broke the silence with a cry and they all whirled. From out of the mouth of the Seraph, something was crawling. Dark and foul-smelling, like a thick trail of oil, it spread onto the vegetation.

"The elementals!" said Wargallow, recalling them from his dream-like experience under the island. The flowing darkness reached the recumbent Ruvanna, spreading around her like a bed. Brannog felt its touch, but it was somehow warm, soothing.

But the girl did not move. The dark mud had become the soil of her grave.

With a terrible cry of frustration and misery, Ogrund raised his war club and made to bring it down upon Wargallow's skull. The Deliverer reacted with instinctive speed, his right arm lifting to meet the club. As it struck, there was a deafening crash and a blinding flare of light that knocked them all to their bellies. Ogrund shrieked in agony and was tossed backward as if made of straw. Wargallow saw the bolt of blue light crackle down and strike at Ruvanna before he could do anything to prevent it. The sounds reverberated from Zoigon's stone face, rolling away until there was silence.

Carac scrambled to his feet and rushed to Ogrund's side. He bent over his friend, but let out a gasp, shaking his head. Ogrund was dead.

Wargallow could hardly see, his eyes still smarting from the light. He stumbled, brushed aside by Brannog, who stood over the dead Earthwrought.

"Ogrund!" he yelled. "No!"

Carac buried his face in his hands, his body convulsed. Brannog felt himself choke, unable to move.

Wargallow saw what had happened. "Why did he do it? Why?" he whispered. "I would not have had this, not again."

Brannog closed his eyes. "Ogrund, Ogrund. Why did you cast away your life? Why could you not accept that you were as worthy a companion as any other of my Host?"

"His life was not wasted," said Dennovia. "And the rod gives life."

Brannog and Wargallow turned together. Ruvanna had opened her eyes. Her gaze fell on Brannog. He rushed to her, kneeling.

"Ruvanna! You are recovered."

She smiled thinly. "So tired, Brannog. But, did we save him?"

He helped her to her feet, then lifted her like a child, taking her away from the body of Ogrund, which she had not seen. She did see, however, the terrible distress in his face.

"Aye, you saved him, Ruvanna. Wargallow is restored. But more important than that, you are alive," he said very softly. "I feared for you." His tears for Ogrund came then, and she smiled, not knowing.

Wargallow watched them, still dazed. As he saw Ruvanna's arms tighten about Brannog, he knew that they, at least, would give comfort to each other.

"You were not to blame," came Dennovia's soft voice.

Wargallow shook his head, slipping the steel hand inside his cloak as he would have done his killing steel. "You think not? This thing that I now carry—"

"She would have died, Wargallow," said Dennovia. "Ogrund would have rejoiced had he known that it was his life that saved her."

Wargallow pretended he had not heard her, his face suddenly becoming a familiar, cold mask. "We must leave this island quickly. Where is the ship?"

Dennovia glanced about her nervously. "And Mourndark. Where is he?"

Wargallow grunted, searching the immediate area and what

he could see of the cliffs. But there was no sign of Mourn-dark.

He has taken your ship, came a faint voice.

Wargallow looked up at the face. "You are yet alive—"

For a while, as you rightly guessed. And I have no power with which to return the ship to my shores.

"Then we are marooned here?" said Dennovia.

"Mourndark could not pilot that ship alone," said Wargallow. He was watching Brannog, who had told Ruvanna of the tragedy. She went to Carac, taking his hand, and together they sat beside Ogrund. Grimly Brannog came to Wargallow.

"Brannog, this is—"

But Brannog shook his head. "Say nothing. Not here, not now."

"We've lost the ship," cut in Dennovia.

Brannog swore. "I should have been more vigilant. If Mourndark sails far enough toward the mainland, he'll find a tide to take him ashore."

Dennovia smiled weakly. "I would rather be here than with him."

Brannog's anger returned. "I'll find him. I vow it."

"Forget him," said Wargallow suddenly. "He is nothing. He has no skill. The Seraph drew it all from him. It remembered him, and saw in him what he had become. The Steel-master can never be what he was. He will never win the support he dreams of. Forget him."

After a while, Ruvanna came to them. Her eyes were misty with tears, but she said nothing to Wargallow of Ogrund's death. Brannog had made her swear not to. "There is a way to safety," she said. "If Zoigon will consider it." She pointed to the somnolent face.

I hear you, Ruvanna. There is so little left. But what I have is yours.

"If you could move, Zoigon—"

Move! I can barely breathe, dear child.

"But if you could, could *you* be our craft?"

Gladly, but it is not possible.

Ruvanna spoke for the first time to Wargallow. "Zoigon is afraid of power, afraid that if he draws it from the rod, the hand, he will desire another thousand years of life, more. It tempts him greatly. When he saved you, he was tormented, torn. Even now, he could take power from the rod. But he fears what it would do to him.''

"If he needs power to take us to land, he shall have it," said Wargallow thoughtfully.

No! The rod is yours. I have rejected it. I will not do so a second time!

"If you try to take its power from me, in its entirety, I will use it on you," said Wargallow.

For a long time the Seraph was silent. When it spoke, there was a faint note of humor in its voice. *Ah, you were a fine choice, Wargallow. Truly a man of steel resolve. Omara needs that. You carry the power of life and death now. How quickly you understood that riddle. At last you see the tragedy of the Seraphim, and of the Sorcerer-Kings, and of the Hierarchs.*

"The curse of power," Wargallow replied, his voice a whisper.

Very well. Give me what I need.

"Where will you take us?" called Brannog. "To Tallwarren?"

If you wish it. But it is a dull place to die. Can you think of no better waters for me to end my days?

"How far could you travel?" said Wargallow.

You suspect treachery? I've no wish to cheat you. But one last journey, a worthy journey, is all I ask. I'll not harm the sea. It will not know I have passed.

Wargallow glanced at Brannog. "Elberon?"

Brannog nodded. "How long?" he asked the Seraph.

Faster than your tiny steeds, though not so fast as the birds of your air. Faster than any ship you ever sailed, Brannog of Sundhaven.

Brannog grunted. "Wargallow?"

"Aye, let it be Elberon."

# Epilogue

THEY TOOK the mud that had been the substance of the elementals and made it a rough grave for Ogrund. Carac vowed that he would bear his fallen comrade to Omaran soil when the time came. Little was said as the grave was completed, for they were all weighed down by a terrible sadness. Even Dennovia, who told herself she had no reason to mourn the dead Earthwrought, shed tears for him. Of the five left alive, it was Wargallow who kept apart from them.

It was a strange journey that followed. Wargallow used the power given to him to hold at bay the decline of the Seraph. His initial fears that Zoigon would attempt to draw all the power into himself were dispelled, for Wargallow found that he had complete control. The Seraph was for the most part silent, but its pleasure at traveling the seas of Omara seeped from it in a way that gave fresh heart to those upon it. South, out of the Bay of Sorrows, they traveled, unable to judge their true speed, for they saw little of land at that stage of their voyage. Most of the power in the island that had so altered the Omaran sea in the past had faded, so that there was no wake of pollution left behind them.

Wargallow was a lone pilot, his attention never wavering between the sea and the navigation of the island. He did not know the seas, nor the currents and tides, but as he gave power to the Seraph, so it returned this knowledge to him. Like a great fish following the migratory instincts of centuries, the island sped on. South into the ice it went, and there were icebergs to negotiate and whole floating floes of pack ice, but the Seraph was able to avoid them with miraculous precision, exuding a kind of joy as it did so. The climate became far colder, but again, the Seraph retained its own warmth, so that those upon it seemed to see the ice and blizzards beyond them as if through sheets of glass, at a distance.

This is how I once roamed my world, Zoigon told Wargallow. *There were many of us then, whole continents, changing, breaking up, reforming. Until the disaster in Ternannoc. This journey has returned to me many memories, things I had forgotten. I shall carry them with me until my last.*

Brannog and Ruvanna wandered parts of the island, mostly to be alone with each other. They had become lovers, both marveling at the intensity of their love. It enabled them, for a while, to put Ogrund's death from their minds, though afterward they felt guilt at having done so. Yet Brannog felt himself coming out of his darkness, his own well of gray unhappiness that had slowly been swallowing him for years. It was only now, standing back from it, that he saw how much it had marked him.

Ruvanna had relinquished the last of the powers that Omara had given her, and she found it like the removal of a burden. The loss still held its fears. "Does it not concern you that I'm no more than any other girl?" she asked Brannog more than once.

Brannog usually laughed. "Power is all very fine. But in the end, who controls it? Sisipher was used by it, and to this day fears what might yet lie within her. And poor Wargallow, who once relished the thought of power, has suffered its weight already. No, I prefer you without power, other than the simple gifts of the Earthwrought. You still have your voice. There is no greater gift."

"How do you think Wargallow will use his power?"

He shrugged. "His judgment is sound. It is true that he is ruthless, but we may need that now."

"Can Anakhizer corrupt him?"

"No one is safe. But Wargallow is the strongest of us. The Seraph knew that."

Ruvanna suddenly smiled. She pointed discreetly to another figure. It was Dennovia, sitting some distance apart from where Wargallow was studying the sea. "I think he has an admirer."

Brannog pushed her gently. "Dennovia is a survivor, like the island. But she is as ruthless as Wargallow. Where there is an opportunity, she will take it. Now that she's free of Mourndark, Wargallow will have to be careful! Mourndark put her aside in favor of greater things. Ironically it is not Wargallow that Dennovia seeks, but his power."

"Will time change her?"

"Perhaps. She understood what moved you. But her own nature may not allow her to change."

Some days afterward, they had rounded the southern ice fields and were moving along the western coast of the southern thrust of the continent. Carac, who had been high up on the island, came racing down to the others, hardly able to contain their eagerness.

"Boldernesse!" he cried. "My homeland." He pointed to the dark mass on the eastern horizon.

"Do you wish to go ashore?" Brannog asked him. "It could be done. A few more days—"

"Aye, I would go. And where better for me to place Ogrund in the true earth?"

He and Brannog went up to the high point of the island. "You shall go, Carac. Speak to your people. Tell them all the things you have seen. Tell them of their new Warlord, the Faithbreaker, and of Brannog."

"But my place is with you and the mistress."

"You serve us both better by speaking of the Host, and of Ulthor. And you will always know where I am."

Carac would have argued out of loyalty, but the pull of his homeland was great. Brannog tried to make light of the pending departure, going to Wargallow and explaining. Soon afterward, the island moved inshore, floating as close to the rocky inlets of Boldernesse as it dared. The coast was not far, but Carac was far too terrified of the sea to risk swimming ashore. Brannog, however, had no such fears, and for him the swim was a matter of ease, although both Ruvanna and Wargallow were apprehensive about his departure. Yet it was only a short time before Brannog returned, rowing a small boat that he had managed to borrow from some startled villagers. These were even more amazed when they saw the huge man return, ferrying an Earthwrought. The people were not enemies of Carac's people, but they were an insular tribe, unsure of themselves and their place in a world that neglected them. They preferred not to hinder their strange visitors.

Brannog and Carac landed some distance from the village, for they did not want to be seen carrying their burden. Ogrund had been carefully wrapped in leaves from the island, and Brannog carried him ashore, again feeling the sting of tears in his eyes. Somehow he yet felt that he had failed Ogrund, that in some way he could have prevented this tragic passing.

Carac held out his arms. "Let me take him, sire," he said. "There is a new strength in me here. My land welcomes me. I hear its voice. Let me take him below. We will give him to Omara with songs and honor."

Brannog did as he was asked. Effortlessly, Carac took the body. "We'll meet in the west," he said, then turned and made for the rocks. As Brannog was about to go back to the boat, he heard a cry.

"Tell Wargallow," called Carac, "that there is no ill will." Then he was gone, blending with the terrain, and for a moment Brannog thought he heard the echo of a song.

When he returned again to the island, he found Wargallow and told him what had happened. Wargallow looked for a moment as if he would speak, as if there were many things he wanted to say, but instead he nodded, going back to his task of piloting the island.

They moved on, around the southern coast of the continent, rounding the mass of Crotac Island before turning back inward, north toward the mouth of the Three Rivers. Two days out from the delta they were hailed by a war galley. It was a ship of Elberon, manned by Ruan's warriors. When they understood what it was that had entered their waters, they were staggered, uncertain whether they should prepare for an attack.

Wargallow sent Brannog and the two girls down to meet the warriors, knowing that Brannog would be known and recognized, by reputation if nothing else.

So this is to be my resting place? said Zoigon softly. *It a good, clean ocean. The journey has pleased me, Wargallow, but I am so tired.*

"If I have not given you enough, if I have been too cautious—"

Didn't you trust me? Ah, but you're no fool. Better that you watched me, Wargallow. Guard what you have. There are things in these very waters that would steal it from you. I have heard them. Their master represents a darker dream than any you have ever had. You'll need your new power. And your allies. You had better leave me. Get aboard that galley.

"And you?" He felt that he had come to know Zoigon better than he knew most of his own kind.

Spare me your pity. It's too painful. Remove the power quickly. Do it at a stroke. Quickly. If you feel you owe me anything, then one stroke will absolve you.

"I wish it could be otherwise."

No. You have your own destiny. Keep to the path you have chosen. Omara knows it. Keep your resolve.

There came a profound silence. Gritting his teeth, Wargallow removed his power from the Seraph, doing just as he had been asked. As he did so, he felt the island sigh. Its life went out of it instantly.

Anger filled him as he climbed down to the sea. Already he could feel the island sinking. The war galley had pulled alongside and a number of faces stared up anxiously. Brannog awaited him, and with him the ship's captain, though it was not a man Wargallow recognized. He did, however, know the Deliverer at once.

"Honored to have you aboard, sire," he said, saluting. His eyes, Wargallow noticed, had been fixed on the hidden right hand before he had remembered his manners and looked elsewhere.

"To Elberon," said Brannog.

"Yes," agreed Wargallow. "The island is going down."

The gallery moved away swiftly, its crew superbly trained. Behind them the island was already two-thirds below the water, and as it went, Brannog caught a last glimpse of its huge face. There was a new tranquility about it now, a serenity it had not known before. He would have commented on it to

Wargallow, but the Deliverer had bowed his head as if in prayer.

Dennovia had forgotten the island already. She was leaning on the opposite rail, eagerly looking landward. "Civilization at last!" she cried. Already a number of the crew had gathered around her, admiring her and trying to engage her in conversation.

Ruvanna smiled, putting her arm around Brannog, who towered over her. They left Wargallow to his thoughts, joining Dennovia and her noisy admirers.

Wargallow was the only man studying the western horizon. Below it there was no more than a curl of foam to mark the passing of Zoigon. The Deliverer put his right hand under his cloak. He may have imagined it, but he thought for a moment the steel had reacted like a magnet, drawn to the west as if by the power there. He forced himself to turn away, but as he went to join the others, he looked over his shoulder, shivering, though the air here was hot.